GRAFT

MADELEINE MARIE-ROSE

1

———

I tried not to mutate, but the rest of the world wasn't making it easy. Sweat trickled down my back as I biked through my neighborhood, the late August sun set to full blast and a back-pack full of groceries cutting into my shoulders. Summer was always a rough season for me, but I probably could've managed if it weren't for the pervasive rotting odor.

It's not a gas leak, I thought, walking myself through the county health department's statement. It's not smoke, or an issue with the sewage system. Sometimes smells just linger in the air before they dissipate. It isn't anything that can hurt you. So it's fine. You're fine.

Did being told something couldn't hurt you actually work on other people? Because even with the bandana covering half my face, I was still overwhelmed. The stench had hung over town for the last couple weeks, and instead of growing used to it, my lungs were still insisting it was poison. It didn't help that in the last couple days, the strong vegetable-decay rotting smell had gained a more... animal note. Musk, maybe. Or meat. I wasn't sure. I didn't *want* to breathe it in even more so I could find out. I felt a full-body shudder on its way and pedaled faster down my street, needing to get inside and out of view before it could happen.

Across the street, my neighbor Matilda had made the perplexing decision of weeding her front yard despite the gag-worthy odor. I envied her ability to exist outside in these conditions, to do things she didn't just need to do, but wanted to; I'd hated every moment of biking to and from the grocery store, and had briefly thought about hiding in the temperature-controlled aisles until it finally felt safe to venture outside again. I knew I had some struggles other people didn't because of my autism, but my sensory issues had been making regular life almost impossible lately.

Matilda's head whipped up as I rolled to a stop. My eyes stung, and I hoped it didn't look like I was glaring at her. It seemed like she was having the same problem, her own eyes damp. I'd planned to be outside as briefly as possible, but I couldn't just ignore her.

"Hi, Ella," she said, sounding exhausted.

"Hey. Nice day, isn't it?" I said politely.

"Name one nice thing about it," she said.

She was right, of course. I'd said it on instinct, reaching for something bland and inoffensive. Noises, sights, and smells that bothered me affected my ability to concentrate, and the current reek was the nasal equivalent of a screeching fire alarm. Not that I was socially skilled even when I was comfortable.

"Obviously, it stinks to high heaven out here," I said, fighting to keep my hands from twitching too much. "I'm very sensitive to strong smells, and while I wouldn't wish this on anyone, it's nice to not be the only one struggling for once."

Matilda's eyes narrowed.

I floundered again. Despite our long proximity as neighbors, I didn't know all that much about Matilda. "I'm surprised the weeds aren't, you know, wilting from the smell like in a cartoon. But I guess it wouldn't just be the weeds affected, would it? It can't be that easy. That bag of mulch looks heavy. Is Brian going to give you a hand later or do you need help?"

"Just go," she said, waving me towards my house.

"I, uh, I hope you have a *nicer* day."

I made a hasty retreat home. Smooth, Ella. Real smooth.

It was good that my parents were out of town; the moment I had our comfortingly solid front door between me and the outside world, I lost control. A violent tremor ran through me from head to foot. I leaned against a wall for support. My short sleeves cut into my shoulders. I tugged at their stitching, barely able to keep an instinctual panic down as the bare skin of my arms broke out into rough calluses. They itched horribly as they appeared, spreading out up to several inches wide like an advanced stage of some new pox. My fingers cramped with the desire to scratch at the calluses, to pinch or peel or apply pressure, anything that would keep them from spreading further. But I knew that wouldn't help. Nothing did. Once it started, all I could do was find somewhere private to hide while my body warped. And try not to cry. Sometimes that was the really tough part.

I took a shower, trying to wash away the stink from outside without touching the latest additions to my body. The calluses were often sensitive, as though they were a deeper, raw layer of me pushed to the surface. Better that they have some sensation than not, so I knew when they appeared, but accidentally brushing or bumping them against something could be so intense a feeling that it was adjacent to pain.

Once clean and scrubbed scentless, I wrapped my arms tight around myself, focusing on my breathing, on being home and safe. Gradually, the rough and raised patches on my skin melted away, shrinking and dissolving. It was hard to describe the process otherwise; if I did it right it was like they'd never been there in the first place, leaving behind the facade of a normal human. Running my hands over my arms, I was relieved to find only smooth skin and delicate hairs. I wiped away the fog on the bathroom mirror, stared into my own brown eyes as I told myself a few affirmations:

You are human.

You are a decent person.

You don't mean it when you upset people.

I got dressed in fresh clothes and carefully arranged my damp, shoulder-length dark hair so it lay just right, creating a dark border, a barricade, at the edges of my vision. It was the one part of my body I could trust not to slip into another shape when I wasn't looking. That wouldn't *mutate*.

I'd been stuck with this... ability for at least a dozen years, and I still wasn't sure what to call it. There were days when it felt like a curse, but to me that implied I'd done something to deserve it. My parents were entirely normal humans, and I seemed to be that way too, until I got overstimulated or upset. Then my body became a free-for-all; surface changes like the calluses if I was lucky, solid lumps of soft tissue if I wasn't, and in a really bad case... let's just say I was fortunate my ability hadn't torn or broken me. At least, not yet. Sometimes it happened while I was in public, leading to moments of silent panic while I tried to figure out what had changed and if it was visible to others. I could reverse these changes with some struggle; I could even deliberately make alterations myself, not that I had any desire to. It seemed like a pointless and unnecessary risk.

If anything about this was normal, I would surely know by now given the countless nights I'd spent desperately searching online, searing my retinas on bright screens and scared to make any noise that might wake my parents. As early as elementary school, I'd known there was no going back once you were labeled as strange. People always had to know *why* you were a certain way. Explaining my neurodivergence could be difficult enough, but this? No. I couldn't risk being *studied*. I knew what happened to new, strange things. They wound up under the microscope, even if they had to be cut into little pieces to fit. I'd kept my secret through annual checkups, changing into gym clothes alongside a dozen other girls, even through the cruel and unusual punishment that was puberty mood swings. I was twenty years old, and sometimes it felt like I had an unbearably long number of years ahead of me where I'd have to keep hiding it.

Having that awful reek outside had been less than helpful, turning my entire town into an environment that triggered my ability, making me go from a few incidents a week to sometimes multiple a day. Another one of my affirmations: You are never more than twenty minutes from home and its comforts. That line had gotten me through plenty of rough days, but lately it had been hard for me to go more than *two* minutes away, let alone consider shelling out for a hotel room somewhere that didn't stink. Today's outing had been my first this entire week.

Speaking of, I had to go through the groceries. Keeping myself fully fed and on a reasonably varied diet was already hard when I found so many tastes and textures off-putting; any trace of rotting smell during a meal ruined my appetite. I used my cell phone as a speaker, needing the strong beat and choral harmonizing of my favorite playlist to help drive me into action. Wearing gloves, I shucked the packaging off lunch meat and sliced bread, undid the triple layer of bags I'd put around the produce, washed and dried sealed yogurt cups. Everything went into clean containers. Even the frozen chicken nuggets I split between several ziploc bags.

My phone buzzed against the countertop, interrupting my music. I glared at it, feeling robbed. I only ever got calls from two groups of people, and one of them was scammers. I shed my gloves and grabbed my phone, wanting my tunes back…

It was the second group, my frustration melting away as soon as I saw the caller ID. I picked up.

"Hey, Mom," I said.

"Ella! Are you holding down the fort alright?"

"Yep, everything's fine. How's Nevada? See any aliens yet?"

She laughed. "No, but if we'd stayed out in the sun for any longer today we might have hallucinated we did."

"If you guys don't come back with a bunch of Area 51 bumper stickers on the car, I'll be disappointed."

"We don't have much bumper space left, but we'll do our best. For now we're stocking up on postcards. Your dad's planning to draw a bunch of nonsense symbols on the back and mail them to your grandfather," she said with a sigh. "Because they already get along *so* well."

My dad's voice was distant and muffled, but it sounded an awful lot like "he won't know they're from me!"

"Who else?" Mom said dryly. "Anyway, you wouldn't believe the landscape out here. Parts of it are dusty, but it smells so... clean? It's hard to describe, but I think you'd like it. There's more life than you'd think, you just have to work to find it. We've seen three lizards today but I imagine you'd have found ten times that."

"Lizards aren't my animal-spotting specialty," I said.

"You could diversify."

"Most furry things aren't venomous."

"Fair. I'm considering drawing two purple dots on my ankle and pretending I got bit by a snake once I get home. Use sick time to avoid office bullshit for a little while longer. Oh! That reminds me. I brought something with us to take pictures with."

I opened the photo she'd texted me and nearly choked. "You *kept* those?"

"Our daughter made them for us, of course we did," Mom said, sounding wounded. "We just, you know. Lost them in a closet for about a decade."

I zoomed in on the lime-green paper mache masks my parents wore in the picture, cringing at each bump. Although they were both far more outgoing than I was, they'd long given up on playing office politics. After hearing them complain about being unable to avoid annoying conversations with their coworkers, a much younger me had made them... what had I called them? Don't-talk-to-me masks? The green alien faces had no mouths. No antenna either, but I couldn't remember if that was because I'd decided antenna were ears, or if I'd just struggled too much to make them. I assumed neither of them had actually worn the masks to their jobs, because they hadn't been fired. "They look awful," I said.

"You were still working very hard on your motor skills back then. Here, your dad's squirming. I'm handing the phone over."

"Hey there. Been locking up at night?" Dad asked.

"Of course. And I always double-check." Being home alone at night made me anxious, though I hid it from my parents.

"You're not feeling sick, are you? I know the county doesn't think it's a chemical spill..."

"I'm fine." I said.

"You could always order in groceries if you—"

"I'm. Fine," I said. "I can do these things. You know I'm moving out in just a few weeks, right?"

"Accepting help with this wouldn't mean you're not ready for college," he said. "It would just mean you needed some extra support while you were going through a hard time."

I swallowed back my frustration, knowing his worry came from a place of love. "How's *the plan* going?"

"Haven't made first contact yet," he said with a sigh.

"They'd better hurry up. You've only got another week to make alien friends and overthrow the government."

"We'll go to Loch Ness next year if it doesn't work out, try our luck there. In the meantime, I'm getting plenty of orange pictures for the Blur, if you want them." He sounded nervous, like he wasn't sure his contributions were welcome.

I wandered upstairs to my bedroom, scrutinizing the tapestry of photos I had taped to a closet door. The Blur was a collage of hundreds of out-of-focus pictures I'd taken, the result of my nature photography hobby and general jumpiness. It was a big ordered mess of motion I was constantly adding to and rearranging into bigger patterns, all browns and greens with the occasional pop of other colors. I traced my fingers along its paths, considering. I couldn't imagine much room for orange in it.

"Maybe they can be the start to a smaller one in my dorm," I said. "Thanks."

"Oh! Once you make some friends, you should ask them for pictures from their homes to add to it."

"I think most people delete blurry pictures immediately. It might come across as a weird request."

"Just be yourself and I'm sure it'll work out. They might not get it at first, but once they see you're passionate about it, that'll change." He paused. "I love you, kiddo. I won't say I wish you were here, because I know you didn't want to come, but... I wish home wasn't so uncomfortable for you right now. Does that make sense?"

"It does," I said quietly. "Love you too. And you, Mom."

We said goodbye and hung up. I loved my parents dearly for doing their best to help me be comfortable, but they weren't on the spectrum and didn't know my secret, so I wasn't sure how much they truly understood. Did they know that I didn't feel like I was a real adult? That the idea of leaving for college felt both necessary and terrifying, despite the two gap years I'd taken? Sometimes I wished the world was just our town and I'd never have to submit to the stress of new people or places ever again—that one, they probably knew. I kept tracing along the Blur, using it as a way to stim and calm down. I'd miss it when I moved to college, but the thought of taking it apart was too upsetting to me.

You'll never be more than three hours away from it, I thought bitterly. Yes, I'd have to make a new one. I knew there were other things I'd bring with me that would be a source of comfort, but it was hard to cheer myself up with that when I hadn't decided what they'd be yet. I hadn't started packing yet, and I didn't start today, either, my trip to the store having exhausted all of my task initiation energy. Finishing putting away the rest of the groceries was all I felt up for, and then it was recovery time. AKA lie in bed for an hour or two time.

Or the rest of the day.

I'm not saying it felt good. It honestly didn't. But getting up for more than snacks and to use the bathroom felt out of reach. And then by the time I was ready to get up and do things...

It was two a.m.

My other closet door had photos taped to it as well. Ella's Enigmas, my parents called them. With only my bedside lamp on, the pictures' glossy finish made their unidentifiable subjects' fluorescent green eyes shine. Even with my parents out of town, I was still quiet as I gathered my camera and put rubber boots on over my pajama pants.

The reek wasn't as bad at night, allowing me to spend time in my backyard in the tent I had set up. I turned on its dim fairy lights and lay on my front beneath a blanket, watching the border between lawn and forest to see if anything would appear. The grass smelled like pure green, blocking out any leftover stench. I still worried there was something horribly wrong just past my neighborhood, something wetly falling apart and spreading through the soil, but right now all I needed to care about was my backyard. That was an easy, manageable place, one I'd known my whole life. This was my home. I knew it, and it knew me.

A wave of motion went through the cluster of ferns at the edge of the yard. I held my breath and waited, taking a picture right as the animal appeared.

The creature that slipped by was fox-height with a too-long snout. I bit back a gasp, suspecting a glitch somewhere between my eyes and my brain. But then the creature stepped fully from the ferns. Six legs. *Six.* Mutant? Alien? Undiscovered species? The last option somehow seemed the most far-fetched. This animal was too asymmetrical, some of its legs sporting more joints than the others. It was covered in a strange mix of textures, splotches of matted fur and damp bare skin.

The creature turned from the light. I followed it into the forest, hoping to get a better picture without spooking it, comforted by the sight of my backyard lights between the branches when I glanced behind me. I liked the idea that my home extended beyond the mowed grass and among the trees—and I was curious about this new resident whose living space overlapped with mine.

I should've noticed the first inklings of that awful rotting reek sooner, but I'd convinced myself that nighttime was better, safer, and I stubbornly clung to that idea until I was gagging on the smell, leaning against a tree to catch my breath. By the time I'd recovered, I'd lost track of the creature.

Something rushed out of the shadows past me. I scrambled away, an attempted shout leaving my throat as a squeak, aware of a yards-long *thing* I could barely see. I stood still, distrusting every tree trunk and swaying branch, not knowing which might be hiding another living thing behind it, or what that thing even was—nothing I'd ever captured a picture of for the Enigma had been quite that shape before. The temptation to call out for help, to let someone else know I was out here and alone and scared, was strong, but what questions might come from that? What else might be drawn to my voice?

I drew in one last deep, polluted breath and ran home, fingers shaking as I locked the back door. My clothes had once again picked up the reek. I kicked off my boots with some difficulty. When I tried to change out of my pajamas, I had to yank to get the pants off, the fabric catching on a swollen knot of tissue around one of my ankles. I dragged myself upstairs, lifting the taped-together tapestry of the Blur so I could take inventory in the mirror hidden behind it.

My whole body felt stiff, similar developments weighing down my knees and shoulders, as if my strange ability had wanted me to freeze until the danger was past. There was pressure against my throat too, tight around my voice. Silent and stationary like a prey animal, even though I had no idea what I'd seen or if I'd even interpreted its size correctly. But now that I was inside and safe, those changes were just nuisances. I was too worked up, the changes too extensive, for a little controlled breathing to fix this.

I pulled my mattress out of its bed frame, retrieving the shoebox I kept hidden underneath. Inside was an instant camera, film, a heat-proof bowl, matches, and a photo album. The album was a reference library of my own body, dozens of pictures from different angles and distances, a blueprint of normalcy. I laid out several pictures of my limbs, and then used the instant camera to take photos of my altered arms and legs. I placed the new pictures into the bowl, comparing them to my album before dropping in a lit match. While they burned, I concentrated on thoughts of soothing and smoothing irritated skin and stress-swollen muscle, a process I found easier ritualized. Let the fire take away the unwanted changes, let them be carried out of my body and home along with the smoke through an open window.

My locked muscles loosened as the new growth gradually melted away, the pressure on my throat easing. I looked in the mirror again. Part of my reflection was still wrong. I pressed my arms together. One was a good two inches longer than the other. I gritted my teeth and made it shrink back, enduring the painless yet distressing sensation of bone and soft tissue grinding and squishing down. I put my ritual tools and photo album away, holding back tears. Growing up, I'd been told by teachers that everybody struggles with something. They probably had meant it to be reassuring, but I doubt they would've said it if they'd known more about me.

I showered and got into bed, still shaking, and checked the newest picture on my camera. My mouth twisted. The single picture I'd taken was underexposed and so out of focus that I couldn't even tell animal from background, yet alone count its legs. In contrast, the glimpses of what I'd seen couldn't be clearer in my head.

Then again, would I mind being wrong? The world would be easier in many ways if it didn't match my understanding of it.

2

———————

You are human.
You are.
You *are*.
You are—

I didn't have a word for what I was right now. That was okay. This was just a dream. I could tell because my altered body was working too well, like a naturally born thing. I wasn't human in the same way a dog or bird wasn't human. They weren't supposed to be human, and so that was no failing of theirs.

My current shape was perfectly suited for the riverbed I was exploring. Water passed over my gills with a heavy comfort. My fins made me agile. The riverbed was tiled with colorful, shimmering stones, and I let the current and my easily-distracted eyes guide me between my favorites, enjoying the scavenger hunt and how the smooth bumpy ground felt against my unscaled belly.

The sound of familiar voices made me stick my head out of the water, the bright sunlight almost too much to bear. My parents were walking alongside the river, holding hands. I knew I was their biological daughter, and it hurt that we were different shapes, that the air they breathed so easily stung my gills. I let the water lap at my chin so it hid the changed parts of me, and called out to them. They were happy to see me, and I them, even though my smile hid a deep fear that they'd join me in the water and see me for what I truly was.

That didn't change that I wanted to be with them. They were my family. They were basically my only friends. They stood on the bank, and waited for me, and I—it was beautiful and comfortable in the river but I was alone there—outside the water *hurt* but—

With a sudden rush of courage I flopped out of the water, awkward, unsightly, and suffering outside of the environment I'd adapted to. My parents looked down, seeing me changed for the first time —

A scream woke me. I lay shivering, wrapped in sweat-soaked blankets. My hands were clammy, my fingers wedded together by a thin sheet of skin stretched between them. I fumbled for my instant camera, hurriedly snapping pictures as someone outside continued to yell. It sounded like Matilda, though I'd never heard her that shrill before. Between my hobbled hands and the panic of the moment, it took me many tries to get a clear photo and successfully light a match. With that frog-like webbing finally gone, I hurriedly dressed, wound a scarf around my nose and mouth, and ran across the street.

"Friggin' animal!" Matilda shrieked. "Hey! Let off!"

I dashed down her driveway. Matilda was on the porch, unstably perched on a rocking chair. I at first thought it was a dog trying to nip at her heels, but she was terrified and the animal had that same patchwork of textures covering its body that I'd seen yesterday. It circled her and, giving off an air of cruel enjoyment, pressed on one of the rockers, sending Matilda wobbling. She caught sight of me.

"Make it go away!" Matilda shrilled. "There's something wrong with it!"

"I can see that." This was an oddly shaped creature, weasel-bodied and twig-legged. It growled at my slow approach and circled behind the rocking chair as Matilda trembled.

I lunged to the left, expecting it to go right. Instead, it climbed the chair. Afraid it would bite Matilda, I grabbed it around the middle, struggling to keep hold of the wriggling creature as I carried it away. I hated the feel of it in my hands, like a furry sack full of loose parts. I was holding it too high up its abdomen for it to bite me, though its short claws pressed urgently against my skin. At least, I thought I'd been holding it close to its neck but the part of its body above my grip was getting longer.

And the part below my grip wasn't getting shorter. I sucked in air as its claws went from a light pressure to the beginnings of pain on the back of my hands. Its claws were getting longer. Not unsheathing like a cat's, but actually growing, an impossible amount of new length emerging from its paws in uneven, jagged angles.

"How are you—"

It bit me. I flailed, flinging it. It hit a tree trunk at an alarming velocity, falling limply to the ground. For a moment I feared I'd broken its back, but it squirmed to its feet and ran into the woods, its gait disjointed but too fast to suggest it wasn't supposed to move that way.

Shaken, I turned to Matilda. She tried to climb down from the chair, but her scratched and mud-stained right leg buckled beneath her, dropping her to her knees.

"Are you alright?" I asked.

She stared at me with a horrified expression.

"I didn't really mean to throw it," I said. "I panicked."

"Your *arms*," she said.

I looked down. My arms were covered in spotty, sandpaper-looking calluses, nearly a quarter inch thick in some spots. My fingers were lumpy and crooked from spots of distended muscle or soft tissue.

"Oh my god," Matilda said. "Inside, now."

She dragged herself to her feet, motioning for me. I felt frozen in place. She wasn't supposed to—nobody was supposed to see me like this.

"Come *on*," she insisted. "There could be more out there."

I shut my slack-jawed mouth and followed her into her home. Matilda stumbled around locking doors while I trailed after her, numbly waiting for the other shoe to drop. She peered out a window into her backyard, hiding behind the curtains.

"I went out to check on the chickens and there was something hanging around by the back door," she whispered to me, on the verge of tears. "Bigger than the one you saw."

"Is Brian home?" I asked. Matilda's brother quite enjoyed target practice with his BB gun in their backyard, a hobby I'd always disliked until now.

"He's in the hospital," she said.

"He what?" I said, startled.

"He got bit," Matilda said. "You know how he leaves out food for the feral cats so they won't go after our chickens? Two days ago, only this mangy one showed up. He went to pet it and it bit his hand. The thing didn't bite like a cat. Tried to take his finger off. I took him to urgent care because I thought he might need a rabies shot, but by the time we got there, his finger smelled putrid and it, I don't know. It's like it started *melting*."

She was shaking. I replaced her at the window, taking my own anxious look at her backyard and the chicken coop. The birds were running around in circles, bumping into each other and squawking. As I watched, one of them coughed up a dark, muddy liquid that clotted in the coop's sawdust. My eye was drawn to movement beyond the coop, at head-height. With how awful conditions outside were, it was particularly difficult to imagine it was someone I knew lurking in the trees that bordered Matilda's backyard.

I shut the curtain before Matilda could see it too. She seemed to think the changes to my body were from contact with that strange creature. The last thing I needed was to seed the idea of a human-shaped... monster in her head.

"Can you get me a damp towel?" Matilda mumbled.

I ran to fetch her one. Matilda tried to wipe away the discolored spot on her leg, only to hiss in pain. She settled for wrapping it around her leg instead.

"We need to get to the hospital," Matilda said. "I don't want to wait here for someone else to show up. Brian's truck is in the garage. Can you still use your hands?"

I nodded mutely.

"I don't think it broke your skin like it did mine," Matilda said, in full panic-chatter. "Maybe that makes it happen faster. We need to go, now. The doctors didn't know what was happening to Brian, I think— I think the sooner we get there, the better."

My throat went dry. My assumption was that hospitals were bad, that doctors were the people most likely to notice something different about my body and investigate. But Matilda needed medical attention, and I hardly wanted to wait around to see if whatever was outside was interested in us.

We went to the garage. Matilda struggled into the truck's passenger seat. I hated how high up the cab was. Driving already stressed me out, and being in a vehicle this size made it worse. A familiar rotting smell was rapidly filling the cab, overwhelming the pine-scented air freshener. From the way it clung to Matilda, I had to assume it was from her injury.

"If animals like that one are the source of the smell," I said, "how many do you think are —"

Matilda hit the garage door remote. "Just drive," she gasped, like she expected a horde of hostile animals on the other side.

There weren't any. I rolled the truck forward before that could change.. Matilda glanced anxiously out her window, constantly reaching up to wipe sweat from her forehead.

"Are your arms —" she started to ask.

"Fine," I said, applying more pressure to the gas pedal. "They're fine. For now."

It was that post-commute pre-lunch time where hardly anyone was out driving. I made the first few turns that took us out of our neighborhood without vehicular manslaughter-ing anyone or anything, pointing us towards the hospital.

Matilda was going through her phone, reading over messages with her teeth bearing down on her lower lip. I flinched when she started playing a voicemail without warning, background noise buzzing from the speaker.

"They don't know," she said after listening to it. How'd she been able to pull words out of the crackling recorded voice, I wasn't sure. "It's been two whole days and they still haven't figured out how to stop it."

"Stop what?" I said.

"His *infection*." She spat the word out like a bullet. "Didn't you just hear? Antibiotics aren't working. They already had to remove two fingers, and they think he might lose the whole hand."

"I, I'm sorry. I couldn't understand what they were saying." It was too much to think about anything other than an apology.

"It doesn't make sense." She was staring down at her leg. I risked a glance down too. Her shoes had been white, but the one on her affected side was getting stained red-brown, the towel she held against her wound blocking my view of anything more.

"They discover new diseases all the time, right?" I said. "Things that were always there and weren't severe enough to notice, or mutated, or jumped from animals to us. Most of them just aren't like, like this."

"I might lose my whole leg," Matilda said. "It's probably in my blood too, so maybe it's in my heart and lungs and brain. They've got Brian on life support, and they can still barely keep him alive."

I was already driving faster than I was comfortable, and over the speed limit. I pressed harder on the gas, figuring all would be forgiven in an emergency.

"So how are you fine?" Matilda said.

My arms were mutated in front of another person and I was shaking from driving an unfamiliar vehicle so fast and on the verge of vomiting from the reek building up in the cab. And my hands...I was not *fine*. I pulled over. Once the truck was stopped, I held up my hands.

My left hand had two dark pinpricks where I'd been bitten, and my palms felt slimy where I'd touched the creature. When I pressed on the pinpricks, my skin dimpled in without rising back up.

Matilda briefly pulled the towel away from her leg, both of us getting a glimpse of muddying flesh before she pressed it back into place with a wince, as if applying pressure would keep her solids from turning into liquids.

"It's still not as bad as mine is, or Brian's got," she accused. "And it doesn't explain the rest of what you have going on. That was instant. You shouldn't... you shouldn't have been strong enough to throw it so hard."

"I haven't done anything wrong," I blurted out. I could feel my body changing with each strike of my pounding heart, skin and muscle and bone lumps on my arms and neck and *face*—

She leaned against the cab's door, hand curling around the armrest.

"Matilda, look, I know there's a lot of weird stuff going on right now..."

"Don't. Start," she said. "You've *always* been strange, and I thought there were times when you were... different, somehow. I just, I don't know, always assumed it was a trick of my eyes. Maybe I needed to see something crazier before I was ready to think... what are you?"

"I'm your neighbor," I said.

"Aside from that?"

I was hyperventilating, desperately needing a more normal appearance. I scratched at my calluses, scraping off layer after layer of nerveless skin, leaving behind an irritated and uneven surface. Matilda watched me in fascinated horror. I dug my nails into the softened skin around my bite wound too, revealing a hot, darker patch the size of a quarter. It came away like damp autumn leaves, and I was relieved to find there was no blood underneath. Showing her my reddened and roughened arms, I said, "please understand, it's not my fault. I don't know why I was born like this. I didn't ask to be."

"I guess I've known you a long time, even if I don't really... *know* you," she said. "You wouldn't hurt me?"

"I'm not a monster," I said, deeply hurt.

She didn't respond, so I took in a deep breath and started up the truck again, trying not to doom-spiral into thinking about disappearing into the woods.

"Why aren't we there yet?" she eventually asked.

"Because we're not," I said, helpless.

She started to cry. I sucked with people. The kind thing would be to reach over and pat her shoulder, but my hands were frozen on the steering wheel.

"You didn't even notice," she accused. "I've been a complete mess since Brian got sick, and you didn't even notice."

"How am I supposed to know these things if you don't tell me?"

"How hard is it?" she said, exasperated. "Don't you care at all about the people around you? You've always been like this."

That hurt more than I could say. Again the skin on my arms toughened and swelled, ready to defend me. Matilda shrunk back in her seat, and stayed like that even after I made the changes go away.

We reached the hospital. I parked in front, staring at the entrance. Matilda watched me, sweat beading on her forehead. She jumped when I used the horn, blasting it for a few seconds.

"Why did you—"

I scrambled out of the truck, fleeing to the trees. Hidden behind them, I stayed to make sure someone came out for Matilda, that she'd be taken care of.

Now what? If she wanted to tell someone about me, there was nothing stopping her. It was all too easy to imagine a life where people knew me for what I truly was—whatever that might be—and there was no longer a place for me here. A place for me anywhere.

There was nothing I could do about that. For now I went home, following the rough path of the road from a distance, trying to balance the danger of being seen while visibly changed with the danger of running into anything strange in the woods. I could feel my body shifting, hardly a surprise given how upset I was, and decided not to even bother checking. I didn't have the emotional bandwidth right now. The reek surrounded me, but it wasn't bothering me as much. I guess it wasn't so bad outside of an enclosed space like the truck. A strangled laugh threatened to break free. Look at me, acclimating.

Someone *did* laugh, their braying voice bouncing up and down in pitch. I went still as a statue. There weren't any hiking trails or homes in view. The occasional sound of a passing car was a low hum compared to how that laugh had cracked the air, though both noises had come from the same direction. I wrapped my arms tight around myself and kept going, shifting my path further from the road. There must've been some little offshoot neighborhood I didn't know about nearby, or a group of people who thought untrodden brambles would make a good spot for a picnic, because the human voice had a sound and range to it that you just didn't hear from animals. And I kept hearing them, wordless calls and exclamations, and changing my trajectory, and —

And the smell changed, gaining a base note of sharp iron. The forest sloped down, its incline dropping me into a clearing. It was empty aside from one large tree standing at its center; leafless, roots swollen above the dirt, bark cracked and leaking red-purple syrup. Small animals milled about it at a distance. While I watched, one that looked like a cousin to the creature I'd found harassing Matilda ran towards the center, dragging a mesh bag of produce behind it. It deposited its stolen food at the tree's base and glared at me, raising its hackles and chattering. The other animals added food scraps and dead rodents to the produce. The dirt beneath this scrap pile shifted, something pulling the collection underground.

I heard a low growl behind me. I puffed myself up and turned around, ready to shout at something knee-height. Instead, I slowly backed into the clearing.

What followed me might've been a coyote once. I'd always thought of them as scrappier, hungrier wolves. But this creature's body carried that extreme even further. Its pelt sagged off its neck and underside, but was stretched taut over its shoulders to the point I could see the skin beneath its fur. The once-coyote flashed its fangs at me in a slow grimace, all the additional muscles in its lower jaw needing time to flex. I hurried back.

"*You're* supposed to be afraid of *me*," I said, terrified. "I'm human, or I'm something worse."

My foot collided with a root. The coyote's jaw dropped open, letting out a cackling laugh.

Climbing up the tree would get me distance from the coyote without running or showing it my back. I turned to the side, eyes still on the animal, questing blindly for a handhold. I found a branch and squeezed it, only to feel that it was mammal-hot. I dared to glance away from the coyote. The branch's bark had come off as dust on my fingers, leaving an exposed section of moist red, like naked muscle.

"Oh," I said.

A cracked and red-dripping branch circled around my leg and hoisted me into the air before I could run, dangling me upside-down a good ten feet off the ground. The coyote patiently watched while more branches waved around me like lethargic snakes, several wrapping around my waist. I held still at first, dumbfounded by what was happening. The whole time, smaller creatures were still bringing in more organic matter, soft plant parts but also whatever meat they could find. The ground beneath these offerings, beneath *me*, churned as if liquid, a hole twenty feet deep briefly opening to the air. At the bottom, its foul smell rising to greet me, was a pool of... it was too many colors, reds and greens and browns, mixed into a slurry. The hole's walls were lined with fist-sized gray points. They seemed too big to be teeth, but too uniform to just be rocks; if I considered what was below me to be a stomach, I supposed teeth made more sense.

I wouldn't, couldn't, process it any further. There was no time. The branches around me tightened, squeezing my legs and torso. My unnatural ability kicked in, my body changing to resist the tree's attempt to crush me. I screamed, hating not just the pain but the sensation of muscle and bone simultaneously being forced inward and growing out. The seams in my sleeves popped and then I was tearing at the branches with strengthened arms. I thought of the weasel I'd held similarly restrained so recently, how it had writhed out of my grip. Curling my fingers around a branch, my nails grew out and cut into the bark, releasing thick, hot sap. The coyote leapt at me, and in a moment of panic I lashed out. It fell to the ground and lay still for a few heartbeats, neck at an odd angle, before the mud opened up to swallow it. I broke the branch around my waist and contorted out of the ones holding my legs. I bolted, barely avoiding the chasm that formed where I'd landed. My world narrowed to the path directly in front of me as I ran. I skirted around streets and houses until I reached my own backyard and fell on the soft, clean grass.

Slowly, Ella. Breathe slowly. I scratched at my arms, building up and shedding layers of skin until I thought nothing that had directly touched the monsters remained. That's what they were, monsters. Them, not me. I didn't recognize my hands, the shape of my legs. My waist felt stiff, inflexible.

I dragged myself inside, got out my instant camera. Just had to go one part at a time until I was done. My nails were thick sharp points; I burned a picture of them first to make it easier to handle the camera. I knew for my torso I'd need to take a photo in front of the mirror, so I decided to undo as many of the other changes as I could before then so there wouldn't be as much wrong with me to see. Legs next, then one arm, then —

I was all out of film. I used up the rest when I woke up.

There wasn't that much in my box of ritual supplies, nothing an extra roll of film could be hiding beneath. Hadn't I bought more? I must've forgotten to. My head felt hot, like I might pass out or throw up. I slammed my bedroom door in a sudden fit. The photos fell from my closet, scattering over the carpet.

"I needed you!" I screamed. My heart pounded in my ears, mercifully drowning out the subtler sounds of grinding bone as my body further distorted. I fell to my knees, trying to separate out Blur and Enigma photos. My misshapen hands were clumsy, my fingers thick and numb. They only creased the pictures.

Impulse took over. I dumped as many of the photos as would fit into my ritual bowl, lighting a match before I could panic over which were Enigmas and which were from the Blur. This was how it worked, right? I burned the unsightly things, and they went away.

"Leave," I said, dropping in the match before I could rethink it. My heart ached as the pictures burned, but this needed to happen. It was all I could do.

As the fire died down, I felt cold and weak. Moving mechanically, I got into my baggiest hoodie and sweatpants, the only clothes that currently comfortably fit, and hid in bed. I clenched my fists, felt little sparks of pain from my palms.

I examined my hands. My nails were once again half an inch longer than they had been, their tips pointed. They extended as I stared at them, slowly and smoothly growing as if they were sliding out from some pocket dimension. I tapped one against my arm, making a droplet of blood well up. At what point, I wondered, did they become claws instead of nails? I tried to put them away, to tuck them back into that hidden space. It wasn't as quick as if I'd burned a photo, but they did gradually shrink, millimeter by millimeter. The way they moved in and out was entrancing, seamlessly lengthening and shortening, like a puzzle piece falling perfectly into place. As if aware of my fascination, they grew out again, and again I tucked them away. I could feel my hastened breathing slow as I concentrated on my nails, the rest of me start to fall back into its normal shape as I calmed down.

But I still wasn't able to completely relax until I peeked out my bedroom window and saw county Fish and Wildlife trucks, followed by a couple police cars, go by—away from me, and hopefully towards stopping whatever was out there.

3

———

My post-meltdown dream was blissfully calm. I sat on our front doorstep, a six-legged mouse lying dead by my paws. My whiskers nervously twitched as Mom and Dad walked up the driveway, finally home; my pointed ears only reached up to their knees, so it was hard to read their expressions as they inspected my gift. I didn't know for sure how they felt until Dad scooped me up so I could nuzzle his face with my furry cheek and Mom petted me, praised me—

I was awake, and I didn't deserve praise. I'd forgotten something, I was sure of it.

The chickens.

I'd forgotten about Matilda's chickens.

I tore open my curtains. It was after midnight, and the darkness felt solid beyond my window. I gnawed on my lip as I considered the likelihood of something lurking out there, so close to more people.

But there was also the chance of Matilda telling someone about me, and it seemed higher if... *when* she and Brian came home, they discovered I'd left their obviously sick animals to starve to death. And the chickens themselves deserved better than that.

I grabbed my phone and shoes, ran across the dark street with my heart in my throat. I stopped by Matilda's garden shed to fill up a bucket with feed, hoping the chickens wouldn't be too sick to eat.

I'd expected the birds to be asleep, but the moment I went around the corner I heard something bounce off the wire mesh of the coop.

"It's okay now," I said. "I'm here, I'll feed you, I'll look up what I'm supposed to do with you—"

Metal squeaked as the wire was hit from inside again. The coop had a solid roof that kept the dim starlight from illuminating inside, but the point of impact seemed to be around waist height.

It really stunk back here.

My hand ignored all of my better ideas and pulled out my phone, turned on the flashlight. I saw the contents of the coop for just long enough before common sense took over and turned the light off to think: *amalgamation.*

A chilling howl echoed over the neighborhood, worryingly close. The creature in the coop hissed and bubbled in response, joining in a chorus with far too many members. One second of thinking about the larger monsters I'd already seen was enough to send me scrambling on top of the coop, moving quick so whatever was inside couldn't grab me, and then onto Matilda and Brian's roof. Lights in a few nearby houses flickered on, weak illumination through curtains and blinds allowing for glimpses of the shadows that raced down the street. One of them paused outside a lit window. There shouldn't be anything non-human and bipedal around here, and that wasn't even mentioning the fanged muzzle. It startled whoever had turned on the light. Their scream was followed by the monster slipping out of my view, and then the sound of breaking glass.

I lay flat against the roof, shivering. Think, Ella. Your best bet is to barricade yourself inside, or drive away. Can't get into Matilda's place without loudly breaking in, so you've got to get home.

Easier said than done when I could hardly tell what was happening at street level. I squeezed my eyes shut. The changes to my body had always been muscle, skin, and bone. I'd never wanted them to happen, which meant I'd avoided experimenting. I didn't know if I was capable of altering other parts.

Come on, I cajoled my eyes and my ears, addressing my closed eyelids. I know you're already sensitive and I've been mad at you for that in the past. But we won't survive this if I blindly trip over a monster.

If asked, I could describe the grinding sensation of bone lengthening, the taut-loose cycles of stretching skin. Those feelings were tangible, the results of clear causes, similar enough to other things I'd experienced. But I couldn't put words to what I felt inside my head besides a fullness that began at the base of my skull and poured out my eyes and ears.

A solid wall of sound broke over me like a tidal wave. The wind rustled through a thousand leaves, my heart and lungs pulsed, creatures breathed and snarled all around me. My eyes flew open. The world lay before me in sharp detail, its colors muted but light enough for me to tell apart. I could see broken windows and doors, watch my neighbors running into the street, hear cars starting up in garages and growling and barking and screaming.

I gritted my teeth. It was too much to handle all at once, making my head pound. But this wasn't a regular headache, or even a migraine. It started as an ache in my molars, the unpleasant buzz of hard surfaces vibrating against each other.

A large mass rounded the corner of the street, knocking aside parked cars and cracking the sidewalk. It resembled a beetle, but the top of its rounded back was level with a single-story home. Overlapping sections of its shell shifted and grated as dozens of black insect-like legs dragged it forward. Its head reminded me of an old-fashioned diver's helmet. Two massive bubble-like eyes stuck out, unmoving and without pupils.

The pain in my head was growing; I nearly fell off the roof when a spark of orange flashed across my vision, impossibly vibrant compared to the current gray-green of my surroundings. More colors popped and fizzed in my sight, glimpses of images gone too quickly to process. A stranger's voice whispered nonsense words, the source seemingly all around me. I thrashed my head, unable to relieve the terrible pressure building in my skull.

This was it. I'd messed with parts of my body that I shouldn't have, and I'd broken them. I was well and truly fucked—except amid the chaos, I saw other people collapse holding their heads. I flinched when a fleeing car swerved into a tree, had to look away from the sight of a monster pouncing on an incapacitated person. I shouldn't have done this. Seeing and hearing more just meant I could see the spilled blood, hear bones crunch. I tried to drag my attention away before I could see any more —

Two insect legs scratched at the edge of the roof, reaching for me. The giant monster's other legs dug out a wall, threatening the house's stability. I grabbed for the nearest handhold, a TV antenna. My brain boiled as one bubble eye loomed closer.

"Fuck off, Pillbug!" I screamed, the name ready on my tongue. I snapped off the TV antenna and swung it, my arm swelling with muscle.

Pillbug's eye cracked like glass. It let out a high-pitched screech that had me in just as much agony as I'd likely caused it. It tore through the house while I rolled down the other side of the roof, flinging myself into a tree whose breaking branches only somewhat slowed my landing.

I fled down the street and into the forest. I couldn't take the pressure in my head, the terrible sounds; I needed darkness and quiet but I'd banished them from my senses. I dashed between trees, wanting their stout trunks to soak up the screaming and snarling behind me.

A snarl in *front* of me had me lunging to the side, barely dodging a misshapen bundle of fur and claws as it pounced. Yes, the screams were getting more distant as I ran, but the sounds of monsters weren't. They were approaching my neighborhood from this direction—and I could hear the heavy footfalls of more behind me. A brightly burning line of pain cut into my shoulder blade. I cried out, stumbling...

My joints popped as my arms shot forward, sending a second supernova of pain through my back, my forearms lengthening. I caught myself with my hands, swinging my legs forward, pushing off, back on my feet and running as hot blood trickled down my back. I knew I couldn't run forever, I just, I just had to —

The forest ran out with little warning, forcing me to skid to a halt so I didn't fall off the edge of a shallow gorge. I twisted around.

Two dozen eyes stared back at me. But some of the eyes were more than two to a monster, so there were actually less than a dozen. Lucky me.

I took one more step back. The edge of the gorge gave way, sending me tumbling down its slanted side. I landed hard on my back in several inches of turbid water. I was tempted to lie there, breathless and still, see if they'd pass me by.

Then the mud started to creep up my sides. I looked beneath the thin layer of water and screamed. Half-formed eyes dotted the muck. I ripped away from its grasp before I could learn if it had a mouth too. The monsters were still in pursuit, taking their own rough trip down the cliff to join me. I frantically climbed up the other side of the gorge, my heart skipping a beat each time I slipped in the mud. As soon as the wall of the gorge began to flatten out I threw myself forward, trying to get my center of gravity away from the edge.

Sharp teeth sank into my left shoulder.

I screamed and beat at the canid monster as it dragged me along the ground. They had carved out the top of the hill, creating a big pit they were filling with more bodies. I saw cloth inside, shoes, panicked. I thrashed, feeling my arms and legs displace from their joints as they warped, hitting the monster's back legs. It lost its balance and we rolled down the slimy hill together—

I was blinded by an explosion of light, and then there was dust in my mouth, dry ground and slick fur beneath me. We came to an abrupt stop, the monster making a too-human grunt of pain as its jaw loosened from my shoulder. My vision recovered slowly, focusing on the closest objects—the monster lying stunned after I'd landed on it, and a flat stone almost a foot wide. I hefted the stone up and brought it down on the monster's head. It stopped moving.

I considered screaming again. Every one of my limbs felt out of place; the cut on my back had hurt bad enough, but now I understood that had just been surface pain; there was a terrible heat in my shoulder, as though the monster had injected me with fire when it bit me. Its teeth were red with my blood, so much brighter than the brown fluid leaking from its head. I was still on top of it. I scrambled away even though it couldn't hurt me anymore, feeling how each movement pulled at my shoulder, my cut, the future bruises from too many hard landings.

And I couldn't stop. I wasn't allowed to yet.

I took in more of my surroundings before anything else could try to kill me. Rock-strewn beige wasteland beneath a bright sky plagued with green and yellow clouds. The ground had been churned by dozens, if not hundreds, of animal tracks, some of them obscured by a flat trail formed by something big and flat being dragged—Pillbug, maybe. The air several feet away shimmered, forming a distorted window perhaps a few yards across, dark as night. I couldn't see through it, but distantly, as though from underwater, I could hear baying and barking.

Had to assume I couldn't outrun them all forever, so I looked for a weapon instead. I backed away from the window, only to trip. A thick, rusted chain lay on the ground. It circled the window, metal links connecting several ceramic plates together. The abandoned chain wasn't the only sign people had been here. A waist-high rock with engraved drawings stood nearby. They depicted a square surrounded by a circle of connected dots. Inside the square were crude renditions of toothy monsters; outside the circle, what looked like people. One of the monsters had its blocky legs up against the circle as if pushing against a wall.

I looked back at the chain. It was broken in one place, a few links snapped. The baying grew louder. I grabbed the disconnected ends of the chain, almost dropping it when they stung my hands like an electrical shock. I wrapped my hands in my sleeve cuffs before bringing the two ends together.

Light flashed, making me jolt back. There was a gray hue to the air in front of me. The color extended up from where where the now-complete chain lay, forming a dome that fully contained the distortion. I cautiously reached out. My hands met smooth, hard resistance as if I were touching plexiglass. I tried to grab the chain again, but the dome was in the way.

A monster rushed through the distortion, appearing as if it was being created from head to tail, suddenly and violently here; it slammed into the dome from the inside, unable to get any closer. It seemed the translucent dome would keep me safe for the moment.

It would also keep me from going home.

I screamed and kicked the dome, the monster and I striking at it from opposite sides—then I got my wits about me. Better away than dead. The monster's furious snarling was muffled, but I could hear much clearer animal calls in the distance. More on their way? I took out my phone. No signal I could use to call for help, and GPS had no idea where I was. Why would it? The sky was fucking green and yellow. Why would there be anything so human as a cell tower in a place that couldn't possibly be Earth?

Someone had created this strange barrier and left instructions. Maybe if I found other signs of civilization to follow, I could find who it was and get help.

I took one last look at where I'd come from. The monster, the nearest thing to a real werewolf that had ever existed on Earth, still clawed at the dome, teetering on its back legs so we were at eye level. Its mouth was packed with several rows of sharp teeth that stuck out at odd angles, like they were meant to maul instead of just cut. Scabs were visible on its gums and tongue as it panted with exertion. No, that mouth had never been meant to close without doing harm. The dome was so smooth that there was nothing for its claws to catch on; blood welled up at the base of its claws as it compensated by trying more force instead of giving up. It obviously couldn't get to me, and yet it was hurting itself to try.

"Just go," I whispered, backing away. "Why did you... just leave us alone!"

It snarled and bashed its head against the dome instead. I hurried back to the engraved stone, trying not to listen as the monster used its own skull as a hammer. There was one more marking on the stone, an arrow pointing out into the wasteland. With no other ideas, I followed it, dragging myself along as fast as I could.

I continued to pass signs that someone else had been here before me, more worn-down stone markers covered in symbols I couldn't read, only their directional arrows offering any help. My adrenaline wore off, and I felt more pain with every step. According to my phone, I made it four hours before I reached the end of my stamina. Longer than I'd've thought myself capable of, but the sky and landscape were unchanging, making it hard to believe I'd made any progress towards the safe destination I was only hoping existed. I stopped at the next indecipherable sign I came across and let my legs fold beneath me.

I passed out for a while and was woken by a short bout of rain. It was cold and soaked through my clothes, but it gave me a chance to drink. My shoulder burned. Just touching around my bite wound was excruciating, the area horribly soft and leaking a murky liquid that wasn't blood.

I swallowed back bile and imagined a healthy set of tissue beneath the injury, scratching at the affected area with unnaturally long nails. The... pulp came away easily. Yes. That was a good word for it. Human bodies didn't contain pulp, so the decomposing stringy bits I was scraping away weren't part of me. When I was done, I thought I could feel a shallow depression in my shoulder.

Again I walked for as long as I could. Again I needed to rest. Again, my shoulder was hot and disintegrating when I woke up. I wrapped my arms around myself, finding that at some point I'd unconsciously built long flaps of skin from them, as if to replace a comforting blanket. They did nothing to keep me warm. I was too tired to try to get rid of them. All my energy had to be focused on moving forward. Hours bled into each other as I walked.

I tripped over a desiccated plank that blended in unfairly well with the ground and tumbled down a ledge. This time, my landing was followed by a surprised shout. I lifted my chin, the rest of me uncooperative.

Two people stared at me. Both looked male, maybe in their mid-twenties. My vision was blurred, my mind worn out. Most of the details my failing eyes could pick out made sense—one of the pair had tanned skin and dark blond hair, the other a darker skin tone and black curly hair. That was totally acceptable, as was the fact that they were trying to get a campfire going in the indented circle between collapsed ruins I'd fallen into.

What made less sense, and convinced me that I had likely started hallucinating, was that the blond one seemed to have *wings.* White feathers, quills of gold. His companion had a green cape over his shoulders.

" 'M fine," I said automatically. I wasn't fine.

The two of them shared a quick back-and-forth in an unfamiliar language before the blond one cautiously stepped towards me.

"How did you get here?" he said in an accent I couldn't place.

"Are you an angel?" I murmured from the ground.

He pointed to himself. "An angel? Is that your word for me?" He looked back at his companion, shared another indecipherable exchange with him.

"That's weird. I don't believe in angels," I said. I tried to push myself up, only to hiss in pain. The English-speaking stranger knelt beside me, maybe to help. I had to keep trying to stand on my own, though, because if they had wings then they couldn't be real, and I'd need to get out of this mess on my own.

If they *were* real, then that was another problem, because it meant they'd seen me changed.

I started to cry.

The other stranger drifted closer, making soothing noises. The blond one touched my tormented shoulder, and his touch certainly felt real, the pain of it solid and sure even as everything else slipped away.

INTERMISSION

A brief break featuring another voice, translated from the misshapen thoughts that torment the mind of Pillbug (or so he is known to Ella):

This could be a home, and the others agree with me. It is free and open and I know I won't find him here, but if I make a home, maybe he will come.

So much work to be done. But I will lead us true and make it worthwhile.

4

———

When I woke up, I was in a strange room. I was tucked into a bed, still wearing my ripped-up clothes. My bite wound and the cut on my back were wrapped tightly. There had been people. Strangers. That helped me? It seemed so, though anxiety still gnawed at me... I was in almost too unbelievably normal a place after what had come before. The room had a high ceiling and light wood panels, dimly lit by hazy sunlight filtering in through the open window and... glass hemispheres stuck to the ceiling. Full of glowing crystals.

Fuck.

Nauseated from a lingering smell of acrid chemicals, I experimentally turned my head to the side, testing how close to actually vomiting I felt. A stray white feather as long as my hand lay on the floor nearby. The golden shaft had two branches instead of being a single line, like no bird's I had ever seen. I reached out to grab it for a closer look, only to yelp when my shoulder twinged with pain.

Someone knocked on the door. That blond guy from before entered. A smile slowly spread across his face. He was incredibly tidy —pressed black slacks, a white shirt whose long sleeves were buttoned neatly at his wrists, delicate fingers. "Awake already? That's a pleasant surprise," he said.

It was difficult for me to keep from gawking. "Dang, you're real?"

He sighed and slumped into a less formal posture. His wings fell as if in disappointment, moving just as naturally as his arms and legs did. How could he look so human—I could see no other obvious differences aside from the addition of wings—and still be... "Yes. I'm real."

"That's... cool." Then everything else I remembered was probably real too. He'd seen me changed, which was bad; but he'd brought me somewhere seemingly safe, which was good. I could feel panic lying in wait, barely contained by optimistic uncertainty.

He touched a hand to his chest. "Veras."

"Ella. Ella Pierce," I said.

"Ella, I need to check your injuries and change your bandages. Is that okay?"

"I have a choice?"

Veras made an awful clicking noise with his tongue, and I twitched. "I don't want to force you through anything. But it is important that I check you. You were covered in contaminated filth. If I've missed any of it, you could get a fatal infection. Even if I haven't, your wounds need care."

I thought of Matilda and shuddered.

"I need to check you," he repeated.

I shifted the blankets off me, looking down. That my clothing only had holes with melted edges after all they'd been through was a sort of miracle, modesty maintained even if they were practically unwearable.

"Sorry," Veras said. "I disinfected and saved what I could. I've never seen clothes fare that well against the rotting."

"They're polyester," I said.

"What's that?"

"A sort of plastic."

His eyebrows knit together.

"Never mind. I'd prefer not to die, so..." I trailed off weakly.

He opened a set of drawers full of jars, thread, and bandages. I braced myself for whatever was coming next. Veras unscrewed one of the jars, and I gagged from the smell. He touched my bare shoulder, his fingers carrying a strange sting, and his vague frown deepened into frustration.

"This will likely hurt," he warned. "You're a species I haven't encountered before. I'd give you painkillers if I could, but I'm wary of having you ingest medicine not made for you. I need you to answer some questions for me. Try to focus on talking instead of the discomfort, okay?"

What a funny request. I fruitlessly tried not to squirm as he peeled back the bandages on my back and began to clean my cuts. Whatever ointment he was using burned, his touch even outside my injuries carrying the sensation of being lightly shocked or poked with needles. I owned dozens of grounding, calming, comforting things that would've helped me get through this, if I'd only had them with me. All I could do was clench my fists and try to keep breathing steadily.

"What species are you?" Veras asked me.

"Human."

"Is that magic you were using normal for your kind?" He looked at me like he'd be naming a newly discovered disease after me.

"Uhhh... yes?" Magic? Me? I hardly had a better explanation for my ability. It sounded better than *horrifying inhuman mutation*.

He raised an eyebrow.

"...No?"

"Do you recall how you arrived here?" Veras asked.

"I'd love to forget."

"If you could please describe —"

I huffed.

"Sorry. I have questions I'd ask another of my kind to check that they're mentally present, but I wouldn't expect you to know what our calendar year or who our current leader is," Veras said.

"My vision's fine, I don't have any gaps in my memory, and I could answer the same questions about my own home," I said.

"Alright. So which part were you confused about? The magic, or if it's normal?"

"Um, the magic. I guess."

"Do you know it by a different name, or is it not normal?"

I didn't trust myself to lie. "It's not normal. We have that term, but to us it's... made up, not real. All fantasy and fairy tales."

"You should tell me what an angel is."

"In some religions, they're winged people who are messengers of deities. They perform miracles and fight evils."

"I see."

"And you're not that," I said.

"No."

"You look almost human. What are you, then?"

"Makhal," he said. "Ours is a relatively common body shape for sentient species, though you're especially similar. We have magic, ways of using energy to change the world around us, but we're hardly anything divine. If we were, the Graft, those creatures you encountered, would've long been scoured from the universe."

I bit my tongue as he washed out one of the deeper scratches in my back, pausing before I responded. Somehow magic potentially being real felt like the least weird thing happening right now, but you know what? Good. I could use a miracle after the nightmare that had brought me here. I could gloss over that bit for the moment.

"But you do fight them?" I asked.

"My species? Yes, we deal with them when we must. Me? No. I'm no fighter," Veras said. "Our last war against the Graft ended about three years ago. The world where we met has been a wasteland for as long as we've known of it. If I'd known there were monsters on 9F, we never would've gone there. How many rifts did you pass through before we met?"

I had to think about that, figuring he meant the strange window of distortion I'd fallen through. "One? Are there very many... rifts?"

"Yes. How advanced was the invasion?"

Invasion was a frighteningly permanent word. I described what had happened.

"I'm sorry," he said quietly when I was done. "I don't know if it'll make you feel much better to hear that your world is far from the first to be invaded, and it wouldn't be the first to fend off an invasion, either."

Or the first to fail to, I imagined. "What'll happen now?"

"You're our guest. We'll take care of you until you're ready and want to leave."

"I meant... thanks. For everything. But I meant to Earth. To my planet. Or, um, my world."

"You're already dealing with a lot," Veras said. "I can tell you later."

"I need to know. It's my *home*."

"I just don't want to overwhelm you."

It was far too late for that. I could feel my body start to twitch and change in protest. I didn't know if Veras understood the word "meltdown," but he seemed to pick up on something being wrong and gave in.

"The Graft are a hybrid of magic, disease, and animal," Veras said. "Something organic gets seeded with contamination—we think this is a mix of infectious illness and magic—and sickens. Without medical intervention, the original life ends, leaving a twisted and hateful being in its place. Living animals become grafted monsters. Plants and dead animals break down and combine into formless biomass, from which new monsters are produced. They're violent towards all non-Graft life, wanting to kill it and turn it into more of themselves. The body fluids and other secretions of graftlings cause new contamination, infecting more beings. They're fortunately limited to animal intelligence and can't use magic like ours, but even with those limitations they've spread across the universe, taking over entire worlds."

Now that. That was bad news. Awful news, in fact, with some serious heft to it, more than I could take in the moment. Grounded. Stay grounded. Focus on the concrete, the information most relevant to my situation.

"There was this gigantic monster, bigger than a house. It seemed to be in charge. Was that something else?" I asked.

"That was likely a Fortress," Veras said. "Fortresses are specialized graftlings. The first ones were large, slow-moving, and heavily armored creatures. They carried large amounts of liquid contaminant in their bodies to spill forth on new worlds, or to kickstart a new horde. Nowadays there's more variation, but we still refer to any large, individualized monster that way."

"They... evolved?"

"We don't quite understand how, but that's just what the Graft does. I just wish it took as long as natural evolution. It's an ecosystem more than a species, and as it takes in new things..." Veras shrugged. "Individual monsters don't reproduce, they continue the ecosystem through contaminating usable material and killing anything that could stop them. They don't need to live long, and there's no real knowing how many different forms of life have contributed to any one monster. You get strange new forms all the time, and some of them get made over and over. Has what I told you made sense?"

It did. It just hurt too much to think about, so I tried not to right then. I had other bases I needed covered. "How are you speaking English?"

"Language magic. It's useful for dealing with patients from other worlds."

"Oh." It seemed like an entirely complete answer to him, but it opened up endless fractals of other questions for me.

"What happened to your hands?" Veras asked with a frown while I contemplated. "They weren't like this earlier."

I looked down, saw my palms were reddened and tender. "I might've scratched them up in my sleep."

He dipped a cotton ball in medicine, and I nearly writhed at the overly minty smell of it. "This topical ointment helps draw the heat out of inflammation. I will use a small amount just in case your skin reacts to it."

Sometimes I wondered if my hands had an unusually high number of nerve endings. They were so sensitive that even my parents hadn't held my hands when I was little, instead guiding me with a touch on the shoulder. The medicine-soaked cotton ball felt like icy pins and needles, Veras's fingers creating too much sensory information where they held my own still. I searched for something comforting to latch on to, a familiar sight or scent or sound, but there was nothing; there was the hard melted edges of my clothing rubbing against my skin, and the aggravating flickering of those strange crystal lights, and those terrible chemical odors. I tried to hold it in and couldn't.

"What's this?" Veras had finished cleaning up one hand and was about to move on to the other. He leaned in to get a closer look.

Veras hissed when he cut himself on a claw that hadn't been there a moment before, lurching away from me. Drops of ochre blood welled up from a small cut.

I sat frozen. Veras stared at me intently, his wings sticking out to his sides, the feathers on edge and trembling.

"I, I didn't..." I stammered. "I didn't mean to..."

"Truly?" Veras said.

I nodded, on the brink of tears.

His gaze broke from me, turning to his palm. Motes of fuzzy white light gathered around his cut. I jerked away from them. Even from a few inches away they seemed to burn without heat, too bright to have so close. The motes of light merged at the center of his cut, sealing it. In a moment it was like nothing had happened. He sat delicately on the edge of the bed.

"Other hand," he said, taking it carefully.

"I don't want to be ungrateful..." I stopped there.

"Magic was the first thing I tried. With my other patients, I can use it to treat cuts, burns, bruises, broken bones, and illness. But your entire body spasmed like you were having a seizure when I tried healing you. Even just trying to sense past your skin isn't working now. It's like my magic can't pass through, even where you're injured. I can clean through sterilizing, but nothing else," he said, voice level rising with frustration. "I've treated half a dozen intelligent species, and *never* experienced that. Probably has something to do with the disgusting changes your body goes through. I almost thought you were already a graftling at first."

I looked away until he was done, trying to keep my ability from going berserk. I'd never known emotions could feel so *physical.*

Veras pointed to a door in the hallway. "Shower. Your bandages are waterproof, and there are fresh clothes for you."

Standing up didn't feel great, but I grew steadier after the first few steps, powered by the desire to be alone for a bit. I locked the bathroom door behind me, trying to convince myself that alone would keep me safe from all the horrible things I now knew existed in the universe. The water took a while to start and came out cold from the shower, but at least it was running, which was impressive given the lack of electrical sockets, heating vents, or any other modern technology I was accustomed to. The hard bar of soap didn't do as much to remove the chemical smell lingering on my skin as I'd hoped, and I eventually had to give up on feeling fully clean. I went through my ripped clothing again, realizing that while I'd seen my shoes (half-melted by Veras "sterilizing" them) next to my bed, I hadn't seen my phone. It wasn't in my pockets, which meant it was probably gathering dust on… 9F. I had to roll up the cuffs of the blue shirt, dark pants, and oversized socks that were left for me. I reached around to touch my back. There were slits in the shirt over my shoulder blades for wings to stick through. I looked in the concave, off-colored mirror and hated the stunned look that was frozen on my face.

Veras had stripped the bed and cleaned the floor while I showered. He tossed me a small pouch when I came back in the room.

"These aren't mine," I said. The pouch held a simple necklace, an inscribed metal plate with chain on either side, and a matching earring. The carved symbols seemed to quiver, playing tricks on my eyes.

"Put them on. My housemate Andras can't translate with magic like I can."

The jewelry felt like it was vibrating too. I held them, disliking the feeling of them against my skin.

Veras sighed and spoke words I couldn't understand. I slipped on the earring and necklace. They buzzed like small motors against my skin, and I wondered if it was Veras trying his healing magic on me earlier that had stung. Leave it to me to have a sensory reaction to something that didn't exist back home. Veras's strange speech gained familiar syllables, most of it still meaningless to me. I tried to relax. The earring's buzzing quieted, and Veras spoke English again.

"—lucky you weren't bitten too deeply, that would've taken the infection further into your body. If you can understand me say in *makhali*, 'no physical exertion for several weeks.'"

"Will it take me that long to heal?" I asked. My words echoed like I was hearing them twice, once as I normally would, and a second time with a delay. The echo sounded different, a similar cadence to the unfamiliar words Veras had been using. Focusing too hard on hearing the difference made my head hurt, so I stopped.

"I'm not sure," Veras said, his words echoing too. "I always use magic to treat my patients, and I don't know what your species's time-line for naturally healing is. At least that translation artifact is work-ing. You'll need to keep it on for Andras."

"Is Andras also a makhal?" I asked.

"Everyone you'll meet on our world, Plesmae, is. Make sure you thank him. Your body is built denser than ours. It took the both of us to carry you here."

"I'm grateful," I said. "I really am. But I need to get home as soon as possible. My parents were away when the monster showed up, but they'll return home to find the neighborhood wrecked and me missing."

He wouldn't meet my eyes. "I'm sorry."

Those two words hurt worse than my aching shoulder. "How do I get back to them?" I asked.

"Unless your species can fend them off, you'd have to pass through a hostile ecosystem."

"What was, there was this broken thing that I think I fixed? It was like a wall I couldn't get through."

"That would be a veil," Veras said. "Unless the supports are destroyed, or someone with specific magic interacts with it, it's incredibly hard to break. You'd have to stand there and hit it over and over for months, if not years, to break it. They're usually used defensively, but we also use them to block access to rifts." He frowned. "There must've been an earthquake or other event on 9F that disrupted its placement."

"So my people don't know about yours because you blocked us off?"

"I'd have to check our records. Maybe we interacted in the past. Nowadays, most civilizations avoid interacting with ones that aren't already aware of worlds beyond their own. There are graftling scouts whose purpose is to find new worlds with abundant organic matter. They're quite skilled at following scent trails left behind by, say, one civilization's people going to visit another's. We try not to introduce the Graft to worlds they're not already on. You'd really never heard of them before? Or other sentient species?"

"Never."

"I'm sorry it's turned out this way," he said.

"So you think the monsters just got *lucky*?" I said.

"It's happened before."

"But that's…"

Too many words came to mind, creating a traffic jam. Awful. Unfair. Bullshit. Stupid. My fists clenched. The muscles in my arms squirmed and swelled.

"Okay!" Veras said. "How about we, uh, go outside for a little bit? Show you where you've wound up?"

I numbly let him lead me through the house. We were on the first floor, the windows' white curtains and wooden shutters open and looking out on an unearthly forest. I'd never visited the California redwoods, but I imagined many of the trees out there were close to the same size. Near the front door and staircase was a kitchen with a wood-burning oven and hand-pumped sink, and a rug-laden area with bookshelves and a couple armchairs. I realized that the ceilings were higher than normal. I supposed being meant for flight could make a person claustrophobic. A few pairs of shoes waited by the front door, half of them polished, the rest working-style boots.

Outside was unpredictable, and therefore the last place I wanted to be. But I felt aimless, like a puppet with its strings snapped. I followed Veras.

The trees were even bigger than I'd thought, stretching hundreds of feet up in the air, roots collecting enough dirt to form small hills and valleys. Their leaves were all different colors, as if it was simultaneously spring, fall, and another fantasy season where the leaves turned blue and purple, creating a backlit mosaic. My neighborhood had been at the edge of the woods, but Veras's house was like a forgotten dollhouse left deep within the wilderness. I looked down, where this new world seemed more manageable, starting with the flower-speckled moss beneath my feet and slowly working my way up to the normal-sized bushes and trees growing in clumps where light passed through the canopy. If I just didn't look up, I'd be fine, but it was hard not to, especially when a plate-sized leaf fell on my head.

"Welcome to the Glade," Veras said. He squinted into the distance. "Follow."

He led me around the side of the house to a fenced-in garden. The plants growing there ranged from almost familiar to absurd. A bench with cushions was under the eaves.

"Just... sit here for a while," Veras ordered. "It takes time to adapt to a new environment. You might as well get to work on that."

I sat. Veras backed away towards the door.

"Andras and I are the only ones in the Glade, and that's not many people to search, so don't wander off and get lost." He rounded the corner, and I heard the front door shut.

I watched the treetops sway, a dark mood swallowing me. If I hadn't almost died, if my parents were here with me, then I'd still need to take this slow, but I'd've been excited about visiting an alien world. I desperately wanted them at my side, safe for at least the moment, instead of on a world that might be turning into a bunch of alien sludge soon. Bile rose in my throat.

What if they were here? I asked myself. What would they do?

Based on the other trips we'd taken, they'd be leading the way, overflowing with excitement so I might absorb their excess. They'd have found pictures of this place beforehand to show me, explained what the weather was like, made the transition as easy for me as possible. They'd be happy that the three of us were exploring together, because I so rarely wanted to travel.

And my job, the one thing they hoped for in return, was that I find at least one cool thing they hadn't noticed to show them. I pretended I was doing that, that they were just on the other side of one of the massive trees. I knelt on the ground and touched the moss. It flaked off on my fingers with barely any pressure; I quickly shook my hand clean on noticing tiny black dots with hair-thin legs crawling over my skin. I found what had to be an alien acorn, except it was fist-sized and spiky. I wandered from the bench, stopping to examine the petals of a daisy knock-off that were solid like a succulent's leaves, exposed dirt that was tinged aubergine, animal tracks with more digits than I cared for.

Pretending didn't work. With each new alien detail, pressure built in my head and chest. Having familiar things around me wasn't a *want*, it was a *need*. I wasn't wearing my own clothes. I didn't know where my phone was. All my comforting things I should've been able to rely on were more than just twenty minutes away; they were on the other side of a giant monster that wanted to make my brain explode.

There had to be something familiar around here, right? Other than a house with a not-angel inside it? I had to find it. Didn't matter what Veras had said, or that I was weak. I could feel keratin pushing urgently against skin as my claws tried to form, calluses attempting to spread over my limbs like a rash. If I didn't find something to calm me down soon, I was worried the changes might reopen my shoulder wound.

It was also entirely possible that none of this was real, and it didn't matter what the hell I did.

I picked a direction and walked, following the natural path formed by the valleys. Ideally I would've kept the house in sight, but the hills and trees made that difficult. I kept walking, maybe longer than I should have, feeling like an ant. An oversized spiky acorn ricocheted off a tree trunk next to me with a *crack*, making me shriek in surprise; I looked up by about a hundred feet to see something sloth-shaped, pipe-cleaner-bendy limbs wrapped around a branch, one clawed paw already weighing another acorn. I'd been menaced by squirrels before, but squirrels weren't as big as a Doberman, and they didn't gather in packs of twenty.

I heard a shout and instinctively huddled down. Far off to my left was someone furiously waving at me—the other person I'd seen before collapsing.

"Excuse me? Could you come over here?" they shouted.

I hurried over to a flat area between the gigantic roots of a yellow-leafed tree. The strangest plants I'd seen so far grew there. Some resembled modern art than anything living, with jarring stripes and harsh angles. There was a complicated perfume in the air, too confusing to analyze.

The stranger was near the back, by the biggest plants. He was a few inches taller than me, and had dark brown skin and eyes, short curly black hair. He seemed warmer than Veras, with a rounder face and easy smile. His wings were blocky in shape, and looked like they had a thick layer of green moss growing on them. He offered me his hand as I walked up.

"Hello there," he said. "I'm Andras. What's your name?"

I said nothing, my brain busy catching up with my eyes. Andras's other arm was stuck up to the elbow in a plant like a giant Venus flytrap.

He still had his hand out. I pointed at the plant.

"Yes, I was going to ask you for help with that in a moment," Andras said.

"Um," I said.

"No need to worry. This buddy eats insects, so its jaws aren't sharp. There's just a bit of acid."

"Acid?"

"For digestion." He gave me a winning smile, as if to say, isn't nature amazing?

The man-eater's jaws had formed a perfect seal around his arm, a foamy substance filling in the gaps between its teeth. I grabbed its jaws, hoping it wasn't poisonous to humans.

"Please be gentle with it, it didn't mean to bite me," he said.

"It's a plant. I doubt it 'means' much of anything." But I was careful as I pulled, not wanting to overextend my hurt shoulder either. The plant's jaws wouldn't budge. "Could you, uh, look away?"

He raised an eyebrow.

"Please." If I gave myself the muscle I needed to free him and couldn't change it back, I wanted to disappear into the woods without him seeing me. First Matilda, then Veras, I didn't want to experience a third person's disgust.

Andras looked away. I watched him for the slightest glance over his shoulder as I slowly increased the strength of my right arm, applying just as much force as I needed. The plant's jaws opened up a sliver, leaking sizzling droplets. Andras pulled out his arm, and I relaxed mine back to normal. His skin was reddened from irritation.

"Thanks for that," he said, once again offering me his hand (the one without acid burns) to shake. His skin had a rough feel that I wasn't expecting, a level of friction beyond a callus. It sent a chill down my spine. "It probably would've spit me out after a few days, but I'm glad I didn't have to wait that long. What was your name?"

"Ella."

"Are you doing alright? I know Veras was worried for you," he said.

"Better than I was. Thanks for, um, not leaving me behind."

"Of course." Andras moved on to another plant, one that spiraled upwards like a hollow unicorn horn. From his pocket he took out a folded-over leaf and shook some dead bugs—too big and with too many mandibles for my liking—into the plant. Nothing happened until he poked the plant. It immediately snapped shut.

"Didn't get me that time," Andras said cheerfully. "Do me a favor and don't tell Veras about this? He's less stressed not knowing."

A hidden stash of murder plants was a big secret to keep, but I said I wouldn't. I'd already annoyed one of the two people I'd met, and didn't want to immediately disappoint the other.

"Is it okay here so far?" Andras asked. "I know you're dealing with a lot, but this is an environment that can work for you, right?"

"I suppose it's like my home, in some ways," I said. "Much bigger than I'm used to. But I do, um, like forests."

"That's a start," Andras said, pleased.

"Are the, um... is there anything out here that might... hurt us?"

Andras raised an eyebrow before glancing up. "Unless you take a plant projectile straight to the eye, you'll be fine. They'll get used to you soon enough."

I looked where he was, spotting the pseudo-sloths again. As I watched, one threw itself from a branch, the shapeless tubes of its arms unraveling into thin, muscular limbs connected to a translucent membrane that let it glide to another tree. The others followed suit. Maybe they'd get used to me, but I doubted I'd get used to them anytime soon.

"Now there are technically some megafauna in the Glade," Andras added. "But I wouldn't expect to see them this close to the edge of the forest. They prefer it deeper in, where there's less of this smaller growth."

"How mega?"

"You won't see them," he assured me.

"Andras —"

"They're herbivores anyway. You won't find a carnivore interested in anything our size. You're not a plant or an insect, so you'll be fine."

I squeezed my eyes shut. No matter where I was, the darkness behind my eyelids was the same; I could use it to delude myself I was somewhere else for a few seconds. "You know your way to the house, right?" I asked.

"Of course. You want to go back already?"

"Yeah. I mean, I like being outdoors, but right now, it's..."

"I forget sometimes that other people have limits on how much time they like to be outside," Andras said.

It wasn't that. Everything was just *a lot* right now and I wanted to be in an enclosed space again. But the reason Andras had come up with was enough to convince him to head back with me. He made a sweeping gesture with his arm. I jumped as the branches of the massive tree we were under creaked and bent, their broad leaves forming a protective shelter around the murder plants. Andras waved goodbye to them before turning away—not the direction I thought we'd come from, which told me all I needed to know about my sense of direction in new places.

Thankfully, Andras walked back with me instead of flying. I was nervous about being around Veras again, but when I saw their house appear between the trees, I almost broke into a run. Only the fear of splitting the stitches in my shoulder kept me from doing so.

"Veras! I'm back!" Andras called out as he opened the door.

He needn't have yelled. Veras was in the middle of deep-cleaning the floor. The liquid he used smelled like weird bleach, strong and burning. He seemed relieved to see Andras, but tensed when he noticed I was along for the ride. I folded my hands behind my back while I told my stubby claws to go away.

I jumped when Andras grabbed my arm.

"You should see the rest of the house. I'll show you around," he said.

I followed Andras back down the hall. He pointed out the bathroom, and at the end of the hall, the room I'd woken up in.

"You already know the guest room. Here's my bedroom." He opened another door, and it was like stepping into another world again. At first I thought he'd worked some sort of... space magic?... to make the room bigger, but no. He'd just filled it with plant life. Vines climbing up walls, bushes and ferns barely contained in their pots, a whole beauty pageant of flowers. A sapling grew through his bed's headrest. I couldn't tell if the floor was carpeted, or overgrown with moss. The smell was pleasant, but the intensity coupled with the humidity was overwhelming. On the other side of the room was a wall of curtain-less windows and a door leading outside.

"That goes to my garden. Want to see it later?"

"Uh, sure. You have more plants than this?"

"They need other conditions, and some of them are big." He lowered his voice to a conspiratorial whisper. "Veras wasn't too happy about the tree. Anyway, there's not as much upstairs. Veras's room, another bathroom, and we have a little balcony. I hope the house is shaped in a way you'll find comfortable. Is it very different from what you're used to?"

"Similar enough," I said.

"How far did you go before you ran into us?"

"Earth, my world, it's eventually walkable from here." In the grand scheme of things, it was no distance at all; in terms of the obstacles present, it might as well have been a million miles away.

"Earth? Not a world whose history I'm familiar with, though we might have different names for it. You should ask Veras sometime, he's studied —"

I fidgeted with my earring. Andras's words turned into unfamiliar rhythms and vowels until I put it back on.

"—also haven't visited other worlds like he has, so I wouldn't know."

I followed Andras back to the living room, only for Veras to pull me aside.

"You're hungry?" he said.

Starving, actually. I nodded.

"Here's the thing," Veras said. "Normally, if I had an alien patient who needed to try our food for the first time, I'd be magically monitoring how their body reacted to it over the next few days so I'd know if they ate something toxic, and could deal with the symptoms. But since my magic won't work on you, I can't do that."

"So it's a crapshoot if I die or not." That was about as kind as I expected the universe to be to me.

"I wouldn't let you die."

"I'm not saying you'd watch me asphyxiate without doing anything, but it's not like you have any human medicine either."

"We'll go slow, do our best, and if it does affect you, I'll find a way to take care of it. Alright?"

I couldn't not eat. "Alright."

I sat at the round kitchen table, where Veras had set out plates of what looked like roasted vegetables.

"Are you a carnivore?" Veras asked.

That way of asking felt hurtful. "I do eat meat, but I don't need to."

"Good. It's the same for us, but it's easiest to be vegetarian living out here."

I nodded, staring down at my plate. Trying new foods was already an ordeal for me. Was I really about to put something unknown, something alien, in my mouth?

"It's okay," Andras said, patting my hand. "We've got you."

I instinctively drew my hand away, not meaning to offend him, but there'd always been a big gap between my intentions and what others saw. "Thanks." I picked up a wooden fork and steeled myself. Why freak out before I even knew if I'd dislike the taste or texture? I speared a bit of something vaguely cucumber-esque and brought it up to my face. Minimal smell? Good.

I looked up and froze. Veras was staring right at me. An even deeper sense of discomfort grew in my gut. I wasn't a messy eater, but having others watch me eat made me uncomfortable. I forced the fork into my mouth, trying to keep my expression neutral.

"You look strained," Veras said.

I swallowed down the vegetable before I could think too long about its mix of savory-smoky and dessert-sweet flavors, which might've been fine on their own but together were just *wrong*. "At home, I'm a bit of a picky eater."

"Visiting new places is a good antidote for that," he said.

Maybe for him, but some of us had sensory issues to contend with.

I tried a bit of something pale orange and almost choked on it, my throat nearly closing off to keep anything going down it. Veras jumped out of his seat, but I was already waving him off. "Just... too sugary," I said.

"Too sugary?" Veras said the words slowly, as if he'd never heard them adjacent before.

"This is a bit less flavorful," Andras said, cutting a slice of bread for me. At least, it appeared bread-adjacent enough that I could tell myself it was that.

I tried it. Yep, close enough. "This is supposed to have toppings, right?"

"I can get you some—"

"No, no, I'm good like this."

I messed with the other things on my plate to make them look touched, but I'd stick to my not-cucumber and bread for now. Just had to chew and swallow quickly. Veras continued to watch me closely, but relaxed somewhat when Andras shot him a pleased look. I ate as much as I could stomach, which wasn't much.

"Can I be excused?" I mumbled.

Veras surveyed my plate like he was searching for crime scene evidence, but nodded.

"Cool." I forced down the urge to make finger guns as I walked away.

"My" room still smelled like whatever medicines Veras had used, and I wanted to give it more time to air out before entering. I found the balcony on the second floor and sat there a while, legs dangling off the side. My stomach cramped and complained with hunger. Darkness came early to the Glade as the fading sunlight was blocked by the canopy. A few glass hemispheres on the balcony filled with a soft white light, but it didn't carry very far. What the sun struggled to do, the moon and stars failed at entirely. Did they even have a moon? Stars seemed required but I couldn't even be sure of that.

The door behind me opened. Andras sat next to me.

"You'll be staying with us for a while, won't you?" he said.

I wrapped my arms around myself. "Do you want me to?"

He smiled in a way that radiated warmth. "Ella, I'm glad to have a guest. It's just been the two of us since we moved here three years ago, and I miss having other people to talk to. Veras can be high-stress at times, and you're not from Plesmae, so I expect there to be some hiccups as we all get used to living together. You've got him a little freaked out at the moment. Just don't ever threaten him, okay? I hate fighting other people."

"I'm not here to hurt anyone," I said, surprised.

"Good. It's nothing personal, I only want to be careful." He turned his smile to the forest. "This could be a good place for you. So much foreign life has successfully taken root here. Here, I'll show you an example," he said.

Andras picked a seed off one of the fallen leaves. I felt him gather his magic, soft and alarming like a furred object unexpectedly brushing against bare skin. The seed split in half, tender pink shoots creeping out from their shell. In a minute, the seedling had swelled into a small leafy plant.

"That's my magic," he said, placing it in a pot and making the roots crawl into the dirt. "Growing and shaping plant life. My hobby, too. Do you like plants?"

"I'm more of a... passive enjoyer, but yes."

"That's great! We'll be sure to get along."

It would certainly make life easier if we did. "Does your magic not work on every plant?"

"You mean the moth-trap? I didn't want to do anything irreversible to it. Growing is easier than trimming back."

Soaking your arm in acid sounded irreversible too, but what did I know about makhali?

"We're mostly on our own out here, but my magic means we're well set up in terms of food," Andras continued. "The Glade might seem frightening at first, but we're safe here. This whole situation might take you some getting used to, but Veras and I are here for you. And if you need to work through some things and we're unavailable, plants are great listeners even if your magic doesn't involve them."

"So can everyone do every kind of magic?" I asked.

"Nope, makhali are born with a specialty. I can work with plants and Veras can heal. He's quite skilled at it too, even with other species. It's a hard discipline to master."

I could feel resentment building in me each time my shoulder ached. "I'm sure it is."

I excused myself, claiming exhaustion, which was true, but I also didn't want to risk insulting one of my hosts right off the bat.

Even at night, they left the curtains and window shutters open. I ran downstairs and through the hallway to the guest room as fast as I could to keep myself from looking out into the dark. I shut the window in "my" room, imagining one of Pillbug's long legs reaching through it to get me. The glass lights turned off when I tapped them. I left one lit. I shoved the translation items in the bedside drawer, grateful to be free of their incessant buzzing.

I got ready for bed, hoping to sleep off some of my physical discomfort. I kept my shirt on, the hem long enough that it was almost a nightgown. It wasn't enough to keep me warm beneath the thin blankets. Even if I closed my eyes, hell, even if I weren't able to hear, I'd know this wasn't my room. The mattress was wider than mine and stuffed differently, the sheets rougher. I thought I could even feel the movement of air in the room as I breathed, and that too was different because of the different shape. I gripped the sheets, claws fraying their edges. I needed to get home to my parents as soon as possible.

5

———————

Waking up to find I was still in Veras and Andras's house might have been the most disappointing moment in my life. I was used to mornings where I had to disentangle real events from vivid dreams, but usually my most upsetting memories belonged to the latter category. Not this time. I was quiet as I sat through a small, stressful breakfast with my hosts, and was less than pleased to get cornered by Veras afterwards.

"Does this really have to happen every day?" I asked as Veras peeled the bandages off my shoulder.

"Yes. Your healing is unusual and I need to make sure there aren't any slower-developing symptoms from your new environment and food."

"Unusual how?"

"It's faster than I would've expected. You're still injured, but the fact that you have a mostly functioning arm at this point is surprising. Is this normal for your species?"

"Don't think so."

"Hmm. Are you experiencing any new discomfort?"

God, yes. Hunger leftover from before the meager breakfast I'd managed to choke down. Exhaustion. The restless sensation that my surroundings were wrong.

I didn't know how much of Veras's poking and prodding I could bear. "No."

Veras appraised me, head tilted, before asking, "how do humans show signs of inflammation?"

I told him about lymph nodes and where some of them were, subjecting myself to his hands feeling my armpits, neck, above my collarbone. His touch was clinical, not lasting a second longer than it had to; I appreciated that, but felt a bit offended by how quickly he pulled away. He cleaned out my shoulder wound again. My feet tensed against the floor through the pain. One knee rose above the other. I looked down at my curled, clawed hands. My left ring finger stuck out an inch further than its neighbors. From behind my shoulder, Veras made a noise of barely contained distress.

"Did you just gag?" I asked.

"No," he said defensively.

I didn't have the tools for my ritual, so I did what I could. I pushed my thumb against the bent joint, applying pressure until something gave. It scrunched back to its original length. We both shuddered.

"Done?" I asked.

He hurriedly finished changing my bandages. I stumbled away on legs that were several inches different in length, finding a quiet corner of the living room to be in while Veras cleaned up. I lay on the floor and willed my body back to normal. One calf shrunk. I pressed my legs together to check they were the same length again. I gave up on getting rid of my claws after ten minutes of failed attempts and stood, thinking I might be less restless if I went outside.

I looked out the kitchen window and bit back a scream. The garden *writhed*. Flowers budded, blossomed, and wilted in seconds, replaced by rapidly swelling growths. I dropped to the ground, hiding behind the counter. My hands covered my nose and mouth, quieting the sound of my panicked breathing, ready to rise up to cover my eyes if... if anything...

The front door creaked open, hurried footsteps coming inside.

"Ella?"

I dared to look up. Andras was watching me, worried.

"That looked freaky, didn't it?" he said softly.

I nodded.

"Sorry. Since we're still figuring out what you can comfortably eat, I thought it would be best if we had more options. Guess I should've warned you there might be some... unnatural growth happening outside."

"Thanks." The word came out hoarse.

Andras offered me his hand. "Would you like to help me harvest my garden?"

I reluctantly took his hand, careful not to scratch him, and stood. We went outside together. Andras handed me a wicker basket.

"Why don't you go through first and pick whatever looks good?" he said.

I walked warily between the plants. Any of them could be fatally poisonous to me. I supposed by that same logic any of them could be safe and absolutely delicious, but that was much harder to convince myself of. I picked one of any crop that wasn't an unearthly bright blue, gelatinous, or shaped like a sea anemone, not willing to even try those. I reached up to pluck an apple-sized purple thing from a vine, only for my injured shoulder to smart. The vine bent over, offering its fruit to me.

"Are you alright?" Andras asked.

"Yes," I said automatically, and then, "ow."

"I'll get the rest. You're doing great, picking out so much."

Hopefully I hadn't picked my own poison. "Couldn't you make them drop the fruit on their own?" I asked.

"I could," Andras said. He wiggled his fingers, and the roots of a nearby plant unearthed themselves to wave back. "With my magic, I could make them do all sorts of things. But there's a point where it stops being gardening, and I like gardening."

"What does it become when it's not gardening?"

Andras tilted his head in thought. "Bullying? It would be overly bossy, at the very least. Magic should enable you to do new things, or do old things better, not make others do it for you."

I must've looked bitter.

"And the best uses of magic," Andras said, "are when you're helping someone who doesn't have your ability. You've found your way to a born healer and gardener, so I don't want you feeling bad about needing us for medical attention and food, okay? Veras and I are in agreement that it's an honor to use our magic for others."

"...Okay." I'd have to take his word for Veras.

I tried to help out in the kitchen, but Andras was concerned about my shoulder. He and Veras had a small bookshelf in their living room, and I was ushered into an armchair and given an illustrated book of flowers to keep me occupied while he cooked. This would have been a fine situation if not for the ever-more-complicated mix of smells coming from the stovetop, and the fact that Veras also got kicked out of the kitchen and into the living room.

"I don't think this translation thing is working," I said, squinting at the jumbled mess of a language with way too many letters.

"I can understand you just fine," Veras responded. He was flipping through an atlas-sized book. I caught a glimpse of something insect-like next to a barricade of illegible text.

"I can't read," I said.

The corner of his mouth twitched.

My face reddened. "I meant this specific language, you asshole."

"Ella," Andras said from the kitchen. "Please."

"Sorry," I said. Veras was kind of an asshole, though. And I'd had too many childhood experiences of people assuming what I was capable of once they learned I was neurodivergent for similar situations to not be triggering.

"Veras, help her understand."

"Those artifacts are sensitive to vibrations. They only translate sound. Most intelligent species struggle with having their senses magically messed with. Hearing's the best tolerated."

"Really? I've changed my eyes so I can see better in the dark before," I said.

He pinched his brow. "What am I going to do with you? Don't assume I'll be able to fix your vision if you ruin it."

"I won't."

"I hope you're being careful in general. Don't do the Graft's work for them."

"I don't understand my ability completely, but I doubt I can re-infect myself."

"I mean making yourself into a monster."

My stomach violently twisted. "Excuse me," I said, making a quick escape.

I locked myself in the bathroom and sat against the wall, considering vomiting. Veras's words had brought up years of barely repressed anxiety. When I lifted my hand to wipe at my damp eyes, my arm was stiff and resistant. The skin of my forearm appeared to be crystallizing, an inch-thick hard layer foaming up and spreading towards my elbow like an infection, keeping me from bending it. The same process was happening in splotches across my back and legs. It was like my body was getting covered in skin-tone lava rock. Telling it to stop did nothing; in the time it took me to attempt some controlled breathing to calm myself down, the crystallization only spread further.

My worrying was interrupted by Veras, waiting outside the bathroom. "Ella? You've been in there a while."

"Do you need to use it?" I mumbled.

"I'm checking if you're alright."

"Go away."

"Look, I'm sorry I brought that up. I know this is all new to you." When I didn't respond, he added, "are you in pain?"

I slammed the hardened back of my hand against the door, the *bang* surprising us both. "Go away!"

He hastily retreated down the hall. I swallowed back tears and watched the off-white growth continue to overtake me. Idiot. I could've —I should've asked for help. Before it could spread further, I got my nails under the edge of the growth on one arm and managed to peel a section of it off. It hurt like pulling off a bandaid, ripping out vellus hairs. The calcified skin, or whatever it was, crumbled to dust once I'd removed it. Taking off the rest became a compulsive action, one that at least helped me get my anxiety and nausea under control. I gathered myself, knowing I should apologize to Veras for snapping at him.

Veras and Andras had set a chalkboard on the living room floor and covered it in clumps of writing and colored lines. All the lines started and ended in the same two places, but squiggled across the chalkboard in different paths. Veras stalked around it while Andras lounged in an armchair, looking half asleep.

"We don't get to just skip to Glashower and back," Andras was saying. "I've told you plenty of times, I'd be happy with either. You're the picky one. Felar or Cannan?"

"Felar was shitty even before the war," Veras said. "At least Cannan has interesting ruins. Tell me even one cool thing about Felar's culture."

"I don't know. I've never seen any of it."

"Exactly! They were so damn insular. Who knows how much of their culture has been lost because they kept it to themselves? Can you imagine that? Though I suppose Felar is flatter. Might be easier for you."

I finally spoke up. "Sorry."

"What?" Veras looked up.

"Sorry. I didn't mean to snap at you."

He stared at me, wary. "Okay."

"Sorry I haven't tried any of your food yet," I told Andras.

"Don't worry about it," Andras said. "It's not going anywhere."

I sat alone at the kitchen table, grateful my hosts were too occupied to watch while I ate. Andras had laid out a good fifteen different foods, peeled and trimmed, seared, stewed. All you have to do, I told myself, is try a cubic inch of everything. One shotgun round of sampling, and then you can go back and fill up on what you like. Or what you hate the least.

That plan went out the window with the first food I tried. My lips went numb, and I quickly spit it out. I sipped on a thick liquid that resembled tomato soup, finding it mostly bland with a sweet after-taste, manageable even though I hated the way its pulp stuck to my tongue. The next solid thing I tried forced a sound of protest from me.

"Are you doing alright over there?" Veras asked.

I nodded around a mouthful of something horribly bitter.

"Then eat more. Andras put a lot of energy into preparing all that for you."

"I'm trying."

"You're hardly eating anything."

"Veras, let her go at her own pace," Andras said. "You know it can be hard."

"She's unwell, and that won't change anytime soon if she doesn't eat. Especially not if she insists on continuing to use her magic."

A wooden fork snapped in my hands as the muscles of my hand spasmed into growth. The noise had been too sharp for Andras and Veras not to notice. I slowly put it down, cringing and halfway wishing they'd left me to my fate on 9F.

"I'm sorry," I said. "I'm not trying to be a bother. If I could go home right now and be out of your hair, I would. You need me gone by a specific time, right? So you can go on your vacation?"

"It's not a vacation," Veras said, eying the splintered fork. "It's important."

My heart pounded in my chest. "So. Deadline?"

"We're working on that."

"Could you at least give me a timeframe? A week? A month? A year?" Those words translated, though I had to imagine they were different lengths of time here than on Earth.

"I wouldn't worry about it," Andras said.

"Please. I don't want it to be a surprise."

Andras eyed the map. "Not until after winter. At least."

I didn't know how long a year on Plesmae lasted, or even which season we were in now, but that must've meant quite a wait. Both Veras and Andras looked put out by the answer.

"Maybe we'll try camping again in the meantime," Andras ventured, though the idea didn't seem to cheer him much.

"Hopefully it'll go better next time," Veras said. "Some new issue always comes up." He said it in the most practical way possible. It didn't even sound like an insult.

I wished it had.

"I could leave," I offered. "There could be people out there I'd get along better with. Maybe, if I'm really lucky, there might even be someone who isn't disgusted just by looking at me!"

"Ella, we're not—" Andras started to say, but I cut him off.

"He is."

"I'm not," Veras said, several seconds way too late.

"Look, I get it," I said. "Accommodating me is a pain in the ass. *I* can't even take care of myself well. I won't blame you for giving up. Just point me in the right direction when I leave."

"It'll be a problem if you run into anyone else," Veras said. "The Graft are enough of a problem that everyone on Plesmae knows about the Citadel's—our government's—policy for off-world visitors. We can't risk missing contamination in a species whose biology is unfamiliar to us. Standard practice is to use sterilizing magic all over the visitor's skin. It's not supposed to be painful, or do harm. I had to do it for your injuries while you were unconscious to remove any infective material, and even in your sleep your body reacted. So if they did that to you, you'd react and surely hurt someone. Then they'd have to figure out what to do with a violent, dangerous alien. What options does that leave them, or you? On top of that, they'd wonder how you got here, which could then fall on our heads."

I bit my lip, a sharp tooth cutting into it. "I was trying."

Andras trailed after me as I stormed out of the room. "I'm sorry about Veras, he's not normally like this. He's probably just stressed because he hasn't treated anyone like you before."

I didn't like how Andras was watching me expectantly. "What do you want?"

He held out his arms. "Hug?"

"Not right now."

"Whenever you want it."

With him gone, I decided the easiest thing to do was sleep through the rest of this hot mess of a day. At least that way, I wouldn't be as much of a bother.

~

FOR MY ATTEMPTS TO stay out of the way, I was punished with dreaming. I was home again, back in my room, hearing the hair-raising cries of monsters as they violated my neighborhood. My vision swam with unnamed colors as Pillbug's rallying screech echoed over the street. I ran downstairs, finding the trapdoor to a basement that shouldn't exist. I hid in the cool, dark room below, waiting for the terrible events outside to stop.

Mechanical noises began, the roar of engines and gunfire, accompanied by inhuman screams. Eventually there was only the sound of vehicles leaving. It would be safe outside now. They'd all been slain. Even my vision had settled, meaning Pillbug was gone. I went back to the trapdoor.

It wouldn't open. I pushed and rattled and scratched at it, but it wouldn't budge. The ground trembled beneath my feet, followed by a low growl. The basement's floor was uncovered dirt. A clawed limb emerged from it, dragging the rest of a newly formed monster out of the ground.

I beat at the trapdoor, but I couldn't break my way out. In a last-ditch effort, I grabbed the handle and braced my feet against the wall. My bones changed as I attempted to leverage the trapdoor open. They grew longer but not thicker, a terrible tension developing in my body as the pressure I was applying to the trapdoor's latch grew. My spine and neck bent until I was looking behind me, seeing the horde of monsters pulling themselves free of the soil they'd been born from.

There was a deafening *crack* as my body broke before the latch did—

~

I HIT THE FLOOR, completely tangled in my sheets. I struggled to kick them off, my legs flexing incorrectly. Even though I could feel that they had contorted, a sliver of desperate hope was still crushed as I finally managed to toss the sheets aside, uncovering my legs. It was like I'd tried to turn into a werewolf or some shit. There was a half-formed joint between each ankle and knee, an extra angle that didn't bend and made me feel like I was walking on stilts. Balancing was all the more awkward because I was hunched over. I couldn't straighten my back without my spine creaking in protest. My skull felt like it was splitting open. I reached up with clawed hands to find a pair of bony bumps sticking out from my forehead. This was the most, the *worst* I'd ever changed myself, and try as I might, it wouldn't go away.

Someone needed to tell me it would be alright. Andras had offered me a hug whenever and I needed it now and if he held it back from me because I looked different I was going to die.

"Andras?" I called out.

I knocked on his door, but he wasn't there or in his garden. I thought about trying to find my way back to his hidden stash of plants, but considered how I'd feel if I saw something like me out in the woods, and shuddered.

That left Veras. I was hesitant to go to him for anything, expecting judgment. But I was tired and life was painful right now and I didn't... I didn't want to go through this alone. Getting help with my ability had never felt like a safe possibility for me before, but this wasn't Earth. Magic existed here, even if it wasn't like mine. I was trusting Veras to take care of my injuries. Shouldn't I be able to trust him with this? I wrapped my arms around myself for comfort and went looking for him.

A nasty burnt smell hung around the living room. It got stronger as I clambered upstairs.

"Veras?" The door leading to his bedroom was open. I knocked as lightly as I could, and heard the rustle of fabric.

Veras sat on his bed, a hand dripping with liquid light held over his other bared arm. His breathing was rapid, like he was recovering after a long run.

My entering broke his concentration. He looked up and froze.

"Could you—" I began.

He scrambled away, backing himself into a corner.

"Veras?"

"Get the hell away from me!" he yelled, and I flinched at the noise.

"Veras," I said, taking a step forward, showing him empty, claw-tipped, hands. "I'm not going to hurt you. Please. I need—"

He summoned a bright light, blinding me. I staggered back, hitting my head hard against a bookshelf. Again I reached out for help.

"I said, *get away*."

Hardly able to see, I felt my way out of the room, taking a painful tumble down the stairs. I forced open the front door and ran away before anyone else could see me.

6

It was strange how quickly the Glade's towering trees could go from daunting to comforting. I felt so small as I fled the house, and my surroundings were so big, that it was easy to think of how unlikely an encounter with another person would be. I needed that assurance right now. I couldn't go home, and I wasn't welcome here. I'd spent my whole life trying to get along with others.

Maybe it was time to stop trying.

I walked aimlessly through the Glade for hours, my unnatural muscle mass gradually melting away, my spine slowly returning to a correct level of curve with only the occasional shooting pain. One of my legs snapped back into shape twenty minutes before the other, leaving me hobbling for a while, but eventually I was miserable and mostly back to normal instead of miserable and changed, which was preferable.

Thirsty, I hunted down a pond. A flash of silver caught my eye as I drank. Fish. Or fish-adjacent. Given my luck, it would probably poison me if I ate it. That was assuming I could get that far, could make a living thing dead and ready to eat, which was doubtful. Even on Earth, I likely wouldn't have been able to survive out in the wild.

Hell, just surviving a trip to a crowded grocery store had been hard for me. I had to be delusional if I thought I could —

I heard the snap of a breaking branch and froze. A woman came over the crest of a hill, carrying an axe over her shoulder. She hadn't noticed me yet, her attention occupied as she went up to the trees, resting a hand against their trunks and tilting her head as if deep in thought. With her heavy boots, pants, and jacket, she would've fit well in a carpentry shop. She had wings, but they were short, reaching from her shoulder blades to just past her waist. They were unfeathered, resembling canvas. She looked middle-aged. Her skin was close to the same color as Andras's, her long black hair shot through with strands of silver and gold. She swung her axe like it weighed nothing, splitting the bark on several trees before moving onto the next; eventually she found one that seemed to satisfy her, collecting branches that were pure white at their cut ends. As she went to leave the forest, we made eye contact.

She stood there scrutinizing me. Feeling self-conscious, I reached up and found that I still had horns. They finally disappeared when I pushed down on them.

"Sorry, am I interrupting something? I tend to do that," the woman said.

That was far too normal a response after seeing my ability. I looked away, hoping she'd get the hint and leave. She stepped closer instead.

"You should stay away from me," I said.

She set her axe aside and held up her empty hands, but given that she must have magic, the gesture did little to comfort me. "I have no intention of hurting you."

I clenched my own hands, feeling my claws bite into my palms. "It's for your own safety. I'm a monster."

"I know what monsters look like, and you're not one," she said with complete confidence.

"You've just never seen one like me before." Even to my own ears, I sounded peeved. Why couldn't other people just make up their damn minds? Why couldn't I?

"I sure haven't, so I'm guessing you're not from around here."

"I'm not. Please leave me alone now."

"You're too polite to be a monster," she said. "And it'll be rather hard to leave you alone, as I live close by. That makes us neighbors."

I began to walk away, wanting to avoid harming, or being harmed.

"Wait!" she said. "I'm Reyna."

"Bye, Reyna," I said, and ran off.

I broke line of sight from her and then stopped, not sure what to do next. If Veras and Andras were the only ones in the Glade, where had she come from? I circled around. Reyna made a lot of noise as she traveled, crunching leaves and splitting wood with her axe. I followed her at a distance, her path bringing me to the Glade's edge. Beyond the baby trees that formed the Glade's frontier were grassy, rolling hills and an impossibly open pale blue sky. A barely-there dirt road snaked into the distance, a lone house visible along its path. Must be hers. Further off was a lone city, tall and contained behind an encircling wall. I knew it wasn't an option for me, and declined to look at it.

Reyna left the Glade, axe at her belt and a bundle of lopped-off branches under one arm. Leaning against a bush was, to my eyes, a motorbike. It had two wheels in the back and the uneasily minimalist look of a prototype, but the core parts I was familiar with were all there. Reyna stowed her belongings in bags on either side, put on a simple padded helmet, and settled into the saddle. It started up silently at her touch and gave off no exhaust as she rolled it forward, more analog bike speed than anything motorized.

Reyna puttered across the grasslands between the Glade and the house, breaking from her previously straight path to drive her bike in big circles. As I watched, she brought the bike to a complete stop in a field of plush grass before deliberately and carefully falling on her side. She lay there with her bike partly on top of her. I watched for a while longer, and while I saw her shift around, she made no sound of pain or panic. I didn't think she was hurt, but technically speaking she had fallen off her bike, and I doubted there was anyone else around to check on her.

Maybe there was a reason for that. Maybe she was completely, one hundred percent, entirely unhinged.

Either way, it didn't feel right to just *leave* her there.

Goddamnit.

Reyna had her head propped up and was reading a book, but hid it in her jacket and flopped back to the ground when I approached. There was no sign of blood on her clothes. Now that I was closer, I saw her jacket was covered in hundreds of embroidered abstract shapes, done in thread almost the same color as the fabric. She wore a belt with tool loops and a strap around each upper arm with... more, tinier tool loops.

"Hello," she said. "As you can see, my invention and I have gotten into a horrific, high-speed accident. I thought I'd be trapped here forever if nobody came to free me."

"Even I can tell you're lying," I said. "And that's saying something."

She smiled up at me. "Help?"

I grabbed her bike's handlebars.

"It's lightweight," I said.

"Do you like it?" she asked, hopeful.

"A lightweight bike sounds less dangerous to crash."

"Makhali are lightweight too. Delicate."

"Your biceps are the most defined I've ever seen."

"Would a monster rescue people or give compliments?"

I made a noise of irritation as I moved the bike off of her. Reyna stood easily enough.

"I might need help walking back to my house," she said. "It sure is a long distance —"

"I don't know if my parents are safe or not right now," I snapped. "If you're injured, I'll help you, but if you're not, don't pretend to be."

"I'm not hurt." She peered at me. "Are they here too?"

"No."

"Did you come here, or did they leave?"

"Came here."

"I've always been a homebody. Never tried foraging in the Glade before, or camping there at night. Is it difficult?"

"Why are you still talking to me?" I said, equally confused on why I was holding up the other end of the conversation.

"Because I'm nosy. And if there's a monster about, then it's safer to have her under watch than roaming the countryside. I'm alone out here, I don't know how to fight..." She lifted her short wings, displaying ragged edges. "...and it would be hard for me to escape. If you wanted to hurt me."

I didn't move.

"Do you have anywhere else to go?" she asked.

"I'm working on that."

"Can't go home?"

"No."

"Still have a home?"

"Not sure."

"Would you like to join me for dinner tonight?"

More than anything. I was also a homebody. And a coward, and a people pleaser even if I wasn't very good at it. Maybe even an idiot, if I was trying the same thing twice and expecting a different result.

"Maybe," I mumbled.

"What's your name?"

"Ella."

She smiled and held out her hand. I didn't take it, but I did follow along as she walked her bike through the grass.

Reyna's house seemed to be built from the bones of a dozen other buildings. One outer wall was brickwork, its neighbor wood planks, she had two sheds stuck on opposite ends, and even what I thought might be a blacksmithing station with a soot-coated fire pit around the back. The inside of the house might've been a similar mix, but I couldn't be sure. There were boxes, cabinets, and stacks of crafting supplies everywhere, making it difficult to see the walls behind them. I passed close to a stack and almost recoiled. Its contents gave off some kind of energy that buzzed against my skin. It didn't hurt, but it did feel how I imagined radiation would, and so I kept my arms firmly pressed against my sides and moved carefully, avoiding coming too close to what I assumed were items with magic in them.

Reyna led me to her kitchen, a mostly open and empty space; the only other one I could see was a neighboring room's workbench whose cleared surface was like the calm eye of the messy storm around it. Above the bench was a framed painting of an old makhali woman with a little girl sitting on her knee. They both had deadly serious expressions. The little girl, wearing a frilly dress and clutching a similarly adorned doll, had sharp eyes that almost glared out from beneath her gold-highlighted black bowl cut. She looked about four years old.

"My great-grandmother and I," Reyna said, catching me staring. "Specific types of magic aren't inherited like looks, but I happen to have the same type as she did. She was a fantastic artisan. Helped build many of the best parts of the capital."

"You both look mad," I said quietly.

"That's just my thinking face. I inherited it from her too. If it looks like I'm glaring, I'm not."

It was good that she'd told me that. Her eyes narrowed as she noticed me staring at her workbench.

"Is everything alright?" she asked.

"I like touching things," I mumbled, knowing it sounded weird.

Reyna considered this before searching through several containers. Soon the kitchen table was littered with pieces of wood, fused glass, metal, and fabric samples. I sifted through them, stroking and weighing and squeezing. Reyna muttered to herself as she did the same, seeming to rediscover materials she'd forgotten she had. With both our gazes down and my hands busy, it was less stressful to be in a stranger's home, even when she asked me to tell her what had happened to my home and parents.

I told her what had happened on Earth, trying not to relive it. "Is there any way I can get help?"

Reyna looked uncomfortable. "Perhaps. We makhali have been at war with the Graft on and off for centuries. It might sound strange to call it that since our enemy isn't sentient, but we're talking the full mobilization of our society. Most would like to be done with such matters. I'm sorry I don't have more answers for you, but I appreciate you telling me all that. Could I also ask how you met Veras?"

I hadn't mentioned him. "What?"

"We were stationed at the same base during the war, and he treated me when I was injured. Veras was the main contact for hospitalized locals, but using his translation magic took away energy he needed for healing. I made a few items for him, including the necklace and earring you're wearing."

I hated talking about him. "We ran into each other on 9F. He took care of me for a bit, but we, uh, had a disagreement."

"Did you track dirt in the house? He hates that."

"I'd had a bad dream, and when I woke up, my body had… it changes sometimes, whether I want it to or not." Even now my arms were callused, possibly a reaction to all that pent-up energy within the house. "I looked like some awful monster, and I couldn't get it to go back. I went to him for help, and he wanted me gone."

Reyna had been fiddling with a metal rod the thickness of a finger. It grew rusty and thinned before snapping apart in her hands. "Oh, I am going to murder him when I see him next."

"That's not needed. I mean, I know I've been trouble for him, and I clearly walked in on him at a bad time, and —"

"That hardly excuses it," Reyna said. "His specialty is treating other species, and he knows what real monsters look like. He should know better."

I'd desperately needed to hear that, but I hid it behind a shrug. "I looked bad."

"If you don't act like a monster, then you're not one," she said.

"What else am I supposed to call what I become?"

"What do you want to be?" Reyna asked.

I wasn't sure. Being human-shaped wouldn't get me home.

"You shouldn't punish yourself for things outside of your control," Reyna said.

I turned most of my attention back to fidgeting, needing to escape this topic. Fortunately, Reyna seemed happy to redirect. She talked while I explored all those different materials, telling me about her work, how sometimes she created items from scratch and sometimes she added magic to things she hadn't made. That was the gist of a long tangent I struggled to follow, anyway. Reyna lived alone, though she assured me it wasn't because she didn't like people. I think I watched her start putting food together only to get distracted at least six times, her attention easily captured by the materials she'd set out, or the beginnings of other projects she hadn't put away.

The meal that eventually made its way to the table was simpler than what I'd seen Veras and Andras serve, though each plate and cup and piece of cutlery was built or decorated in a different way. Most of the food was unfamiliar to me, but some of it that resembled bread was the same as I'd eaten before, so I focused on that. The whole go-with-the-evil-you-know choice didn't end up working in my favor. I soon wound up doubled over with nausea and with Reyna's hand patting my back.

"Is that a bandage I feel?" she asked.

"It's taken care of," I said, taking in slow breaths as the nausea finally passed.

"Are you ill, or is it a reaction to the food?"

"I did hit my head earlier, but I don't think it's from that."

"What?"

"It's just a little tender."

"Those aren't clothes you wear when you're recovering."

Five minutes later, I was wearing a set of soft borrowed pajamas—the shirt and pants containing an astonishing dozen pockets between them—and was getting settled for an early night on Reyna's couch, which stood like a pier against the rising tide of objects around it.

For a long time I lay there, listening to my surroundings and translating them in a way that the magic items at my throat and ear couldn't. Floorboards creaked as Reyna moved throughout the house. The outside noises of hopefully small and harmless animals. An irritating buzz I couldn't tell if I was hearing, or just feeling against my eardrums from the magic-packed supplies around me. And somewhere, a regular thumping noise, as if Reyna had some machine powered on. I put my hand below my sternum. Not a machine. My heart, beating like a rabbit's in an open field.

A shameful idea entered my mind, impossible to ignore. The creaking had settled down. I was quieter than Reyna had been, stepping close to the furniture and stacks where the planks were too pinned down to complain.

Reyna had left her bike outside, beneath a three-walled shed. Her helmet dangled from the handlebars. I donned it and straddled the seat, touching all the movable parts until I pushed a button on the handle and the bike silently rumbled to life beneath me. It had that same vibrating stillness as the translation items she'd made, an uncomfortable sense that the object in question was bigger than it seemed, that it had two surfaces overlapping and colliding with each other. At least the bike was quiet as I drove away, hoping it would carry me across 9F before I could tire or succumb to dehydration as I almost had previously. It felt like I was witnessing my actions from outside my body as I rolled it towards the Glade. As I stole it.

You're already doing the bad thing, I thought. So make it worth it. Dig beneath the veil if you have to. Throw yourself at it until it breaks, or you do. At some point in the future, I would unpack my guilt, the fact that even if I wasn't a monster, I was still a horrible person. I'd do what I could to make it up to Reyna, whatever that meant. But there wasn't room in my mind for that now.

I got a decent enough grasp of the bike's controls and balance and sped up, racing across the grassy hills. I had to slow down in the Glade and drive carefully around roots and bushes, but I eventually came across a sign. Its writing was alien to me, but the bold and frantic-looking symbols next to an outline of a door were a clear enough warning. I ignored the warning, following it and several other signs to the rift, rolling through its hazy lime-green and gray turmoil that was flanked by two carved stone pillars. My vision strobed as I passed from night to acid-colored, searing day.

"Andras and Veras went partway there and back without getting horribly lost," I told myself. "Mind you, they can fly, but..."

Makhali, I decided, must share some psychological traits with humans. They thought naming or describing places brought them under control. And they liked things to be idiot-proof. Someone had put up a big sign with a map carved into it, simple drawings marking what I hoped were the ruins where I'd met Veras and Andras.

I drove across the cracked desert, recognizing the ruins I passed. I could find my way back home. I hadn't walked *that* far, not when I was hurt and weak. From there I'd make a plan on what to do about the veil.

As it turned out.

I didn't need to plan anything.

I left the bike a short walk from the rift, where it would stay clean, and proceeded on foot. My first idea had been to dig through the hard earth below the veil's chain, try to move it out of alignment. But I'd been beaten to it. My shoes squelched through a disgustingly hot and thick ooze.

Sludge spilled forth from the rift like a giant busted pipe. It had softened the ground, turned it into a sinkhole, destroyed the veil's foundations so there was little more than a few flickering and failing sections left. I couldn't tell if more ooze was coming out and creating a small current as it spread, or if I was stepping in something breathing or beating or pulsating. There must've been tons of the stuff, which, from a logistical and totally-not-about-to-panic perspective, implied a far greater volume of it on the other side.

And nothing keeping anything clawed and fanged from coming through anymore.

I wanted to run away. I wanted to push forward. Of course this meant I froze up, torn between two terrible options.

Wow, I thought, still feeling like a spectator of myself. I really have no survival instincts.

I should've been thankful it was Veras yelling that shook me out of it, and not a monster eviscerating me, but I was still sullen as I turned to face him. He dove out of the sky, landing just beyond the ooze's reach. For a full minute he just stood there, catching his breath, looking windblown and exhausted. But it turned out he had plenty of energy left.

"Why are you just standing there?" he screamed. "Are you trying to die? Waiting for your body to rot away from the legs up? If it's wet, it can and *will* kill you."

"I need to go home," I said, my one defense for doing, well, everything I was doing.

"I knew you'd try coming here at some point. Get over here. Now."

I took careful steps away from the rift, so I would get out of the sludge close to the bike, and away from him.

"Here. In front of me," he ordered. "You're not thinking straight. If that much is flowing through the rift, then —"

"Do you think I haven't had the same thought?" I yelled back. Being on solid ground was good. It meant I could stomp. "I'm already having to consider my entire home being destroyed, that I maybe can't ever go home. Being stuck between that possibility and you makes me want to test out that theory."

His head and wings jerked back as if I'd slapped him. "Don't compare me to that."

"Don't make me feel shitty like it does!"

"I'm not *that* bad."

"You are exactly the type of person I have spent my entire life avoiding," I said. "Thanks for turning out how I expected. Doesn't listen, no empathy, only pretends to care about someone like me because it makes you feel good about yourself —"

"I'm trying to take care of you as we speak! Whatever more you have to say, could you let me make sure you're not actively dying first?"

I sat on a rock and folded my arms, making sure my claws were visibly out as he approached.

"Kick off your shoes into the sludge," he said.

I obeyed. Veras checked my ankles and socks.

"Just a little spot on your leg here. I can't believe you keep getting this lucky."

He put his hand near the dark spot on my skin, but I shoved him away. I pinched myself above the area of slowly spreading contamination and, concentrating, peeled up a strip of skin several inches long.

The area beneath it was thin, not ready to be exposed to the open air yet, but it was unmarred. I threw the strip into the sludge too.

"There," I said. "Not dying."

"Is that Reyna's bike?" Veras asked.

"Do other makhali have bikes?" I asked.

"You stole Reyna's bike," he said in disbelief.

"I was going to take it back after I went home."

"How?"

"I..." It hadn't been a lie. I really did want to take it back. I recognized that without being able to fly, traveling for Reyna was probably a lot harder than for other makhali. "I don't know."

"So you weren't going to," he said.

"I will!" I said. "I've never stolen before, and I've never hurt anyone, including Reyna, in case you were going to accuse me of that next. I'll make it up to her as soon as I find my family."

He pursed his lips. "Can you do that? Realistically?"

"Am I a dangerous monster, or a fragile patient?" I snapped. "Why can't you make up your mind?"

"I let you into my home and gave you care without knowing anything about you. Can you blame me for being frightened of you? I don't even know what you are."

I didn't know either. What was a useless little affirmation compared to what my body could do? There was a hole in my chest where a firm, decisive answer should be.

"You screamed at me," I blurted out, the piece of pain that was easiest to voice. "Why did you do that?"

He blanched. "You came in at a bad time, and I overreacted."

"You overreacted," I repeated.

"Yes. I've gotten over it. Look, you already know you can't survive that," Veras said, gesturing to the rift. "And Plesmae is an alien world for you. It could hold dangers you're unaware of. You have to—"

"What? Go with you?" I said. "I don't want every time I walk into a room to be a crapshoot between whether I'll be treated kindly, or made to feel like a stupid, dirty animal." I could feel my body changing with my distress, and clamped my hands around my forearms, crushing them back down to a smaller size. "You're right that I shouldn't throw my life away. But that doesn't mean I have to put myself through the torture of your company."

And then, because arguing deeply hurt, I walked away. I walked away from the rift, which hurt even worse. It was probably too late to return the bike without Reyna noticing its absence, so I'd burned my only other safe harbor.

I was saved from thinking on this any longer by almost stepping in a monster footprint.

7

I stared down at the tracks, muddy indentations connected by a snail-trail of slime. Veras made a choking sound. His face had gone from flushed to horribly pale.

"That's pointed straight towards Plesmae," he said.

"Did you see that at the rift to the Glade?" I asked. "Because I didn't. I'm assuming you left after me."

"I wouldn't have left if there were signs of the Graft almost on my doorstep," he said.

We both eyed the tracks, and then each other.

"Ella, I—" Veras started to say.

"I don't want what happened to my home to happen anywhere else," I said. A large part of me wanted to pick a random direction and drive until I found a new place to try existing or collapsed, but I supposed I had a stubborn streak in me too. It was saying that I couldn't turn my back on this.

Veras pursed his lips. "You're following it?"

"Aren't you?"

He nodded, and as disgusted as I was with him, the appearance of the tracks seemed to call for a temporary ceasefire until we knew where they led.

I followed the trail on the bike, and Veras followed me in the air. The trail curved at random, but its overall heading was still the same way I'd come from. I came to a halt next to Plesmae's rift, finding disturbingly moist muck there, glistening against the desiccated ground. Veras landed beside me. I rolled the bike forward.

It was still night on Plesmae. Veras summoned a bright white light in his hand. I lurched away from him, ready to throw down.

"Put that away," I hissed.

"I can barely see without it."

"Your eyes will adjust if you let them. We have to assume there's something here. Do you want to be seen from a mile away?"

His fingers tightened protectively around the light. "It's all I have."

I gritted my teeth. "You'd better know your way around at night."

"Did you know every detail of the landscape several miles out from your home? I'm doing my best."

I followed him, walking with the bike. His light didn't reach very far, making it almost useless, though I supposed for him it was better than nothing.

I caught wind of a rotting stench, dropped the bike, and grabbed Veras's arm, making his fingers crush the light out of existence. He made a startled sound, so I covered his mouth. He stared at me, shaking. Veras was lightweight in a way humans weren't, almost like a bird. That and his fear made forcing him to move easy. I needed him to cooperate right now as I tried to put distances between us and *it* while staying hidden.

This quadrupedal graftling reached up past my waist. Its dog-like head was equipped with large paper-thin ears and a crevassed blob of tissue at the end of its muzzle I just barely recognized as a nose. On its back were several deflated pockets of tissue. I led Veras along at a glacial pace until it found something of interest in the distance and went to investigate.

Veras's fingers trembled as he moved my hand from his mouth. "I didn't even realize it was there," he whispered.

"I could smell it." I took in a deep breath, trying to focus on the subtler smells hidden beneath that reek. Sweat. Whatever soap we'd both used at his house. New green life, pollen, the gentle decay of leaf litter. Scents that had been barely a trace just a moment before, now magnified, distinct, weaker odors that had been covered up now available to me. The experience was almost too much sensory information for me to handle, but I'd put up with it for the sake of survival.

Veras was going through his own internal thought process that I tuned back into. "...means more will come. Could be others here right now. We have to find Andras. He's still looking in the Glade for you—"

I was already running on strengthened legs, Veras lagging behind me, letting my sense of smell guide me on an erratic path between the trees. As best I could tell, we were far away from Andras's hidden garden, yet my nose picked up on its confusing scent. I followed it, hoping it would lead to the person who tended it.

There—a dim light, gray-green, in the distance. Andras carrying a basket of softly glowing leaves. My night vision picked up something low and creeping at the edge of the light. At the frightened noise I made, Veras shouted a warning.

Andras turned around in time, slammed his foot into the ground. The monster was struck from below, lifted up by the roots and branches of a tree that hadn't existed a minute ago. Veras and I skidded to a halt and watched as the rapidly swelling limbs of the tree curled in and squeezed with an audible *crack*.

"Jesus Christ, Andras," I said. "You never mentioned you could..."

Andras clutched his chest and gasped for breath. Veras dragged him away from the dead monster, arms and wings wrapped protectively around him. Eventually Andras caught his breath and gently pushed him away.

"Veras, I'm sorry. But I need you to deal with it." Andras squeezed and opened his hand.

The tree's branches uncurled, revealing a shattered body. Andras's mouth was set in a hard line. Veras mumbled a curse and stepped up to it. He held his hands above the graftling's body. Pinpoints of white light formed in his hands, igniting into a white fireball that dripped over the dead monster and burnt away its flesh.

Andras took a few difficult steps over to me. "You're okay?"

No would've been an honest answer, but recent events had reminded me just how much worse I could be doing. I nodded, unable to look away as Veras's magic melted through skin, fat, and muscle. I was no expert on anatomy, but the layers I saw made little sense to me; the monster's body had dozens of bone chips throughout it, seemingly embedded in its muscle tissue without being attached to anything. The cluster of organs within its abdomen —god, but they stunk as they burned—were strange as well, some appearing shrunk in on themselves and atrophied, others hugely swollen to the point of looking cancerous. I felt lightheaded, like I might faint or throw up, especially because some parts of the head were the last bit for Veras to destroy, and I thought I saw a vestigial third eyeball lurking beneath the monster's skin before it too was gone, only hole-ridden bones left.

"I need to stop saving the worst part for last," Veras mumbled, appearing just as queasy as I felt. His lower lip trembled.

"What happened to just having light?" I said.

"It's exhausting and takes too long to be useful as an attack," Veras said. His shaking hands poked some of the larger bones, turning them over and revealing a small strip of remaining muscle that he immediately burned away. "This is a scout. They leave some kind of scent trail wherever they go that other monsters can follow. They're built for crossing large distances through abiotic environments."

"Like a camel?" I asked.

"What's a camel?"

"They have big stores of fat concentrated in specific areas so they can go longer without food or water."

"Like a... camel, sure. They're not the worst warriors the Graft has, but they can still easily kill. There's at least one more out there." Veras gently touched Andras's face, eyes focusing on something distant. "You've had a shock, but you'll recover with rest."

I didn't trust Veras's, well, anything. "Andras, what happened?"

"I just used too much magic, too fast. It's part of a chronic condition I have," Andras said.

Veras grimaced. "We should get out of here."

"This is where I can best defend us," Andras argued.

"Until you get too worn out, and it seems like you already are. We don't know how many are out there. Outside of the Glade, we'll have a better chance of spotting a graftling before it tries to kill us. We can get help."

Andras's shoulders slumped, but he nodded in agreement. I didn't speak up. I just fell into line with them as they walked, Veras clinging to Andras's arm. I was on high alert, but thought we were alone. Fortunately, the two of them guided us to the grasslands in a much more direct path than I'd previously taken. From there, I could guess where we were going. Knowing there were monsters out there removed the option of splitting up.

By the time we reached Reyna's house, a period drawn out by Andras's slow steps, my fear of being torn apart by monsters had morphed into the fear of being yelled at. Veras nudged me towards her front door while he checked on Andras again. I rocked on my heels, my sense of dread rising as I heard Reyna bumping throughout the house on the way to answer my knock. Her gaze flicked from me, to Veras, to Andras, eyebrow rising further at each new visitor.

"I, um, I took your bike," I said softly. "And I was going to bring it back once I had all my other shit figured out, along with a bunch of sorry-for-taking-your-bike apology gifts from Earth, and then I couldn't go home because there was a bunch of Graft biomass in the way and Veras showed up and we realized the monsters had wandered back towards Plesmae and they were in the Glade and we had to move quietly and I'm the worst person ever for taking what must be like a mobility aid for you and—"

"Ella, breathe," Veras said.

I didn't want to at first. With Reyna's front door open, all the smells of her home, leather and fresh-cut wood and something like wool and polish and a million other odors, were hitting my heightened senses. She pulled me against her, my face pressed into her shoulder, her own singular smell of woodsmoke and natural glue drowning out the rest, making it easier to breathe until I'd dialed down my senses.

When I was better, she gently pushed me away. "Monsters, here?" she asked Veras.

"Not *here* here," he said. "We're safe. Unless they follow us. Sorry, I know that doesn't help."

Reyna took in her own series of calming breaths. "Who are you, and are you alright?"

Andras introduced himself and told her he was just worn out. Reyna ushered us all inside, scanning the hills behind us. I split up from the three of them before she could turn back around. There should've been a million places to hide in Reyna's house, but somehow she'd managed to fit things together so tightly that they were more like walls, and I couldn't pull them apart to make a niche for myself without causing an avalanche. I needed the privacy, a place where I could sulk without being seen. Everyone in this house probably hated me for something, and I hadn't even tried surviving on my own yet because I was too pathetic. Shame filled me, but there wasn't enough room for all of it. I felt it rise to the surface of my skin even before the calluses formed, rough and the sickly green of a bad bruise.

Reyna must've been living alone for too long. The sound of surprise she made was loud enough to hear across the room.

"Please don't look at me," I said.

She turned her head. "What's wrong?"

"It won't go away," I said, fighting back tears. "It happens on its own, and then it doesn't, my body doesn't listen to me, ever, and—I can't stay. I shouldn't. You were kind to me once already and I took advantage of you immediately."

"I'm not throwing anyone out to the mercy of monsters," Reyna said. "You'll have to stay and live with the discomfort of knowing you did a bad thing instead."

"I'm sorry," I said. "That... I have to assume that was something irreplaceable that you needed."

She just sighed. "One thing at a time. Can I do anything for your skin?"

I had no idea what was in Reyna's stacks of supplies, but I highly doubted there'd be anything like an instant camera. What would be the next best thing? I asked for paper and something to draw with, sketching out a stick figure and smudging the graphite on its arms and legs before ripping out the page and throwing it in Reyna's burning fireplace.

She darted forward, snatching the paper from the flames and stamping out the smoldering edges.

"Don't do that," she snapped.

I flinched back. "I, I'm sorry, I wasn't trying to start a fire or anything—"

"It's not about that. It's about you destroying yourself."

"That paper isn't me."

"It was supposed to represent you, right? Close enough."

"Is that a makhali belief?"

She joined me on the floor, suddenly very close. "It's *my* belief. And I believe it's especially bad for someone so young to do that. You don't even fully know who you are yet."

"I stole your bike." She'd tried to tell me I wasn't a monster; to me, what I'd done meant the same thing, but it was a more obvious fact that she couldn't argue against.

"Were you expecting to do that?" Reyna said.

"No."

"See? You don't know yourself. You shouldn't throw something away without knowing what it is first, or you'll regret it later. So no more of this." She pointed to the burned page.

I looked down at my arms, still in dermatological distress.

"We'll come up with a better way for you to fix yourself," Reyna said. "If you stop burning pictures, and bring back my bike if it's safe to do so, then I'll consider us even. You *did* escort a friend of mine away from danger. Deal?"

I nodded numbly.

Reyna went to her workstation, bringing me a fist-sized gray lump of clay. It was cool, slightly moist, dense, and smelled like earth. I held it like a fragile egg, not sure how to proceed.

"Whatever feels right," Reyna said. "Your magic is a natural part of you. It knows how it should be used."

I passed the clay between my hands, crushing it until it squeezed between my fingers. It made a horrible stress ball. I wanted the spring of rubber, something I could shove between my teeth and gnaw on until my jaw grew tired. I wanted my goddamn camera and an endless supply of film and matches.

The closest I could get to a picture of myself with Reyna lurking over me was stippling the clay's surface with my nails until it was rough, and then pressing it smooth between my palms. I repeated this a few times, the clay warming in my hands, as I thought about how malleable both it and I were. Soon the calluses on my limbs faded.

"Isn't that better than what you were doing before?" Reyna said.

I wanted to say that this was my body, my experience, and that I didn't appreciate her interfering with my coping mechanisms. But I couldn't risk alienating her. I owed her so much, and needed another person's support too badly.

"You know magic better than I do," I said.

Reyna stuck out her hand. I supposed it made sense, that species with similar anatomy might share some customs. I shook her hand as briefly as I could, hating how it felt, which brought out my claws. I squeezed my hands shut, but it was too late to hide them.

"You don't need to worry about frightening me," she said. "Would a monster sleep on my couch in borrowed pajamas?"

Even I had to admit the idea was a little ridiculous.

She gave me a drawstring bag for the clay. "You take your time with that. Veras and I are going to have a talk about how to manage our... situation."

I took the clay with me outside, wanting a break from the over-whelming visual and magical clutter of inside. Andras was already sitting in the grass nearby. He held out his arms for me, letting them awkwardly fall to his sides when I didn't accept.

"I'm sorry we messed up," he said.

"I didn't leave because of you," I said. "You made me feel welcome, just... not enough to balance out everything else."

"Could we talk for a bit?"

I joined him. Andras's breathing was better, but his complexion had a gray pallor and his wings sagged.

"Veras and I went looking for you because we wanted to help," Andras said. "From what I've heard, he didn't communicate that intention very well."

"No," I said.

"I'd get if you didn't want to be around him, but will you at least accept my help?"

"I'm not used to others being able to help me," I said, trying to change my original thought of *there's nothing you can do for me.*

"I know what it's like to be forced away from home," Andras said. "I came here because of the Graft too, and while I love it in the Glade, it's not the same. We're from entirely separate worlds, but I'm sure there are some similarities between what we've gone through. Please, let me help you feel comfortable here."

"I don't know if it's even possible for me to be comfortable," I said. "I've never had to be afraid for my parents before. I've never even gone this long without talking to them. I *need* familiar things, and I don't have any, and it's cold even in your house and there are weird noises outside that I don't know the cause of and you've been nice enough but you killed something in front of me and I'm glad you killed it but I, I've never liked and been afraid of the same person before."

He stared at me blankly for a moment. Yeah, that had been a lot, and some of it had come out against my wishes. I drew my knees against my chest, wondering what Andras was capable of making grass do.

But all Andras did was reach into his pocket and pull out my phone. I snatched it from him, desperate to have its familiar weight in my hands.

"Sorry we didn't give it back earlier," he said. "Veras and I didn't know what it was or if it was dangerous, so he wanted to hide it until he'd met you, but then he felt awkward about admitting we took it. Kind of forgot I had it there with everything else that happened. I hope that at least helps with one of your problems."

As pathetic as realizing it made me feel, I'd been desperate for the feeling of smooth plastic. Pressing the power button did nothing. The screen was cracked, but clean.

"As for the last of your concerns... that wasn't the first graftling I've killed, and if it ends up not being the last, then so be it," Andras said. "All I can say to reassure you is that I wouldn't hurt someone unless they wanted to hurt me first." He watched me spam my phone's power button. "I am, of course, assuming that item isn't actually dangerous."

"It's not," I said.

"Is it supposed to be doing something?"

"It won't turn on. And no, it's not dangerous even when it's working. It's for communicating with people and looking up information." Not that those functions would've worked without a signal. "And you can take pictures... you can preserve images with it."

"Images of what?"

"Beautiful things. Important moments. People you care about," I said.

"I'm sorry it's not working," he said.

"I still appreciate having it back." I tucked it into my clothing, both to feel its familiar plastic surface against my skin and hide it before anyone else could take it away.

"That's two problems solved, then," Andras said.

"Andras, you don't have to—"

"It's a huge weight on your shoulders, isn't it? Not knowing what of the thousands of strange things on this world could hurt you. I know you don't like Veras, but he's been terrified for you. He'll worry about your health and environment whether or not you're in front of him. If you come back, Veras will share that weight with you."

"I don't know if I can trust Veras enough to share what's bothering me with him," I said. It wouldn't be the first time someone deliberately triggered my sensory discomfort.

But Andras was, if nothing else, an optimist. "Promise you'll consider it?"

"Fine."

"Thank you," he said. It was hard for me to look right at his smile. My gaze shifted to one of his blocky wings instead.

"Is that a fern?" I said.

He patted its sawtooth leaves. "If that's your word for it."

"Your wings change?"

"It's called being fashionable."

"Does that mean your wings are just dirt underneath?"

"Um, Ella, you can't just ask people if their wings are dirt. But no, they're not."

"Ella? Could you come inside?" Reyna called out.

Andras waved me off. I joined Reyna and Veras, both of whom looked grim.

"We need to ensure our own safety, but graftlings are a threat to everyone," Reyna said. "The best solution we can think of is getting help from the Citadel. Most of us have returned to a civilian lifestyle, but there are some soldiers and first responders on reserve. Once they know about the monsters, they can send someone to deal with it. The unfortunate part is, that means going to the capital, with the possibility of being hunted by a monster who followed your trail from the Glade."

"I'll go," Veras said. "Andras needs to rest. And, Reyna..."

"I'm sorry about the bike," I said again.

Reyna shook her head. "That's not what he's getting at. I've only had one close-up encounter with a monster. I don't know if I can... function outside, knowing there could be more."

"Someone should stay with Andras anyway, in case he gets weaker," Veras said. He turned to me, fingers nervously knotting together. "Ella? You saw how I would've blundered into that graftling earlier. Nobody's forcing you to go. I'd understand if you wanted to avoid danger after all that's happened to you. But if you were willing, I'd appreciate the backup."

"Aren't the Graft kind of a time-sensitive thing?" I said. "Wouldn't I slow you down on the way there?"

"Some graftlings can fly," he said quietly. "They're less common, but they're out there, and if you've taken out even one monster before, that's more than I have."

I didn't want to leave the house, but sending him by himself didn't seem right either.

"I'll go with you," I said uncertainly. "I just know you're not supposed to have me here."

Reyna went to dig through one of her many piles, returning with new clothes for me, shoes and pants and a shirt she said would fit in well at the capital. She also took a long cloak and sewed a thick piece of cloth to the underside, to create bulk where my wings would be if I was makhali.

"Stay covered up," Veras advised. "I need you to pretend you're one of us for a little while. It'll make life much easier if you can blend in."

I nodded. That was definitely my best skill, blending in with other people.

8

Being on the lookout for monsters was an easy excuse for Veras and I to avoid speaking as we made our way through the grasslands. Although I kept my eyes and ears sharp, the only noise of concern was Veras's huffing and puffing. I seemed to have better stamina than him on foot, though even I was surprised that I hadn't passed out by now. We were lucky that the grasslands had little in terms of sound, sight, or smell that could've hidden a monster from me, and as we drew closer to the makhali's capital city, I allowed myself to put thoughts of immediate danger aside for the moment.

"Why's it look so lonely?" I asked, an inside thought that slipped out as I stared at the walled city.

"We had smaller towns in the past," Veras said. "Hostels next to natural landmarks, farms better situated to grow specialty crops, accommodations next to mines. They were all abandoned or destroyed during our last war. Our capital, Pellior's Landing, was the only place that was truly safe." He nodded to the city's thirty-foot walls. "There's space enough for everyone inside, and they can sleep easier knowing they're protected."

"It's been a couple years though, right? If they're not too far away,

I'd rather be near one of those landmarks. It's just boring grass out here."

"You and Andras," he said with a sigh. "That's the one thing that grew back easily after these fields became contaminated swampland, and then scorched earth. You should appreciate its resilience."

I'd appreciate it more if there were animals I could see enjoying the grass, but there wasn't, at least near us. "Do we need to worry about avoiding crowds once we're inside?" I didn't want to literally bump into anyone and have them realize I wasn't quite shaped like them.

"No. There are about five thousand residents in the capital, and it's not like they'll all be out in the streets at once."

I was taken aback. Five thousand didn't sound like a capital city, it sounded like a tiny town. It seemed too elaborate for that, to the point that I almost asked Veras to confirm that our numbers were translating right. Pellior's Landing was made smaller by the absence of further development outside it. Everything I could see within that container was beautiful, white and pale gray skinny tall buildings that struck me more as towers than skyscrapers. The one in the city's center rose above everything else, tapering to a point. I sharpened my sight, but even then I couldn't make out any more detail.

Veras saw me squinting. "Don't strain your eyes. The veil can be hard to see from far away, but it's there. That's the Citadel in the middle, where we're going."

"I didn't realize they could be that big." The veil attached to the tip of the Citadel and floated over the city, arcing down to connect to the top of the wall.

"It's the largest we've ever had, and different from the one you previously encountered. Matter and magic can pass from the inside out, but not the other way around. Wouldn't do to have everyone trapped inside during a disaster."

The closer we got to the capital, the more its walls seemed like that of a stronghold. The walls slanted outwards higher up, seamless and and covered in finger-length dull spikes; I was reminded of zombie movies, of undead hordes climbing over each other to reach their prey.

Stepping through the gates was like returning to a more peaceful world, but even if there weren't that many makhali here, I'd only been in the company of three people recently. I could feel tension brewing under my skin as I thought about being around more strangers.

"Will you be alright here?" Veras asked me.

"Sure," I said, not actually certain.

"You could wait outside the walls if—"

"I don't want to be alone in a new place," I said.

Veras nodded. I stuck close to him as we continued through the city, passing by clusters of shorter buildings broken up by the occasional tower. Everything was clean and spacious, the upper of two-story homes smaller than the lower to leave space for rooftop walkways, plazas and gardens. If I looked to either side at intersections, I could sometimes see what looked like farmland, the makhali's food source also within the wall's protection. Shadows flicked across the ground from wingborne air traffic. I tried not to stare. To a makhal, all of this would be normal. I could only hope there wasn't some kind of rule, some social law taught since birth or consequence of makhali biology, that I was breaking without realizing it. After all, people at home had always seemed to pick up on my being *different* somehow.

I could feel stress building inside me, and my sensory issues certainly weren't helping. As we walked by shops with items proudly on display, by a playground full of shrieking children, by other people just going about their lives, I felt the sting of magic. It was like salt on my tongue, the fizz of a sparkler held a little too close to the business end. Not pain itself, but an omen of it. I crowded even closer behind Veras. I compulsively grabbed the tip of one of his wings, fingers gently closing around a strange mix of soft fluff and hard spots, the gold lines of each feather like pencil lead with stuffing glued to them. Veras jolted and glanced back at me.

"Sorry," I mumbled, letting him go.

"You seem more stressed here than when we were worried about graftlings," he said in disbelief.

I lowered my head. There wasn't magic in the flat stones lining the streets. I liked that about them.

"You shouldn't have come here," Veras said.

"You're welcome, asshole," I said.

"I mean—you're so frustrating. For your own sake, you shouldn't have come here. I'm trying to say I'm grateful. Walk next to me, so I can keep an eye on you."

I wasn't sure how to respond, so I kept my head down and stuck by him. A few minutes later, we had reached the open double doors of the Citadel. I flinched as we stepped over the threshold and the intensity of magic around us increased.

The Citadel's center was hollow, the ceiling visible hundreds of feet away. A staircase spiraled around the inner circumference of the building's thick walls. I hoped there would be at least one helpful person behind the many doors I could see before the staircase's landings blocked my view. Our footfalls were uncomfortably loud against the white stonework that made up the building. Across from the doors was some kind of receptionist desk.

Veras watched me tremble beneath my cloak. "Now isn't a good time to freak out."

"I'm not." I followed Veras to the makhal at the desk. The, I don't know, secretary had a large spread of documents and notes in front of him. Veras approached the desk, wings unnaturally stiff and straight.

The secretary glanced up at him without interest. "May I help you?"

"Yes. I'd like to meet with an officer of the Citadel. There are important security matters I need to discuss with someone."

"Do you have an appointment?"

"No, um..." Veras glanced at a placard on the desk. "Saela. Can I make one?"

"What did you say your name was?"

"I didn't, I, um, Veras."

Saela's eyes narrowed in thought. "Have I heard that name recently? What do you do?"

"Medic corps."

"The medic corps has been disbanded for two years. What do you do now?"

"Not all that much, I suppose."

"Veras. Veras. Where have I heard that name?" Saela murmured to himself. "*That's* where. You broke restricted travel guidelines."

Veras was sweating. "Not really a law, is it? And I didn't go that far."

"Are you the 'important security matter'?"

"No! It's something else. Well, it's complicated."

"Why aren't you just saying it?" I whispered.

"There could be consequences if we're blamed for anything following us," Veras hissed back. "And I don't want to cause a panic if there's no need for one, okay? Everyone's been afraid of this happening for the last three damn years, if it can be dealt with quickly and quietly —"

Saela cleared his throat, getting our attention. "Commander Berith's schedule is booked for the next two months. The rest of the Citadel's leaders only convene monthly."

Veras scratched at his arm under his sleeve. "I'm not proud of this situation, but —"

"Who's your companion?" Saela asked, seeing me fidget under my cloak. He leaned in over his desk, tilted his head. A purple ring formed over each of his eyes. "What the hell is your magical signature? I've never seen anything like it. Take your hood off."

I knew my upper canines had lengthened when a little blood trickled down my chin. My fists were balled up in the fabric of the cloak. Makhali had governments and secretaries. I didn't want to find out if there was makhali jail too, or what might happen to an alien held there. "Veras," I whispered. "Unless you have a way to defuse this situation, we need to go."

"This is a time-sensitive matter," Veras said. "It's not what I wanted either. Take off your cloak."

I took it off, wincing. The lights floating above us were incredibly bright. Saela jumped up from his chair. "What did you bring here?"

Shit. I'd unintentionally built up my claws and the muscles of my arms and shoulders. I let them dissolve away, slowly raising my hands in a gesture of surrender, trying not to hyperventilate.

"She's not infected," Veras blurted out.

"Has she been decontaminated?"

My whole body went rigid, muscles visibly squirming in my arms.

"She's not infected," Veras repeated. "I examined her myself."

Saela was furious. "You brought a non-decontaminated alien equipped with magical items into the center of our city? Into the same building where our leaders meet? What is *wrong* with you?"

"We have a bit of an emergency on our hands! Can we just speak with someone higher up? Please?"

"She needs to be checked out first. That isn't optional. And *you* obviously need to relearn some of the responsibility you've forgotten since the war."

I was locked in place. I noticed a few other makhali in the lobby approaching. When one of them went to remove my translation artifacts, their hand brushing against my face, I snapped.

A problem with claws, I realized, is that it doesn't matter if your swing is a reactionary, open-handed one without any real force. They automatically turned any unexpected movement into a potential attack.

Someone else grabbed my arms, locking them behind my back. A bewildered Veras was held in place as we were separated. I kicked and flailed as I was dragged away, stuck in a purely instinctual and reactionary state. They took my translation items, but even with them I probably couldn't have processed what the people carrying me away were saying anymore.

They didn't decontaminate me, at least not yet. I scratched too many people for them to attempt it. Instead they shoved me into a windowless small room, shutting the door behind me.

I beat at the door, the pain of bashing my stupid sensitive hands against it triggering a cascade of physical changes. My arms and legs swelled with mass. Some of it might have been muscle; if there was anything actually useful in them, instead of just fat and fluid, it wasn't of much help. They were cold, numb, my misshapen fingers barely able to curl into fists. I slammed the flat of my forearm against the door like a club, hoping if I couldn't feel it then it couldn't be hurt, only to cry out. A stray piece of bone, free-floating in my arm, jabbed against my original flesh. There were chairs and a table I could've swung at the door instead, but I didn't think I could have taken that noise on top of everything else.

I kept hitting the door until someone yelled at me and started to open it, and then I was kicking it shut again because people were waiting on the other side and people were bad, almost pinning someone's hand between door and frame.

Surely I could find or make another way out. I pressed myself flat against a wall, sidling along it, listening and feeling for any sign that outside might be easier reached in another direction. I didn't find anything promising, but we were in full-blown freakout and that didn't matter. I grew keratin plates stemming from my arms and reaching past my hands, using them to try to carve at the walls. I was distantly aware I was crying.

I didn't know how long it took for another person to enter the room, just that by the time it happened I was exhausted, most of my extra mass melted away, my not-claws broken from being repeatedly forced against the wall and slowly disintegrating. When the door opened, I stumbled back into a corner, hunching up.

The makhal who came in was alarmingly tall, easily six and a half feet. He wore a simple white shirt, charcoal pants, and black shoes. His hair was steel gray, his eyes dark with epicanthic folds, his skin a warm beige. His wings hardly looked organic. Smooth bone-like sections connected to his back, forming the leading edges and ribs. The rest was a barely visible membrane that resembled cellophane. He looked old, well-worn, but he had a presence that seemed to fill the room, pinning me in place.

He took me by the hand, starting to gently pull me out of my corner. I froze, willing to stay still if it would just mean this was over, until he touched something magical to my face. In a moment of animal panic, I bit his arm. Shockingly sweet blood entered my mouth. He released me. I pressed back into my corner.

He looked from his arm to my face. A blue haze formed over his arms and chest, coalescing into a translucent layer that floated over his skin. He slowly knelt and slid a couple items across the floor to me. My translation items. I started to cry again as I put them on.

"I want to leave," I said. "I want to leave and if you let me I'll never bother anyone ever again. I'll find a quiet empty corner to die in and you'll never have to see me if you just let me go."

"Why would I want you to die?" the makhal said.

"What *do* you want?"

"To know why and how you're here. And to take care of your injuries. It seems you have quite a few cuts and bruises," he said.

I glared at him.

"I mean you no harm, and I promise nobody else did either. We created certain rules during a very dark time, and not being able to follow them created a bit of a panic." He sighed and sat at the table, taking out a medical kit from beneath it. The magic around him dissipated, allowing him to clean and bandage the four punctures in his arm. "Didn't hurt at all," he said. "You just surprised me. I'll sit at this end of the table, and when you feel ready, maybe you could sit at the other end? We'll get you looked after as well."

"No."

"To what part?"

"No healing magic. It doesn't help, it just feels bad."

"It's not supposed to feel like anything," he said, puzzled.

"It. Feels. Bad."

I could feel my body starting to shift again, and fought to keep it under control.

"Please sit?" he said. "I have perfectly non-magical bandages here as well. Whatever you have to say, I'll listen."

I crept into the chair, allowed exhaustion to take care of the changes to my body, and hesitantly held out my hand. I tried not to squirm as he washed blood from the pinpricks my claws had made in my palm. He reached for my face with a cleaning pad. I took it from him. My split lip had already sealed shut. Hopefully I hadn't just traded blood with an alien.

"There," he said. "Your bruises appear superficial. My understanding is we heal similarly enough, minus the magic."

"You know about my species?" I said.

"Barely. The rift to your world was sealed off soon after it was discovered for the safety of your species. I know that you exist, and that you should not have been able to come here unless you found some other way off your world. What's your name?"

"Ella."

"Berith," he introduced himself.

"Oh." I looked down at my bruised arms. "Well, at least we got your attention."

"An unexpected alien visitor being held captive will do that, yes. Could you tell me what led you here?"

I explained about the monsters that had shown up on Earth, and now in the Glade.

"So much to go through in such a short period of time," he said. "And now this. You look barely out of childhood."

"I'm an adult," I said, gaze drifting down to his bandaged arm. "I... I am responsible for my own actions."

"I imagine anyone put in your situation might be driven to lash out," Berith said. "I understand panic, and self-defense. This can be left in the past."

"Thank you," I whispered.

"I imagine you want to be reunited with your companion?"

I shrugged and nodded at the same time. Better the devil I knew.

Berith motioned for me to follow, and I stuck close to him when we left the room, still not trusting that the door wouldn't shut before me if I left too big of a gap between us. But he must've gotten everyone else to clear out. He approached the secretary, who had a firm   if-I-just-keep-to-myself-today-will-not-get-any-worse   look to him.

"Saela," Berith said, "I want a team sent to the Glade imme-diately."

"Dorian was nearby and waiting to give you his monthly report when they arrived. He took the liberty of going to examine the problem on his own."

"Of course he did," Berith said. "And our other guest?"

Veras was brought out, looking disgruntled but unharmed. Most of my bruises were fading or gone, since they'd formed in extra tissue I no longer possessed, but I imagined I must look pretty rough.

"What happened?" he said.

I didn't want to tell him I'd been punching and kicking walls because I knew it would make me sound stupid.

"Did a person do this?" he asked me.

I shook my head.

Veras had my folded-up cloak under one arm. He carefully draped it over my shoulders, pulled the hood up over my head.

Berith drew Veras aside for a minute, talking with him in low tones, the conversation clearly an apology. It ended with Veras nodding and Berith squeezing his shoulder before rejoining me.

"Shall we see what can be done?" he said, and I dared to feel a little hope.

9

———

Berith led Veras and I to a small meeting room several flights up. It was a strange anachronism for me to see the relatively familiar shape of a conference table with chairs and know none of it was made using electricity. Although, considering there were makhali like Reyna whose magic was focused on crafting things, I probably shouldn't use that as a reason to doubt their building skills.

"I believe I understand the situation as you know it," Berith said. "That leaves Dorian's update when he returns, as well as the Citadel's response. Some of our reserve soldiers will patrol through the Glade every couple days for the foreseeable future. We'll also send a group to track down where the graftlings you found came from."

"They probably came from my home," I said.

"That, or the same source," Berith agreed. "Ella, I will be honest with you. The team we'll send is experienced in fixing veils that border combat zones. In my youth, paths between worlds were kept open, and transportation between them maintained. I'm sorry to say that the universe is a darker place now than it was then. Leaving the rift to your world open only makes it easier for the Graft to invade others."

"You're putting it back up?" I said. I thought somewhere in his copious words I must've experienced a hiccup with either my translation items or my own auditory processing skills. I had to have heard wrong.

Some of Berith's calm, cool exterior faded. "I'm sorry. But you deserve transparency."

"You know you can't go back even with the veil down," Veras said. "You'd be handing yourself over to them. Wouldn't your loved ones rather have you here and safe than dying in an attempt to return home?"

"Cutting Earth off benefits it as well," Berith said. "It stops more monsters from entering. Throughout many conflicts, there have been times when we were on the verge of wiping out a local population of monsters, only for them to be supplied with more biomass and recover. I've witnessed raw Graft biomass moving like a tidal wave between contested worlds, looking for certain makahli victories to turn into complete losses. Do you understand why this has to happen? For the sake of everyone in this universe?"

I nodded. It did make sense. And then I slipped out of my chair and under the table, because the world was spinning and it was quieter and darker down there.

"Ella?" Veras said.

There were too many words inside me. If I tried to say anything, they'd all try to crowd out at once and choke me in the process.

Veras shifted in his seat, the tip of one of his folded wings poking my leg. I drew myself in tighter.

"Is there something we could get for her?" Berith asked. "I can only imagine that she needs comforting at the moment."

"I have no idea what she likes. We could leave the room and give her some space, but..."

"Her most recent time alone did not go well."

"No," Veras said, sounding exhausted. "No, it did not."

They carried out a stilted conversation about changes in the capital and what it was like living in the Glade. I stayed where I was, stimmed with my claws, and tried not to panic spiral.

The door slamming open startled me out of it. Still beneath the table, I watched as another makhal came striding in. This newcomer wore silver armor. His hair was crimson, as were his wings, which seemed to be covered in a short, velvety-looking fur texture of the same color. His face was sharp and pale, his cheeks flushed gold from exertion, brown eyes glaring. His hair was a couple inches long, much of it pulled into a thick braid going from his temple to the back of his head.

"Dorian, welcome back," Berith said, rising to greet him. "You're alright?"

"In one piece and reporting for duty, sir," Dorian said.

"What did you find?"

"Half a dozen graftlings in total spread between the Glade and the region of 9F immediately connected to it, all quadrupedal scouts, all neutralized," Dorian said. "No new traits that I noticed, no significant growth in either area, no other monsters spotted from a distance. The situation was caught very quickly."

"Doesn't seem like he's all that observant," Veras murmured.

"About?" Dorian said coldly.

I saw Veras flinch, legs twitching beneath the table, and figured I had to come out at some point anyway. Dorian had been turned away, showing me that the back of his wings were covered in stiff white feathers, but he whipped around as I emerged, his gaze immediately going to my clawed hands.

"What are you, and how did you get here?" he said.

"This is Ella, a human from one of the worlds past 9F," Berith said. "Dorian, your monthly report?"

"Nothing new on my end."

"Then I must go make the other arrangements we discussed." He laid a fatherly hand on my shoulder that I almost flinched away from. "I will have the 9F expedition check on the rift to your world often. Should the contamination on the other side be cleared, you'll be one of the first to know."

I looked down at my lap and pressed my claws against my arm, just short of the amount of pressure it would take to draw blood.

"Expedition?" Dorian asked, perking up.

"By some of our reserve troops," Berith said.

Dorian slouched.

Berith left the room. I wondered if someone better than me—better at charisma, at talking, at being a person—could've changed his mind. Every passing second closed the window of opportunity for me to run after him and beg him not to do this, but I knew I wouldn't be able to convince him.

Dorian leaned on the table next to me, his chin propped on his elbows. "Is it that bad on your world that you came all the way here?" He sounded too interested, he'd gotten too close; he'd asked me a question, but I didn't know what he actually wanted from me.

"Leave her alone," Veras said, irritated.

"I'm one of the soldiers responsible for keeping you safe. I want more information in case I end up needing to deal with it."

"Do you live with this every day?" I said. "The knowledge that at any point, a horde of monsters could show up and make your home into theirs?"

"I do," Dorian said. "It stops feeling so bad once you know how to prevent that from happening."

What could I have possibly done? Nothing, most likely. I was tired of being so... malleable. Of having to adapt to the universe instead of it adapting around me. I was too soft. I needed more substance if I was ever going to stand up against anything. I looked up to see Dorian about to leave.

"Wait!" I called out.

Dorian swiveled.

"You really killed the monsters you found?" I said.

"Are you calling me a liar?"

"No! I just, I want to do what you do. I..." I couldn't do anything about the veil being back up. I could only prepare myself for a day when it wasn't. "If killing monsters is what it takes to go home, I'll do it."

"Have you never been shown how?" Dorian asked.

I shook my head.

"What makes you think you're capable of it?"

I held up a hand and grew out my claws more, getting a raised eyebrow from Dorian. "I can change my body. Become stronger, faster. Sharpen my senses too. I've only taken out one monster so far, but I kept myself safe in the Glade by detecting a monster before it could detect me."

Dorian put a hand on his sword.

Spontaneously formed muscles let me spring backwards as he swung the blade. The skin on my forearms swelled into thick calluses. I doubted they would protect me from getting cut, but I appreciated the effort, just like I appreciated Veras's delayed yell of *what are you doing get away from her.*

"Not bad," Dorian said, sheathing his sword. "You've got quick reflexes, and finding your enemies before they can find you is a useful skill."

I started trembling. His blade was a few inches too short to have hit me even if I hadn't jumped back, but I hadn't known that at the start.

"Was that too much?" Dorian asked. "I guess that was a bit much."

I wrapped my arms around myself and took a few calming breaths. "It was."

"Hey, you did good. Though you know you'll have to face far worse," Dorian said, and I *think* he meant it kindly.

"I do."

Veras was making every universal gesture for stop-what-are-you-DOING possible.

Dorian regarded me, head tilted. "Do you come from a society of warriors?"

"Uh, I guess some of us are? Nobody I know, though."

"How much experience do they have against the Graft?"

"It's new to us."

"Damn," he said. "People make big mistakes the first time they meet them."

"I'm aware," I said miserably.

"Having even one knowledgeable, experienced person in the right place can make a huge difference. Is that what you want to be?"

Veras tried to interject again. "Ella, you can't—"

"Shut up," I snapped at him, making him flinch. "This isn't your business. It's my life, and my home, and my family. I know you don't think much of me, but I have to at least try."

"It's a big universe," Dorian said. "It could always use more people keeping it safe. We just don't have the capacity to take care of other worlds anymore, but you're here, I'm here — preparing you to take care of your own world is something we can do. In return for some favors, I'll teach you how to fight."

"What kind of favors?" Veras said.

"Not your business, healer. Also, I haven't decided yet. I'm the leader of an elite task force, sometimes I need work done. Sound good?"

"Yes," I blurted out. "Sure. When do we start? Where?"

Dorian pulled aside a curtain, revealing a glass door and a small balcony. He waved me over. I held onto the doorframe, leery of getting too close to the unfenced edge given that we were multiple stories up. Dorian pointed, past the wall and the veil.

"There's a rift in that field to world 7C, where you'll find Vanguard Base," he said. "Stop by whenever. I'm always practicing. It'll be nice to have something new to spar against."

"You'll be careful with her, won't you?" Veras asked from behind us, making me jump. "Ella's body is resistant to healing magic."

"I know what I'm doing," Dorian said. He smirked at me. "See you later, girl."

He stepped off the balcony, wings catching the wind and quickly propelling him out of sight. I inched my way back inside, relieved to shut the door behind me.

Veras started to speak. "I can't believe you agreed to—"

"Stay out of my life," I said.

He balked.

"You saved my life, I saved yours. Given that neither of us likes the other, I figure we can ignore any other details and call it even. I don't want or need you looking out for me, even if you were any good at it. It should be safe in the Glade now. You can go without having me escort you."

"Could I have one hour?" Veras asked.

"One hour of *what*?"

"When we were separated," Veras said, "after a while, they told me you were having some kind of fit. I didn't know if seeing me would make it better or worse, and if I have to ask that, then I haven't been a good doctor. Maybe you won't ever want to see me again. If that's the case, I'd appreciate you giving me one last hour to try and set you up with what you need."

"You don't know what I—"

"A toothbrush," he blurted out. "Something for you to write down the things that bother and hurt you so you can keep track of what to avoid. If you need it like some younger makhali do, supplies to deal with bleeding cycles. I'd like to get those while we're in the capital. And then I'll go back to Reyna and Andras, and you'll... I don't know what you'll do."

"I don't understand you," I said. "Don't you hate me? Aren't you afraid of me?" I'd almost rather he pick one option, even if it was a bad one, and stick to it so I'd know what to expect.

"It's not hate," Veras said. "And I wish it wasn't fear. I have someone I need to protect, just like you want to return to your parents. When I saw that monster near Andras, I, I couldn't have helped him myself. I don't know what I would've done if he'd died. Having someone new in the house, someone with strange magic..."

"When did it ever seem like I might want to hurt Andras?" I said.

"You didn't—I—losing someone I care about to contamination, having them turn into a graftling, that's my worst nightmare. And it's what was on my mind when you came to me. The best tools I have to prevent that from happening don't work on you. I panicked and assumed the worst because in that moment, I was scared of losing everything." He reached under his sleeve cuffs, scratching at this arms. "It was supposed to get better once the war ended, but I still can't relax. The anxiety just attaches itself to other things, or apparently other people, even if that's not fair to them. I know you're not *bad*. Are you going to live with Reyna?" he asked suddenly.

"I don't know," I said. "That's her choice first."

"I don't want you starving and freezing outside at night. And, if you'll already be learning how to fight, you like Andras, right?"

I cautiously nodded.

"If you're around," Veras's voice cracked. "Will you help me keep him safe?"

I stared at him.

"I don't want you putting your life on the line for us. Just, if you see any new contamination, let us know? Mark it for the patrols? Please? I don't know what I might have that's of value to you—"

"I can barely breathe in Reyna's house," I admitted. "I doubt I could stand to spend very long there, which sucks because I like her much better than you."

Veras paused to catch his breath. "You know, normally I value honesty. It feels different coming from you."

"That might be the autism," I mumbled.

"...Autism?"

Shouldn't've said anything. "Don't worry about it."

"Is it some kind of condition?"

"It's not medical. It's just something certain humans are."

He tilted his head, watching me. "Is it important to you?"

I sighed. "Humans who are autistic have some differences in how our brains function. A couple common effects are struggling socially and processing sensory information in odd ways, like it's more intense or even distressing." I didn't want to even mention how common anxiety was too. "And then the real fun, unique part about being me is that discomfort makes *this* happen." I held up my clawed hands.

"Was the environment in my home so awful for you that it made you change that much?" Veras said.

"Last time was from a nightmare. Everything else just kept me from being able to relax."

"Like what?"

"Are you sure you want to know?"

"I do," he said. "Especially if you're coming back."

"They reek," I blurted out. "All your medicines and cleaning supplies. Just being near an open container makes me feel like my nose and lungs are getting chemically burnt."

He stared at me, open-mouthed. There went cohabitation attempt number two, and in record time. But Veras managed to gather himself. "They're that bad?"

"Can't you smell them?"

"Of course I can. I just don't think they're bad. They bothered me a little when I first started medical school, but I suppose I've—"

"Makhali have medical school?"

"They don't let just anyone do it."

"Huh."

"Anyway, I got used to them. During the war, we had to keep our hospitals perfectly clean. If infected material touched a patient's wounds, it could mean a death sentence and a new monster. I have a bit of a fixation on hygiene for that reason. It's stressful when I'm in an unclean environment. But I can avoid using them around you from now on."

"Will that work if you need them to feel comfortable?"

Veras shrugged. "We can only try."

He held out his hand, and I gingerly shook it.

"Do I get more than the one hour?" he asked.

"I guess so. Just please don't give me anything else with magic in it. Sometimes I can barely put up with the translators."

He paused. "In what way?"

"Magic seems to give me bad sensory input? Which is kinda funny, because what were the chances of me ever finding that out if the Graft hadn't appeared?"

"I thought you just weren't used to it. When you flailed in your sleep the first time I tried healing you, I... have I hurt you?" he asked with horrified urgency.

"It's not actually painful."

"That's not a no."

This was the unfortunate reality of my neurodivergence, that people could be doing things completely ordinary and harmless to them that caused me anxiety or distress. "Too much is overwhelming, and I expect overwhelming things to hurt, so there's the anticipation and stress of that. And sometimes I get a headache."

"That's harm," Veras said. "Harm we can try to avoid unless it's the lesser of two threats to your wellbeing. It must've felt even more like I was threatening you, didn't it? When I spoke of decontamination."

"You assuming I would harm someone else felt worse. And when you yelled at me and I ran off, I did... fall down the stairs and hit my head."

He winced. "I wish I could offer you more than an apology and some cold gel. What about your shoulder? Is it alright?"

"It's still sore," I said.

"May I take a look? No magic, I promise."

I let him peel back my bandages through the gaps in the back of my shirt.

"Your temperature and range of motion is normal, and you're not bleeding, so it's likely just soreness. Let's quickly take care of business here, and then let Reyna and Andras know we're safe."

I followed Veras around the city as he made his purchases with stamped clay tiles. Soon I had a bundle of items tucked under one arm, a toothbrush, cloth pads, a journal and pencil, some other hygiene-related items, and we were passing through the gates of Pellior's Landing just as the sun set.

Veras surveyed the land before him. His wings lifted halfway, then fell. "I don't think I have the energy left to fly," he said, and began trudging towards Reyna's house.

"Does walking take less energy?" I asked.

"Depends on the weather and terrain. But flying also uses magic, and I had to use mine on Andras earlier. And I haven't been sleeping well."

"Oh," I said. "Spoon theory, but magical."

"Spoon?"

"Each day you only have so many spoons you can use to get

things done, and if you're already tired, in pain, or overwhelmed, you'll start with less spoons than someone who isn't."

"How many spoons do humans need in a day?" Veras asked, bewildered.

"It's just the item the person who described it that way used."

"I suppose it makes enough sense."

"How does that work if you have multiple types of magic?" I asked. "Is it weird that you do?"

"It's all one reserve of energy. I'd say it's attainable for plenty of makhali to learn a second kind of magic if they dedicate themselves to it, but it's uncommon. Healing is what I was born with an aptitude for, and then trained in. Language took a lot of studying during my spare time. I got lucky that it came to me as quickly as it did. I always knew I wanted to learn other languages, but I found new ones I was interested in far faster than I could learn them without magic."

"Is it for when you travel?"

"That was what got me started, but even with healing magic, it's hard to properly treat someone without talking to them. Plesmae used to have plenty of visitors before the last war, and I wanted to help if they got sick. I was hoping to eventually study other species' medicine, but given the current state of the universe, I doubt that'll happen anytime soon." He saw my look of confusion and added, "we know of many dozens of worlds, and the Graft have been on almost all of them. Two of our closest neighboring species were forced to completely abandon much of their home worlds during the last war, and there are other civilizations we haven't had contact with since. As you saw with the veil around the rift to Earth, we have our ways of preventing passage, and I'm sure other species have theirs. They've probably cordoned themselves off too."

"How bad was it?" I asked. "The last war?"

"We lost about a thousand of us. I told you we have about five thousand in the capital right now." Veras sighed. "I didn't tell you that the capital is all that we have."

"Fuck," I said before I could stop myself. I hadn't realized they were literally endangered. The idea of losing one in six people...

"Yeah," Veras said quietly. "There were so many more of us just a few generations ago. Our species didn't begin here. Plesmae was just a colony when our original home was lost to contamination. Not everyone… most of our species didn't make it off-world in time."

I wanted to grieve, for the past I'd just learned about and the future I was terrified of. Stupid of me to hope there could be any fairness in the universe.

"Anyway," Veras said, tone neutral. "Wasteland worlds, like 9F where we met, or 7C? Their names come from the lowest number of rifts it took to reach them from our original homeworld, and then alphabetical in order of discovery."

He seemed to be trying to set the conversation on a softer path, but it was too late for that.

"Are you overwhelmed right now?" he asked me.

I nodded.

"Is there anything I can do about it?"

I shrugged again.

"Are you alright with Reyna and Andras hearing about your needs and…?"

"They can know about it, it's just a conversation I'm tired of having."

"Only if you're sure," Veras said. "I try to respect others' privacy. And I do need to ask that you do the same for us as well. Particularly Andras."

"Like how Reyna didn't know about him?"

"Reyna is fine. But other people, they might not —"

"Veras," I said, "I don't think I can describe how little interest I currently have in meeting more strangers. I don't need to mention Andras being in the Glade to anyone else, and that's all the energy I want to spend thinking about it."

Even tired, he seemed so uptight, one thing right after another stressing him out. I mean, I was the same way. I just tried to keep it inside more. That didn't make either of us better than the other. It just meant I was now dealing with both our stress.

At least it wasn't for too much longer. Soon we reached Reyna's house, where she and Andras were waiting on the porch. They spotted us on our way over. Andras came running over and embraced Veras, and then turned to me, holding out his arms. This time, I accepted his hug. I closed my eyes and wished I was home, that it was my mom or dad holding me.

"A soldier already did a brief patrol through the Glade, and over a few neighboring miles of 9F," Veras explained. "He found a handful of monsters to use his sword on. We were promised repeated patrols through the Glade for the time being, and a group sent to 9F to..."

"To find all their sources and block them off," I finished for him.

They seemed to hear the unspoken part just fine. Veras drew Reyna and Andras aside to talk while I sat by myself in the grass. If I looked only at the sky, sunk my fingers into the wild green, and tuned out the alien language being used nearby, I could pretend to be home.

You went somewhere not-home and will learn new things, I thought. Just like was planned.

I'd much rather be suffering through a degree in Communications with a minor in Debate.

Reyna approaching shook me out of it. "Veras explained it wouldn't work for you here, long term," she said.

I nodded.

She tucked a stray lock of hair behind my ear, fingers brushing against a small section of rough, altered skin on my face that I hadn't noticed. The sensory feedback from it was intense. I wasn't ready to be touched there yet, even gently. "Don't be afraid to return to me if you need anything."

"Thank you," I said. "For keeping a space open for me. I'm bringing your bike back tomorrow."

I don't know why I thought that would be it. Reyna filled a satchel with clothes that would fit me better than my former baggy castoffs. She had several closets' worth, all new designs that she'd been meaning to eventually bring to the capital. I still felt bad for taking them, but it was one less thing for me to worry about.

Andras must've rested while we were away, his recovered stamina letting us return to his and Veras's house much quicker than we'd left it. Andras smiled when we were within a few minutes' walk of it, letting us know his garden was untouched; the monsters hadn't made it too close. Once inside, he steered Veras to one of the armchairs, fiddling with his sleeves.

"I can do it myself," Veras said.

Andras shook his head. Veras sighed and held out his arms, letting Andras unbutton and roll up his sleeves. His bronze skin had scaly, irritated patches on his forearms.

"You know about my fixation now," Veras said, catching me staring. "It's hard to sanitize skin and be gentle at the same time."

"You can't heal it?" I asked.

"I could, but that just enables me to do it again. I'm trying to dissuade myself by living with the consequences."

Andras took out a jar of medicine, a thick cream that smelled far nicer than anything I'd been subjected to, and applied it to Veras's rashes. "Make sure you let it sit for the full ten minutes before washing it off this time. Looks like we're running low. I'll harvest more of the roots tomorrow."

Veras pulled his sleeves back down. "Andras... I know this is the best place on Plesmae for you to defend yourself, but even so it would be safest if you and I limited how often we're alone away from the house."

Andras wilted.

"I'm so sorry."

"We're safer now than we were," Andras said. "That's nothing to apologize for."

The two of them embraced. "Now let's take care of you," Veras, who must've been exhausted, said, and I thought it would be best to go to my room.

I took out the journal Veras had gotten me. He'd had his idea for how I should use it, but I'd never needed help remembering what bothered me. Instead, I started writing a letter to my parents. It felt like the natural thing to do, but also horrible, like I was preparing my final message to them. I'd just have to write another letter tomorrow, so it wouldn't be the last. And the day after that. And the day after...

"I'll see them again," I told myself. "I have to."

I made myself write.

Mom, Dad,

If you're reading this

I went to erase what I'd written. The charcoal eye at the end of the pencil leered at me. No eraser. I crossed it out and started again.

When you read this

I crossed that out too.

I don't know if you'll ever read this, but I have to believe you will. I have to believe I'm coming home. I don't know how, or when, but the if is non-negotiable.

When I didn't go to college right after high school, you were worried that my world wasn't big enough. My world got way bigger recently, and I don't like it. I had to run from what was happening at home, and somehow I've wound up on another world, with two aliens named Veras and Andras as my hosts (I suppose I'm the alien in this situation). I remember a couple bedtime stories you told me about meeting aliens and exploring the universe, but there wasn't as much gross stuff in them. And in those stories, you never mentioned the food. Alien food is like gross dessert, which I didn't think was possible.

My mouth quirked into a smile. Here I was, on an alien planet, experiencing alien things, and *complaining*. Mom and Dad would be appalled if I didn't mention anything good. I wrote a bit about what I'd seen so far, describing the Glade, Pellior's Landing, and Reyna and Dorian.

Tomorrow, I wrote at the end of the letter, *I'll collect some alien moss to bring home to you.*

Love you always,

Ella

As soon as I finished the letter, an irrational anger seized me.

"They don't have ziploc bags here," I said. "How the fuck am I supposed to bring something fresh home for my parents?"

I clenched my fists, then had a thought as I felt the prickle of my claws. They felt small in comparison to the monsters we'd seen, puny compared to Dorian's sword. As horrible as it had been, watching the monster Andras killed burn away had reminded me of the hidden layers of my own body.

Instead of just working with my fingernails, I reached into the bones of my hands, asking them to grow, asking everything else in its path to get out of the way. Bone spurs broke through my skin, fusing with my nails to form longer, stronger hooks. My fingers broadened to support the two-inch-long weapons.

I took Reyna's clay, pinching out spikes of it and then smoothing them down as I thought about my claws disappearing. Some of the extra growth was drawn back inside. The rest crumbled into dust. I thought I caught a glimpse of the underlying muscle and bone before the skin reformed over where it had broken. Hopefully I hadn't. But I still dreamed that night that all my skin was gone, needing Andras to wake me from my terror.

INTERMISSION

This new world welcomes exploration. Even now its rivers carry us to new places, and its winds bring us scents and signs of other environments. Everyone loves it here already. Like me, they have come from far across the universe in search of a home. Their natural instinct is to separate, to disperse, but I say no. I advise them, let at least some of us stay here and lay a strong foundation. There will be world enough for all of us, there is no need to rush; we have never found the edge of the universe, and I do not believe it will happen in my lifetime.

Of course I am selfish in choosing to remain where I am, even though I do believe it is the wisest course. For us to find each other, it is best if one of us stays still while the other searches. For now I will be here, and if I leave before he arrives, he will hear from others that I am nearby and have somewhere comfortable to wait for me.

10

———

It was hard for me to get a full breakfast in the next morning, both from a continued distrust of the food available to me, and nerves. Veras seemed equally jittery, constantly switching between keeping an eye on Andras and I; Andras was better than he'd been yesterday, but still lethargic and wheezing occasionally. I kept expecting Veras to come up with some excuse for why I couldn't go, and considered avoiding him, but in the end I built up the courage to ask for help. He noticed me lingering and raised an eyebrow.

"Do you have medical books?" I asked.

He nodded.

"Can I look at them? I need to learn about anatomy," I said.

"You don't read our language," Veras said.

"I'm hoping one of you can help me with that."

"Sure," Andras said.

"Besides, there'll be drawings, right?" I asked.

"But not of you," Veras said.

"I'll take whatever might help me figure out how to use my ability."

"Doesn't it just happen on its own?" Andras asked.

"Well, yeah, but it doesn't always go right," I said. "I think it'll help if I get a better sense of which muscles do what and how they connect. It surely can't be worse than blindly guessing."

"I thought it was more instinctual than that," Veras said, suddenly extremely concerned.

"I wish."

Veras took in what I had to assume was a calming breath before perusing the bookshelf. "Most of my books are focused on treating illness or injury, not general anatomy." His hand hovered over a thick book's spine. He hesitated. "This might not actually help."

"Worth a shot, isn't it?" Andras said.

Veras pulled out the giant book he'd been reading earlier. "I don't have anything else like it. Treat it well."

"I'll be gentle," I said. I opened it to a random page. "Is this...?"

"There are plenty of other intelligent species out there. You're not in it, but you might be able to use it for inspiration." He seemed to regret the words immediately. "Please be careful. With yourself, not just the book."

He excused himself, casting worried looks over his shoulder as he went upstairs, probably wanting to avoid seeing me contort myself. Andras, on the other hand, eagerly sat by my side as I flipped through the super-special alien book. A few species looked bug-like, others like they belonged underwater. Some, I had trouble picturing as sentient. It was a little dizzying, learning how much other life in the universe there was.

"My parents would be so jealous," I said. "My species, as far as we know it's just *us*. Mom and Dad always had... I know even now they have hope there are other people out there."

"Someday you'll get to tell them they were right," Andras said.

I wanted him to be right so badly. "Should I? They'd boast so much."

"They're proud?"

"About most things? No. About this? I'd be hearing *we told you so* for the rest of my life. They're the sort to drag me out to an empty field, in the rain, in the middle of the night, to take turns squinting through a telescope at a cloudy sky. And then, because we didn't see anything, obviously we have to spend the whole trip home listening to alien conspiracy podca... oral storytelling so they can get their fix." I sighed. "At least I'd get to tell them they were looking in the wrong damn place for aliens. The rifts feel more like some kind of fairy bullshit, they'd hate that. I mean, I'm sure they hate the Graft too, but they'd be especially put out by the rifts." Even if they were safe, they had to be so afraid...

"Is it hard to talk about them?" Andras asked.

"A bit. I feel like, they had so much hope our family would be special. That against all odds, we'd be first contact, or discover a cryptid in our backyard, or meet Sasquatch while out on a hike."

Andras politely nodded despite not knowing what Sasquatch was.

"I don't mind that part," I said, and could've stopped there, but the words burned and needed to come out. "I mind that I was the closest thing to an alien or cryptid they were ever likely to find, and I hid it from them because I didn't know what would happen. Part of their dream was that no matter what we found, getting other people involved couldn't possibly go wrong, for us or for... the creature." That was why my favorite genres had always been fantasy and sci-fi that took place entirely somewhere else; it felt so much more realistic than anything speculative going well within the world I knew. I held up the book, trying to force a smile. "But, some good news for the probability of me just being a weird human, I'm not seeing anything in here that's Ella-shaped. You've really never heard of a makhal, or anything else, with magic like mine?"

"I haven't."

"Shame." Knowing there was somebody else out there like me, that I could be one of even just a pair... the thought affected me more than I wanted it to.

"I'd consider that a positive, not a negative," Andras said. "It just means you're unique."

"I guess," I said. Whether that was positive depended on *how*. "What's this caption say?" I pointed to a picture of a squat, armored species.

"It says 'in order to ... must compensate for ... builds up over their lifetime.' " I understood a few words, but the rest was nonsense to me. Andras looked proud of himself.

I tapped at my earring. "I think it's struggling."

"Guess I didn't pronounce most of that right," he admitted.

"I couldn't've done any better." I turned to the next page, a diagram of the armor's layers. I looked expectantly at Andras.

"Chitin," he read. "Over a sponge-like layer to allow for blood circulation and cooling." He looked at me expectantly.

"Would you, um, mind turning around? I don't want to be seen… in-progress."

He did, and I fought down the urge to send him away. It was too late to prevent discovery.

I was new to making deliberate changes. A normal body had always been my goal, but that wouldn't get me home. I wanted to try thickening the top layer of my skin, recreate that slate-over-honeycomb structure from the diagram. I focused on my left forearm, fingers crossed as if that would help.

My skin hardened, gaining a sheen. I twisted my arm. The shiny layer ripped. It crackled as I scratched it off, a complete wash.

"Are those success noises?" Andras asked, still facing away.

"No," I sighed. "I've always made simple changes, adding soft matter or growing what's already there and hoping it works out. I don't know if I'm capable of anything more."

"Didn't you have longer legs once? That worked."

"I have done that, but that was luck. There was just as much chance that I ended up with something numb and hard to move. It's like, I can see certain changes happening, and connect that to what I'm feeling. I know what growing bone and muscle and skin feels like, and recreating that feeling is how I do it on command. I can't see veins or nerves changing, and if it's happened before, I certainly don't know what it feels like. Clearly it's not always happening on its own."

"You might just have to trust that part of the process," Andras said. "That was part of my learning to use my magic, closing my eyes and checking afterwards if the effect I wanted actually happened."

"That sounds riskier for me than it does for you," I said.

"I'm not saying to leave it up to chance. When I was learning, I've accidentally told only parts of a plant to grow, and left out an important component. A tree trunk that thickens without forming more bark isn't a happy one. I didn't get better until I understood each part I was trying to affect, but I don't need to think about them individually anymore. Is your situation at all like that?"

Was it? Part of the reason using my ability could be uncomfortable was that there was so much sensory information involved. I didn't feel a limb lengthening as just one sensation. It was multiple at once, some more strained as they outpaced others, packed densely into the same space.

"Until you can learn more about your own anatomy, why don't you try visualization?" Andras suggested. "I like using metaphors. Veins forming could be like roots, or underground rivers cutting through the ground, or even worms digging—"

"*Please* don't mention worms while I'm thinking about my body," I said.

"Could you think of it like a growing forest instead of an individual branch?"

I shut my eyes and tried. All the metaphors Andras used were natural events. I wasn't used to comparing my ability to that. Using it had always seemed more like taking a sledgehammer to a statue. How many times could the pieces be glued back together before they didn't connect right?

But I had to try. I liked the growing forest metaphor best. I needed protective bark, thick skin. I needed sap and water flowing beneath the surface, blood and lymph. I needed anchoring roots and a sturdy foundation, tendons attached to bone—

I opened my eyes, had to swallow back a scream. The skin of my left forearm was crystalizing again, an inflexible layer spreading from an epicenter halfway between wrist and elbow. Panic started to set in, but I pushed back against it. I'd be fine. I'd had this happen before. And if I wasn't fine, Andras was right there. He'd help me. It would be fine. I could do this.

I don't need you there, I thought, glaring at my hardening skin.

Above the wrist, below the elbow, back of the arm only. *That's* where I need you.

The hard layer stopped growing. It was difficult to twist my arm with it there, my skin uncomfortably taut. The tightness eased as I built up a softer layer beneath it, padding with more give and flexibility. I tapped at the shell, my claw bouncing off it. I didn't recall making that. My claws were starting to feel like a normal part of me. I dared to make one more change, thinking about a tree growing tall, doing so evenly; my forearm lengthened by several inches.

"You can..." I swallowed down my nerves. "You can turn around now."

He did, and didn't scream in horror, which was a great start. "Better than before?"

I nodded.

Andras's answering smile was a huge dopamine hit. "Good job."

Before I could start to worry about my arm being stuck like this, I imagined the shell dissolving away like a sugar cube in water, its padding deflating until only regular skin was left, relieved when my body actually obeyed me. My arm shrunk down to its normal length, a process I learned felt much less distressing when I pictured every element—muscle, bone, veins, skin—moving as one. I was surprised to find that my face was hot. It was an odd feeling, having someone outside my family be proud of me.

One last thing to do, and then.

And then.

And then I would learn how to fight.

I let my enhanced nose guide me through the Glade, seeking woodsmoke. Reyna's bike lay where I'd abandoned it, thankfully untouched; mere yards from it, a new clearing had been carved out, smaller foliage razed and the trees bearing burn scars wherever a monster must've come in contact with them. I rode the bike through the oversized forest, trying not to overthink my and Reyna's impending interaction. Maybe I could just leave the bike outside her door? No, that wouldn't be right. Even though the bike seemed fine, I was assuming it ran on magic. *Reyna's* magic, energy from her body she'd saved just for this. Energy I'd wasted.

My head hung low when I reached her home, summoning her to the front door with a knock. She perked up at the sight of her bike. I watched her inspect it, her relief clear when she found no damage.

"Looks like you took it quite a ways," she said.

I nodded.

"Was it a good ride?"

"It's a bit bumpy over the uneven ground of the Glade," I said, and then realized now was not a good time for criticism. "But I couldn't believe how quiet it was. I hate driving at home, and I've never been on something shaped like this that goes that fast, but it was nice to... I don't know. Travel without disturbing anyone?"

"What do you drive at home?" she said, confused.

"A car."

Several silent seconds passed between us. They should've been filled by the sound of two gears failing to mesh.

"You're headed somewhere else now?" she said. "Ella, you have to come back. I'm looking forward to hearing about your world. Don't leave me waiting too long, okay?"

I nodded, a little stunned. If I hadn't been so antsy to go see Dorian, I would've blabbed on about Earth tech right then and there until I'd made my theft up to her.

The rift Dorian had pointed out stood in the middle of an open field a few miles out from the capital, thankfully not too far from the Glade. 7C wasn't much to look at. The ground was a mix of dust and dirt that soaked up sunlight and spat out dry heat, a seemingly endless plain of slate gray with meandering ribbons of red and brown. Vanguard Base was a perfectly rectangular bunker made of smooth gray stone, neighbored by several watchtowers. It sat atop a hill, the only significant change in the otherwise flat landscape, a system of trenches surrounding and leading out from its base for drainage. There was a disturbing lack of anything I could identify as alive no matter which direction I looked.

I heard a shout from one of the towers. Dorian leapt from the top, diving towards me. He landed nearby with a spray of crimson gravel. I tried not to flinch at the commotion.

"Something wrong?" Dorian asked.

"It just seems kind of dead here," I said, really identifying with the fact that I was a pathological New Place Hater.

"Nothing for the Graft to take root in, except for us," he said.

He beckoned me over to a flat section of bare and pounded-flat ground where circles of increasing diameter were marked with chalk. Dorian unbuckled his sheathed sword from his waist and reverently set it down before stepping into the smallest of the circles, which was about the size of a boxing ring. I joined him, anxiously eying the many cracks and scorch marks around us. They gave me the same inkling of dread that spotting the burst remains of tires always did when I drove.

"Here's the plan," he said. "We'll start with teaching you how to fight back. Before you learn anything else, you need to know how to survive. Fighting between people isn't the same as fighting graftlings, but everyone has to start somewhere. Your goal is to work on your reflexes, your magic, and your nerve. You won't know if you can handle the real deal until you're in the thick of it, but we can give you the best chance possible. You ready?"

"We're doing this right now?" I said.

"Of course. Don't worry, I won't use my magic. You're not ready to face that yet."

He briefly held some in his hand, and it was like dark red fire and lightning forced to coexist in the same space. I backpedaled, startled. I wasn't sure what I'd been expecting from this training, but I hadn't fully processed until now that I was *absolutely* going to get hurt in the process.

"I said I *won't* use it," Dorian said patiently, as if there weren't other ways to cause pain. He removed his metal gloves, but kept on the rest of his armor.

What other options did I have? I built up my muscles and drew out my claws, trying to practice that morning's lesson.

"Please remember, I'm very new to this," I said.

"You got it," Dorian said.

He swept my legs out from under me. In a moment I was gasping on the ground. I released my modifications without meaning to.

"Get up," he said, offering me a hand.

I crab-walked away from Dorian before standing.

"Have I offended you?" I asked.

"It's nothing personal. You know what it's like to get thrown to the ground now. Try to get up faster next time. Having a monster on top of you is an easy way to die."

He was giving me the opportunity to learn. It was up to me to take it. There didn't seem to be anyone watching us, and he'd already seen me changed. I wasn't worried about someone like him, someone armed and dangerous, getting scared of me and responding with violence. I wasn't. Really. I took a step forward, hesitated, wondering if that was too aggressive, reminded myself we were supposed to be fighting, hesitated again anyway.

"You know they won't wait for you to approach them," Dorian said.

"Then maybe you should just come at me instead," I said. "It'll be more realistic that way."

He shrugged. "If it's realism you're after, I should try to rip your throat out."

"No, that's, uh, that's fine." I flexed my fingers, considering that the bodily changes I chose had to be made with monsters in mind. To kill them, or to keep me from getting killed.

"I'll just fight normally then," Dorian said cheerfully. "Don't worry, I'll hold back. You have a good reaction time, but let's see if you know how to react correctly."

"By that do you mean dodging, or?"

"That's for you to decide."

He threw a punch at me. It was much slower than his sword had been the other day, which gave me more time to panic. I held up my hand to catch it. The muscles in my arm bulged, veins sickeningly colorful under my skin. I shuddered, and they squirmed and settled back into their normal thin, undefined shapes, just in time for Dorian's fist to collide with my hand. My very sensitive hand. I all but folded at the waist.

"Is that what you want your magic to do?" Dorian asked. "Waste your energy showing up and then disappear right when you need it?" He watched the still-baggy skin of my arm draw itself tight. "What was your plan?"

"I didn't really have one yet," I gasped.

"So you wanted to buy time. Can your body extend any part of itself?"

I nodded.

"But doing so is tiring, I take it? Muscles take lots of time and effort to build normally. Have you tried making fat instead? If you just want padding, that might be easier. Here, try that and then hit me somewhere."

"You're sure?"

"Do it," he ordered.

Most of him was covered by his armor. I rubbed at the soft pad of tissue by my thumb, imagined it spreading between the skin and bones on my palm and fingers. I weakly slapped Dorian's face before I could think twice. I should've been at home right now, making complex trade deals with my dad over who would clean out old stuff in the fridge before garbage day. I hoped this would somehow return me to that life.

Dorian didn't flinch. "Did that hurt?"

I shook my head. It was hard to bend my fingers like this. I decreased the fat around the joints, replacing it with strengthened tendons to prevent injury.

"Didn't hurt me either, but that's what we'll work on next."

"I'm not hitting you with my claws out."

"That's right! Claws. You could have blades in so many fun places," Dorian said, delighted.

"If I grow them out elsewhere, I think they'd have to break the skin," I said. "And that's just not cool."

"I disagree. That's very cool. But would it be an actual wound?"

Hesitating, I searched for the body part that felt safest to try it on.

I settled for my elbow, bending my arm and extending the bone out through the thin skin there. A twinge of pain was followed by a few drops of blood beading at the tip of my elbow. I flinched, straightening my arm a little, the small sharp point I'd made dragging through a half inch of skin. I made the bone shrink back to its regular shape and size and applied pressure to the spot until it started to scab over.

"Maybe that'll be more of an advanced technique for you," Dorian said. "I suppose you already have enough to practice right now. Are you ready to go on the offensive this time?"

I looked Dorian in the eyes.

"You'll get there eventually," he said, and threw another punch.

I lasted half an hour against him. I'd experimented wildly with padding to block his blows and protect my fists when punching, and even tried higher bone density to add weight to my kicks and keep my balance. Dorian still sent me to the ground frequently enough that I gave up on counting. He had not given me any new feedback or instructions, and I suspected this was some kind of breaking-in. Or hazing. A one-time event, hopefully. It didn't feel like he was getting enjoyment out of dropping me. He backed off when I chose to stay on the ground for a little while, trying to convince myself the hard, sunbaked ground felt good on my back.

"Why are you stationed on such an uncomfortable world?" I asked. "I thought the war was over."

Dorian finished aggressively chugging from his canteen. "Commander Berith ordered it. This is a stepping stone between Plesmae and plenty of other worlds. Someone has to stand guard, and I prefer life as a soldier."

"How many others?"

"Want to see?"

"Would it involve a lot of walking?" I knew I'd have to make my way back to the Glade after this, and my body was already complaining. My feet felt tighter in their shoes than they had when I'd set out, making me wonder if I'd unintentionally built up extra cushioning on their soles.

"It doesn't have to."

Dorian seemed excited, so I followed him into the bunker, which smelled somewhat of sweaty musk. The rooms were too big for how little furniture they held, the lounge unoccupied.

"That way is the barracks," Dorian said, "and there's our armory."

"How many of you live here?"

"Eight."

"Is that a normal amount for a base?" It barely sounded like anyone.

"We had some other occupied bases, but I think we've left them all over the last few years. Too much danger without enough benefit to keep them active. So, yes."

"I guess you must be the best, then."

"Damn right. Here's the command center."

That didn't sound like a place I should be allowed into, but Dorian clearly didn't care. When we stepped over the threshold, the waist-height stone pillars on either side of the door made high-pitched whining noises. I covered my ears. I recognized the stones from the rift that went from Plesmae to 9F, but those had been silent. A female makhal with dark skin, short-cropped blue hair, and wings like wisps of clouds was working on another pillar, etching lines into the top. She reluctantly touched a button on the wall, turning off the alarm.

"Do we have to keep your sensors right there?" Dorian asked.

"They have an important function," she said. "When they go off, someone's come to bother me."

"It's my command center too, Bliss." He clapped her on the shoulder, turned to me. "This is my second-in-command. We served in different units during the war. I've always been part of the Vanguard at the front lines, and Bliss was usually in charge of defensive camps, but I'm glad to have her as part of my unit now."

"Don't touch me," Bliss said. "We're not friends."

He removed his hand. "We have company. This is Ella."

She looked up for a second. "I'm Bliss. Dorian and I aren't friends. Don't touch anything glowing and I guess you can stay."

I hesitantly stepped further into the room. Half of the command center was plastered with paper maps, dozens of worlds hanging in an empty background like a confused solar system. The other half was ordered, thin pieces of sheet rock stacked on top of each other, pulses of light trailing through carved channels. Some were connected with wires to standing stones with similar designs.

"Wait here," Dorian said. "I'll see if there's anyone else who wants to hear about my work." He ran off.

The search seemed to take a while. I rocked on my heels and waited until Bliss finished whatever she was doing.

"So you're what Dorian was so excited about," she said.

I blinked, not sure how to respond to that.

"Did you have fun training with him?" she asked.

"Sure?"

"Don't."

"Oh. Okay."

"Try not to encourage him. If he gets too worked up, he'll want us all to join in."

"I thought you were a military unit of Plesmae's best soldiers."

"Don't say this around Dorian unless you want a meltdown, but we're not out here to be heroes. I wanted to focus on my research somewhere quiet, the rest of the team doesn't have much to go home to, and society wasn't ready for Dorian."

"May I ask a rude question?" I said.

"Sure."

"Really?"

"You should learn to be aggressive," Bliss said.

"Am I safe when I train with Dorian? He's... very intense."

"So long as you don't fall and hit your head too hard. He can be shitty towards people he doesn't respect, but not violent. He saves that for graftlings. Were you worried?"

I shrugged. "I haven't ever met anyone like him."

"The best and most infuriating thing about him is he's genuine," Bliss said. "Lets me tear into him whenever I want. But definitely not someone I would've picked as my commanding officer or housemate, and certainly not both."

Dorian returned soon after that, all in a huff. "Nobody else wanted to see my progress on the maps."

"Why would they?" Bliss said. "You can't draw for shit, and it's not like you've been anywhere new in the last three years."

"It's part of our mission."

"I don't remember Berith ordering it."

"I did, and I'm in charge."

"Good for you," Bliss said, and went back to her magical wiring.

I took a closer look at the largest map. Two dozen large circles were clumsily drawn in pairs, for twelve planets. What I assumed were rift locations were drawn in with thick black ink, from which hair-thin lines sprouted to connect locations on other worlds. Two worlds sat at the center—Plesmae and a smaller 7C, I assumed—with six other worlds connected to 7C.

Dorian pointed at a smaller-drawn world ready to fall off the wall. "That's you."

"What?" I wouldn't have known it from the map. The only detail was a single rift, two hops away from Plesmae, the largest on the map.

"I had the rift on 9F already, but I added a page for your world," Dorian said. "I expect you to tell me more about it later, as one of those favors."

Seeing Earth's place in the universe should have excited me, but I couldn't find the energy. "Have you been to all these other worlds?"

"I've fought on a handful. The rest, I plan to explore someday."

"Do makhali have..." I realized the words "astronaut suit" would probably give the translator some trouble, "ways to deal with other atmospheres and gravity and stuff?"

Dorian shrugged. "That hasn't been an issue yet."

I stared at him. I wasn't as big of a space nerd as my parents, but they'd still exposed me to plenty about our solar system and other planets. "That doesn't make sense. What are the chances that these dozens of worlds would all be habitable for you?"

"Yeah, they're pretty conveniently placed. Sometimes it's a bit of a step up or down, but could be worse."

"Do you know what I mean about habitable?" I said.

"I wouldn't want to live on most of them, but—"

"I'm talking about no *air*, Dorian. Or gravity strong enough to instantly crush your bones, or unshielded solar radiation that would fry you, or, I don't know, storms where shards of ice are flying around at top speed."

Dorian blinked. "Haven't heard of any of that, no."

"Sounds fun," Bliss said. "You should go looking for one of those, Dorian."

"I feel like a habitable world being connected to one like that would probably make most of them unlivable," I mumbled. "I mean, how *did* you guys get rifts?"

"We didn't," Dorian said. "They were already there. For a while we thought that they formed naturally near large amounts of magic."

"But there's at least one on Earth, where magic doesn't seem to be a thing," I pointed out.

"Situations like that are why we no longer think that. So we don't know how or why they formed, and we've never witnessed a new one forming. Imagine how much more we'd be able to explore if we'd been the ones to make them, but no."

"As far as we know," Bliss muttered from the other side of the room.

"Sounds like a hard thing to forget," I said.

"History gets lost all the time," she said. "Sometimes intentionally."

"Keeping that much power a secret would be difficult," Dorian said. "We've tried to close and widen them and never been able to get enough energy to. So for now, it's a mystery. The Great Question. Well, there's actually three. The others are how life and magic started."

"Three and a half," Bliss corrected. "Why magic and life combined to create the Graft."

"I see," I said, trying not to sound distracted.

Dorian heard my stomach growl anyway. He pointed at me, hand uncomfortably close to my face. "Have you been taking care of your body?!"

"Just let her live her life, Dorian," Bliss said, exasperated.

"You're no good in a fight if you're starving," he said.

"I'm an alien, remember?" I said. "Not everything here agrees with my biology, or my palate."

"I'll introduce you to the most bland food there is."

He took me to the "mess hall"—a couple plain tables next to what could at most be called half a kitchen—and presented me with a crumbly tan cube an inch across. I bounced it in the palm of my hand. It was light and dry.

"One at a time," Dorian said. "Or you might give yourself a stomachache."

"Seriously?"

"It's ultra efficient. Everything a soldier could ask for. Well, it's a little low on vitamins."

I sniffed it before biting off one of the corners. It was odorless, tasteless, and melted away, nothing objectionable aside from how boring it was. I braced myself for the immediate reaction I'd had to some makhali food, but it settled alright. I ate the rest and actually started to feel full.

"Nothing about makhali makes any sense," I told Dorian.

"Oh, that's not us," he said. "That's the universe. You'll get used to it eventually."

By the time I'd returned to Veras and Andras's house, I was considering giving Veras's anatomy book back. If I focused, I could probably find each individual muscle in my body thanks to how sore they all were. Based on my hosts' expressions when I came inside, my getting knocked down so many times had left bruises.

"Do I need to kill this Dorian?" Andras asked bluntly.

"No," I said, "it was actually really useful getting to try out new things in a fight without being afraid of dying. I think he was just scaring me straight. He was holding back."

"If he hadn't, would you have come back at all?" Veras said.

"Remember how I was when we first met?" I snapped. "I'd rather take some bruises now if it'll help me avoid that again."

Veras held up his hands in irritated surrender. "Bed. Now."

I sat down in my room, wincing as I discovered, yes, the muscles involved in sitting and being propped up against pillows. Veras grabbed a bundle of blankets that had been waiting at the foot of the bed and squeezed them to his chest, eyes narrowed in concentration.

"What are you doing?" I asked.

"Makhali magic without direction is just energy, and it can leave as light or heat." He draped a wonderfully warm blanket over my legs, tucked another behind my back. "This is the best I can do for you, and make sure that asshole knows it."

"I'll tell him. Look what he gave me, though. I think this'll make it easier for me to eat enough each day." I took out a bag of that bland food Dorian had packed for me.

"Really?" Veras said, disappointed. "You want to eat *that*?"

"What's wrong with it?"

"That's rations for soldiers who don't take the time to eat real meals."

"Well, it's helpful," I said, angry that he was judging what I considered a solution to my eating problems on Plesmae.

"Whatever you need," he said, tired. "I suppose it'll keep you fed. Now, *sleep*."

He turned out the lights on his way out, and I spent some time glaring up at the ceiling. It was harder to stay mad at Veras when I was still wrapped in those warm blankets. He'd be easier to get along with if he left my makhali version of microwave chicken nuggets alone. Eventually I dragged myself out from beneath the blankets to change into pajamas, settled back in with one light dimly on, and took out my journal.

Mom and Dad,

The universe keeps getting bigger. There are dozens, minimum, of other civilizations out there. The idea of telling you this makes me want to panic, but I'm learning to fight from Dorian, a makhali soldier, who's working on maps of the universe. Yes, I'm aware I haven't even done any regular sports since PE classes, let alone tried martial arts. And that I hate confrontation. I don't think I'd even be able to practice if I was learning how to fight other people, and normally the thought of hurting an animal would make me want to curl up and die, but I can make an exception for graftlings. I wonder what they're being called on Earth right now? I hope to find out sooner rather than later, and I'm assuming I'll have to deal with some danger to get home, so this is my next best option.

I borrowed a reference book on other intelligent species from Veras. I regret to inform you that I did not see anything in it that resembled gray aliens, but it's not like the makhali know everything. To my understanding, there could be inhabited worlds on the "other side" of Earth from Plesmae. Veras doesn't have any references on alien animals, so I can't report on the existence of, say, the Loch Ness Monster. Hoping to ask around. Dorian feels like the safest bet, but if he does know about any creatures like that, it's probably because he got into a fight with one. He seems like the kind of person I absolutely would've avoided at home, but here we are.

Trying to stay positive even though it's hard. Hope you're in a position where you can do the same.

There was a quiet knock at the door.

"Come in," I said.

Andras entered. "Wasn't sure if you were still awake," he said.

"Not for much longer. I have to take care of myself so I can beat up Dorian."

"You do that," he said. "I brought some things that might help you sleep easier. Wanted to check before I, you know."

He'd brought a set of thick curtains, which I appreciated, though he waved away my offer to help hang them.

"There," he said. "Fewer noises and less light from outside. We aired it out while you were gone too, in case it still smelled like Veras's cleaning supplies. Do you prefer things that smell nice, or don't smell at all?"

"The first option, so long as it's not too intense," I said.

Andras smiled. "Got some friends for you to pick from."

He brought in a couple scented houseplants. I liked one that smelled like almonds, which he set on the bedside table.

"Good?" he said.

I nodded. "Thanks for all this."

"Veras was very nervous while you were gone," Andras said. "As was I. Did he... ask anything of you? He seemed to be feeling guilty."

"I'll be passing through the Glade a lot as I go to see Reyna and Dorian. Plus I hate being cooped up. He just asked that if I see anything bad, I tell someone."

Andras seemed to relax. "You'll be careful?"

"Always."

"Sleep well," he said. "If you wouldn't mind, could you check around, you know."

"Seems like the carnivorous plants could hold their own," I said. "But yes, I will."

He excused himself, and I curled up in bed. It was a little easier now to let myself pretend it was my room at home.

11

____

My body was sore enough the next morning that I immediately knew I wouldn't be returning to 7C that day. Not wanting to spend hours just wallowing, I had a quick breakfast of ration cubes before venturing through the Glade, armed with brightly colored chalk and a heightened sense of smell. I found more spots the patrolling makhali had burned, though thankfully nothing fresh—otherwise I would've marked the area and let Veras know so he could tell someone in the capital. Telling Dorian would be an option too, but I was a little afraid he'd burn the whole Glade down if he got too excited.

It was chilly out, there being a significant jump in time between when the sun rose and when its light properly heated the forest floor, and I retreated to the living room. Andras was reading in one of the armchairs next to an already-lit fire. I took the other, wanting to get warm, and then sat there feeling stumped. I supposed I could go see Reyna, though I didn't particularly want to travel that much on my sore legs. So what the hell else did I do all day?

Andras was going slowly through his book, fitfully running a hand through his short curls. On one of his regular glances at the windows, he noticed me watching.

"What are you up to?" he asked me.

"Literally nothing," I said.

"Is that a normal Ella hobby?"

I scowled. "No."

That got him to smile. "What would you rather be doing?"

Photography. Movie night with my parents. Video games. My eyes strayed down to his book. I wished I knew what the symbols on the cover meant.

"I could teach you to read," he pointed out.

"I..." I had to accept I would likely be here long enough to make that effort worthwhile, which was depressing but realistic. "You'd do that?"

He dragged his chair closer to mine. "Of course. I'm also a bit pressed for activities at the moment, and it'll make your time here easier."

"Is your written language hard to learn for other species?"

"Writing might be hard," Andras said. "But reading should be easy if you do it out loud. It's a phonetic language, so once you know how to say a word, your translators should do the rest. This is one of my favorite books. I could read it out loud for you so you start getting used to the sounds?"

"If you don't mind."

He opened it to a bookmarked page and began to slowly read, finger tracing below the words. I took off my earring so I could hear him untranslated, connect symbols to raw sounds. I focused on a couple at a time, ones that appeared at the start of words. There weren't actually too many more letters than English had. But I quickly got confused. Andras seemed to be making several different sounds for the same letters.

"I thought you said it was phonetic," I said.

"It is."

"Are you teaching me to read wrong?"

"Why would you think that?"

I squinted at him.

"That's quite the accusation." Andras sighed. "I'm not... I just realized this book isn't the best choice. It's a novel written by another species soon after their first contact with the Graft, so it can be a bit depressing."

"That's one of your favorites?"

"Yes. I see it as a reminder that no matter where someone comes from, it's all of us versus a common enemy. Does that sound weird?"

"I can't judge. I came from people with weird taste in TV. My mom chooses to watch these sad shows that make her cry, and my dad..." Even if I was on Plesmae until the day I died, I would never forget the music from the old Westerns he loved. They haunted me even now.

"What's TV?"

"It's hard to explain if you've never experienced it."

"This one-sided cultural exchange isn't fair."

"I'd love to share something with you if I had it."

"I suppose for now I'll have to settle," Andras said. "So. More cheerful fiction, or horticulture?"

"Fiction if you're willing to read it twice so I can follow along with the story."

Andras got a new book and read to me again for a while. If I was rolling with the assumption I'd be here a while, there was something else I ought to know.

"Are you and Veras a couple?" I finally asked at the end of a chapter.

"No," Andras said. "Not yet."

"Are you trying to be?"

"I am, and as far as I can tell he's receptive to the idea. But some things just grow slowly." Andras shut his book. "You look like you might fall asleep soon."

It was true. I felt ready for a nap. "I slept better last night. Shouldn't be this tired already."

"I bet you used lots of magic yesterday. And the days leading up to it were hardly restful."

That was an impressive understatement. I had to take the chance to rest now, because I knew the days ahead might be just as chaotic.

I SHOWED up at Vanguard Base the next day, ready to try taking Dorian down a peg. It was good for me that he had other plans than immediately jumping into the ring this time. He seemed excited when I arrived, though for a moment I thought he was going straight for emotional damage rather than physical.

"This," Dorian said, gesturing vaguely at my head, "is going to be a problem for you."

My face went red.

"Your hair," he clarified. "It'll keep getting in your eyes. That's a hazard on the battlefield."

I instinctively brushed it out of my face. I preferred my hair to be somewhat in my way, like a barrier between me and the rest of the world. But I knew he was right. "Do I have to cut it?"

"'Course not. Here, turn around."

I tried not to yank away when he touched my head, hands sweeping back my hair. He stood behind me longer than making a ponytail should've taken. When Dorian stepped away, I reached back to find he'd braided my hair, a bit of ribbon holding the end in place.

"That should do it," he said.

Even temporary, I didn't like it. Not having my hair at the edges of my vision made me extra jumpy.

"You can undo it as soon as we're done," Dorian said.

"I feel vulnerable like this," I admitted.

"I know a fix for that feeling."

By that, he meant taking me to the armory and putting a fucking bladed weapon in my hand. I stared at the two-foot-long sword, wanting to drop it but fearful one of us would lose a limb if I did.

"Is that your style?" he asked. "Or would you prefer a spear?"

"Dorian," I said slowly, "back home, the only place where I would see anything like this is in a museum. This room is full of sharp heavy things that make me very nervous."

"What do humans use to fight monsters, then?"

"We don't *have* monsters. There aren't any big threats to human life other than natural disasters and ourselves. When our militaries fight each other, it's from a distance, with either..." I looked around the room. Swords, spears, axes, bows, but no guns. "Handheld long-range weapons, or bigger versions of those that take more effort to move around."

Dorian looked deeply confused. "And you're not at war with any other species?"

"We haven't met any others yet. We haven't found any life off our planet, let alone another sentient species."

"Your world is connected only to lifeless planets?"

"I don't know about through rifts. Maybe some secret government department knows they exist, but I only recently learned about them. The one that was near my house seemed to have been buried until the Graft came through it. We looked in space."

Dorian slowly pointed upwards.

"Yeah."

His wings twitched all over, which made me worry he was on the verge of a conniption.

"It's really dangerous, and only a handful of people have been up there," I rushed to add. "It's not, like, an everyday thing we're doing. There's still a lot we don't know."

"You can't just drop that on me and then say you can't tell me much about it," Dorian accused.

"I didn't think—we've only been on our moon! You've been on more unique planets than all of humanity put together."

"So have you, then," he said.

I flinched. "Holy shit. You're right."

"But we didn't cross through space to do it!" Dorian yelled, throwing his arms up. The stiff white feathers on the back of his wings were on edge, reminding me of a porcupine. "That's different!"

"Could you please take this from me?" I begged, feeling my arm start to shake.

Dorian replaced the sword on its rack. He spent a minute just breathing deeply.

"You good?" I asked.

"You're going to tell me more about this later," he said. "Right now, we'll train. I understand that using anything here feels strange to you, but when you find a weapon that suits you, it's life-changing. For example..." He reached for his scabbard, unsheathing the long, straight blade he always carried with him. "A gift from Berith after I lost my own. The best weapon a soldier could ask for. But I'm sure we can find something acceptable for you." He handed me a blunted practice sword. "More comfortable with this?"

"Yeah."

"Then let's see what you can do with it."

"I'm serious. This isn't working for me," I said.

"Have you tried holding it the right way?" Dorian asked. "The way I've showed you a dozen times?"

"It doesn't feel right." I adjusted my grip on the hilt again. My fingers waited until I wasn't looking to stray.

"And you're thinking about it wrong," Dorian said. "Act like it's an extension of your arm." He swung his blade through a slow arc.

"Can I just use my ability?"

"It doesn't seem to be a question of if you can, but if you're willing to. You seem afraid of it," he said, pacing around me in a way I found aggravating.

"I don't know all it can do yet, and I have to be careful. I'm screwed if I mess up anything vital."

Dorian rolled his eyes. He only seemed able to imagine pain and death as coming from outside the body. I tried to hand him the sword, wanting to be done with it, but when he tugged on the hilt it wouldn't leave my grasp. We both looked down to see that my fingers had developed curved hard plates on the outside, locking them into position around the sword. I dissolved the plates, shaking the stiffness from my hand. Dorian set it out of the way before throwing a punch at me. I caught it; he'd been deliberately slow, and I had time to pad my hand and arm.

"Did you screw up anything that time?" he asked.

"No."

"Then why don't you trust yourself with your own magic?"

"If you'd charged into battle the moment you picked up a sword, wouldn't you be dead?" I pointed out.

"Seems like you've had your magic for more than a moment."

I gritted my teeth. He didn't know how lucky he was to grow up on a world where his magic was normal. "I think we've already established that our species and societies aren't the same."

"No, they're not. How high do you think you can jump?"

I did a pathetic little hop.

"Flight is an important part of makhali battle tactics that you unfortunately can't take part in."

Dorian launched himself upwards, wings catching the air. He had to beat them hard to stay in place ten feet off the ground.

"From here, I could safely bypass or retreat from a grounded enemy, or fall on them from above with my weapon," he called out. He smirked. "Or..."

Red lightning crackled around his sword as he drew it. Dorian suddenly dropped, swinging his blade as he fell. I shielded my eyes as he struck the ground, his magic flinging gravel everywhere. The air seemed to be full of invisible sparks threatening to singe my skin.

"Or I could do that," Dorian said.

"How do you do it?"

"Energy enhancement. I can build up heat, or increase my force and momentum to strike harder and faster." Red lines curled around his flexed arm. "Works a treat for burning away contamination too."

"What else can you use it for?"

"What else do I need?"

I shrugged.

"We've got a mix of offensive, mostly ranged magics here," Dorian said. "Throwing fire, creating lightning between their hands, that sort of thing. Your magic's only good for close combat, which isn't ideal against graftlings. Let's get you something ranged to work with."

Much too soon, I was holding a bow. An experimental tug on the string told me I'd need more than my natural strength to fully draw it.

"Go on," Dorian said. "No arrows yet. Let's just get you used to the motion."

I slowly pulled on the string. As I drew my arm back, my growing muscles burned and then eased, burned and eased, until I had the string pulled back to my ear.

"Good, but you'll want to do that much quicker. Holding the string taut for too long can—"

I glanced to the side, saw my arm was grossly swollen with lumps of muscle, and released the modification. The string fought my weakened grip, friction-burning my fingers as I let go a moment too late.

"—hurt you," Dorian finished. "You alright?"

I shook out my arm. "Yeah."

"Why don't you want to see your magic?"

I froze. He'd figured it out. "Dorian—"

"I know, we're not the same. Don't talk about it if you don't want to. But better to look like that than whatever the Graft would turn you into."

I tried not to glare at him as I changed the subject. "What do you do, since your magic's also only good for close combat?"

"I've never had great aim with a bow or crossbow," Dorian said. "You can slow a graftling down with one, but it's harder to kill them from afar since the location of their vitals isn't consistent. I stick to what I do best."

"How do you..." Visions of horrible ways to go out danced through my head. Dorian had his armor, and I imagined plenty of skill and experience, but that didn't seem like enough defense against a graftling horde, or the possibility of getting infected. "...not die?"

Dorian took off a piece of armor on his forearm, showing me what looked like a wetsuit underneath. "Our artisans make seamless, water-resistant underlayers. There are a couple pieces that overlap for full coverage. Contaminated fluid could eventually eat through it and reach my skin, but it would take a while, giving me a chance to remove it first." He pulled more of the fabric out from beneath the armor around his neck, bringing it up to cover his nose and mouth. "Bit hard to breathe through, though. And we have helmets. The good news is, a lot of graftlings aren't as tall as us. They tend to be lopsided, so we don't see bipedal forms as often. Unless you go down, it's your torso and limbs you have to worry about. If your underlayer does tear and some leaks through, it helps to never put yourself more than ten minutes from the nearest healer."

"There's nothing else you can do to disinfect it?"

"Before my time, there was this salve that was supposed to do the same job. Burn it all away before it could reach the bloodstream. But even if you got the chance to use it before it was too late, it didn't have restraint like our healers do. The salve burned *everything*. Then you've got a chemical burn I've heard feels like it's eating right through to your bones, and if the medics are in triage mode, you aren't bleeding or infected so you get to wait to be seen. Worse, people weren't thorough enough with the salve and would miss spots of contamination. We don't carry that around much anymore."

Yikes. "What about your wings?"

"We have a few options to protect them, but they need to be uncovered to fly well. Don't want to crash land in enemy territory. We just do the best we can. It's a very common spot for injuries." He tugged at the hem of my shirt. "If you're going home, you'll need more than this on."

"I know."

"Got a source for it? Everything we have here belongs to someone. Wouldn't fit you."

I hesitated. "Can I hold a piece of yours?"

"Only if you promise not to run off with my vambrace." He handed me the piece from his forearm.

I turned it over and squeezed it, getting a feel for its thickness and weight. I again pictured the top layer of skin on my arm peeling up, growing out, hardening, forming a shell. The resulting calcified matter was perhaps half an inch thick.

"Armor?" Dorian said.

I nodded.

He slapped it.

A firework exploded on my arm. Not from his magic. And not the heat of it. But the gunpowder-crack and suddenness of one going off, the *intensity*. I shrieked. The sensation of it was bigger than my arm, big enough to get lost in. My knees went on break. I barely felt myself hit the ground, landing on my back. I'd reached my limit for how much I could process at once.

"You good?" Dorian asked, bent over me.

"Everything is bright," I whispered.

He shaded my face with one wing. "Better?"

"No." He didn't understand, but I didn't know how else to put it.

"Did I break something?" Now he sounded worried.

"Armor isn't supposed to have nerve endings in it," I said.

"No, it really isn't."

"I accidentally put a lot in there."

"Rookie mistake?" Dorian said.

"It didn't hurt," I said. "Just... a lot." The sensation was already melting away, as was my makeshift armor.

Dorian pulled me to my feet, giving me a pat on the shoulder and brushing the dust from my hair. "Let's call it a day for you. Go home."

That was the goal. It might seem impossible, but that was the goal.

Going from 7C to Plesmae meant stepping from mid-afternoon to nearly sundown, so I stopped at Reyna's for the night. I lounged beside her on the couch while she worked on a commission, the silver thread she was using to embroider a long jacket so fine that I could only see it when it caught the light.

"So how normal are weapons and armor to your people?" I asked, a question I hadn't trusted Dorian to accurately answer. "I know you make them, but is everyone used to them?"

Reyna shrugged. "They weren't before the last war. Nowadays?

Plenty of former soldiers around, and even support members know they might need to use them someday."

"Huh. It's not like that where I come from. Holding a weapon like that just... it doesn't feel like it should be real. But my other option, changing my body, I don't like that either."

Reyna seemed to be fighting back a smile, and failing.

"What?" I asked.

"Isn't your body changing just a natural part of life? I don't look how I did back then," she said, gesturing to the painting of her and her great-grandmother.

"This is more drastic. And unnatural."

"Why is it unnatural if it's the magic you were born with, and a reaction to the situation you're in?"

"Please don't try to convince me they're the same," I said.

"You can't deny that even now, your body is going through small changes. It's a fact of organic life."

I knew she was right about that, and I had to admit it was a little ridiculous to get hung up on things like appearance when I was preparing to fight monsters to the death. I just didn't know how to get over that, especially the worry that, physically or on a deeper level, I wouldn't be my parents' daughter anymore by the time I fought my way home. Positive examples, maybe?

"How do you think you've changed as you've aged?" I asked.

"Well, once upon a time I was about knee-height—"

"As a *person,* Reyna."

"—and I had slightly more destructive tendencies. Great-Grand-mother gave me a whittling knife on my fifth birthday. My parents felt I was too young for it, so they took it away once she'd left the party. They left me alone with my other new toys for less than an hour. By the time they returned, I'd set half of them on fire in protest. Nowadays I try to calm down and think a bit more before I break things."

"Only slightly more?" I asked.

"I'm still me. And you'll still be you, regardless of how you reshape yourself." Her eyes narrowed into a glare. "Maybe you won't need a traditional weapon, but you should absolutely have armor and an underlayer if you're going near graftlings. A set that shifts and grows with you, so it doesn't restrict your movements. That's quite the challenge. Let me go grab my notebook."

YES, I screamed inside. "I couldn't ask you to do that for me," I said instinctively. "I'm sure that would take up a lot of your time and materials, and I can't pay you."

"Doesn't matter. Now, how much weight do you think you could comfortably carry for a full day?"

"I..." I wanted this. I needed this. Why was asking for help so hard?

"Ella, I don't want or need money from you. I'm well set up here. It's been ages since I've had a project worth getting excited about. You're not going to take that away from me, are you?" She made it sound like I was stealing her child.

"I suppose not," I said with fake reluctance.

"Besides, even though I don't have the ability to help in your fight, I'm still on your side. I don't think there's a single person on Plesmae who, if they understood, wouldn't be."

I had no response to that. The idea didn't just feel new, it felt impossible, and the fact that it felt impossible was upsetting. How did I deal with that?

I chose to focus on another idea instead. "Actually, I maybe *can* pay you, but not with money. If Veras hasn't thrown them out, would you want some materials from Earth? They're, um, synthetic fabric made from... I don't even know how to describe where polyester comes from. But it's not organic, and it melts instead of burns while still being a comfortable material to wear. They're all torn up, and I'm not saying that should completely cover the cost of —"

Her jaw dropped, and I felt the need to lower her expectations.

"By materials, I do just mean my old clothes," I said. "Nothing that special."

"I'll start right away," she blurted out. "Ella, I've never been this excited to turn in a project."

"You can have them before you finish, they're too trashed to wear."

Reyna was already out of the room, hunting down several note-books, pens and paper, measuring tape. I held still as she lassoed different parts of my body with the tape, muttering the numbers to herself like I wasn't there. She tugged on my arm.

"How long does this get? Is the new length evenly spread out, or focused above or below the elbow?" Her teeth clicked against the pencil sticking out of her mouth. Reyna was suffering from a terminal case of only having two hands.

"It depends? I don't have a good answer. You're absolutely sure this won't be too much work?"

"New and different work hardly feels like work at all. Besides, I don't have to worry about some other tough bits I normally do. You don't fly and your body density is different, so there's more leeway with weight and how it's distributed. And no keel plate! Those take forever." The measuring tape went taut against my back. "Those are flying aids that sit under the wings. Makes it less energy-intensive to stay in the air, but requires a lot of magic to create. You just need pieces that overlap and expand, which requires more planning, but much easier in terms of handwork."

I let Reyna continue measuring me. I told myself it was wonderful to be around someone who accepted my body's changes as nothing more than a design detail. Unfortunately, I failed to listen to myself. I pulled my arm from Reyna's grasp, needing both hands to cover my face.

"Oh dear," she said. "I'm so sorry. Can you tell me what I've done?"

"It's not you," I said. "Just having a moment. I miss home."

She guided me to the couch, hands on my shoulders. The way she looked at me suggested she needed her curiosity satisfied, or she wouldn't be able to think of much else.

"I find the feel of certain clothes extremely upsetting," I said. "I hate necklines that touch my throat, cuffs that go too far past my wrists, or dresses that restrict my movement. But it can take a while for those things to really affect me. When I was little I'd try on clothes at the store and love them, and then twenty minutes into wearing them at home I'd freak out. My dad was always trying to make sure I was physically comfortable. He learned to sew, just for me. He wanted to do a good job, so he'd always take measurements, and it just—yeah." I tried to smile. "I wonder if he'd be frustrated if I told him about my ability. All those hours spent hemming sleeves when I could've just made my arms an inch longer."

"I'm sure he saw it as an act of love." Reyna hesitated. "Am I understanding correctly that your parents aren't aware of your magic?"

"Humans aren't supposed to have any. I've kept it a secret."

"That answers my follow-up question. I was wondering if you'd ever met anyone else with the same ability. It's a shame you haven't. Once I started meeting people with similar talents, it drove me to improve. But sometimes it's easier to be around people with different skills. Speaking of, I don't suppose Veras and Andras have much free time?"

"I'm away from the house a lot, so I'm not sure," I said, not wanting to make promises for anyone. "Do you need, um..." I wasn't sure how to put it. "Continuing care? For your wings?"

"No, I'm fully recovered. Our healers speed up the normal healing process, they can't make us regrow parts of limbs. I do still stretch and exercise my wings, but only because I don't like the idea of them getting weak. My work and hobbies keep the rest of me strong." She flexed one arm, showing off her muscles.

I copied her, attempting to develop some muscles myself. The tissue beneath my skin squirmed like a bunch of rats running beneath a sheet.

"Do you ever play with your magic?" she asked.

"Play with it? I fiddle with my claws sometimes, but that's about it."

"It would be interesting to see what you could do if you didn't have utility in mind." She was watching me expectantly.

"Oh," I said. "I, um, I've been too tired lately to have the extra energy for that."

"Maybe one day, when you're home safe. It's a good way to test what you're capable of."

I nodded, only agreeing with the second half of her statement.

I rested on Reyna's couch that night, not getting much sleep because of the constant sensory information from all the magic crammed into her house. My sleep schedule was thrown off by spending time on two separate worlds, and so it was just before dawn that I left for the Glade, jogging through the dew-covered grasslands to keep warm. As the sun rose I was treated to the occasional glimpse of red, orange, yellow, and pink sunrise through the Glade's canopy, the colors almost neon when viewed through my night vision.

Once beneath the trees I slowed down, trying to enjoy my walk. I stopped here and there on my way back to the house, gathering leaves, flowers, sprigs of multicolored flora. I wasn't an artist. I didn't think I could make a drawn version of the photographic collage I'd made at home, which sucked given that I wanted something I could lose myself in as easily as the Blur. I could ask Reyna for scraps, but I didn't want to take anything else from her. I tucked the plant matter in my pockets, trying to keep them out of sight —

"Back already?"

I flinched, startled. Andras had surprised me, stepping out onto the porch. I kept my hands over my pockets. His gaze drifted down.

"I'm sorry," I said. "I know I should leave the plants alone, I don't think any of them were ones you cared about but I could've asked, I hope I didn't kill anything, I —"

"Ella, you're allowed to exist here."

I blinked back tears.

"The Glade isn't mine," Andras said. "You have just as much right to it as I or Veras do. Are you alright? You look upset. I know you can have trouble telling, but I'm not mad. Nobody's going to kick you out."

"I know that," I said. "I just... need to be told things that sound obvious sometimes." That was what having sensory issues could feel like, that an environment, or the people who shaped it, wanted to keep me out.

"That's okay. In return, could you help me understand something that's not obvious?"

"What?"

"Why you have twigs sticking out of your waistband?"

I tried but struggled to describe the Blur, because going into any detail made its importance to me sound a bit ridiculous. But Andras nodded along.

"So you want to put all this together in a way that feels right to you?" he said.

"I do."

"Easy enough."

He knelt down and traced his hands around a square two feet wide, lifting up a separated chunk of moss still clinging to dirt. We went to my room, where Andras made the moss adhere to a wall. I placed the plants, and he made them attach to the dirt so they could draw up nutrients and water. When we were done and surveying our work, a thought occurred to me.

"Will Veras be mad we've put literal dirt on the wall?" I said.

"Veras," Andras said carefully, "is trying very hard to give you the space you need. He gets anxious about the people around him and wants to check on them, but we both know he's better off not seeing certain places. Especially where I've brought the outdoors inside."

"So don't tell him?"

"I wouldn't invite him in without good reason. And make sure you wipe the wall below it clean after watering. Actually, do you mind if I add a couple plants around the edges? I can't guarantee there aren't any little occupants in the moss. I wouldn't add anything that bites, just plants with sticky lures."

I hesitated.

"You could pick where they go?" Andras added.

I nodded, and followed Andras to his room. I hadn't been there in a while, but the sheer amount of life inside was still surprising to me. Andras's plants seemed... wilder, somehow. As if they'd all been perfectly sized to fit the space before, but now they were so overgrown that they were curling back in on themselves, at risk of choking.

Andras offered me a tired smile. "As you can probably guess, Veras has already been conditioned not to enter other people's bedrooms unless necessary. What's wrong? You look upset again."

"Are you alright?"

He chewed over his response. "Just feeling a bit cramped, I suppose. It's frustrating to see all that," he waved at his window-wall, "and not be able to freely enjoy it like I'm used to."

"There's still your garden?"

"I feel it the worst out there. I didn't want the fence around my garden. It seemed cruel to me to keep plants from growing where there's open space for them, but..." He shrugged. "Have to watch out for things that would eat them. Or me, in this case."

He picked his way across the room, reaching up to remove a few stems from a basket hanging from his tree. They reminded me of sticky dandelions. He added them to the new Blur where I pointed.

"You'll appreciate these as the weather gets cold," he said. "Bugs try to get inside the warm house once the temperature drops, but it gets stuffy inside and you'll want to air out the room sometimes. Hopefully making an example out of the first intruders will keep the rest away."

"Damn, dude."

He gave me a wide-eyed, innocent look. "Too much?"

"It was just dramatic."

"Pests cause problems for my plants."

"But aren't they an important part of the ecosystem?"

"Yes," Andras said, "which is why I haven't been mass-breeding my carnivorous plants to spread over the entire planet. They enter my territory, that's it."

"I suppose I don't mind violence directed at bugs." Or monsters named after them.

"That's the spirit. How is it? Learning to fight?"

Training with Dorian was at least giving me some confidence that I might not immediately die in a fight. In the moment, it felt like learning how to survive; outside of my training, in quiet moments like this, it felt more like being trained to kill, and that was so at odds with my life before this that it hurt. "It's going well for something I never wanted to do. I'm trying not to focus on why I need to learn."

"Does having something familiar help take your mind off that?"

I nodded.

"Happy to help." Andras fought back a yawn and glanced out the window. "Looks like we'll both be going to bed right as the day begins. Enjoy."

Once Andras was out of the room, I gently leaned against the new Blur, feeling a dozen different textures against my skin. The softness and springiness of moss. The prickle of bare twigs. The silken luxury of giant flower petals. Each was accompanied by its own set of smells, even their own small sounds as they brushed against my clothes. I missed my Blur back home, but that had only been visual. This worked with so many other senses, and it was alive. It pleased me to think it could have even a little capacity to like me back.

Feeling grounded, I lay in bed. I'd never been able to properly capture my old Blur on a phone screen, and I knew this one would be even less portable.

Unless.

I shut my eyes and imagined all those wonderful textures first brushing against my bare arm, and then as part of my arm. Tiny wrinkles packed tightly together in a patch here, a bit of fluid collected under hairless skin there, thin stripes of callus laid parallel and millimeters apart.

After a minute, I looked. My skin was still the same color, but from elbow to wrist it was a medley of textures. Smooth and raised spots here like stones in a riverbed, knobby and rubbery in another area like some succulents. A solid band around my forearm resembled the organically uneven lines of tree bark. I pressed a fingertip into its center, moving the lines around so that they spread out in echoing circles. These were useless changes, of course. But maybe it would be good to experiment more, in the name of learning control.

To play, just a little bit.

INTERMISSION

Trouble has appeared on what I had hoped could be a paradise. Settlers are sent out, and we do not hear from them again, though many of them are at least able to send their families back to the safety of the foundation. I want to call them all back, but I can't. Something greater than my own desires is happening, and I can't slow or stop it, only direct its progress. It seems we've been here for such a short time, yet so much has happened. It is not a home yet, but it could be soon. I am pleased that others have been able to settle down and be happy here, to start new families—have they? No, I am mistaken. We surely haven't been here long enough for that. Regardless, I will set out myself, follow the silenced paths of settlers, ensure this is a world where we can all be safe.

12

———————

ay 12 on Plesmae: Surprised Veras is letting me keep learning to fight. I've gotten some bruises (nothing major I promise) but he gets this disapproving look on his face EVERY SINGLE TIME I come back. Maybe he would try to stop me if he wasn't so focused on Andras's happiness. While we should be safe, there's a non-zero chance of running into a monster in the Glade, so Andras and Veras have been mostly staying inside. Being cooped up's got A incredibly frustrated. Spent some time outside with him after training today to have safety in numbers just in case, though even then we didn't go far from the house. He's doing a lot to keep me comfortable and I wish there was more I could give him in return. Was originally going to spend more time with Reyna too, but I gave her the scraps of my old clothing and she immediately went into Focus Mode. I feel like there are lots of sci-fi stories about the dangers of doing exactly what I just did and I only thought about it afterwards. I don't know. Maybe it's patronizing of me to worry about it, like I'd be "protecting" a somehow lesser species from our superior one. If their society was given the exact same amount of time as we were, without the existential crisis they faced when losing their original world? I imagine they'd have a similar technological level as us, though maybe in a different shape because, you know, magic. The people I've met here are just as intelligent as anyone at home. I thought Reyna would want me to explain how the materials were made to her, something I'm not sure I'm capable of, but she jumped right in with examining it with her magic (I think?) so chances are she knows more about it than I do by now.

∼

Day 16: Dorian's given up on teaching me to use weapons. Guess I'm lucky I can make my

It's weird having a pencil but no eraser. Or using a journal without easily being able to order another online. I still don't know how hard it is to get certain things—new clothes or fabric, flour or whatever similar thing they have here, clean water—and it has me nervous about waste. I don't want to be a problem for Veras, not when I still feel like I'm walking on eggshells around him.

Learned to punch and kick properly this week, and to be comfortable rolling when I hit the ground. Dorian's holding back, but he's not babying me either.

I can feel it growing colder here, and I know the same must be happening at home too. At this point I'll take whatever connections I can get. Wish I had a camera here for the times I've come across wildlife so I could make a new Enigma. Running into something is scary because there's always a moment before I know it's a monster or not. But aside from the smell, Dorian assured me if I don't have a graftling trying to rip out my throat in approximately half a second, I'm safe. According to him, violent monsters have only one speed and it's INSTANTLY MURDER. I guess hearing that made me feel better for now. Asked him about small monsters but he wasn't as interested in those. V says those are more for gathering and exploring early in an invasion, before there's enough biomass to start pumping out bigger creatures. Usually infected native species instead of made from scratch. I think I accepted that info too easily for his liking, had to explain to him about zombie stories from home, that the idea isn't super new to me. He seemed appalled. Might think we're all sick in the head for finding that entertaining. It's too close to the reality he's always known.

~

Day 21: *Dorian had the audacity to DIVE BOMB me when I arrived. I think he was trying to startle me into developing something new. He was unsuccessful. Told Veras I appreciated him for not doing things like that to me, and how much effort he puts into keeping things clean. Seemed to startle him a bit. Laundry without electricity SUCKS. I've been doing my own, and some shared stuff to try to contribute something to the household, but not sure I scrub them well enough for V's liking. Tried to talk to A about making a plant-based lint roller but sticky things are apparently the bane of V's existence. The man deserves a vacuum. And I'm mad that I don't have an ereader full of books to give to A. I think he's read everything in the house twice over, at least.*

~

Day 28: *Sorry I haven't been writing as much. There's something a little unnerving about how easily I've slipped into this new life. When I search the Glade for contamination, or train to fight, I'm fully considering the dangerous side of our universe that I've learned about. And I'm choosing to get closer to it. That's what I need to do, but it makes me feel like I'm someone different. Remember how long it took me to get my driver's license? Or apply to college? Even just to get on a bike when I was younger? It feels almost impossible that I could be both people at once. That your daughter could be doing this.*

I'll try to be good and write more often.

~

When I reached Vanguard Base today, something felt off. Bliss was outside, using quick bouts of wind magic to dust off the bunker. At the sound of my footsteps she slowly turned around, a massive scowl on her face.

"Oh. It's just you," she said, expression neutralizing. "I'd get out while you still can."

"Get out of what?" I asked.

"Servantry."

I tilted my head.

"Berith and some of the other senior citizens from the Citadel are inspecting the base in a few hours. We're cleaning up."

"I do owe Dorian some favors," I said. "Can I help?"

"I won't stop you. Your lack of self-preservation is none of my business."

It was odd to pass by other makhali as I searched the bunker for Dorian. They side-eyed me but didn't object to my presence, so I guessed they'd heard about me. They all had a much more... Dorian was hardly formal, so it felt odd to call them casual by comparison. Less alert wouldn't have been a fair descriptor either. Maybe it was just that Dorian behaved as if he was always on duty.

That was true even when he was mopping the hallway. He was moving at a considerable speed, pale face flushed, at war with all the dirt and discoloration on the floors of Vanguard Base.

"Ella! I know you came here to train, but —"

I held up a finger. "This counts as one of my favors." Which, I now realized, we'd never agreed on the number of. Damn.

He nodded and got me a mop. Together we worked our way through a couple rooms.

"Do these inspections happen often?" I asked.

"No. That's why we have to get it right."

Bliss breezed past us, not looking at Dorian.

"I hope you didn't just track in more dust," he said.

She flicked her hand, sending a light wind to muss up his hair. "I'm not an animal. And before you say anything, I'm done. The exterior's as clean as it'll ever get."

"Fine."

"By the way, your thing's outside."

Dorian's mop clattered to the ground. He ran, sliding on the wet floor, towards the entrance. I followed, not sure what was happening. Outside, Dorian clambered up the watchtower's ladder, a wild mix of limbs as he used his wings to propel himself upwards.

When I joined him up top, Dorian stood on the railing, wings twitching to keep him balanced as he shaded his eyes and stared across the rippling dust.

"Does 'thing' have a connotation I'm not aware of?" I asked, panting.

Dorian pointed. The unchanging landscape made telling exact distances near impossible, but the wolf had to be massive. Not as large as Pillbug, mind you, but at least ten foot at the shoulder. It was currently little more than a canine-shaped silhouette, but it needed a name in my head and that one came readily. I loved dogs, but something about that animal was off-putting.

"You're not going after it, are you?" I said.

"I've tried before, but it's damn fast," Dorian said. "It shows up every few weeks, but it's never been around during one of Berith's visits before. If it's found a way to live off of this barren world, he'll want to know how."

"I think you just want to fight it because it's giant."

He didn't disagree, but he did crouch behind the railing, pulling me down with him. "Here's the plan. It's interested in the base, but it never gets close to people. You let me know when it's nearby, and I'll ambush and restrain it before it can run off."

"What happens after you restrain it?"

"I show it to Berith when he arrives."

I must not have worded the question right, because I'd more meant, what's to stop it from tearing your head off? But Dorian placed his hand to his mouth in a clear gesture to be quiet.

I sharpened my hearing until I could hear the delicate crunch of gravel under paws. It was definitely getting closer. Without being able to see it, I couldn't tell if it was casually loping or maliciously creeping. My breathing and heart rate accelerated. The last time I'd hid high up, senses sharpened, from something dangerous... I wanted to latch onto the railing, certain the watchtower would start shaking and collapse at any moment, but I couldn't move. If I did, it might see me.

Dorian poked me. "Now?" he whispered.

I met his eyes. Dorian grimaced. He put his hands over my ears, and I dulled my hearing.

But instead of flinging himself off the watchtower like I'd expected, he stood and shouted over the edge, a wordless yell. Gravel scraped and scattered.

"Let's get you inside," he said, nudging me towards the ladder.

I shook my head, hiding my face against my knees.

Dorian stepped away. A minute later, I heard him from below.

"Ella, I'm at the bottom. It's gone." When I didn't respond, he added, "do you need me to get your healer? Var—Veras?"

"No," I said in a small voice.

"Ella?"

"No," I said, louder this time.

"Come down, then. You can do it."

It was alright. I was safe. Dorian was here, and his team close by, and it was broad daylight instead of night and not Pillbug and...

Midway down the ladder, my nails turned into awkward, over-sized claws, making me lose my grip. I swung my arms out, imagined filling the space between them and my body. And then I hit the ground.

"You made it most of the way down," Dorian offered. "And look, you made something new."

I tried to whack him. The skin-tone, delicate tissue that went from my wrists to my armpits limited my reach. I was like a pathetic bat.

"You should see if you can separate it from your arms, so it's closer to wings," he said.

"Pretty sure I twisted my ankle, asshole," I said, feeling my foot smarting.

"Which is something we'll get taken care of very soon," he assured me. "But give it a try first."

Whatever. The stuff was already there. I imagined the join between arm and... flap...splitting apart.

The membrane near my wrists thinned, became translucent. Blood vessels criss-crossed blue before tearing. The rips were barely half an inch long, but they bled an alarming amount, making me fear I'd opened the large veins in my wrist.

"You should probably stop," Dorian said.

I dug in my pocket for clay, not trusting myself to undo the modifications without it while I was panicking. When the extra skin melted away, it thankfully closed the wound, leaving a line of stressed skin from my wrists down my arms. And I hadn't gotten any blood on my clothes. Veras would've thrown a fit if I'd come home bloody.

Dorian knelt facing away from me, let me loop my arms around his shoulders, and slipped his hands under my legs. I brushed against his wings. The inner red down really was soft like velvet, while the white feathers on the back were sparse and rough.

"Is this okay?" I asked.

"This is nothing for me." Dorian glanced off in the distance one more time before carrying me back to the bunker. He set me on a couch in what I supposed was the rec room. "Be right back."

Dorian returned with a box of medical supplies, and Bliss on his heels. "You'd better replace whatever you—are you alright?" she asked.

I gave her a thumbs up.

She turned her ire on Dorian. "What's *wrong* with you?"

"It was an accident," Dorian said. He wrapped a bandage tight around my ankle.

"You always push others too hard," Bliss said. "See if she comes back now."

Somewhere in the base, a door opened. I could hear Berith's voice as he talked with one of the Vanguard.

"Shit. That should be me," Dorian said. "Bliss, hide Ella. Berith doesn't know she's training with us. He'll be furious if he sees an outsider got hurt here. And we both know how you get around Citadel members."

She rolled her eyes. "Can you walk?" she asked me.

The bandage didn't feel like enough. I imagined new strips of muscle holding my ankle in place before I tried to stand. It ached, but held my weight. "Not quickly."

"Come on, I can practically hear the cracking of arthritic knees," Bliss sneered.

She took me to a room near the back of the base. I saw the punching bag and weights, and thought it was an exercise room. Then I realized it was a bed in the corner, not a workout bench.

"Are we allowed to be in here without Dorian?" I asked.

"He's got nothing to hide," Bliss said. She plunked down on his bed while we waited. I sat at his desk, looking over the drawings he had pinned to the wall: maps, multiple attempted paintings of the same drab red and gray landscape, sketches of the wolf. "What did you think about Dorian's crush?"

"You don't mean he's actually..."

"No, it's just all he talks about for days after a sighting. Damn thing's been throwing my rift sensors into chaos. I'm tired of deploying just to find a landslide or lost animal set one off, so I'm working on more accurate ones. Berith's taken an interest, so I'll admit he has some sense."

"I hope I haven't been giving you more interference every time I visit."

Bliss's gaze turned analytical. "I want my sensors to distinguish between makhali and other magic. You could be a good stand-in for a graftling scout when I get to that level of accuracy."

"Thanks," I mumbled.

"What? It's true, and I didn't mean it as an insult."

"Is not apologizing for speaking the truth part of how you got stationed here?"

She smiled and patted my head. "You're starting to get it. There's a good expression, it's just like Dorian's when I tell him to shut up about his pet."

"Maybe it works differently for makhali, but humans don't fight their pets."

Dorian opened the door, seeming unsurprised to find us here. He had a box tucked under his arm and a grumpy expression. "Berith wants to hear about your experiments."

Bliss shot me a smirk before she left. I hoped I hadn't pouted *that* much.

"They'll leave after talking to her," Dorian said.

"What's the box?" I asked.

"Berith brings everyone gifts when he visits." He opened it and first removed a plant in a clay bowl, gently setting it on his desk next to a stack of what I realized were empty pots. "They don't get enough light inside, but it's too dry for them outside. Berith promised me we'd find something capable of living here eventually."

He unpacked thick paper, bright pigments, a new shirt, pants, and pair of socks. The last thing in the box was a bag of small pink crystals. Dorian stuck several in his mouth and offered me one.

"Candy," he said.

I sucked on it and nearly gagged. It was like someone had compressed powdered sugar into a diamond.

"Is everything makhali eat pure sugar?" I asked.

"You say that like it's a bad thing."

"Cavities?"

"Not if you brush often."

"Do you?" I asked.

"It gives you a good energy boost," he said instead of responding, eating a few more.

"Insulin resistance," I countered.

"What's that?"

"Never mind."

"You sure do enjoy keeping information from me," Dorian said.

"I don't enjoy it," I said. "I just sometimes bring up things that would take too long to explain and you wouldn't actually find interesting, and next thing you know I've ruined the conversation."

"I could stand to hear you talk about something new for a while."

"Are you, um…" It struck me that he kept looking at his empty pots and was binge-eating candy and maybe those two things *meant* something. "Is everything okay?"

"You ever have a moment where you realize you're in the same place now that you were last year?"

"Sure." It was what made me apply for college.

"Did it make you feel like garbage?"

"I don't think I had as many... pressures in my life then as you currently do."

He sighed.

"Sorry."

"It's not about you. I'm glad if my being out here means more people on Plesmae can have a normal life. But when you've chosen a life of action, stagnation is frustrating. And they're *still* not planning any new missions for us. Berith knew I had potential when we first met and I was at a low point. I just wish he'd let me live up to that potential now, when we're in a better place." There was something trained in the way Dorian brought energy and vigor back into his voice, his movements, his face. "At least I have you here now. I don't think I've thanked you yet for being available for me to spar with."

"*You're* the one training *me*. And I'm not coming back until my ankle's better," I warned him.

"Of course."

"But I do seem to heal fast."

Still, even when braced with a (Bliss-applied) splint and extra muscle, I moved slowly on my trip back to Veras's house and had to stop by Reyna's. She answered the door wearing a heavy apron and massive gloves, fumbling with the handle. "What happened? Here, come in and sit."

I sat on the couch and propped up my aching ankle on a folded stack of canvas. "I fell off a ladder. Landed wrong."

"So much for you getting along with Veras," Reyna said. "He'll be upset."

"Tell me something I don't know."

Reyna smirked. I didn't like it when she smirked. On her, that expression suggested she had machinations grander than I could ever anticipate in progress. "Guess what I've been working on."

"I hope it hasn't been too much effort," I said, still feeling bad.

"Right now it's more about the planning than the execution, though it'll of course require testing. But I think it's going great. Obviously the armor can't cover all of you if you significantly change in shape or size, but in terms of staying on without being restrictive, it should be able to accommodate your limbs doubling in length."

"That's... wow. Reyna, I don't... I don't see myself ever doubling the length of my limbs."

She shrugged. "If it works perfectly at that much of an increase, it should work perfectly at anything below that. And while my main intention with this project is to keep you safe, I might be able to apply the same design principles elsewhere. I'm especially excited after examining the materials you gave me. Whatever your clothes were made of, if I could recreate something like it, I might be able to make a stretchier, more flexible underlayer. And the shifting, connected pieces I have in mind for the armor, maybe I could even apply them to other inventions I haven't thought of yet... here. Before I get any further lost in thought. Tell me what you think, if they're what you had in mind." She offered me a sheaf of papers.

I flipped through them. Reyna had indeed been busy designing my armor. The shape of the armor was the same on each page, but they each had individual decorative elements. A braided cable design on some greaves, a piece to cover my back that had a pattern like cherub-sized feathered wings engraved on them. I figured I'd just tell her to keep it plain, or do whatever she most enjoyed making if she insisted.

The sketches on the last few pieces of paper weren't about armor. They were more like fashion illustrations, obviously non-protective clothing on the outline of a person—one whose proportions kept changing. My eyes stopped at one of a dress that clung to the model's form before swooping out to the sides, right at a level that would draw attention to claw-tipped hands dangling at the end of extra-long arms.

"What's this?" I asked.

Reyna glanced over. "Almost forgot about those. I told you, I appreciate a design challenge."

"Have you started making any of these?"

"No, I've been focused on your armor and underlayer."

My throat wanted to close up. "Please don't."

"Why? If you're worried about payment again, look around you. What more could I possibly need? If anything, I need less. You taking things would —"

"Reyna, I don't want this."

"I suppose I've never seen you wear a dress."

"It's not —" I bit my lip, almost drawing blood with a sharpened canine. "Reyna, it's not about the type of clothing, it's what you want it to do."

"Suggest that you're proud of your magic?" she said.

How the hell was I supposed to respond to that? I couldn't in any good way.

"All of *my* clothing is comfortable to wear, fits with my magic since it has pockets for tools and materials, and it looks good on me. I thought you might want the same. What are you planning to do, Ella? Hide part of yourself away forever?"

"I just want to be safe," I said.

I doubted Reyna completely understood what I meant by that, but I almost choked on the last word, and she backed off.

"Alright," she said with a sigh.

Reyna took back the papers, marking off ones that showed things they shouldn't. She went back to her other sketches of machinery that didn't yet exist on Plesmae. I sat quietly, waiting for some of my tension to leave me. It was hard for it to in this room so stuffed full of magic. Having her plans to work on seemed to be all Reyna needed to destress. Eventually I stood up, feeling I should leave, and she glanced away from her work.

"Let me give you a ride?" she said. "I made a second helmet."

I still felt sullen, but for the sake of my ankle, I agreed. I sat behind Reyna on her motorbike and clung tight to her. She was confident on the bike despite the Glade's winding and hilly ground; it wasn't until we were almost to Veras and Andras's house that she slowed the bike to a painful crawl.

"Do you think they want to see me?" she said.

"I can't imagine them saying no," I said.

"But that's different than wanting."

"Reyna, I wouldn't ever rely on my read of a social situation."

"If it's not obvious, I don't want to risk it. I do want to visit sometime, if only to make sure Veras is taking care of the place properly, but I suppose I should wait for him to initiate. I wouldn't be surprised if he's scrubbed the varnish off the floorboards. That Andras, he's good to be around?"

"I like him."

"Let him know I'd like to get to know him better someday. Come back soon?"

I nodded and got off the bike. She took my hand for a moment, turning it over as if hoping to find it was changed in some interesting way; it wasn't, and she released me.

By the time I'd reached the house, I was hobbling. I'd hoped to reach my room without bumping into Veras, but there was no possibility of that. He was in the garden with Andras, a tarp between him and the ground, awkwardly holding an obviously unused trowel while Andras did the actual digging.

"Welcome back," Andras called out. "Want to join us?"

"Maybe some other time. You two keep having fun." I walked a little faster.

"Are you *limping*?" Veras shouted.

Faster.

Veras tracked dirt into the house running after me, which I guess meant he cared, even if I didn't enjoy him glaring down at me as I lay in bed with my leg elevated.

"No training until this is better," he said.

"I know," I said.

"If you're ever hurt, tell me immediately. Even if you have to interrupt what I'm doing."

I nodded, ashamed.

"I don't see you as much anymore. Are your needs being met? Do you need more supplies for your... what was the word? Menstruation?"

"I'm not worried about that," I said. "I haven't gotten my period since I arrived here."

Veras's eyes went huge. "Were you supposed to?"

My face flushed. "I'm not—that's a normal human thing, to skip bleeding when we're not doing great. And I hardly mind. It's a nuisance."

He went from amped up to miserable. "Your body isn't carrying out its normal functions because you're not getting what you need?"

"Or sometimes we skip it if we're exercising a lot," I added. "Which I certainly have been, with training. Too much energy needed elsewhere."

His shoulders were still sunk low.

"What were you and Andras planting?" I asked desperately.

"Please don't change the subject," he said.

"Why not? I don't even want to have it, and you can't do anything about it anyway. Gardening?"

I saw it as giving Veras the freedom to not worry, but he seemed frustrated instead. Still, he let the conversation move on.

"I got him seeds from the capital. The seller wasn't even sure what they are, so hopefully they're still viable."

"If anyone can make them grow, it'll be him."

"Do you think I'm doing enough?" Veras asked.

"He seems happy."

"Would either of you tell me if you weren't?"

"Go back out there with him. You already know I'm fine," I said.

"About that. I don't know how much time I'll have for you in the near future. It's a... seasonal thing, as we get closer to winter."

"Oh. Okay."

"But I'm still here for you, if you need anything."

I nodded.

"Thanks for understanding."

"Yeah."

That put a damper on the day. I went to get something other than a ration cube to eat later, only to find Andras in an armchair by the fire, eyes closed, and Veras with a hand on his back. Neither of them looked up when I came in. Veras's eyes were narrowed in concentration as white motes of light gathered around his hand.

"Let me know how long it lasts this time," Veras said. He looked over and jumped when he saw me. "Why do you have to move so damn quietly?"

Andras smiled, though it seemed empty compared to his usual ones. "It's alright, Veras." There were rough-looking patches beneath his eyes.

"Can you tell me honestly if I should be worried about you or not?" I said.

They looked to each other, their eyes speaking a language I couldn't follow. "There's history involved that you're not a part of," Veras said.

"And I don't want you to worry," Andras said.

"That's not a no," I said.

Andras sighed.

"You deserve privacy," I said. "But you're also my—"

"If you really believe that, then you need to stop asking," Veras said.

So I gave them their privacy, retreating to my room, spending time with the Blur to destress. Most of my appetite was gone, hunger replaced by emotional discomfort. Sometimes it still felt like I couldn't go a day without making trouble with Veras. And while I was getting better with my ability, was that useful if fear shut me down the moment I was in real danger again? If that was the case, and I was back to square one...

Were any of them actually my friends?

13

Idreamt I was in an empty space that had once been pristine white, but the Graft had ruined it. The sky wept painfully, blood falling like rain and becoming clotted liquid contamination by the time it hit the ground. Pillbug rose from the resulting muck like a breaching whale, its many legs pulling it onto solid ground. Its glassy eyes were shattered, leaking more contamination in a constant river.

"That looks like it hurts," I said.

Pillbug barreled towards me. I barely rolled out of the way in time, almost getting crushed as the semi-truck sized monster charged past. I tried to land on my feet, only for one of my legs to crumple beneath me; my foot was melting, the pale bones of my ankle exposed. There was no way I could crawl fast enough to escape. Pillbug was already circling around for another charge.

Fly. That was the obvious solution. I leapt into the air, my fingers somehow catching on nothing as I pulled myself upwards. Pillbug screamed in frustration, but its cries soon turned to excitement. My hands were tiring too quickly, struggling to hold on as they became slick with falling blood. I was slipping down, barely able to keep myself out of Pillbug's reach. I needed something else to keep me aloft. I didn't know how wings worked, but I had to figure it out fast—

I WOKE up to eye-scorching brightness. There was a strange noise, loud as a windstorm. I opened my eyes as little as I could and realized the source was Veras at my bedside, attempting to make soothing sounds. His hand settled on my shoulder.

I recoiled from his touch. I'd seen him move slowly, but my body told me each pat was a physical blow. Calluses blossomed beneath my shirt, and the harsh scraping noise they made against the fabric when I moved drew a shudder from me. Everything was taut, the smallest sensations ratcheted up to full intensity.

Veras took several full steps back, looking at his hand like he expected my blood to be on it. "Are you okay? Did I—"

"Quiet," I whispered as low as I could. "Don't touch me."

"What?" Each syllable he spoke felt loud enough to rupture my eardrums.

"Don't. Touch. Me," I said, louder this time, spacing out the words to make them easier to bear hearing. "Quiet. *Please.*"

I'd propped myself up on my forearms to get away, but needed to lie down again to take pressure off my hands. The cacophony of noises that movement made left me overwhelmed and trembling. I curled in my fingers so they shielded my palms without touching them.

Veras knelt beside my bed. He held a hand above my forehead to block out some of the lights he'd turned on, and then dramatically held his eyes wide. I managed to do the same for a few seconds before needing to bury my face in my pillow, nearly blinded. Veras rushed to dim the lights, his steps loud enough they should've shaken the house.

"Why haven't you undone it?" he said from further away.

I tried, but couldn't. It was like trying to concentrate when surrounded by wailing, flashing sirens. "Can't."

"Just wait here. I'll figure something out. It'll be okay."

He left the room. Veras and Andras probably thought they were being quiet as they whispered at the end of the hall, but I could hear every word.

"She's done something to her senses," Veras said. "Her hearing, sight, and touch seem to be strengthened to the point of causing her pain."

"Poor girl," Andras said. "That doesn't sound like something you can fix."

"It's not. My ability to help her has always been limited. But I can at least try to make her comfortable. I'm going to Reyna's to see if she has anything that could help."

"Should I sit with her while you're gone?"

"I'm not sure. It might only upset her. My magic's at its best when I'm confident in what I'm doing. If you react poorly to what she did to her back, it might make matters worse."

My back? I shifted, wincing at the chorus of sounds that came from different textures rubbing against each other, and reached around to touch whatever was there.

Fluff that rubbed off on my fingers. Rough patches of skin. Something spongelike, soft and springy. I traced my hands along them, confused.

"Ella?" Andras asked from down the hallway. "I'm here, okay?" He took a few steps closer. "If you need anything, you just have to say."

My sense of smell had grown stronger too. Andras smelled like sun-warmed earth and bark, but also stale. He inched towards me, eventually standing by my bed. His breathing was shallower and slower than Veras's, calmer but hoarse. His hand grazed lightly over my head. I blindly reached out for the bedside table. Andras opened it for me, the drawer sounding like a tree being sawed in half as it slid out, and tried to press my clay into my hands. I recoiled and dropped it, unable to handle its clammy grit.

"Are even good things bad now?" he whispered.

I gave the tiniest of nods.

Andras minced in and out of the room, taking out the fragrant plants whose smells were now too intense for me, returning with enough blankets that he could wrap me up like a porcelain doll. He held a cup of water close to my face. It sloshed, making nauseatingly wet noises. I tried to take a small sip. Through squinted eyes I could see the water was clear, but it tasted like dirt and plants and too many other things. My gag reflex made me spit it out. Andras took the cup away and sat with me, unable to do much for me but be present.

What felt like an eternity later, I heard two sets of steps, one stomping business-like upstairs, only to be shushed by Veras. The steps drew closer, and I braced myself to be touched again. A gentle hand brushed my hair out of my face and lifted my head. Something was put over my ears, and the world became mercifully quiet. I felt contact on my temples.

"Can you open your eyes?" That was Reyna, sounding muffled.

Wincing, I did so. She'd put a shaded visor on me, giving me limited vision without being completely overwhelmed. Veras and Andras stood off to the side, waiting.

"Nod if you can hear me," Reyna said.

I nodded.

She hugged me, stopping when I went stiff. "Touch, too?"

"It doesn't exactly hurt," I said, trying to speak at a normal volume. "It's just intense, and then I expect it to hurt..."

"Sounds close enough to pain for me," Veras said.

I twisted around, trying to look at my back.

"You shouldn't do that," Veras said.

Too late, I'd already seen them. A pair of... I supposed they were meant to be wings. They dangled limply from my shoulder blades, about four feet long but only half a foot wide. They didn't seem to contain any nerve endings, bone, or muscle. It was like I'd taken pieces of all my friends' wings and stitched them together into a patchwork mess.

"Now that you're more comfortable, can you undo your magic?" Veras asked.

Trying to calm my senses almost triggered a fight-or-flight response in me, as though giving them up would be dangerous, and

I couldn't make myself do it. I'd hoped my wings would reabsorb as easily as my claws did, but they refused. Squeezing my eyes shut, I focused my attention on where they connected to my back. I pictured the soft tissue there, where there should've been flat skin...

And found that if I truly concentrated, I could more than imagine it. I knew humans had some sort of sixth sense, the awareness of the body's position and movement, but this went beyond that. I picked a muscle in my arm and followed it as though I were tracing a finger along its length, aware of the veins and fat tissue that neighbored it, horrified and fascinated, trying to build a 3D mental model of it. I turned to my wings, becoming aware of the skin, connective tissue, and veins that made them up.

Yet I still couldn't get rid of them. No matter how many times I visualized them melting away—bold spring growth retreating for winter, high tide rolling back out to sea, any method—they wouldn't budge. An animal part of my brain screamed that I might need them to get away, while a more medically aware part questioned if I could split and reconnect those veins I was now aware of without bleeding out beneath my skin—

"You're panicking," Andras said. "Take a break."

"It feels permanent," I said, scared. Now that I'd started, it was hard to stop repetitively tracing the haphazard tangle of veins that passed through my wings and wove into the gross core of my body.

"Ella, I'm sorry," Veras said. "If you can't make this go away, I don't know what I can do for you. You know I don't practice medicine that much anymore. Not to mention, you're another species. It's possible another could find a way to help that I missed. There are many other doctors in the capital—"

"Don't send me out there like this," I said.

The three of them seemed to have a whole conversation through eye contact alone.

"On my ride here, there were signs of another graftling scout having arrived," Reyna said softly. "You're incredibly vulnerable right now. It would be best to get you out of the Glade until that's dealt with, and we both know my home is always one clumsy step away from becoming an avalanche."

As much as I hated this idea, I hated being torn up by a monster even more. Reluctantly, I nodded.

"Let's go, then," Reyna said.

Veras fiddled with his sleeve cuffs. "Andras and I can't go with you," he admitted.

"You're her *doctor*," Reyna said, pissed.

"I want to, but—"

"And you're her friend, aren't you?" Reyna said, turning her ire to Andras. "You probably know what she finds comforting or distressing far better than I do."

"I can't travel right now," Andras said. "I'd give an arm to come and make sure everything turns out okay, but I don't have that option. If it weren't for our safety concerns, I'd keep her right here and reshape the entire damn house to make it more comfortable."

He seemed on the verge of crying. Reyna's glare—and this time I didn't think it was just her thinking face—returned to Veras.

"What about you?" she said. "What's your excuse? You're making a habit of not keeping up with your patients."

He looked like she'd stabbed him. "*Reyna.*"

"It's not that far of a trip for you to come visit me, you know?"

"You said you found a good doctor in the capital."

"I did. That doesn't mean I don't want to see you still."

"I told you you're always welcome."

"Am I actually, though?"

"Yes!"

"Do you understand why I struggle to believe that?"

"...yes," he admitted. "That doesn't change that I care about you and Ella. Or that I have to be here."

"Fine," she said, clearly not satisfied. "Come on, Ella. I'll get you taken care of."

Reyna kicked Andras and Veras out of my room before helping me change from my pajamas into other clothing. I was grateful that makhali clothes involved wraps and buttons; pulling a t-shirt on or off over my head would've been awful. It was still a painfully slow process, as was her helping me to limp outside on my injured ankle. I couldn't tell if doing something felt better than doing nothing, but if I gave up I doubted I'd be able to start again, so I kept going.

Reyna had taken her motorbike here. I sat behind her with my arms around her waist, face pressed against her back. Every time the bike jolted over a tree root I thought my teeth would smash apart.

"You know you're doing amazing, right?" Reyna chattered. "Not much longer to go now. We'll have to go through some of the city to get through, but that'll be quick and I know you can—"

"Reyna. Thanks, but please stop."

She fell silent. I couldn't tell if she was stressed from knowing there could be monsters around, or if I was just hearing her breathing more than usual. Despite my recent training, I knew I'd be helpless like this in a fight. We'd be safer in the capital, but I still felt awful when we arrived there. I wore a cloak again, not wanting to show off the twin messes hanging from my back. Reyna did something with the bike and then we were walking through Pellior's Landing. I shut my eyes and wrapped my hand in the hem of the cloak, pressing it into Reyna's, letting her lead me around. With everything hypersensitive, I felt like I was in a completely different environment. She could've been taking me anywhere, and I wouldn't be able to do anything about it—it wasn't that I didn't trust her, but being so overwhelmed made every step feel like a fight for my life. I could at least tell by the change in sound when we stepped into a building, and squeezed her hand.

"We're so close," she said. "You'll get to lie down in a nice, quiet room. I'll make sure they keep the lights as dim as possible."

And then she slipped away, leaving me isolated and shivering. Reyna had a long exchange with another person where she reported the monsters in the Glade and tried to explain what had happened to me. I chose to tune most of it out after they explained that, per protocol, I'd need to be decontaminated, and she said that might actually kill me.

More being led around by Reyna, this time with a different

person's hand at my lower back. Then, nobody. I stood stock still, feeling unanchored. I risked opening my eyes and removing the headphones. The lighting was low enough that it only stung instead of seared. I was in a small room, what seemed to be an examination table in one corner, a couple chairs and some counter space the main other features. I sat on the table and took off my cloak. Slats on the sides of the table swung out, probably to lay a patient's wings on. It was alright that I had them. It was normal here.

A doctor slipped into the room, a gentle smile on her face. I'd have expected her to be disgusted by me, but in a post-Graft-war society, she must've seen worse.

"Are you okay if I turn the lights up a little?" the doctor asked.

I nodded and turned so most of it was out of my face. Her smile faltered when she saw my back. She probably hadn't been able to really see it in the dark.

"How badly does your back hurt?"

"It doesn't. My head does." I had a horrific migraine.

She guided me into lying on my front. "Let's start here."

I waited for ages while she looked at my "wings," lifting, pinching, poking. They were numb to physical sensation, but her touch still smarted. When she examined where they met my back, the smarting became a burning.

"Stop," I gasped. "It feels like you're trying to worm under my skin."

The doctor drew her hand away. "You shouldn't be able to feel that."

"It's absolutely awful."

She circled around me where I couldn't see, and I felt the brush of magic against my lower back. I slapped at the spot, feeling a new callus form.

"That's not normal," she said. "Try to relax. I just want to take a look. My magic won't go past your skin for some reason."

She tried to use her magic on me a few more times without any luck, eventually giving up and calling in another doctor to try. I felt outnumbered with two of them in the room, and asked for Reyna.

With her there I tried to make it through the doctors' examinations, but none of them had any more success.

After the fourth near-identical assessment, I snapped. I looked the next doctor, a younger one who seemed quite excited to treat his first alien, dead in the eyes.

"I am going to bite the next person who puts me through this," I said very softly, a tone that seemed to add to the threat rather than reducing it as I'd intended. He paled and excused himself.

An intense wave of shame rolled over me. Not for reclaiming the space I needed, but for bringing violence into it. What if they kicked me out for threatening a doctor? What if I got locked up again? Why was it so much to ask for a body that didn't hate me?

Reyna ghosted a fingertip against my shoulder. "Do you want me to stay?" she asked, uncertain.

I didn't care if it felt awful. I hugged her. Having emotional support in any situation that involved my ability was still new to me, precious.

They moved us to a room with two beds, and I was grateful for the lack of machine-noise I would've expected on Earth. I dissolved a ration cube in water, making a thick slurry, and managed to take little hummingbird sips of it over time. I tried to sleep, and barely managed to doze for a few hours. As soon as I could feel myself drifting off, I'd unintentionally shift and displace my headphones, the sudden increase in noise waking me. But eventually I figured out a position where I wouldn't move as much, and fell into a deeper rest.

Then the universe exploded. A vibration so strong I thought it would boil my blood and atomize my bones, all sight and sound and smell drowned out by the supernova that was happening inside my skull.

I kicked, breaking off some kind of contact. The awful buzzing abruptly ended, but it was still with blurry vision and ringing ears that I took in my surroundings. My first doctor from yesterday was picking herself off the floor, hands over her ears and grimacing. That was how I realized I was screaming. It had been like having Pillbug in my head again.

Reyna had been out of the room but came rushing in, a few books under one arm. She all but dragged the doctor out of the room to have a shouted conversation that was too loud for me even with my headphones on.

"Are you trying to kill her? What were you doing?"

"Figuring out why she can't be healed! She's actively preventing anyone from working on her."

"How would she even do that?"

"From what you told me, she changes the physical makeup of her body. It could be related. I didn't get the chance to look at her false wings, and it's hard for me to tell if there's anything wrong with her brain since I don't have a control to compare her to—"

"There's nothing wrong with her head," Reyna seethed.

"It ultimately doesn't matter. If she's keeping that up, we can't help her. Magic resistance means she's beyond our abilities."

"But she does fine with..." Reyna paused. "She manages small magical artifacts alright, I think. Ones with a much lower energy than I've heard healing takes. She doesn't... she's always scratching at them, and sometimes you have to repeat yourself a few times with her, but that might just be how she is."

"I'm telling you, it's like there was a wall up when she was awake that kept my magic out, and it was gone while she slept. Maybe it's unintentional, but she's still doing it. Until she gets over it, the most we can offer her is a quiet room."

When Reyna came back again, I'd wedged myself into a corner, worrying away at my patchwork wings.

"I should've stayed with Veras and Andras," I whispered. "I hate hospitals. I'm scared of doctors."

"I'm sorry that happened. I just went out to see what food options they had for us, and grab some entertainment. She wasn't trying to hurt you, you know that, right?"

I scrunched up further. "I should've known something like this would happen."

"Why?"

My face burned. I hated explaining myself. But I knew Reyna meant well. "Humans aren't supposed to have magic."

"Sure."

"Don't you see the problem?"

"You seem like you'd prefer a quiet life, so I get that you wouldn't want to be known as special among your species. But everyone here has magic."

"Reyna, nobody at home would see me as *special*. I'd be a mutant, or anomaly, or mistake. It'd probably be a doctor that found something wrong I forgot to hide, and doctors that would take me apart. I'd be studied, not celebrated, and I bet if they didn't immediately cut me up they'd cage me like an animal to see what I did under stress, and they'd say I'm not actually a full person so they could—"

"Ella," she said, quietly shocked.

I shut up. I'd never voiced those fears out loud before. They were out in the universe now.

"You poor dear," she said. "Nobody should have to be scared of their home."

"I'm not." I couldn't be. I just couldn't. That would be at odds with the very real love and support I had from my parents, the genuinely happy memories I had of home, but the words had created a puzzle frame my memories were easily slotting into and I had to make it stop. "I don't want to talk about it."

"Do you want me to take you back to Veras and Andras?"

"Will he hate me once he knows it's my fault he can't heal me?"

"I don't think he will," Reyna said, but she said it with a slow care that emphasized it was only her opinion. "But I won't be the one to tell him."

And I didn't want to be either.

"Do you want to leave?" she asked me again.

"I don't want to move." That blast of magic in my head had completely burned me out. I didn't think I could take even a moment of the sensory overload that awaited me outside.

"Can I get you into bed?"

I nodded. She helped lift me up, got me arranged semi-comfortably, adjusted my messy hair so it didn't get between my ears and my headphones.

"You're staying here for now," she said softly. "I'll make sure you get the space you need, and in return, I need you to eat and drink at least a little today, alright? And I'd understand if you weren't able to trust anyone else to look at you after that, but can you try to trust that tomorrow... has the potential to be better?"

I would never tell Reyna this, but I agreed only because I was terrified of losing her support.

14

_____

Day 32: Have been at a makhali hospital for last few days because of overstimulation and back problems. Feeling very low. There was a point where just existing was incredibly hard, and though that's gradually gotten better, back isn't better yet. Haven't done much, or had much to do, but sleep. Hospital staff appears to be scared of me, have mostly let me be in a quiet place, which is what I needed most. Reyna has stuck by me the whole time. Hoping A and V are safe back in the Glade. Hate that the monsters can just keep showing up from somewhere else. Universe is unfair but you already know that.

I put the pencil aside, not wanting to write anything more. It felt strange to dance around describing my ability in my letters to my parents, but what else was I supposed to do? Trying to write down what had actually happened made my hand violently cramp up, so I gave up. Even though my senses had slowly decreased down to their usual sensitivity over the past few days, I was still stuck with my fake wings. I shifted, needing to pull one out from underneath me. My ankle had recovered, leaving me restless, but I was anxious of tripping on one of my stupid dangling wings or catching them on something and whatever new medical emergency might follow.

I was distracted from doom-spiraling by distant shouting, needing to actively stop my hearing from sharpening to make out what was being said and potentially sending me straight back to square one. Reyna went to see what the commotion was, only to almost have the door swung into her. Dorian pushed her out of the way.

"THERE YOU ARE!" he yelled at a volume that would have made me crave death if my hearing was still augmented.

Reyna looked to be winding herself up into a lecture, but Bliss saved her the effort by bringing her fist down on top of Dorian's head, toppling him.

"You said this would be a stealth mission," Bliss snapped. "Have you forgotten what those words mean?"

"Reyna, this is—" I began.

Dorian sprang to his feet. "Your rescuers. Let's get you out of here."

"This is a hospital room," Reyna said. "Ella's here for a reason."

"Whatever's wrong, I'm sure she'll be better off at Vanguard Base, she likes it there."

"Nobody likes it there," Bliss said. "And you're the opposite of a doctor."

"It can't be that bad if she's awake and talking. Let me see." Dorian spread my "wings" out. "You tried making wings again?"

"Not on purpose," I said.

"Do they hurt?"

"No, they're just *wrong*. I hate them."

He poked at a dark red section. "I've seen *this* color somewhere before. Could you remind me where?"

I was worn out and frustrated and didn't exactly want him here, but I couldn't help it. I smiled weakly. He was treating my fake wings as if they were nothing to hide. I supposed it was better than the alternative.

A healer stuck their head in, likely drawn by the commotion. "Sir, ma'am, all visitors need to check in at the front desk."

"We're not visiting, we're taking her home with us," Dorian said.

The healer frowned. "She hasn't been discharged yet."

"Don't worry about it, we'll handle it."

"Sir, you can't just trespass and then steal patients."

"We're not stealing," Dorian said. "This isn't a good place. She's not actively dying, right? Then she'll do better somewhere else, where she won't be poked and prodded every half hour."

"Actually, they've mostly been leaving me alone," I said. "I had trouble with some heightened senses earlier, and I still have this extra growth on me, but—"

"Hardly any point to being here, then," he said.

"If you don't leave, I... I'll call security..." The doctor's eyes roamed to Dorian's hip, where he had his sheathed sword. "I'll call your commanding officer." They looked beseechingly to Bliss, who grimly pointed up. "I'll do it!"

"There's no need for that," Dorian said, starting to get his arms under my legs and shoulders to pick me up.

"Guys, seriously. I'm fine here," I said, scooting away on my bed.

"This is fine?" Dorian said, now touching a downy spot on my wings. "Look Bliss, she admires both her commanding officers."

"Never look up to authority figures," Bliss said.

The doctor was no longer in the room. Reyna was looking between the three of us as if wondering how she should intervene.

"I really don't want trouble," I said, growing upset. "What are you even doing here?"

"The reserve soldiers needed a break, so we were tasked with patrolling the Glade for monsters," Bliss said disapprovingly. "He wanted to invite you along, you weren't there, here we are. I couldn't stop him. He'd just go the moment I turned my back."

"Did you find anything?" I said.

"Just some smaller monsters, nothing above knee-height. I believe we found all the areas they'd contaminated too. Thankfully it was caught early."

"You're welcome," Reyna muttered, annoyed.

I let myself relax a little while Dorian went into an overly long recount of his and Bliss's admittedly few and short battles in the Glade. It sounded like Veras and Andras would be safe.

"Why don't you want to leave?" Dorian insisted when he was done. "Your healer couldn't help you, can these people?"

"No," I said.

"Look at this empty white box, there aren't even windows in your room."

"I'm anxious, okay?" I snapped. "I have been physically and mentally bad, and that makes me want to hunker down. No, I don't like it here. But at least I know what to expect."

"What if I told you what to expect outside," Dorian said, "and then I made sure it happened?"

Bliss made a noise of disgust. "Dorian, you do not have as much control over the universe as you think you do."

"I'm not saying I'd turn the sky purple, just that I'd ensure everything went alright. You know I mean it, right?"

Could I trust in him to do that? "Dorian, I—"

The door was thrown open, almost hitting Reyna again.

"I called him!" the doctor crowed in triumph. Then they took a good look around the room and decided to dip. I didn't blame them. I wouldn't want to be standing between an irritated Commander and the subjects of his potential ire either.

Berith's eyes went on a journey around the room: Bliss cleaning under her nails with a knife, Dorian trying to herd me out of bed, and finally Reyna wedged into the corner by the door. The expressions his face went through were what I imagined mine would as I was getting a headache.

He pointed at me. "What happened?"

"My magic hates me and I hate it," I said miserably.

"You're in pain? Sick?"

"No, just... shaped wrong."

He skipped over the soldiers to pull Reyna into a side hug.

"You could've told me you were in the capital," he said, upset.

"I didn't want to leave Ella alone. She needed an advocate."

"You two know each other?" I asked.

"We're old friends," Berith said.

"Reyna, I totally understand if you didn't feel safe going out, but

Veras and I going to the capital last time might've gone a lot smoother if you'd told us that," I said.

"I," she said, "did not consider that."

Berith turned his attention to Dorian and Bliss. "Why did I get called out of a meeting to address two of my soldiers going rogue in the hospital?"

"I'm just chaperoning," Bliss said.

"I can't even be in the capital?" Dorian said, hurt.

"The issue isn't that you're in the capital," Berith said. "Any member of the Vanguard is welcome to come here whenever they want, so long as there's coverage at the base and you're being fair about it."

"Not that we're actually welcome," Bliss muttered.

"The issue, Dorian, is that you've trespassed into the hospital to harass a recovering patient."

"They're clearly not helping her, so I thought I would," Dorian said.

I wish I had Berith's ability to arch an eyebrow on command.

"Just look at her," Dorian said. "She's obviously miserable here. Ella's a creature of the outdoors, she needs fresh air."

Creature. Great.

"And how do you know any of that?" Berith asked. "I didn't think you two would interact again after the day we met her and Veras." His gaze drifted across the room, settling on a sketchbook Reyna had brought with her. It was open to a diagram of armor. "Dorian, I know life had slowed significantly since the war, and that's been difficult for you. But we've talked about this."

"Talked about what?"

"You trying to train new soldiers. I told you I've gotten complaints from parents."

"They were months away from being fully grown adults. And they came to me and asked."

"Dorian, *please* tell me you haven't been training her," Berith said.

"I haven't been training her?" Dorian said.

"I suppose I should be grateful you can't convincingly lie to me."

Dorian deflated a few inches.

"I do want to go outside now that my head doesn't feel like it'll split open at the slightest noise or light," I said, only half-convinced I did actually want that, but feeling bad for Dorian. "I can't stay in this one room forever."

"See? It's good that I came," Dorian said defensively.

"If you're feeling up to it and your medical team allows it, you're welcome to go out in the city," Berith told me. "So long as a certain individual doesn't do anything to put you in danger. Do you want to go?"

Screw it. I nodded, committing to it.

"Dorian..." Berith sighed. "Go show Ella around. Make sure she enjoys her time here. That's an order."

"Yes, sir," Dorian said.

"Bliss—"

"I don't do half-assed jobs," she said. "I'll keep him out of trouble the rest of our trip. Come on Ella, let's give those two a chance to catch up, and get you out of here before the old man changes his mind."

She herded me out of the room, Dorian at her heels. The doctor who'd called Berith was lurking in the hall.

Bliss pointed at me. "She wants to go outside now." It wasn't a question.

They shrunk back and nodded.

"Good. I'm sure you have other patients to check on."

That earned us an empty hallway. I did my best to neaten up, trying to smooth down the mishmash of textures on my wings, make them look less... mutated before I put on my cloak. It didn't accomplish much. I wanted fresh air, but going outside to see things meant that I'd be seen too.

Dorian tried to take my hand, but Bliss stopped him. "She's not a baby, Dorian. Let her try on her own first. We'll be just around the corner."

We'd left the door open behind us. After a few minutes Berith came to close it, perhaps for a private conversation, and found me standing there chewing my lip.

"Where are Dorian and Bliss now?" he asked wearily.

"Waiting for me ahead. I'm, uh, experiencing a struggle."

"There's always tomorrow. The capital isn't going anywhere."

"I'm starting to feel stir-crazy. And... there's this giant journey ahead of me. If I can't even walk around a peaceful city, then how will I have the confidence to do anything else?"

"I know that exploring a new place can be overwhelming," Berith said, and I suspected he was trying to be comforting, but his statement was such a simplification of what I was experiencing that it made me resent him a little more. "There's something I can do that might make it easier, but it involves magic and I know that's not always comfortable for you."

"...okay," I said, nervously agreeing. I didn't want Dorian to have to come back for me.

"May I see you arm?"

A point of light glowed at the tip of his finger. He drew a complicated pattern on my arm, finishing it with a flourish. His steel blue magic sat on the surface of my skin, itchy like a rash. Berith pulled my sleeve down over it.

"That'll help if you get lost," he said.

"What was that?" I asked.

"You don't understand it?"

"I barely know anything about magic."

"It's..." Berith tilted his head, contemplating. "It's like a protection charm, but it only works if another makhal activates it. Keep it covered unless you need it. Sunlight will make it fade."

"Magic can have conditions for it working?"

"It's very old and complicated magic. Wash it off when you're back."

Of course Berith would be able to use stuff like that. No more excuses, Ella. I adjusted my cloak, strode down the hall before I could think twice, and was almost scared out of my wits by Dorian jumping around the corner to pull me along.

15

I walked between and a step behind Bliss and Dorian. The former looked moderately disgruntled and the latter energetic.

"Where to?" Bliss said, and if she were a human on Earth I'm sure she'd've been distractedly looking at her phone when she said it.

"I figured we'll just wander," Dorian said. "We're here to relax, and show off to our favorite alien. Look, Ella." He gestured to a bubbling fountain that cast water high into the air, creating a light mist over the surrounding garden.

"Wow," I said, not sure what reaction he wanted.

"She's already bored, Dorian."

"She's not bored, she just hasn't had the wonders of magical engineering fully explained to her."

"It's a nice fountain," I said. "We have them at home too."

"You do? How do they work?"

"Electricity? Hydraulics?"

"I suppose you didn't just come crawling out of the forest. Your species must have its own advancements." He threw his arms into the air. "The veil, Ella! An entire city kept safe, always aware of the protection overhead."

It certainly had been impressive, the first time I saw it. I wasn't sure what kind of reaction he wanted from me.

Dorian drooped somewhat. "Hmmm," he said. "Bliss, your commanding officer requires assistance."

She steered me to a mural. "The Vanguard does its work so other people can have the security they need to make art like this," she said. "Someone as... busy... as Dorian doesn't have time to work through all the crappier works of art required to reach this level of talent. Can't paint if you're dead."

"No," I agreed. It was a beautiful mural, different shapes and colors of feathers drifting in a breeze. I just felt uncomfortable standing in an open space for long enough to appreciate it.

"Oh! I grew up here," Dorian said, redirecting us down a side street.

"Are you just now remembering?" Bliss said.

"I actually do have a functioning brain in my skull, Bliss."

"Where'd your family move?" I asked.

He smiled in a way that was so forced even I could pick up on it.

My face reddened. "I'm so sorry—"

Bliss punched Dorian in the shoulder, almost knocking him over. "Do you want to impress her or not? Show her your favorite spot."

That got him to perk up. In a plaza set between a residential zone and restaurants was a larger-than-life-sized statue of a makhal striking down a graftling, her foot pinning its neck, her sword stabbed into the base of its skull. I thought my eyes were having issues again until I realized the whole statue was slowly cycling through a set motion, her hands lifting the blade in and out, the monster's legs bracing against the ground as if to rise and overthrow her, but never succeeding.

"Could humans make that?" Dorian asked proudly.

Surely, but even with our technology it would be difficult and Dorian seemed desperate for a win, so I shook my head.

"That's Ilona, an old hero of ours. She helped end a skirmish with the Graft several generations ago. My house was just a few blocks from here, so I'd come see the statue all the time as a kid."

"Dorian's fate was sealed from a young age," Bliss said. "Still want to walk around this area, brave leader?"

"Something to eat first?" he said, pointing to a cafe.

I wasn't hungry, but I figured Bliss and Dorian would probably be happy to have a real meal instead of rations. We sat at an outside table and waited to be served. Many of the buildings around us were multi-story, the ground floors bricks or stone and upper floors painted wood, often with garden rooftops. A soft wind swiveled the weathervanes every house seemed to have on a roof or balcony.

"Does everyone have weathervanes around here?" I asked.

"You've never launched yourself into the air and gotten slammed by high wind speeds into a wall," Dorian said. "It pays to check first. Plus, it's art." He clapped his hands. "Bliss, for the watchtowers—"

"The air is always still and you aren't touching my tools to try and make one," she said. "You can buy one yourself if you want to waste your allowance from Grandpa Berith."

"It would be a souvenir for the team."

Bliss rolled her eyes. "You think about that. Ella might as well learn about other makhali building choices while we're at it. See how the windows are always above the ground floor? It's Graft-proofing. No easy entryways, no wood for them to contaminate or chew through. If you ever make it home, these are the sorts of lessons I want you to take with you."

"Do we have to talk about this now?" Dorian asked.

"Someone has to. If you want to focus on the 'exciting' things, you can, but at least a few of us have to use our brains. I won't apologize for preparing Ella for reality."

"That's what I've been doing."

"No, you're only training her to fight. You should be teaching her what our civilization has learned the hard way so hers doesn't have to."

"We were going to get to that later."

"Were you? Because it looks like you let adrenaline take over the moment she shows up."

"Excuse me."

We looked up. The makhal who'd approached had a fidgety look to her.

"My family is sitting right over there," she said in a soft voice. "Could you please not have this conversation in front of my child?"

I glanced over. There was another woman bouncing a toddler on her lap as constant movement would stop him from hearing us. Makhali wings must not grow to their full proportion until they were older, because his bounced with him like a duckling-down capelet. He was staring at us. At me specifically. I adjusted my cloak, wondering if he'd seen my fake wings. If I looked like I had some exotic, infectious disease to makhali who were strangers.

"Why not?" Bliss said. "We're discussing the universe he was born into."

"He doesn't have to know that yet."

Bliss shrugged. "If it's your goal to make him feel cheated later rather than sooner—"

"Bliss, please don't," Dorian said.

"You don't give me orders when we're off duty."

"I'm asking."

Bliss stood with a huff, glaring at the mother and coldly saying, "you're welcome for our service." Dorian and I had to sprint to catch up with her power-walking away.

"This place gets worse every year," she complained.

"It's not that bad," Dorian said.

"Really? Name one thing worth staying here for."

He looked taken aback. "I... you know I haven't been here much since I enlisted."

So he'd hardly spent any time here between the war and getting stationed at Vanguard Base. And he could visit, he just... didn't, it seemed.

"Would you be back at your base right now, if not for me?" I said.

Bliss nodded.

"Would you *prefer* to be back at your base?"

"You say that like you think we're uncomfortable here," Dorian said.

"I'm not trying to suggest that. You can be alright in one place but better in another."

"We're both better suited there," Bliss said. "And Dorian, you have a report to write about our time in the Glade. I'm not doing it for you."

"That sounds important," I said.

I wondered if I'd looked how Dorian did now when high school assemblies had let out early. Or if he'd known he would be this uncomfortable here before deciding to show me around.

"I'm terrible about getting those done in a timely manner," he said. "Ella, if you're alright here...?"

"I am. Leave if you need to."

Bliss started walking away, but Dorian hesitated.

"I get that you're still recovering," Dorian said. "But whenever you're ready, you know where I'll be."

I gestured to myself. "Are you not seeing this?"

"Well, yeah. I meant after you get that sorted out."

"Dorian, I think you might have too much faith in me." And I'd probably had too much in myself. Until very recently, I'd been living a quiet, unemployed life with my parents. Trying to craft a warrior out of that...

"Why'd it happen?" Dorian asked.

"The creature... the Fortress who invaded my home, we got close up and personal," I said. "Not just physically. It felt like it was trying to invade my brain. Between that and almost getting torn apart by the graftlings following it, you won't be surprised to hear it's given me nightmares." I held up my fake wings, touching them as lightly as possible; they'd lost much of their looser fluff from being handled too much by other people, leaving behind bare skin. "In my dream, I tried to get away. Then I woke up like this."

"So long as you know that Fortress is out there, it'll probably keep haunting you," Dorian said. "I don't want to go against Berith's wishes, but if there's this obstacle between you and your goal, I want you to be able to handle it. He's a bit old to have a nemesis, you know? He might not fully understand that part. I know what I would do in your position."

"I know what you would do too," I said. "We'll see."

They took me back to the hospital, dropping me off outside. I hurried inside, not wanting to be without someone I trusted to hide behind. I slunk past the front desk, the staffer and I doing an excellent job of politely pretending the other didn't exist. The hospital really was a quiet place without Dorian here. Whether because there were only so many makhali, or because healing magic and makhali medicine was just superior to human medical science, most of the rooms I passed on the way to my own were empty and open.

I stopped outside one. A question had occurred to me, curiosity over whether makhali healers ever needed to do surgery. I wandered into the empty room, cleaning my hands at a sink before starting to open drawers.

Well, they certainly had scalpels. I turned one over and over in my right hand, my left toying with the tip of one false wing. I had the desire to put down the scalpel, to hit the brakes, but it was weaker than my desire to be *done* with this whole mess. It was all that damn Fortress's fault. Veras had removed the contaminated material from my body, but I had to wonder if there was somehow a piece of Pillbug stuck inside my head. The nightmare, my terrified reaction to the wolf, the sensory hell I'd been through, and these damn wings—I hadn't seen Pillbug since the invasion, but even now it was making my life miserable. Killing my neighbors and destroying my home hadn't been enough. It might as well have reached across worlds to reshape me.

This isn't you, I told myself. The parts you don't like, they don't have to be you.

I sliced at the tip of my wing with the scalpel to prove it before I could lose my nerve. The blade painlessly parted skin. The smallest drop of blood welled up, but nothing compared to what would've come from a cut elsewhere on my actual body. Which this wasn't. I sliced again, applying more pressure this time. The wing's tip came off, disintegrating into a few specks of tan detritus between my fingers.

It was okay if I couldn't draw all this growth back into me like I normally did. I didn't need to. I could just get rid of it.

I set the scalpel in the sink, knowing I wouldn't be able to cleanly use it as the wings got shorter, and unwilling to ask anyone to help me. They'd be upset, I imagined. Reyna certainly would be if she found out, but she didn't have to know. I squeezed the fake wings, emboldened by the fact that they felt like nothing more than worn sheets in my hands. I pictured the wings' cells—not part of me, not myself—breaking. Each one splitting in half, cytoplasm evaporating without walls to contain them, protein-built machinery crumbling.

My fingers met my palms as the matter between them crumbled into dust, gone before it could fall to the floor.

I shortened both wings inch by inch, finding it almost alarmingly easy to do. In a final rush of courage I grabbed what remained and deteriorated it all at once. I gasped as my back burned, expecting a hot trickle of blood, but there was none. It felt like I'd scraped myself, fallen on gravel or tarmac, but a few thin layers of new skin over those spots protected whatever delicate cells had been exposed to the outside world.

I slipped my fingers through the slits in the back of my shirt and felt my shoulder blades, finding only smooth skin. This was how I was supposed to be, and I savored the feeling, running my hands over the uninterrupted planes of my back, trying to ignore the residual ache there. Maybe I'd been correct earlier, back before I'd encountered the Graft. Maybe training myself to abstain from my ability was the only right choice. I hadn't gotten any braver. If anything, I was even more scared, and an ability that incapacitated me in the face of my biggest enemy was a liability, not an asset. I just wanted to be myself and safe, and those two criteria were easiest met if I wasn't changing in ways that hurt me.

I felt ready to be done, and the fact that I wasn't entirely sure with what scared me. My ability. It had to be my ability. The rest of the consequences and implications, I could think about later, but I wanted to stop messing up the body my parents had given me, and I wanted out of this city. I ran back to the hospital to find Reyna, pulling her away from a conversation with Berith.

She embraced me, making my back burn in protest, and said, "I knew you could do it! What helped you make them go away?"

"I tried meditation," I lied.

"Sometimes you just need to try a different tool than you're used to," she said, sounding proud. "Let's get you discharged."

Berith wound up accompanying Reyna and I to her house, apparently not done catching up with her. Outside the city gates, Reyna straddled her motorbike and patted the seat behind her. "This is what I was telling you about, B. Come on, give it a try."

He examined it carefully, taking his time, while Reyna watched him like a hawk.

"What do you think?" she asked, hopeful.

"It's beautifully made, and you know I trust the quality of your work," Berith said. "But that thing makes me nervous."

"Ella and I have ridden it just fine. It's an early model of a technology I think could really change things. Once I've worked on it more, could you show it off to other artisans for me?"

"You made it. You should be the one to do that," Berith said.

"I'm the weird hermit. They might not listen."

"There isn't much point in them listening to me if I don't know what to say."

"I'd coach you."

"Why not just use that time and energy to tell people who'll actually understand what you're talking about? I'm sure they'd like it. In the meantime, I'm glad this project makes visiting the capital easier for you. It's been far too long."

"Visit me," she ordered.

"I'll try to get away more often."

She nodded. Berith and I both felt like walking, so she rode alongside us. The two makhali chatted until we reached Reyna's house.

"Thanks for being there for me," I said to her.

"You'd better let me know if you need help again," she said.

We hugged and parted ways so I could return to Veras and Andras. A lump caught in my throat. I *did* have friends here. Real, caring friends.

Once she'd shut herself inside, Berith turned to me.

"Have you been inside her home?" he asked.

"Yes."

"Is the rest of it... consistent with the entryway?"

"You mean the clutter?"

He grimaced. I didn't have the heart to tell him the entryway was more open than the rest, so I just nodded.

"Clearly others can find their way out here if she's accumulated so much," he murmured to himself. "No excuses."

"She really would love the company," I said.

He nodded. I took that as enough of an end to the conversation, and turned towards the Glade. Berith took a few paces in the same direction.

"Where are you going?" I said.

"Where are *you* going?" he responded.

I pointed to the Glade, which I'd thought was obvious.

"Yes, that was my understanding," he said.

"I'm fine on my own."

"There were monsters in the Glade far too recently," he said. "I'm accompanying you."

I frowned. It was Berith's orders to fix the veil around the rift to Earth that kept me from going home, and while I wouldn't have denied Reyna his company because of it, I wasn't interested in being around him more than was necessary. "I'm sure Dorian and Bliss got it all cleaned up."

"Ella, this is my world to protect. I need to see for myself what's at risk. Besides, it'll be dark soon."

I froze. The Glade would be pitch black by now, and it had just occurred to me that I wouldn't be using my night vision. I'd just, well, I supposed I wouldn't be coming and going at any time of day as freely as I had before, which was disappointing. While I didn't enjoy that Berith was the one with me, I didn't mind having makhali-created light to see by. I just had to make sure he didn't see Andras. "Fine."

Once we were properly in the Glade, I was surprised by how comfortable I felt. So long as I could see, I could find my way, relying on natural landmarks, which side of the trees had rougher or smoother bark, whether the ground trended higher or lower in elevation. I'd traveled through it plenty of times now, at all hours of day and night, to go between Veras and Andras's home, Reyna's, and Vanguard Base. I knew what was normal for it, what to expect. Despite the dark, and the sounds of animals moving high in the branches above us, I found myself relaxing.

"You truly don't mind being out here at night?" Berith asked. He eyed the towering trees and waving branches, made monstrous by the magical light in his hand. He twitched as an acorn struck a bush next to him, likely thrown by pseudo-sloth annoyed by his light. "I'm sure I would've been frightened at your age."

I shrugged. "Back home, outside at night was where I didn't have to worry about being seen by others if I... didn't look right."

"You felt the need to hide from others in the dark?"

"At times." I should've just said no. But it was hard for me to see his expression, or for him to see mine, even with the light he held. It made being honest easier. Also, I'd bitten him. There was little I could say that would match up to *that* level of weirdness. "Don't we all?"

"I wouldn't mind fewer early-morning meetings," Berith admitted. "I'd say it's because I'm an old man now, but I've always hated them."

"You don't look *that* old."

"Do you know what the potential lifetime for my species is?"

"No."

"Then I'll take the compliment and not tell you."

"Fine. Leave me to live in ignorance."

"It's the burden of a leader to protect others from what might hurt them."

I thought he was joking but couldn't be sure, so I didn't respond. We walked in near silence until Veras and Andras's house—my home for now—was in sight.

"My understanding is that being in the capital is uncomfortable for you," he said. "But this is the second time graftlings have been found in the Glade. It's not your or Veras's job to be an early warning system. I'm sure something could be done to make a decent living place for you within our walls, where you'd be safer."

"Veras and I have our reasons for staying," I said.

"Are they worth your lives?"

I was taken aback by that. If Andras insisted on staying, then I was sure the answer for Veras would be yes. And I... of the places I'd been so far, the Glade was where I most felt like I could be myself. Did I know what that meant? Not really. But it was the easiest place to find out.

"I'll let Veras know about your concern, but I don't see us moving in the immediate future," I said. "In the meantime, we appreciate the patrols you ordered." I hated some of the other decisions he'd made, but it was best to be diplomatic.

Berith sighed. "Be careful around Dorian."

"I've got it under control." He could leave now. His job was done.

"And stay safe," he added.

"Of course."

"Then I'll take my leave."

"Bye."

Except he hung around for a moment longer, so when I stepped onto the porch and Andras came running out of his garden to tackle-hug me, he saw it. In Andras's defense, it *was* the most efficient way to reach and hug someone, but it might've looked like he was trying to murder me, especially if he saw me gasp for breath when I landed on my shoulder. I gave Berith a double thumbs-up before realizing that might not mean anything on Plesmae, but he seemed to get the message.

"Whoops," Andras whispered in my ear as Berith left.

The front door opened. "If either of you hurt yourselves doing that..."

"Hello to you too, Veras," I said. The ache was already fading. It would go away on its eventually. I had to trust that my body was better off without any more meddling.

He gave me a hand up, Andras still clinging to me, and a pat on the back. "All better?"

"I think so."

"Were they able to help you in the capital?"

"Not really," I said.

He seemed disappointed. I would've thought it might bring him some relief that I was a problem patient, rather than it being his own failure.

"I was able to get the time and quiet I needed for it to improve, though," I added.

"If there's anything that would help to have around..." Veras said.

"It shouldn't happen again."

"I hope you'll forgive me for having some doubt about that."

"Really," I said. "I'm done with my ability. No more accidental claws, ugly rashes, or weird lumpy muscles. And no more—well, less overstimulation. Can't get rid of that entirely. But the rest of the gross changes, I'll train myself out of."

"Won't that be difficult?" Veras asked.

"Maybe, but it's what I've been doing my whole life before coming here, so it's not like it's new to me. Now that I've experienced real consequences, it should be easier."

Veras once again wasn't happy about this like I'd expected. "I see. Whatever you feel is best."

"But how will you—" Andras started to ask.

"Not now, please," I said, forcing a smile. I couldn't face that pain yet.

And I couldn't really face Veras either, not when I knew why his magic hadn't worked on me and he didn't. I didn't see myself ever being able to get past that obstacle. And while I might've been over-thinking the situation, if I really was well and truly stuck here...

I didn't want to risk him hating me. Better to let him think it was a problem with my species.

So I tried to let it be a good day. This wasn't my real home, but it was still nice to be back. That night, as I put on the pajamas I'd worn enough times to call my favorite and enjoyed the scented plants Andras had returned to my room, I decided to copy Berith's fading blue sigil onto a folded piece of paper that I tucked into my phone case before washing it off. There were powerful forces in the universe and maybe, if I was lucky, I could find one that would return me safely to Earth.

I'D MISSED Andras during my time in the hospital, and went looking for him the next morning; I'd slept through him and Veras having breakfast, and hadn't seen him yet. An odd papery sound preceded him answering his door.

"Thanks for taking care of the plants that were in my room," I said. "Especially the Blur. It's looking very healthy, much better than any plants that have ever been in my care."

"Of course," Andras said. "I wouldn't want you coming home to desiccated friends. That would be a horrible discovery."

I hugged him. I wasn't sure how, but Andras was comfortingly solid compared to Reyna or Dorian, even though they had more muscle than him.

"I wasn't sure if you wanted to, um, Andras, why is your room brown?" I asked, distracted.

"Oh, they're out of season," Andras said, surveilling the wilting plant life in his room with me. "Happens every year."

"I thought your magic and them being inside would make that not matter," I said.

"It's cold and they need the rest."

Andras knew more about them than I did, but some of his plants looked dead rather than asleep. "Would it be better for them upstairs? Might be warmer there."

"Having to repeatedly go up and down the stairs to take care of them would be a bit much for me once we're deeper into winter," he said.

I balked. Would he really get that weak? I'd seen him wiped out after using his magic, but when we'd first met he'd seemed so active. "I'd help," I said.

Andras picked a wilted leaf out of my hair; some of his hanging plants were shedding. "You're sweet," he said. "But it's okay. I…"

He suddenly leaned against me. Not sure what to do, I stood straight like a supportive pillar.

"The last few winters," Andras said, "I've lost some of my carnivorous plants to the cold. Going out there to take care of them gets to be too much, and if I make a shelter around them to keep them warm, fewer insects get in, and they starve. The feeling of checking on them for the first time each spring, not knowing how many will be left…"

"I could take care of them." Assuming, of course, that I would be here still.

"I'd never forgive myself if you lost a finger during a feeding," Andras said. "No, I'd like to move them closer by. Could you help me bring them back to the house? Best to do it now, before it gets any colder."

Before you get any weaker, I thought. "Sure, I'll lend you a pair of hands. Unfortunately I can only have one at a time now."

The joke seemed to make him sad. "I'll take whatever you'll give me."

We went to his hidden garden. Andras gave his plants cautious touches that made them unroot themselves and turn their hungry mouths inwards. He deliberated over the several dozen plants.

"Thinking of where they'll go?" I said.

"Wondering what looks the least hostile. I don't want to freak Veras out," Andras said.

I picked up one that looked like a squat, stemless pumpkin. Andras gathered a drooping set of vines into a basket for himself. He hesitated again once we were in front of the house.

"Give Veras some credit," I said. "Maybe he's cooler than we thought."

"He *is* cool," Andras said.

"Is he though?"

Andras's expression was firm. "Yes."

I put my plant down. He sighed and did the same, and we went back for more.

On our final trip back, we found Veras surveying his moss lawn, confused.

"What are these?" Veras asked.

"Some of my other plants," Andras said.

With Andras tired and Veras unaware of the danger, I took on the task of replanting Andras's sharp-edged children. "Where am I putting these?" I pulled a few strands of my hair free from one's sticky tendrils.

"Somewhere we don't normally walk would be nice," Andras said.

"I'm sorry, what exactly is Ella planting in front of our house?" Veras asked.

"Carnivorous plants."

"...what *kind* of carnivore?"

"Mostly bugs, but some of them eat small animals," Andras said. "They lure their prey in with scents and visual trickery. They won't be a problem unless you stick your hand in one."

Which was a habit of Andras's, I thought to myself. I really hoped Andras was right about Veras being at least a little bit cool, because that would be put to the test come the first feeding day.

"Why have I never seen them before?" Veras sounded confused. Maybe even a little hurt.

"I guess I didn't want you to see how much I loved them," Andras said. "They're my favorites."

"Ah." A light bulb in Veras's head had yet to turn on.

"They feel *smarter* than any plants I've seen in the Glade. I mean, I know they're not. It's just evolutionary luck. But I take what I can get, you know? It's just unfortunate that the way they appear smart is by catching meat. Being dangerous and violent."

Veras was quiet for a minute. "I don't know if I ever told you, but there's really no such thing as a makhali born with healing magic. It's magic that I use *for* healing, but it's not... by its nature, it's invasive and capable of doing so much harm. Just about all magic has the capacity to hurt others, but mine's the worst among them. Learning how to handle it, and to be careful with it, is what makes it healing magic. So long as that same care is taken with other potentially dangerous things... they're okay. I can live with them, and they make you happy. No more needs to be said." He watched a hungry root snap at my fingers. "But please, put them at least twenty feet out from the house, would you?"

Andras hugged him. "Thanks for understanding. I've really enjoyed those alien seed packets you brought me. You never know what you're going to get. Some of them just shouldn't be sold to random people, for their own safety."

Veras nodded. "I guess we won't have to deal with as many bugs in the future."

"They're very good at what they do. It hasn't happened yet, but I always hope I'll get a species from home."

"I thought they were alien plants," I said.

"They are," Andras said. "Like me."

I laughed, assuming it was a joke.

"That might not have been the best way to tell her," Veras said.

"What?" I said.

"I put it off for long enough," Andras said.

"But you have wings," I said. Though given what I'd done to myself, maybe that didn't mean much...

He spread them out. Moss rustled and split. In a moment they were long zigzags, then tubes, a shape like grasping hands, and then they were wing-shaped again. He took them off, and they were nothing but sheets of plant matter. "I'm a hamadryad. My kind can connect with plant life and control its growth."

My mind hit a rough patch, trying to make mismatched pieces fit into one cohesive picture. I stared at Veras. "You told me everyone I'd meet on Plesmae was makhali. Did you mean, because we met on 9F...?"

"I wasn't trying to be clever," Veras said bluntly. "Andras's wings are a lie, and so was that. Reyna doesn't know either, unless she's guessed and hasn't said anything."

"I don't know how much longer you'll be with us, but I decided that I'd rather you know," Andras said. "At first, we thought the easiest thing would be to have you think I was makhali, in case you wound up talking to anyone else. We're well past that point now. You have my trust, and... and I hope this hasn't changed that I have yours."

"I'm not upset," I said, and I really wasn't. "I mean, I've been hiding my ability from my parents ever since it started. I get that sometimes you need to keep secrets to protect yourself. I guess I'm just confused. I'm an alien here too. I know you didn't want that little fact getting out when we first went to the capital, Veras, but you seemed to accept it happening."

"I've been trying to stay in the Glade as much as possible, and avoid other makhali," Andras said. "My species has a way of keeping a connection with our home, no matter how far away we travel. The region of Glashower, my home world, I'm from is contaminated, and so a part of me will always be as well. To a healer, I read as contaminated. Someone trying to make me better might accidentally hurt me in the process, so I avoid other doctors." His hand drifted to Veras's shoulder. "I'm chronically sick, but Veras's magic and being around so much healthy plant life helps me manage it. It's harder as everything goes dormant for winter, but he takes excellent care of me."

"I'm trying, anyway," Veras said, sounding tired.

"You're succeeding," Andras said, momentarily tilting his head so his cheek brushed against Veras's. "Aside from my health issues, I'd understand if other makhali would be less than pleased to come across a hamadryad who survived and made it to Plesmae when their own loved ones didn't."

"That's not a situation your fault," Veras said.

Andras shrugged. "Anyway, yes, it may've been fine to tell you from the start. But I've been keeping that part of myself to just Veras and I for three years now. Continuing to hide it felt easier, even from someone in a similar situation."

I considered that. If, before all of this had happened, I'd met another human on Earth who had anything like my ability... would I have approached them? Explained that we were the same? I couldn't imagine myself doing so, even if that person more than any other should've been safe.

Andras squeezed my hand. "Now that you know more about me, I just want to say that I know what it's like to be desperate to go home, even if you're happy where you currently are. You know that you have my support, right?"

"And mine," Veras said.

I nodded and thought about Andras's insistence on keeping me comfortable and entertaining me.

"You don't have anything from home, do you?" I said.

"Just myself," Andras said. He made eye contact with me, and I thought I saw a request for help in his expression, and did my best.

"So Andras, your being a hamadryad, does that, like, change anything?" I asked.

"How do you mean?"

"Between you two."

"Oh, Veras has always known. He was stationed on Glashower, and took care of me when I first became sick. I missed the opportunity to leave with other hamadryads, so I moved here with him."

"But does it *change* anything."

Andras looked down in coy shyness, not answering.

"What do you mean?" Veras asked, wary.

"You know," I said.

"I'm afraid I don't."

"Denial won't get you anywhere."

"Why do you have to be so difficult? Are all humans like this?"

"Visit Earth sometime and find out."

Veras's face fell.

"I'll figure it out. I'm not sure how, but," I shrugged, knowing I didn't sound very convincing. "As much as this past week sucked, I've at least learned more about myself."

"So optimistic," Andras said. "I know it's hard to keep that up."

"Please don't say that."

"Sorry."

I leaned against him, accepting a hug.

"Do you know what you can do?" Veras asked me. "To work on going home?"

"Keep training, I guess. With weapons this time. Should be interesting."

"So long as it's interesting in a safe way. Or as safe as you can be around someone like Dorian."

"I'll be careful, I'll be careful. Why does everyone seem to think I'm attracted to danger?"

Veras gave me *a look*. "Aside from your choosing to be around someone who swung his sword at you the first time we met him—"

"Training is for business, not pleasure."

"—I'm never sure what you'll be up to the next time I see you."

"At least I'll always be the same shape now," I said.

"It's more about what you're doing than how you look. Yes, I tend to overly worry about the people in my life. With you, it feels warranted. Not reminding you to be careful feels like a dereliction of duty."

"I'm not that bad," I said. And then I surveyed the many carnivorous plants I still had to replant. Maybe I was.

"There is such a thing as worthwhile trouble," Andras said, amused. "And we're it."

If I was going to be like that regardless, might as well be part of a group.

16

———————

*D*ay 33: *Had trouble picking up the pencil this morning. I know I'll figure out a way to return to you, but I've definitely hit a setback with my training. Back is feeling better. Don't know if I could take it being bad like that again, ever.*

It's seemed to get much colder in the Glade while I was away, and now there's frost on the grass some mornings. Most of the trees here don't drop their leaves, which is why I didn't really understand when Veras told me it would be winter soon. The Glade is dying back in different ways, the moss crunching like little bones beneath every step, the smaller foliage hunkering down. Some of the wildlife is building nests, woven domes of sticks glued together with sap showing up like warts on the trees. Had to scare something bird-like away from trying to do the same on the house. I don't know if it'll snow, but there's a different kind of weather, the outer layer of bark on the big trees drying out and some of it drifting down as a powder. Andras is also withdrawing. He seems to have something like seasonal affective disorder. I'm worried about him but don't know what to do. I feel helpless.

～

Day 36: Went to spend a couple days with Reyna. She still finished the first few pieces of armor she'd promised me. Feel bad that their most interesting feature will go to waste, but it's nice to have something made for me to wear again. She's turned my ripped up clothing into some kind of melted-down yarn to experiment with, and I only realized afterwards it was pants you shortened the cuffs on, Dad. Reyna was so excited about what she could do with this new-to-her material and I just had to nod along and pretend to not be upset.

~

Day 39: Going to see Dorian today. Hope he isn't too disappointed. Remembered I was supposed to be collecting stuff to bring home to you. Going to gather some red dust in a paper pocket. It'll look nice out of context.

When I arrived at Vanguard Base, Dorian seemed excited to see me. He paced back and forth in the training ring.

"Well? C'mon," he said. "Monster up."

I wished I'd pre-planned this conversation. "No."

"Do you want me to, like, turn around first?"

"I'm not using my ability anymore. It really messed me up last time, Dorian. You didn't see how I was at the start."

"Then how will you fight your way home?"

"I haven't decided yet," I said.

"You need a plan before you can fully prepare," he pointed out. "If you can no longer—"

"*I know.*" I didn't want him to push me for an answer. I wanted him to tell me it was still possible, that I could still do it, even if it wasn't true.

He changed the subject. "Where'd you get all that?"

"A friend made it." I wore the armor Reyna had put together for me. Weight-wise it didn't feel like much. A chest piece, backplate, a few pieces on my sides, all of them connected with straps that, like the sleeveless two-part underlayer I had on beneath them, were flexible and stretchy so they would pull apart when I changed instead of crushing me. Was it still crushing in that case? Unclear. It no longer mattered anyway.

"So you have armor now, but not a weapon," Dorian said. "Lucky for you I've got plenty of spares. You do still want to learn how to fight?"

"Still want to go home."

He made finger guns as he went to fetch a wooden training sword, and I thought, oh god, he's picking up after me. Had I really been here long enough for that to happen? I turned the practice blade over in my hands. My fingers looked normal, but they must've been messed up. I just couldn't get them to hold the hilt with any amount of strength.

"Not today?" Dorian said.

"I don't know what's wrong with me," I said.

"You feel defeated?" he suggested. "You came back here, and that was the first step. Maybe you're just not ready for the second one yet."

I nodded and handed him back the training sword. "Sorry to bother you for nothing. I know you have, um, reports to write. And stuff." Smooth, I know.

"You don't have to go yet," he said.

"What else is there to do?"

"You could help me fill out my maps. The only detail I have for Earth is the rift you came through."

"I don't think today's a good day for me to do that."

"Then pick a direction and we'll walk."

"How far?"

"As far as you'll go. I've got time."

I chose randomly, and the two of us went for a walk. There was barely anything worth seeing and we didn't really talk, but I preferred spacing out while moving versus while sitting, or worse, bed-ridden. And Dorian choosing to spend time with me helped quiet the voice accusing me of wasting so many hours and so much of his energy helping me to refine a tool I'd chosen to abandon.

We eventually scaled a small ridge. Dorian grabbed my hand,

which was one more hand-grabbing events than I wanted to endure today, but I understood why.

Perhaps a few miles away, the wolf let out a hair-raising howl. I could see why Dorian was fascinated by it. It seemed unreal, like a living mirage. You hardly dared blink in case it disappeared.

We sat and watched for a while as the wolf sniffed and dug at the rocky ground. It eventually loped away in search of the unknown. Dorian realized he was still touching me and let go.

"Are you going after it?" I asked quietly.

"No," he said. "I want to, but I have a duty that comes first. Otherwise I'd have chased it halfway across the universe by now."

It must be nice, I thought, to have a purpose that could be fulfilled. Guarding the rift to Plesmae was boring, but it was achievable.

"I've been thinking about when we first met," Dorian said. "When we talked about how important having more people who know how to deal with the Graft is. I'm one of Berith's soldiers, and I'm proud of that. But you aren't."

"I hope you're not about to ask *me* to chase after it," I said.

"Without me? Never. The point is, we all serve a higher purpose. You, me, Berith, the rest of the Vanguard, your healer, everyone else to ever live, we have a duty to our people, but above that, we have a duty to our universe. Right?"

"Sure?" I liked the idea of it, anyway.

"Nothing ever happens here, and I know the rest of the Vanguard dislike me. Bliss keeps telling me to give civilian life a try, but I hardly feel at home on Plesmae anymore either. We all have this shared experience of the last war, but it's like everyone else is trying to leave it behind."

"Wasn't it absolutely terrible?" I said.

"I'm not arguing with that. I'm just saying that if *you* remind people of the war, then they don't want you around because you bring up the bad memories for them, even if you dedicate yourself to keeping them safe. So I don't want to stay here or go back there. But," Dorian said, as if interrupting fast enough would keep his words from getting too heavy, "that leaves me with the rest of the universe. Whatever the Graft has taken, I'll take back."

"All on your own?"

"You're more than welcome to come along."

"I don't know. I'm hesitant to leave the one place I know is safe, but I do need to keep training."

"I wouldn't go far to start with. Maybe 9F, check in with the expedition."

"You could run into some nasty customers," I warned. "Like that Fortress I told you about."

"You were right about my wanting to fight something large." He had this weird little smile, like he was actively fighting to keep it from spreading across his entire face. I must be missing something.

"Wait," I said. "Are you saying you'd take me home?"

"There's a lot of universe," Dorian said. "I have to start somewhere. Your training's not done and I know you're not content on Plesmae, so this is the most efficient plan. We'll catch up to the expedition and have them let us through the veil to your world, and then I'll get to discover a new path between your world and Plesmae on my way back."

My emotions were slowly catching up, threatening tears. "Really?"

"Really," Dorian said. "You're going home. And I'm going to see worlds no makhali ever has before. Maybe even ones the Graft hasn't either. New environments, perhaps new sentient native species, new ecosystems..."

"New big animals to fight?"

"Only if I'm *really* lucky," he said, grinning. "But I have to make a house call on Earth first."

I sniffled. I could find my parents. Maybe Earth would already have the invasion under control, but if we didn't yet... oh my god. Maybe I could help. Things were happening so fast, I thought I could feel the ground start to spin beneath my feet. It was everything I wanted, and... and Dorian was taking a huge risk to give it to me.

"What if it goes poorly?" I asked.

"We'll figure that out in the moment."

"Okay, but Dorian, I just... thank you. *Thank you.*"

"So you're ready?"

"Now?"

"Any situation involving the Graft only gets worse with time, and I need to keep you safe."

I thought of Reyna, Andras, and Veras. I knew they wanted me to go home, and I... I knew I was a source of trouble for them. "Will Berith be upset if you leave?"

Dorian looked troubled. "Berith's put a lot of trust and confidence in me. I don't want him to think I'm deserting, but if I go tell him what I'm doing, he might... I could see him wanting to slow me down because he doesn't understand how ready I am."

"I can't leave without telling Reyna and Veras first. She knows Berith, so we could have her pass on a message."

"That'll work. Let me tell Bliss and get some stuff from the base."

We walked to the base, thoughts of home churning in my head. Dorian squared his shoulders before entering, returning with a pack stuffed full and a spare sword strapped to his side.

"She was disappointed, but not surprised. Race you to Plesmae?" he said, shaking off his dismay. "Foot race only. Make sure you're back in shape."

I shrugged and settled into a lunge, legs tensed and ready. Dorian got into position next to me.

"I'll let you give a countdown," he said.

"Three, two, one—"

"You look great in armor," he whispered.

I froze. Dorian charged forward, getting a head start. It took me a few seconds to recover, and I wasted my breath yelling at him, English curse words piercing the quiet night of an alien planet. He only laughed. He reached the rift with me right on his heels and leapt through it, the two of us suddenly on Plesmae in golden sunlight, continuing to run.

We stopped by Reyna's house on our way to the Glade. Dorian

scribbled out a quick letter to Berith and gave it to me, choosing to stay outside and sit in the soft grass.

"Look what you have on!" Reyna said, holding me at arm's length. "How's it feel?"

"It's comfortable," I said. "You're sure I can't give you anything else for it?"

"I'm sure," she said.

"And now I have a new request. Sorry. Could you give this to Berith?"

Reyna took the letter. "Of course. Not planning to visit the capital for a while?"

"No." I knew I should tell her I was leaving, but the words wouldn't come. Maybe I was scared I'd jinx it and fail to go home. I hugged Reyna instead, catching her by surprise, breathing in her warm metal and woodsmoke smell for what might be the last time. I tried telling myself that I could come back and visit once the universe felt less fucked up, but the thought of dragging myself away once I was actually home again...

"Thank you," I said about a million times. "*Thank you.*"

"Of course," she said, puzzled. "Take care."

I met back up with Dorian. "That was quicker than I thought," he said.

I shrugged. "Didn't know how to say things."

"Saying goodbye well takes practice."

He was right, and I knew I'd have to say *something* to Andras and Veras, but thinking of what hurt. I curled my hands into tight fists and concentrated on not letting my claws come out instead. Walking beneath its distant canopy, I knew I'd miss the Glade too; Earth forests would probably feel puny in comparison to it. I wished I'd tried climbing one of the massive trees using my ability. I probably wouldn't have made it very far, and likely earned myself a volley of thrown acorns for invading the pseudo-sloths' airspace, but it would've been worth it for the sake of enjoying the Glade in every way I could have. I hoped I could hold onto my memories of it, the look and feel and smell of it...

Uneasiness grew inside me. It was so quiet. Even the trees seemed unnaturally still. The temptation to sharpen my senses was strong. I never would've described myself as confident, but if being without my augmented senses made me less sure of myself, then they must've been a reassurance to me.

I turned to Dorian instead, hoping he could talk me down from my paranoia.

"Dorian?" I whispered.

"What is it?"

"Aren't you getting a strange feeling from this place?"

"You know the Glade better than I do," he pointed out.

"I'm not sure. I mean, something *is* different, but I don't know if it's... a real problem or not." If my sense of smell was heightened, I could've noticed if there was a rotting odor in the air. I was on the verge of hyperventilating, as if my body thought quantity could make up for quality.

I caught a glimpse of stained purple between the trees. Dorian heard the small noise of surprise I made and spun, sword arcing out to strike down the graftling mid-lunge. It was dead on the forest floor and he was tossing me a blade of my own before I could fully react.

"Get the healer," Dorian said. "I'll ward them off."

We split up before I could question if that was a good idea. I broke into the clearing to discover that a dozen monsters had beaten me there. Some were canine in appearance, muscular legs studded all over with barbed claws; others were—

That was a person. *Was*, past tense. The former makhali were bloated, their faces mercifully distorted into something animal, swollen tissue having pushed apart their armor, their wings rotting off the bone. They seemed unfinished, whatever sick evolution they were going through still deciding if they would be better on two legs or four. A few unlucky graftlings had fallen victim to carnivorous plants, but the rest were free and vicious. Andras's window-wall was broken, sporting a hole that would've fit a bear. I charged past the approaching monsters and through it, shoes crunching on broken glass. His bedroom door dangled on its hinges. I raced around the corner to the base of the stairs, finding a muscular monster whose rough skin was already growing over the shards of glass embedded in its shoulders—

The wall between the hallway and Andras's bedroom smashed inwards, struck by a bundle of branches clutched together like a fist; they forced the monster against the stairwell, breaking its bones. I shrieked.

"Ella?" Veras called out.

"Downstairs!"

The branches withdrew, the monster's body falling limply to the ground. I leapt over it and raced upstairs, finding Andras and Veras crouched behind the railing. Andras was gasping for breath. More glass shattered on the ground floor. I shut my eyes and grabbed Andras's arm, letting the warmth and rough feel of his hamadryad skin remind me that this wasn't like last time. I was better now, I had to be. It had to go differently.

"How many are there?" Veras asked.

"Too many to fend off," I said firmly.

We went to the balcony on the other side of the house and dropped down. Andras landed heavily, taking long enough to recover that the monsters outside came running at us. One leapt at Veras, but Andras swept out a hand. The roots of a tree sprang from the ground, smashing into the graftling scout. Its bones audibly snapped. The grass beneath the remaining monsters grew long, individual blades twisting together to form rope that lashed around their legs.

But the grass quickly began to brown, and Andras failed in his struggle to get up, his fake wings becoming desiccated. The largest of the monsters, a canid creature with bony growths on its head, ripped free and lunged.

I tackled into it, grabbed its half-formed antlers, braced a foot against its neck and kicked out. The beast moved no more. I clenched my augmented muscles, hated this whole situation, hated what I was turning into to address it. Reyna's armor had shifted and expanded as promised, but the scabbard strap over my back was too tight, constricting, as if angry I wasn't using it.

One of the grafted makhali trapped in plants broke free. Half its body still coated in the plant's digestive fluids, it dragged itself forward. With its face down it looked more like it could still be someone, just a person who needed help, and if it managed to get to its feet I could maybe fight it but the idea of striking it while it was down was too terrible to consider.

I pulled Andras onto my back. Hamadryads were closer to a human's weight than a makhal's, but I had adrenaline and magic pumping through my system.

"We can't leave," Andras said. He reached out, making the plants around us sway, but had to stop because of a coughing fit before they could do anything.

"There isn't another choice. More are coming," I said.

"Ella—"

"Don't make me be this any longer," I begged him.

At that, he stopped struggling. I moved out of the clearing as quickly as I could while carrying him, Veras running alongside me as we tried to escape the Glade before any of the other trapped monsters could free themselves. I couldn't carry Andras for long, needing to set him down as soon as I thought we had a little distance from any potential pursuers.

"Fly out of here," I told Veras.

He shook his head, too out of breath to respond.

"Veras, you could reach the capital quicker and—"

Veras grabbed Andras's hand. At first, Andras tried to push him away, clearly agreeing with me, but Veras clung to him with a death grip, and Andras gave up. I didn't blame them. I didn't want to split up either. Veras and I each wrapped an arm around Andras's shoulders, trying to support him as we fled through the Glade.

Not too far behind the scouts were flocks of drab birds cawing out death knells, which ignored us but made it feel less like a single attack and more like they were planning to move in permanently, bringing a whole food chain with them. I heard wood snapping, a sound that suggested the arrival of something far bigger than those pests, and pulled the three of us into a hollow among some tree roots.

That wouldn't have been a good hiding spot from a terrestrial creature, but *it* moved high above us. The blasted thing was horrible to look at, an ovaloid pink sack thirty feet long, suspended in the air by claw-tipped tentacles that wrapped around branches and pierced tree trunks, pulling it through the air. Its skin was somewhat transparent. I figured the liquid I could see inside wasn't anything anatomical, but pure liquid contamination. The seeds of a new army.

Andras made a terrible, desperate sound, his fists clenching, but the flora around us didn't respond. I waited for the monstrosity to pass, and then it was onwards again, Andras essentially dead weight between Veras and I.

We pushed through the edge of the Glade and into the peaceful grasslands. The boys both sat down, unable to go further until they'd had a break.

I was already making plans. "We'll grab Reyna and go to the capital. Andras, can you regrow your wings? I know you're tired, but we don't need any extra problems right now."

"I, I don't know if I can," Andras said, looking completely drained. "When I reach for my power, it isn't there."

"Shit. Never mind. Let's go get Reyna."

I had to slow down on the way to Reyna's house. It was that or abandon two of my closest friends. My senses were so strained, they seemed on the verge of breaking. I didn't know how else to describe it. White spots danced across my vision when I whipped my head around. I could hear Veras and Andras's ragged breathing and heartbeats.

Reyna quickly answered my pounding on her door. "What's going on?" She looked between the three of us. "You came to see me?" Her hopeful expression disappeared when she saw the blood on my boots.

"We're getting out of here," I said. "Invasion in the Glade, don't know how many."

Reyna stood there for a moment, her eyes unfocusing as she processed that. She slammed the door in my face.

A moment later she flung it open again, a bag slung over her shoulder. "Sorry about that, I think I'm panicking but I've shoved it down. Please continue."

"Capital?"

"Sounds good." Reyna got her motorbike from the shed, starting it up with the press of a button.

"Take Andras with you," I said. "He's unwell."

Andras awkwardly straddled the bike behind Reyna. She leaned it from side to side a little, and I could practically see the gears in her head turning, that for a makhal this amount of weight wasn't adding up, but she started the bike, rolling forward. Veras and I jogged alongside them to Pellior's Landing. I glanced over my shoulder as we went, hoping to see red and white wings in the sky, Dorian catching up to me, but there was no sign of him.

He'd want you safe, I thought. Just like your parents would.

I could only hope they were all still alive, and capable of wanting.

17

On arriving at the capital, we were surprised to find several dozen makhali gathered in a large courtyard just inside the entrance. Some bore weapons and wore lightweight armor. They were grouped around Berith, apparently going over orders. They turned to look at us like we'd just crashed their party. Important words had to be said, but I saw the size of the crowd in front of us, Berith was somewhat familiar to me but he seemed so different in full Leadership Posture, and Saela the secretary was giving me a strong *the fuck do you want now* look. I froze. Our little group got eaten up as Reyna and Veras told Berith everything he needed to know and I lurked over Andras's shoulder like a bodyguard.

A staticky noise pulled my attention away from the conversation, not because it was loud—it barely registered before I focused on it—but because I'd never heard anything that electrical-sounding on Plesmae. We'd been followed by a winged graftling perhaps the size of a medium dog. It had landed partway up the veil and was slowly sliding down its smooth surface. Where its claws made contact, the veil bubbled, making that strange sound. Nobody else had noticed yet; it was too quiet, and the monster was little more than a speck unless you were looking for it.

"Reyna, is it supposed to do that?" I said, hoping this was just something special the larger veil at the capital did.

"Ella, not now, please," she said without turning around.

"It just really feels like it shouldn't be doing that."

I was being quiet, I realized. I didn't want to be the outsider who raised a fuss about nothing while an invasion was happening. But any monster had to be dealt with, right? I sidled up to Berith's secretary, who gave me a wary look that suggested he'd rather I give him several blocks more personal space.

"Hey, I am *so* sorry," I said. "Potentially dumb question here, just need a quick yes or no. Is that normal?" I pointed.

Saela stared at the veil a moment, then looked at me as if I was a lower order of life form than him.

"You're not looking in the right spot," I said. I held my hands in a circle centered over the monster. "That."

For patiently guiding him to see what I was seeing, I was rewarded with a surprised shout right next to me hearing-sharpened ear. I think I might've blacked out for a moment. When I came to again, Berith was calling out information and orders, quickly marshaling the gathered makhali. An arrow struck the monster, sent it tumbling to the ground. The veil's surface calmed. The armed makhali were already on the move, I assumed towards the Glade.

I looked to Reyna. "Not normal?"

"No, Ella, it's not normal for a monster to start breaking through the veil like that," she said softly. "You know how your translation artifacts are engraved? There are much larger engravings built into the capital's defensive wall that shape the veil. Some might be damaged now. If they get too cracked, you end up with a permanent hole in the veil until it's repaired. It takes a lot of force to do that amount of damage. I don't see how a monster could have that much of an effect that quickly without magic."

"Is that what happened to the rift to Earth too? We thought its supports were shifted or had eroded, but maybe..."

It was only then that I realized Reyna might be holding back tears. "I don't know how we can protect ourselves if we can't trust the veil."

I wasn't sure how to comfort her, and my mind was too far away to puzzle through a solution. Most of the makhali around Berith had cleared out. I startled him by reaching up to tap his shoulder.

"They're safe here?" I said, pointing to my friends.

"You are," Berith said.

My intention must've been written on my face, because he grabbed my arm as I tried to bolt, anchoring me in place.

"I have to go back," I said. "I left Dorian behind."

"Dorian is at Vanguard Base."

"He's not. He was going to take me home, and then we saw monsters in the Glade, and we split up, and I *left* him, and—"

"We already sent out a small group of warriors, and Saela's going to summon more," Berith said firmly. "They'll get there before you could."

I looked over at the bike. Reyna had a death grip on it.

"I'll help you make a new one," I said. "I'll teach you everything I know about human technology. Just let me take it."

"It's not about the bike, it's about you," she said. "I'm not letting my invention carry you to your death."

I burst into tears. Berith handed me over to Andras and Veras as if worried I'd disappear if someone wasn't constantly restraining me. He gave Reyna instructions, handed her something. She came back, locked an arm around me, and marched towards the center of the capital. Behind us, Veras helped Andras along, treating the bike like it was a walking aid. Reyna led us to a home just a block away from the Citadel, unlocking the door and letting us all inside.

"There are a couple spare rooms, do whatever you need to," she said. She looked at our surroundings—neat not in the compulsive way Veras kept things, but minimalist, empty—and sighed. "He was always telling me he'd make this into more of a home someday."

She parked her bike in the entryway, lending Andras a supportive hand as he staggered down the hall. Once he was settled and Veras tending to him, she made eye contact with me and removed several parts from her bike, each separating out with a pop of static, then pressed the ignition to show me it would no longer turn on.

"I'm sorry," she said. "Ella, please don't try to leave."

Reyna guided me to the couch, took off my boots, put my legs up on a pillow. She wiped my face dry and spoke to me very calmly, saying I was panicking. She was probably right, and I didn't *want* to be panicking, but if I wasn't panicking, then I... I was going to...

It was a while before I could even start to think in complete sentences again, let alone move myself. I dragged myself to my feet once I was able, unaware of how much time had passed. Everything from my waist down felt like lead, and the rest like paper mâché. Arms wrapped around myself, I went to find Andras in one of the guest rooms.

He was propped up in bed, his hands worrying at his blankets. His wings lay wilted and abandoned on the floor, kicked under his bed. It was only now that he smelled of sterile medicine that I realized he normally had a sweet scent to him. Beneath the overpowering *clean* was a hint of rot.

"Could you open the window for me?" he asked.

I pulled aside the curtains and unlatched the window. Thread-thin lines of smoke wafted up from the direction of the Glade.

"They'll be burning parts of it," Andras said miserably. "Only thing you can do when it's not safe to bring makhali with the ability to cauterize in." He moved closer to the window so that more of his body could be in the light and shifted his blanket off his chest. I imagined the sunlight and outside air soaking into his skin and bringing him what he needed. He surprised me when he spoke again. "This is why Veras was reluctant to let anyone else treat you." He pulled down the collar of his shirt, showing me a patch of skin over where a human's heart would be that was strangely glossy and pale. "Even trained healers can get confused when alien anatomy is involved. If

Veras wasn't so sensitive to others' pain, he might've kept going and killed me."

"I didn't realize it was that bad."

"You did a good job, you know," he said.

My brain was firing on zero cylinders. I didn't understand.

"With getting us out of there quickly," Andras explained. "You're stronger than you realize."

"I feel like a child right now," I said.

"I think that's everyone at the moment, Ella. And you might never stop feeling that way. But you're healthy, and capable, and you've been learning how to survive." He made harsh eye contact with me. The edges of his irises seemed muddy, as though they were leaking into the whites of his eyes. "When you get your next chance to go home, you take it. Run, and don't look back."

"Andras?" He was unsettling me.

"Veras and I would have both given you our blessing to leave, so long as you can get home safely," he said, his expression softening.

"I don't know if I can anymore," I said, and I meant it. Attempts one and two had gone so poorly. There was always so much more trouble waiting for me than I expected.

"You'll do it. At least one of us needs to go home."

Veras returned with a bag of medical supplies under his arm, interrupting our conversation. "Is the sunlight helping?"

Andras nodded. Veras sat close to him on the bed. Very close.

"You're alright, physically?" Veras asked me.

"I'm not hurt." My head and ribs ached, but that was different. It felt like their contents had been entirely exhausted. "I'll give you some space to, um, focus."

I knew sleep had to be in my near future, but I was too antsy with Dorian still out there. I found Reyna in what had to be the main bedroom, going through a dresser drawer full of clothes that were far too short for Berith.

I hesitated to ask what was on my mind. "It seems like makhali are... really hospitable."

"Many of us try to be," Reyna said.

"Even people in positions of power?"

"Berith and I became each other's comfort near the end of the last war," she said bluntly. "Fear of your entire civilization's death is a great motivator, but so is having somebody to come home to. The two of us happened to click when he visited on Glashower. And when the war was over, a lot of things slowly got better, but some didn't, so I put distance between me and the problems." She met my eyes in an uncomfortable way. "Dorian was really taking you home?"

I nodded, feeling ashamed.

"That explains our last meeting. You don't know how to handle any of this, do you?"

I sniffled.

"I didn't mean it as a judgement, Ella. Just that I need to look out for you, and looking out for others isn't a strong skill of mine."

"Don't," I said. "I'm tired of it."

"Of what?" She was reaching for me, like my mother might.

I lurched away. "Needing help. Needing people to look out for me. Being so..." My claws were biting into my palms. "How can I be capable of this and nothing else?"

"Everyone needs help sometimes, Ella."

"He's still out there."

Reyna stared at me, and something in her seemed to harden. She threw a fresh set of clothes at me.

"Get changed," she ordered me. "Wash your hair so that when he gets back, you smell like something other than the ash and death he's been around. You don't have to be doing well. You just have to look enough like it that he doesn't try to take care of you when he returns, because I know he looks up to Berith and that's what Berith would try to do, no matter what state he came home in."

I hugged the clothes to my chest. I didn't want to be touched or talked to but I wanted the clothes to smell more like Reyna did.

"I'm not saying it's good advice," Reyna said, tired. "But it's something you can do."

And it was about all I could manage at that point. I did as instructed and then hid in the other spare room, fighting off what might've been another inbound panic attack, until I heard the front door open. I nearly toppled over after leaping to my feet, but it would've taken broken bones to keep me from rushing out. Reyna was there a few seconds quicker to see Berith and Dorian come in.

I grabbed Dorian, surprising him with a hug. He smelled like scorched metal and burnt hair and other awful organic odors but he was here and alive. A dozen thoughts ran through my head—you don't know him that well he's fresh out of battle and probably doesn't want to be grabbed even if he does you're doing it in front of his leader—but he collapsed on the couch leaning against me. Even with his armor on, he didn't weigh enough. I needed him to be sturdier on the inside. There was at least some strength in his embrace. It felt like we were competing for whose shoulder was supposed to support the other's head, but I let him win.

"Shouldn't've left you," I mumbled against him.

"I wasn't alone for all that long before backup arrived," Dorian said. "And there weren't too many fliers at first. I was able to avoid getting surrounded. Took out as many as I could." Coming from Dorian, it should've sounded like an obvious boast. It scared me that he was too drained for that.

"You smell like you got hurt."

"A couple bruises, nothing more. Got some Graft blood on my wings, had to get it cleaned up." Dorian pulled away, carefully looked me over. "Did you manage what you were trying to do?"

I nodded.

He managed a tired smile. "Then that's a win for you and I."

"What about the rest?" I asked.

He glanced to Berith, who had been in his own embrace with Reyna. They were slow to release each other.

"The rest is... ongoing," Berith said. "Non-combatants are to stay within the walls at all times. We have hope that there's just one massive wave of graftlings to deal with, but we don't know what else is on its way to us. A lot will depend on if we can clear the Glade before it becomes a breeding ground for them. For now, we've prevented too many monsters from congregating around our walls."

"Have there been more attacking the veil?" Reyna asked.

"They've been trying. From what I've heard, your great-grand-mother was a stubborn woman, and her work takes after her. We have food, water, and protection. Nothing large has arrived or formed yet."

Fear seized my heart. "Will Pillbug show up?"

They all stared at me. With no way of knowing what a pillbug was, or that it was my name for a monster, they might've thought my mind had snapped.

"Pillbug is the Fortress that came to Earth. A pillbug is an animal on Earth, about this big," I held my thumb and finger half an inch apart, "and they have a bunch of legs and armor on their backs so they can roll into a protected ball. The Fortress kinda looks like one but way bigger and leggier."

Berith blinked owlishly. I immediately regretted exposing this tired old man to the concept of "leggier."

"Pillbugs are sometimes called roly-polies so I think I did a good job naming it," I added.

"You saw this Fortress firsthand?" he asked.

"It was taking a stroll through my neighborhood."

"I am sorry."

"Is it normal for your head to hurt from being near a Fortress? Like it's about to split open?"

"I've never heard of it."

"Lucky me, I've discovered something new." If it did show up here, then what? Would the makhali kill it for me? Dorian would try, I believed. "Dorian, you're not going back out there, are you?"

"Not right now," he said. "But once I've rested, I'll be needed."

I wanted to destroy the monsters that were hurting my friends and keeping me from my loved ones. I had the ability. Didn't that give me an obligation to act? "I want to—"

Berith gently took me by the shoulders. "I promise there's a place for you here, but it's within these walls, not outside. Too many young lives have been lost in our wars with the Graft already. Having an outsider die defending our world would be an additional tragedy. You had a sword with you earlier?"

My traitorous eyes automatically glanced to where I'd left the sheathed blade leaned against a wall like an umbrella. Berith took it outside with him, and came back with empty hands. Dorian looked like he wanted to argue, but wouldn't.

"You're welcome to stay here," Berith said. "That goes for Veras and your other companion as well, though you might be woken up at night if you do. This will be a quickly evolving situation, and I imagine someone will call on me soon. Does anyone need anything?"

Silence.

"I will be getting whatever sleep I can. Wake me if that changes."

There was a slight stagger to his walk, compounded by his height. Reyna followed after him. I looked down at my lap, unsure what to do. A soft weight settled over my shoulders as Dorian draped a wing around me.

"I should go to the barracks," Dorian said.

"Why?" I asked.

"Veras and someone else are in one of the rooms, right? That just leaves one more, for you."

"I'll sleep on the couch," I said.

"You don't have to."

"You're hurt, I'm not. And I want to know you're safe."

Dorian hesitated.

"You can go with Berith whenever he has to leave," I said.

He gave in. As tired as I was, I stayed awake on the couch while Dorian showered, unwilling to lie down until I heard him enter the other room and knew he was settled in bed. Even after that, sleep wasn't my friend.

Hours later but still too early, I heard a knock at the front door and woke Dorian, letting him get Berith up and pretending to be asleep when they left because I couldn't stand to speak with Berith at that moment. Eventually, the pretending became true.

～

I RAN down an endless gray hallway, my shoulders aching with every step as if a great weight was attached to them. A dry slithering sound accompanied my footfalls. I turned around to find there was a skin-colored tube six inches wide growing from my back. It stretched down the hallway from where I'd come. I couldn't see the other end, but I could feel it. I willed it to disappear, but it wouldn't.

Apprehensive, I retraced my steps, the tube growing slack until I was dragging it in a pile behind me. It looked like a giant worm. I kicked it away from me in disgust, then doubled over in pain. Like it or not, it was part of me; most of my mass at that moment was contained in it, the head, torso, and limbs I thought of as myself merely a minority. I gathered the tube in my arms, scared it would catch against something and tear its many yards of veins. I could feel my own heartbeat in it through my palms, enough distance between the spots I held in each hand that the beats were desynchronized.

The tube was yanked from my arms. Giant black insect legs rounded an invisible corner, dragging a shapeless shadow between them, my new growth speared on their tips.

I ran away but quickly reached the end of my tether and was pulled off my feet. Pillbug drew me towards it. I crawled forward, claws anchoring me in place, and felt something in my back give. The tube tore away, and as I lay on the floor limp and bleeding, I saw the severed end spasming, my heart and lungs stuck to it.

Serves you right, Pillbug thought as it loomed over me, its words echoing in the excavated cavern of my chest.

I WAS SHOCKED out of it by Reyna shaking me and yelling. I shoved her away, rolled off the couch and slipped behind it. I touched my back, terrified of what I'd found, but although its surface was bubbled over with fluid-filled pockets of soft tissue, I was in one piece.

"Ella? Can you come out from there?" Reyna asked.

"Why?" I asked.

"So I can make sure you're alright. Your eyes were wide open but you were barely breathing. I thought... you had me worried."

I wormed, no, I crawled out from behind the sofa. Reyna knelt nearby. She held out her arms, and I hugged her. A separate hand patted my head. Andras had dragged himself out of bed. He looked grim.

"You're okay?" he asked.

I nodded.

"Go see Veras. I made him let me check on you first. You'll understand."

I took in a few deep breaths, my back slowly reverting to normal before Veras could see it, and entered the spare room Veras and Andras had first collapsed in. Veras, standing so tensely he looked like he might spontaneously combust, relaxed a tad when he saw me.

"Can I examine you?" he asked.

I hesitantly nodded, and sat on the bed with him.

He touched my forehead. "This feels like a good temperature for you." Gentle fingers against the side of my neck. "Consistent, strong pulse too. This is all very good, Ella."

"I only had a nightmare. You know I'm fine," I said.

"It doesn't hurt to make sure."

If I hadn't been so stressed, I would've nodded along. "It makes me anxious."

"I'm sorry. I just needed to have a checkup that wouldn't go poorly," Veras said, and I was horrified to see his eyes growing wet.

"He'll be okay," I said uncertainly. "He needs us both to be sure he'll be okay."

"It's not just Andras. I'm sure our hospital is already over its limit, and I know I should help, but I'm scared to and I don't know if they'd even *want* me there. I should go and ask, it's just, I didn't know just walking somewhere could be so hard."

"Do you want me to go with you?" I asked. "I know that's not much, but..."

He wrapped his arms around me. He was thin and bony and he was squeezing sort of hard, but it was, in fact, still a hug.

Pellior's Landing was full of hectic order, and while the veil seemed to keep any smoke from the Glade from reaching us, the air still had a heavy, ozone-like quality to it I assumed was from large amounts of magic being used. As Veras and I walked to the hospital, I watched supplies being transported and people hurrying by, trying to understand what was happening beyond the walls, and then something in the distance exploded and I didn't want to know anymore. I refocused my attention on Veras.

"Do people, um, know about Andras now?" I asked.

"Reyna does. She doesn't like that I didn't tell her earlier, and it doesn't change that I should've visited her more, but we made up a bit. I have his blessing to tell the other doctors too. If someone else needs to take care of him, I have to make sure they do it right. Otherwise, they might..." Veras squeezed his eyes shut. "If they don't understand his condition, they might be afraid he's at risk of becoming a monster, and hurt him while trying to stop it."

I was shocked by the idea of someone trying to hurt Andras, especially while he was bedridden. Then again, I supposed they wouldn't be seeing Andras. They'd be seeing what he might become if they happened to miss even the slightest bit of contamination.

"You kind of *were* on the front lines, weren't you?" I said. "Working in the infirmary."

Veras frowned. "I wouldn't say that. I never had to defend myself."

"If you messed up with one patient, it would've put everyone else in danger, though. You *had* to be thorough, or else. You had to be afraid all the time, even if you never saw an actual graftling. You probably felt like you could never rest," I guessed. "And now you're returning to that work."

"I'm trying not to think about those things," Veras said quietly. "It's easier if you just focus on the tasks themselves. If you always do it right the first time, you don't... you don't have to think about the consequences."

"I think you're brave," I blurted out.

"Brave? I keep remembering how it was three years ago. The incinerators for used bandages and bedding, the assistants who check you over for contamination at every hallway, the soldiers stationed in case someone *turns...*"

"You're trying despite that," I said.

"If they'll let me."

We entered the hospital, discovering its entrance had become a checkpoint. Curtains had been hung up to create changing areas, soldiers stood outside the door, and there were bins of clean white accessories that smelled like chemical death. Veras took in a deep breath before approaching an orderly.

"Veras," he said, holding a hand over his chest. "Former member of the medic corps. Here to offer assistance if it's desired."

She stared at him as if he'd grown a second head. "If?"

"Well, it's been quite a while since I've, you know..."

She gestured at the bins. "You remember how to put all this on?"

Veras nodded.

"Suit up as quick as you can. We'll put you to work."

Veras looked back at me. I gave him a thumbs up. He hesitantly copied the gesture. I waited while he went behind a partition, returning wearing strangely waxy clothes. Between the face mask, hair covering, multiple sets of gloves, and a jacket that wrapped around his tightly folded wings, he hardly looked like himself anymore.

"I'll see you soon," I said, and then, "I promise," which kinda made it sound like I expected him to die, not the vibe I'd hoped to give off. Veras nodded. He passed inspection and disappeared beyond a guarded door.

When I returned to Berith's home, Andras was asleep despite Reyna's loud pacing in the sitting room.

"When will he be back?" she asked, seeing me return without Veras.

"I, uh, I don't know," I said. "Not sure how busy the hospital is, or... I just don't know."

Reyna stared at me with blank eyes, and I wondered how the past day must've felt for someone who'd experienced war but didn't know how to fight. I bit my lip and, slowly, with the same care I would use if dangling a piece of raw meat before a lion, showed her my phone. It left my hand faster than I could blink as she gave in to pure Id, touching it, attempting to gently bend it, wrapping her magic around it.

"What is this? Why haven't I seen it before?" she asked.

"I was worried you'd want to dismantle it." I was actually still worried about that, but at least it was working as a distraction.

"I wouldn't want to dismantle it so much," she said, frustrated as she turned it around, "if everyone could just agree to be decent and make the mechanisms visible from the outside. What does it do? Is it broken?"

"It might just be out of electricity," I said. "Back home it can do a bunch of things, like store information, communicate with people who are far away..." My chest ached. "It, um, you don't think you'd be able to charge it, would you? It has pictures of my family in it."

She flexed her fingers. Magic sparked between them. "It might not be so different from how I put energy into magical items."

"You'll stop in time if that'll fry it?"

"This is an alien object to me. I'll do my best, but I can't make any promises."

Now that the possibility had occurred to me, I needed this too much. I nodded.

She stuck a piece of wire in the charging port, using it to send her magic in while I anxiously watched. I could barely resist snatching it from her the moment the screen turned on. I kept my eyes shut while I unlocked it with my thumbprint so I wouldn't see the date and know how long I'd been gone. Reyna leaned in to watch over my shoulder as I opened up my pictures.

Mom, Dad, and I on my twentieth birthday. Him meeting a stranger's adorable dog. Her and the results of a beginning painting class she took. Most recently, a picture they'd sent me mere days before everything went wrong, them on their trip standing in front of a road sign with a small town's stupid name.

"They were traveling when it all happened," I said. "I should've been with them. But I was scared if we were all in a hotel room together, I'd change in the night and they'd find out about me."

"Maybe another outcome would've been better for your family," Reyna said. "But if you'll allow me to be selfish, Veras, Andras, and I would likely all be dead without you." Her inexperienced hands copied my swiping touch on the screen, moving back to my parents and I together. "I'm sure they're waiting for you. Look at that, they clearly love you."

I turned my phone off before I could start crying. "Should save the power."

"I could charge it up whenever you want," Reyna said. "It barely uses any of my magic."

"I appreciate that," I said. "But I can smell burning plastic, and I don't want to push my luck. Could you hold onto it for me? Otherwise I'll be constantly turning it on and run out of battery quickly."

She put it in her bag. "Can you do something for me in return? I'd like to help with repairs on the veil. Walk with me there?"

I linked my elbow around hers. We went to the wall, a section of it thankfully far from the main gates and whatever awfulness was happening on the other side. The veil must've been under bombardment, window-sized sections of it hazy or flickering or loosely woven, and Reyna picked the direction of the worst area. A group of makhali were already working. Having removed a bunch of panels from the inside of the wall, they used magic and tools on the inscribed patterns that had been hidden away. I stepped closer with Reyna, who seemed reluctant to approach the group alone, and nearly recoiled. The uncovered wall radiated magic strong enough to make my fingertips and tongue burn. Maybe I could hand her off to someone else?

Reyna watched the veil. "Do you ever feel like you've already lost the one person in your life who'll truly understand you?"

I stared at her, nauseous. The set of her mouth and eyes seemed vaguely angry. I didn't think she was really asking for a response. She might not even have been aware she'd said it out loud. It was all I could do to not start crying.

"Do you know anyone here?" I asked.

"Yes." She went to an unoccupied section of wall and began laying out her tools. I fled once her face settled into a look of isolated concentration.

Everyone was on weird schedules, and I found Dorian crashed on Berith's couch when I got back. He'd been drawing when I came in, but quickly shoved the paper beneath him as if I'd caught him doing something inappropriate.

"What were you drawing?" I said.

"Things out there," he said. "If you haven't already, I don't want you to see them. "

"Where'd they come from?"

"There are two things you need to understand about the Graft. The first is that it only takes a single mistake for everything to go wrong. The second is that now and then, it feels like we're fighting... more than a big group of animals. Something that strategizes and prepares. Based on the number of pre-formed violent monsters in the invasion, this is one of those times. We've got soldiers sweeping the veil and artisans fixing it around the clock, and we're trying to keep clearing out the monsters that congregate, but... we've never had to focus on defense this much before. It's infuriating. But we also can't let offense slip, because if enough gather outside our walls—" He cut himself off.

"You can tell me," I said. "It's my reality too."

"We don't want them... squeezing too tightly together and potentially fusing," Dorian explained. "Otherwise we risk getting, ah, it's really hard to kill something that big with dozens of hearts and lungs..."

I shouldn't have made him told me, but my mind was full of terrible questions. "For a monster that started out as another creature, do they stay that shape forever? Or will they keep changing?"

"They may keep mutating, but you might still be able to tell the original form. I'm guessing you saw the remains of the last expedition. I was hoping you hadn't. I'm sorry that I wasn't able to... that I can't take you home right now."

"You're needed elsewhere. You don't have to apologize for that." I squeezed my shoulders, arms tight against my chest. "I'm using my ability again."

"I'm glad you still have that tool. I hope you won't need it, but... it didn't go this badly in the Glade last time. I don't understand how we're doing worse." He sighed. "Who is it that I've heard coughing? I don't recognize their voice."

"My friend Andras."

"And he's not in the hospital because...?"

I gave Dorian the quick version.

"Can't believe your healer secretly brought *two* aliens here," Dorian said.

"Yeah, which is weird because I don't think he goes looking for trouble? But here we are. The rest of the Vanguard, are they alright?"

Dorian nodded. "Pissed off at me, understandably, but alright."

"Does that mean you'll be staying here?"

"If Berith's okay with it."

I relaxed a little. I didn't trust the universe. I needed to see and hear and touch things for myself, or for all I knew they might stop existing. I knew the time Dorian wasn't here would be difficult for me, but at least I could expect to see him every day, if nothing went horribly wrong.

18

———————

For several days, I walked Veras and Reyna to work, waited up for Dorian, kept Andras company, and tried to avoid Berith. Sometimes, when Andras slept and nobody else was around, I left Berith's house to sneak a look over the wall; there were stairs leading up to the ramparts, and I'd wander until I found one that wasn't busy. No matter where I looked, the land past the city was blighted with different ailments, churned and melting grass broken up by areas that had been burned. On occasion there were pyres, and I could barely fight the compulsion to sharpen my sight and see what kind of bodies they contained. The part of the wall that faced the Glade was always the busiest, preventing me from getting a better view in that direction, but I could still see the constant smoke trails.

And then I'd return to Berith's house and find Andras worse off than when I'd last seen him. His increasingly poor health didn't stop him from fussing over me. He made sure I ate, tried to keep me engaged in something other than despairing. I wore one of Reyna's sweaters so he could pull the cuffs down and hold my hand through the fabric. Even with his calming presence, my body changed often and without warning, driven by stress and frequent nightmares. When I needed a ritual, I smoothed out the wrinkles in Andras's sheets or wiped the sweat from the back of his neck with a washcloth, trying to put the both of us right. It worked for me, and only me.

After a particularly bad dream in which Pillbug skewered me to the capital's walls, Andras woke me up. He stood beside me, legs shaking from exertion.

"You don't have to be afraid," he said. "We're safe here."

"Back to bed," I said, helping him over to it. *I* was safe here. Andras wasn't. The top layer of his skin was peeling up like shedding bark. I thought he was starting to smell like mildew, and had to swallow back the urge to scream and sob.

"I'm fine," Andras assured me. "Just tired. I'm not in pain."

Even I could tell he was lying. "What would it would take for you to recover?" If that was even a possibility.

"Hamadryads have an organ called a taproot that we can physically separate from our bodies while retaining a magical connection to it. When we find somewhere we want to settle down, we bury it, let it form roots and connect to the plant life there. We care for the flora, and it cares for us. A taproot collects energy from healthy plant life, which we receive over that connection. Serious damage to one can instantly send a hamadryad into fatal shock, no matter the distance." He grimaced. "I never wanted to leave Glashower, even once the war started. It was the Graft's first time on our world, and we didn't understand how screwed we were until it was far too late. I was probably the equivalent of your age when it happened, and hadn't found a place to settle down yet. As part of choosing to stand with my world, I finally buried my taproot. But Glashower fell, and the soil where I buried it is contaminated. Leaving with Veras kept me from dying, but it didn't fully save me. So I'd need to either safely return to a place like the Glade, where I can draw from the plants around me, or have my taproot treated."

"So you're fucking dying," I said.

"Language," he said. "I choose to believe there's a post-Graft future for all of us." He reached for a book Reyna had brought him. "Try to relax for a bit. If you don't like the story, just tell me and I'll come up with something better."

As Andras read out loud to me, all I could think about was that he was trying to protect me, even as he fell apart. And I'd almost *left* him.

"Ella?"

My fingers were in my mouth. I returned my sharpened canines to normal. "Sorry about that. Are you okay if I go? There's something I have to do."

"Of course. Please be gentle with yourself."

I gave a noncommittal nod and left the room, eased the door shut. Waiting for Dorian to get home was painful, but it gave me time to start making plans in my journal. I started with *give Andras his taproot* and worked backwards from there: I had to get his taproot. I had to get to where it was. I had to know where it was. I had to avoid or fight monsters between myself and there, and not die of starvation or dehydration along the way, and relying on shedding my own tissue to get rid of contamination couldn't be relied on without other medical supplies either...

It was good that Dorian had only stepped out to restock Berith's pantry, because I gave him no chance to rest when he returned.

"I have good I need to do elsewhere," I said. "And I'm not sure just how I'll do it yet, but the doing isn't up for debate. Do you think you could draw some maps for me?"

Dorian and I covered the sitting room floor with notes, our two languages detailing packing plans, distances, and potential paths. When Veras and Reyna returned, we were bent over our plans like wild animals defending their territory. Veras took one look at the papers, similar enough to his own trip planning with Andras back before I really knew them, and must've immediately understood.

"This way would be the most efficient," Veras said. "Since we're not traveling with Andras's current physical limitations."

"Traveling where?" Reyna said, and once her questions were answered, she was instantly involved. Dorian hadn't told me he was coming yet, but he didn't need to. I knew how antsy he was here.

Vanguard Base had always been a bad fit for him. For someone like Dorian, returning to the same point over and over—even if it was after winning—would always feel like defeat.

I felt pretty good about what we were doing, until Andras walked in. Like Veras, he understood what we were planning with a single glance.

"No," he said. "You're not doing this."

"This was always the plan," Veras said.

"Not like this!" Andras shouted. "Putting you at risk was bad enough. But the rest of you—"

"Watching you wither away is worse than when I was hospitalized," I blurted out.

"I would've thought the last thing you wanted was to die on an alien world," Andras said.

"This isn't only about you," Dorian said. "Other work needs to be done out there."

"I have to," I said.

Andras snatched Veras's hand and muttered to him too quietly for my translation artifact to translate, though I could just make out the shapes of his words and tell they weren't in the makhali language. Veras responded in turn, eyes downcast, letting Andras pull him into a room to talk.

"Other work?" I said to Dorian.

"Yeah. I'm still working through how to say it to Berith," Dorian said.

"Better figure it out quick," Reyna glanced over at the groceries he'd brought back. "If you don't mind, I want to take some time to go through his things. Make sure none of it needs mending. He's the sort to have a very few things he uses all the time until they're completely trashed, and it hurts me as an artisan to know he's probably been wearing shoes with thinning soles and cooking with dull knives. Call me when he gets home, would you?"

She scurried off, and Dorian was furiously writing down his thoughts. Veras stuck his head out in the hall, motioned me over.

Andras was propped up in bed. Veras sat on its edge, interlacing his hands in different ways.

"Why do you have to go?" Andras said.

"There are many awful things between me and home," I said. "I have to get stronger and learn what's out there. And I can't just stand by and watch you decline anymore. I... I'm scared for you like I am for my parents."

Andras mumbled something in that second alien language again, the words translating to "what happened to the sapling I carried?" His eyes looked past me, glassy with fever. Veras stroked his face.

"Don't put me to sleep," Andras accused.

"I'm not using my magic," Veras said. "You're exhausted. If you need the rest, then take it."

"Can't. You'll leave."

"Not while you're asleep. I promise."

That small bout of resistance seemed to wear him out even further. Andras sank back into his pillows, collapsing into sleep.

"I don't get what he told me," I said quietly.

"To my understanding, hamadryads have a responsibility towards any plant they bring to a new environment, even if they hand it off to someone else," Veras said. "When we first met, Andras helped me carry you to Plesmae. He transplanted you here, and now the Glade is overrun with monsters and you're heading into more danger because of him."

"Did he give us permission to go?" I said.

Veras sighed. "He said that if anything happened to us, it would haunt him forever. He's accepted he can't stop us, but he couldn't let us go without a fight."

Both our heads turned at the sound of the front door opening.

"That's one person convinced," Veras said. "Time for the second."

"Do we actually need to?" I said.

"Berith could prevent us from leaving, for our own safety."

Just what I excelled at, being persuasive. I minced back to the living room, Veras a step behind me.

Berith looked fatigued. I hadn't heard him in the house for a while, so he must've just gotten back from a full day, if not longer, of crisis management. Dorian had the nervous look of someone mid-reality check.

"I agree there's work to be done beyond Plesmae," Berith said. "My issue is with who would be going. Everyone on our last exploratory mission died. I can't just send out whoever feels like it."

"We need to be fast and stealthy. A larger force would attract too much attention, and we have all the different skills we need between the four of us," Dorian said.

"Explain."

"Three goals. We deal with the fact that your fifth house guest is dying, which requires us to go to Glashower. Clearly the Graft have been hard at work coming up with new traits if they've found a way to wear down our veils, so along the way we learn what else they've been up to since the last war before it reaches us, giving us a chance to prepare. And on our way back, we block off whatever rifts we can, hopefully stopping or at least slowing any more waves of inbound monsters. I scout, Ella's our monster-detector, we'll have a healer—"

"I've studied different species' anatomy, so I can help with that research," Veras interrupted.

"—and Reyna... will also help," Dorian finished, as if he'd realized ninety percent of the way through that he didn't actually know what she could do.

"Someone with my skills *has* to go," Reyna said. "I can get us through any veils in our way."

"I didn't know you had that skill," Dorian said.

"It's why I was on Glashower. They needed people with it on all our frontiers."

"So you're a sort of," my earring glitched as it struggled to translate Dorian's words, "jack of all trades?"

Despite a height difference of several inches (and not in her favor) between them, she got right in Dorian's face, actually making him lean back to get away from her. "I can't believe you don't remember me. At Berith's request, we spent several hours together while I took your measurements and tested your range of motion so I could make your armor. The sword you bear was also made by my hands. I am not an amateur at many things, I am a master of my craft and I happen to be pretty damn good at some other things too. Understood?"

Dorian nodded frantically.

"Good," Reyna said. She turned to Berith. "B, I need to do this." She held up a finger, keeping him from interrupting her. "And we both know that if I want to go somewhere, there's no substance in the universe that can stop me. We'll be back soon enough, won't we?" She slung an arm over my shoulder, nudged me when I didn't say anything.

"Quick as we can," I spit out. "Someone had to go eventually, right? If something happens to us, you didn't order us to go so it wouldn't be your fault."

For some reason, that didn't seem to reassure him.

"Commander, if I take someone with me, I'll make sure they return home," Dorian said. "That's what it means to be a leader."

"Dorian, you're..."

"I was one of your best soldiers during the last war. That's because I wasn't stuck doing defense, which you know I'm no good at. Bliss is far better than me at strategy and resource management. The Vanguard will be best off in her hands, and I'll handle this task instead."

"Be honest with everyone here," Berith said, frustrated. "You've never been on a mission like this before, where you'll be cut off from the nearest source of help by entire worlds of hostile land. When we first met, I was worried about your lack of confidence, but now it seems you might've swung too far in the other direction."

Dorian looked like he'd been slapped. "When you describe it that way, yes, I suppose this is... new to me. But I'm still one of a small group of makhali whose only focus has been preparing for battle over the last three years—"

"Dorian, I don't want you dying alone, violently, stranded in some awful corner of the universe." Releasing those words seemed to shrink Berith down by a full inch, as if he'd been carrying them around for too long.

"That won't happen." Dorian's voice was full of certainty.

"Why?" Berith asked.

"I..." It was as though Dorian had expected an answer to automatically present itself, but none did.

"It doesn't matter if it's fair," Berith said. "It doesn't matter what you've already suffered through. It doesn't even matter how skilled or experienced you are. If you throw yourself at an enemy that's too large, or for too long, eventually your chances will run out. I don't want that fate for any of you."

"We both know this is necessary," Dorian said desperately.

"And we're not jumping into this without preparation," Veras said. "I've been planning this journey for years. I have a route and everything."

"I mean it about breaking things to get out," Reyna said.

Berith's gaze fell on me, and we held eye contact for a few seconds. I slunk over to him, motioned for him to lean down so I could whisper just to him.

"I am going to die inside if I don't do this," I said. "I have a copy of my life before all this happened in my mind, and if I fail, I think I'll go inside it and not be able to leave, because it'll be easier to escape reality than deal with the consequences of letting my friend die."

He was unhappy about it, but I think he understood. I returned to my friends.

"When you're in their territory... please consider what it'll do to others if you never return," Berith said.

He hugged Reyna, and put a fatherly arm around Dorian's shoulders. A shoulder squeeze and tired acknowledgement for Veras and I. He must've been beyond worn out. I hated seeing him like that, less because of who he was, and more what he was. About five thousand makhali, I reminded myself. How many could be lost or break down before there wasn't anyone left who could do their job? And soon it would be just four of us setting out. I could barely keep myself from imagining how many graftlings we might encounter on our journey, how many fights lay ahead, how much danger we'd be in. Maybe Berith had been making the same awful estimates, weighing the statistics of our survival, but his position meant he couldn't turn that part of his brain off. Maybe he had to face those numbers.

"There were once days in my lifetime when we'd celebrate sending expeditions out into the universe," Berith said. "I'm sorry that's not... that it came to this. None of you were even born yet."

"I don't think I'd enjoy a big send-off," I said. "Too loud and crowded."

Given the way he looked at me, I regretted speaking up. I'd intended it as consolation, but it only seemed to make him sadder.

"I never even asked if you were comfortable here, as my guest," he said. "I knew just existing in the city was a struggle for you, and I never—"

"Berith," Reyna cut in. "Go rest. You look about to collapse."

"Other people need you too," Dorian said.

"I need to do more to prepare you," Berith said. "The things you might come across out there—"

"*Berith*. We're going partly because you *don't* know what's out there," Reyna said. "We'll be careful, okay? Yes, we missed out on the days when this kind of travel was something to look forward to. But that also means Veras, Dorian, and I, we've never imagined the rest of the universe as being safe. Maybe it's different for Ella, but we know she's adaptable, and she's seen firsthand what to expect."

"At least let me see you on your way," he said.

"No," Reyna said simply. "Go lie down. I patched your favorite leisure clothes. I'll come visit you in a minute."

If he hadn't swayed on his feet, I think they would've stood there arguing until the Graft broke through the walls. He looked almost beaten as he retreated down the hall. It wasn't the note I imagined any of us had wanted to end the conversation on.

Dorian clapped his hands, a grim look on his face, as if he had to clear the air before we could move on.

"You lot can meet me at the gates in two hours," Dorian said. "Gather whatever you need by then. They're doing timed counterattacks on the Graft to keep too many from accumulating, it'll be safest to leave right after that."

"I need to wake Andras," Veras said.

That left Reyna and I alone. She wouldn't meet my eyes.

"So even once the veil was back up, you could've gotten me through," I said.

"Only a few makhali know how to," Reyna said. "Technically all of us have the capability to learn, but artisans like me find it easier. You have to resonate with the veil, which is easier if you're already used to putting your magic in other materials. There's me, maybe a couple dozen other artisans, and Berith, because our leaders always learn how." She flexed her fingers slowly, as if regretting they were empty. "I didn't know you would try to go home that first night. And after that, it seemed like you were focusing on your training. Like you knew better than to—I'm sorry for saying it that way. For even accidentally implying you'd have been stupid to try to go home. I want you to succeed, but if you're not absolutely ready then I'd rather you not try than fail and potentially die. So I thought, if I made you armor first, and you finished your training, I'd take you then. And I probably should've told you earlier, but I was scared of what would've happened if you'd asked to go then and I said no and you..."

"Did you think I'd lash out?"

"No. I just thought you'd hate me. Not that I expected hiding the truth to have a different outcome."

No matter what she did, Reyna would always be the person who made me my armor, and pretended to crash her bike on the slight chance that I'd see, and went with me to the hospital. I had a similar feeling towards Berith. Twice now he'd made it harder for me to go home, and despite knowing he'd done it to protect me and others, I was still frustrated with him. But he was also the man who hadn't been angry when I'd bitten him in fear. I was used to people not acting for my benefit, and it being uncomfortable; for them to be trying to help me and it still hurting was something new and horrible, but I had to live with it.

"I don't hate you," I said. "If I'd asked and you'd said no, it would've been because you don't want me to die. And asking you to go anywhere near the Graft... Reyna, are you really okay with taking this trip?"

"The reasons we talked about are enough," she said. "Beyond them, I have my own."

"Which is?"

"If I tell you, you might... well, you might actually hate me."

"Reyna," I said, "please stop worrying about that and go do whatever your relationship with Berith calls for."

"Don't wait for me," she said.

I knocked on the door to Andras's room. Veras answered.

"He's awake for the moment," Veras said. "After you talk to him, I'll do one last check-up and then go to the hospital. Someone needs to look after him while I'm gone, and I need to make sure they do it right." He took in a deep breath. "And get supplies for our trip. I'll give you two some time together."

I stuck a smile on my face before entering the room, but Andras saw right through it.

"If it's not too much for you, I could use someone to hold my hand right now," Andras said.

I slipped my fingers between his, putting up with my discomfort so I could memorize the feeling of his rough skin.

"I really am glad you came to live with us," Andras said. "My body isn't infectious, but there's still this fear that if I touch people, I'll contaminate them. You were a relief. It felt safer for me to touch you. I hope I never made you uncomfortable."

"You didn't. I needed that too."

"Good," he said softly. He placed his other hand over his chest. "It's been so long, I don't know if I'll feel it when someone touches my taproot. I know it's still out there, because I'd be dead otherwise. But I'm worried what you'll find. I hate that I'm not strong enough to go myself and find it first so nobody else has to see it if it's ruined."

"Veras is a doctor. He won't mind what he sees so long as you end up alright."

Andras sighed. "I'm scared for all of you, but especially him. So many things could go wrong, and I know you won't have control over many of them, but can you make sure he's not scalding his arms?"

"Of course."

"And please try to get along with him, you'll need each other. He does care about you, even when he's upset." Andras closed his eyes. "I hope you know you're family to me."

I hadn't. Being told so sent a jolt of happiness through me, but it also hurt. Aside from my parents, Andras was one of the people I felt safest and most comfortable around. Without him, I wasn't sure what would've happened to me. I certainly couldn't imagine myself staying with Veras or Reyna if he hadn't been there. My heart was relieved to have permission to feel the same way about him.

So how hadn't I known he felt that way?

"We haven't known each other that long, in the grand scheme of things," Andras said. "But when I click with people, it's fast. It seems like you didn't know. I'm sorry I didn't say it before. When you get back, I'll try to be more direct about what I'm thinking and feeling, okay?"

He cupped his hand next to my face, and I leaned into it. Leaving, even if it was the best chance of helping him, felt cruel. But I had to. I did the only other thing I could think of.

"May I see your arm?" I asked.

"Sure."

"I'm going to give you a charm to keep you safe. All you need to do is rest." My magic wasn't like a makhal's, but I could still try. I imagined my body heat becoming concentrated at the tip of my finger, like ink at a pen's nib. I flipped through my journal to the reference I'd made of Berith's charm, tracing the same complex series of symbols on Andras's arm. He felt cold, so that instead of the roughness of his skin creating warm friction, it was like touching dead bark.

Andras watched, quiet. "Do you know what it says?"

"No, but Berith said it could help to keep people out of harm's way."

"I guess we didn't get too far in our reading lessons."

"I did a bit on my own, but this is different from normal writing."

"Yes, in a way, but..." Andras smiled. "Berith's right. It's a very powerful charm. Thank you. Please put just as much energy into keeping yourself safe."

"I'll keep an eye on Veras, too," I promised.

"I'd like to see him now."

Stepping out of that room was one of the hardest things I'd ever done, but I knew he and Veras needed their time together.

I met Dorian at the gate. As we waited for the others to arrive, I took out my journal. I'd explained my reasoning for going on this journey already, but even so, my next letter to my parents was difficult to write.

Day 42: Things have gotten bad on Plesmae. Every now and then I get this flash of anger. I was supposed to be SAFE here, but I'm not. I can only imagine everyone else here feels the same about having the enemy they beat three years ago at their doorstep again.

I'm leaving with a group of friends to try and help Andras. He'll die if we don't. I'm just realizing now that nobody brought up the idea that he'd be fine if he could return to the Glade before his illness goes too far. I guess they don't expect it to work out that way.

I hate that I'm going away from you, but I have to. I can't return to you right now either way, and if I did make it home with Andras dead, it wouldn't fully be me returning. There'd be a part missing. There are already parts of me I've never shared with you. I'm hiding myself again right now, because even though I've addressed all these letters to you, I wouldn't have written that if I knew you were going to read it. I don't want to have even less of myself available to you.

I'm sorry that I haven't—

I scratched out that last sentence, let the letter end there. I'd write more to them later. I'd figure it out.

Reyna showed up soon, wearing three separate tool belts clasped over a worn-in shirt far too long to be hers. We strapped supply bags to her bike: rations, water, materials for whatever she thought might be useful, medical supplies once Veras joined us. He and Dorian set off together, taking advantage of a sky momentarily empty of flying monsters.

As Reyna did her final checks on the bike, we were both surprised by Berith approaching. Reyna barely had time to turn around before he scooped her up. I expected her to disappear from the translucent cocoon of his wings he had her wrapped in, like a magician's assistant vanishing into a trick box, stored somewhere safe. But he eventually released her and turned his deeply upset gaze my way.

"I thought you wanted to go home," he said, and I suspected he was mad at me.

"I will," I said. "I promise, I will." Logically, I'd known that I was going further from home. I just hadn't felt it until now, and it made me weak.

Reyna stepped on a nearby rock to get the extra height she needed to kiss his cheek, and then joined me on the bike. The engine hummed to life and then we were actually through the gate, and all the sights and smells and sounds of a brewing war were upon us. I was overwhelmed by charcoal and ozone and filth. Slain and torched monsters dotted the landscape. I couldn't resist looking over my shoulder at the Glade. My first thought was *oh look, they relocated some of the trees away from the front line, how wonderful* and then I screamed. The trees were relocating all by their damn selves, trunks split into tripods at their base, literal giants slowly grinding their way towards the capital, and it was all too much.

The last thing I saw on Plesmae was Berith watching us leave, small and blurry in the motorbike's imperfect mirrors, and then I pressed my face against Reyna's back, holding back sobs.

INTERMISSION

There is no shortage of habitable worlds in this universe, yet this one feels like an especially good fit. The temperature, the light, it's all familiar. It reminds me of my childhood, when I had no responsibilities and could spend as much time as I pleased running through fields and wading through streams. The sky is different, but I have never seen a sky like the one I grew up beneath anywhere else.

I must stay on my guard. Part of that familiarity comes from the structures I've encountered. There is other life on this planet than myself and my companions, and it is this life that has killed some of us. Before I left our foundation, they had already fallen into the awful cycle of self-defense becoming offense becoming the other side's self-defense. These strangers will not listen to me, will not hear reason, and so my companions do what they must. I hate that we've brought war to this—

No. We did not bring war. We would not do that. I would not do that. The strangers arrived after us, antagonized us. Yes. It is not our fault if we must raise more than a shield.

The strangers stay away from me, moving on their own two legs or in strange carts the likes of which I've never seen. I just want to talk. Eventually I manage to get close to one, the exhausted participant in a skirmish. I marvel at how similar our bodies are, the near identical proportions of their limbs, head, and torso. I press my hand to theirs, our palms and fingers lining up, and say, "I wish it hadn't come to this. Are you alright?"

They don't respond to my touch or voice, making me worry they're badly hurt, but eventually they get up to speak with my companions. It sounds like they've seen the error of their ways. Hopefully more can be convinced.

I want to wait for him, but he'd understand that I have a responsibility to stop bloodshed wherever I can.

19

____

Reyna and I made it to Vanguard Base unscathed, catching up with Veras and Dorian and collecting more supplies, including sleeping bags and some extra clothing. I already felt like I wasn't contributing, since all I had to bring was the armor Reyna had made for me, the clothes on my back, my journal, and my near-useless phone. It was night there, and Dorian noticed me shivering. He took out a dark jacket from our supplies and wrapped it around me. The hem went almost to my knees. Along with the wing slits in the back I was already accustomed to, the front buttoned up, as did the sides from the hemline to my hips. It felt slick, hopefully water-resistant, but surprisingly soft and insulated on the inside.

"There," Dorian said, satisfied despite it being several sizes too big. "A fitting coat for Plesmae's newest warrior."

"She's not one of your soldiers," Veras said.

"You've never fought, so I wouldn't expect you to understand true camaraderie."

Veras rolled his eyes and motioned me over. I let him give me a quick checkup.

"I know there have been times when you wanted to avoid my attention," he told me. "That can't be how this trip works."

"Mmmm."

"Ella? I need you to promise me. This is important." He squeezed my shoulder.

"Sorry," I said. "I think you've got some magic on you." This close to him, I could feel the edges of it, soft against my brow. I'd gotten distracted because it didn't feel like Veras's usual white-hot magic.

"Andras put a little of his on me," Veras said, brushing a hand over his forehead. "It's normally a makhali gesture, a bit like a blessing. Anyway, do you promise?"

He seemed a little... fidgety as he said it. I raised an eyebrow, and his face flushed.

"Sure," I said.

Veras cleared his throat, getting Dorian and Reyna's attention. "How long do we have supplies for?"

"Couple months if need be," Dorian said. "Plenty of condensed food, plus what we need to purify whatever water we find. What's in the rest of the bags?" he asked Reyna.

"Tools, some loose materials, a couple notebooks, and whatever else I need to fix or break veils." She'd slung them around like they were nothing. I needed to stop forgetting that Reyna was a blacksmith.

"I hope the seats on that thing are comfortable, because you ladies are going to spend a lot of time in them. As for you, healer, stick close to me when we're in the air. We need to be ready for anything."

I looked between my three friends. I felt so small compared to the rest of the universe. I had to be big enough to keep them out of danger—or kill the danger with my bare hands, if need be. I'd do it. For them and Andras, I'd do it.

And I knew they'd do it for me too.

As much as my stomach was curdling with nerves, I tried to keep my chin high as I followed Dorian. I could let myself slink and skulk later, but for this first moment, I wanted to at least look like I could handle myself.

The next rift was nearby, bordered by a burned-out wooden structure Dorian explained had been a way-house for travelers once. We stepped through it into a bleached sandy desert that stretched to the edges of my vision, the bright sun forcing me to squint. The dry air scratched the inside of my nose and mouth. We at least started off with some relief from the heat, because next to the rift was... it reminded me most of a large bus stop.

"Really?" I said. "That's all they have to mark the path to an entire inhabited world? And you guys barely have anything either."

"We used to, but it was destroyed in the last war," Dorian said. "And while we may have practically been neighbors with Felar, that doesn't mean we enjoyed seeing each other. I don't think their goal was to be welcoming."

My eyes were slow to adjust to the light and dryness. Much of our surroundings reminded me of a ruined painting, someone having accidentally smeared the near-identical shades of tan, beige, and sandstone together, destroying all the detail. Rocky plains bled into crumbled buildings that faded into distant mountains. Miles away was a churning, screaming dust storm that seemed too big to be real. It was large enough to contain a city. I squinted even harder.

It *did* contain a city. I could see the outlines of rectangular buildings slanted at odd angles. The ground between us and it was mostly flat like it had been bulldozed, clusters of low-lying domed buildings blending into the identically colored environment.

"Did you do that?" I asked. "The storm?"

"We did, once the surviving inhabitants were all evacuated," Dorian said. "There were too many hiding places to make destroying all the Graft possible any other way than making it too dry to live here for long. Felar's native species isn't shaped like us. They had a lot of underground spaces that needed to be smoked out too."

I gave him a scandalized look.

"The Graft ruined it first, and its surviving residents fled off-world. It's not like they're around to be upset by it."

"This was done right after we passed through," Reyna said, nodding to Veras. "The storm's self-perpetuating. Took a bunch of solar-charged magic-generating panels. I take it we're returning to

Glashower on the same path we left? Through the middle of the city?"

"Same one. Figured it was best to stick with what we know," Veras said.

"That's nice. I was hoping to see the building they constructed around the rift again." Her smile faded. "Though I suppose it'll be in much worse shape than before."

Veras nodded. He looked overwhelmed too.

"Do we know how much of a hurry we're in?" I asked, trying to put it gently.

"It's... hard to know exactly," Veras said. "We have plenty of reasons to hurry."

No matter how long we were gone, I'd have to imagine Andras in the same state we'd left him in. Constantly sleeping, unconscious but unchanging, at the worst. The thought of returning to find him or my parents fully *gone* was unbearable. I knew Andras was in one of the safest, most well-guarded places in the capital, and that he'd have round-the-clock care... if the medical staff didn't get too busy. And if none of them, exhausted from weeks of being under siege, forgot what he was and how his condition worked, and acci-dentally—

No. I'd already decided we weren't going to think about that. I had to assume the same was going through Veras's head. I gave him a hand squeeze that might've been a bit harder than intended; it star-tled him, and if he had been stuck on the same train of thought as I'd been, I hoped it snapped him out of it.

The boys took wing while Reyna and I drove. The sound of the bike's wheels on the ground alternated between rough and smooth as our straight line of travel took us over old railways now covered in sand. I knew I was making assumptions, educated guesses at best, about what we were seeing, but I couldn't help but assign familiar names to them. Felar had once had something like monorails or streetcars connecting a network of suburbs to the greater city ahead of us. Now they were just rusted carcasses and buried mounds. The occasional post or half-eroded metal item still flashed with light in a way that seemed too glitchy to be magical, the last functioning electrical machines slowly burning themselves out.

"Why don't you guys have this stuff?" I yelled to be heard over the rush of the wind. Even at its top speed the bike only went about thirty miles per hour, but having been away from cars for a while, it felt incredibly fast.

"They wanted to sell, not share, and for a high price," Reyna called back. "Wouldn't even let us on their vehicles, and by the time nobody was around to protest if we did, everything was broken. Some of us *tried* to learn before Felar fell, and got banned from visiting."

"Anyone I would know?" I said dryly.

"Perhaps."

"For doing what?"

"I may have attempted to covertly dissect a street lamp."

"*Reyna.*"

"I would've put it back together when I was done!"

"You're lucky you didn't get electrocuted."

"Whatever they were doing was destroying their natural resources anyway. This place wasn't always a massive desert. Their technology didn't mix well with magic, and it didn't save them from the Graft."

It was hard to tell from the ruins whether Felar used to have more or less advanced tech compared to home, if they were even similar enough to compare. If Plesmae weren't under siege, and Andras's life on the line, I would've loved to poke around and find out for myself. Instead we passed by it all, and in the several hours we spent driving, it became easier for me to see the buried and eroded technology as just shapes beneath the sand instead of mysteries to uncover. The want was still there, but needs came first.

I was just starting to wonder if we should've agreed on some signals for communicating between sky and ground when Veras separated from Dorian, gliding down to land near us. Reyna brought the bike to a halt, accidentally spraying him with sand.

"The hell's Dorian off to?" I said.

Veras held up a hand, panting as he caught his breath. "Scouting the city. Told me to regroup with you."

"Can he fly alright in that storm?" Reyna asked.

"He said he could, and for us to keep going and he'd meet up when he was done." Veras's words were followed by a dusty cough. "Air's not great."

"Well, the further we go, the less far Dorian'll have to fly back," Reyna said. "We won't reach the city before sunset regardless, and I need to make masks for the two of us." She nudged me. "Remember to use your underlayer when we enter."

I pulled the loose fabric around my neck up over my nose and mouth. It made breathing a little harder, but it was better than choking on dust. It was good that Dorian had the same beneath his own armor.

Veras was worn out, so he rode on the back of Reyna's bike at a slower pace while I jogged alongside them. Nightfall soon turned the distant dust storm into a writhing mass of shadows, and we stopped for the day, finding shelter in a sort of covered amphitheater. The lowest levels of the terraced pit had filled with sand, but there were padded seats higher up that offered a softer place to put our sleeping bags. There were some of those dome-shaped buildings nearby, and up close they seemed similar to adobe houses. Nobody suggested we try to enter one, which I found a little odd, but it wasn't like I was comfortable doing so either. Probably best to get used to sleeping outside anyway, because based on Dorian's maps I expected that would be the case for most of our journey. One upside to being on a dead world was that we could light a fire without worrying about being spotted. Reyna had brought a tin of some gelatinous substance that served as fuel. We clustered around the fire, the heat needed as the air grew cold. Veras kept rubbing his shoulders and adjusting the drape of his wings.

"I don't know how Dorian keeps it up all day," he said. "He's been flying for ages. It's a big city for one person to search."

"He should be back soon," I said. "I don't like that he's on his own, but I'm trying not to worry."

"I didn't say I was worried about him. He's an asshole, why would I be? If anything, I'd be concerned he's going on without us."

"Dorian's usual work requires a support group, and even he knows it," Reyna said.

"It's bad enough being back in this dump again. Relying on Dorian only makes it worse."

"The first two times hardly counted. We were only passing through."

"Those were more than enough."

"I thought you liked travel," I said.

"We can be honest, since none of the original inhabitants are still around," Veras said. "Felar sucks now, and it sucked before the war too. There are too many wonders spread across the universe to waste your leisure time here."

"You weren't like this the last time we passed through," Reyna said.

"It's attached to bad memories now. Andras had never been off Glashower before the war, and seeing dried-up garbage worlds like Felar made him fear he'd never find a good place to call home again." Veras managed a thin smile. "Once on Plesmae, I got him out of the capital as quickly as I could. He was delighted with the Glade on first sight."

"It makes sense now, but I still can't believe you moved out there," Reyna said. "You were such a city boy."

"I know. I think I'd only been there once before on a dare, even though it's so close. It certainly wasn't easy, especially because we only had a tent at first and I didn't know my way around yet. Every time I went to the capital, I was worried I'd get lost or Andras wouldn't be there when I got back, but..."

"But?" I said.

He wiped at his eyes.

"Sorry. I didn't realize."

"It's alright. I may need distracting sometimes, that's all."

"I do have to ask. You did dares?"

"I was young and fun once," he said defensively.

"Veras, you *are* young," Reyna said.

"Well, I was younger, and desperate to fit in with the other new students at med school. At that point there hadn't been a war with the Graft in our lifetime. We didn't really understand when our teachers spoke about the ways doctors needed to be brave. A bunch of us visited the Glade after dark to show off and, ah, had a bad time. We got lost and spent the entire night there, which was cold, wet, and full of nocturnal wildlife—wildlife that evolved without any reason to be afraid of makhali. They were *very* curious about us." He drew his wings in tighter around himself. "I hope we don't repeat that experience on this trip."

"I want to see non-Graft animals," I said.

"No pets," Veras said firmly.

"I didn't say I—"

"No. Pets."

Reyna was trying to hide a smile. I scowled at Veras and put my head on her shoulder while we waited.

Dorian found us soon after that. He landed close by, his boots hitting the packed earth with a satisfying *thump*.

"How was it?" I asked.

"Food first," Dorian said, so I supposed everything was fine. He tore open a pack of rations. We'd waited to eat until he came back.

Veras swallowed some of the ration cubes whole, washing them down with a long swig of water. He caught me staring. "Why do you look so surprised? We didn't have time for nice, long, hot meals in the trauma ward."

"Are they better like that?" I asked.

"They spend less time in your mouth."

I tried it and nearly choked, needing to wave him away as I chugged water.

"So. The city?" Reyna asked.

Dorian grimaced. "Dust up to your knees, and everything looks on the verge of falling apart. Streets are clear but I'd expect some environmental hazards."

"Is your throat okay?" I asked. "You sound a little hoarse."

"Just dehydrated."

"Are we taking turns sleeping tonight?" Reyna asked.

"Always."

She took a long chain beaded with carved ceramic tiles from her supplies and walked around us, encircling our little camp with it. When she connected the two ends, a small veil about fifteen feet across flickered to life over us. The air around the chain buzzed uncomfortably against my skin if I got too close, but there was enough room within our sanctuary for me to avoid it.

"It won't stop much for long," she said, "but it's something."

"Why doesn't Vanguard Base have something like this?" I asked.

"We'd need someone to let us in and out all the time," Dorian said. "And one that large would've needed a lot of maintenance. Bliss isn't a born artisan, but she probably could've kept one running. She felt it wasn't a good fit for us, and I'm glad." He shuddered. "I know she would've constantly locked me out if we'd had a veil around the base. She's probably enjoying time without me around."

"Speaking of going in and out, I won't be held responsible for the consequences of others' poor bathroom timing," Reyna said. "I'm a deep sleeper. Consider yourselves warned."

Between the four of us, Veras and Dorian were the most tired, so Reyna and I took the first shift of the night. I pulled Veras aside before he settled in.

"Can I check you over?" I said. "Andras asked me to."

"He did?"

"He did."

Veras let me roll up his sleeves to check on his arms. Given his recent work in the hospital, I wasn't surprised to see they were a bit scalded. He applied a soothing balm to them himself.

"How are you holding up?" he asked me.

"I've had a little on-and-off chest tightness, but I think it's just from stress," I said.

"Keep an eye on it, and tell me immediately if it gets worse. Flag me down out of the air if you have to." He sighed. "Ella, I have no idea what we'll see on this journey, but it won't be good. Don't feel weak if any of it... sticks with you. I didn't specialize in psychology, but I'm here if you need me."

I just nodded, not wanting to think about what lay ahead.

Dorian had already fallen asleep, still wearing his armor, and soon Veras was quietly snoring. Reyna had started working on masks for her and Veras, appearing deep in concentration. I sharpened my hearing and wrapped my jacket around my shoulders, settling in for several more hours of wakefulness. There was an ill wind over the desert, and I watched the flames recoil from it. A bubble in the gel popped, the sound like a gunshot to my augmented hearing. I spasmed, accidentally getting Reyna's attention. Thankfully, she quickly understood what had happened.

"Ella, you don't need to sharpen your senses just to keep watch. People manage just fine with normal sight and hearing, and the veil will give us time to react," she said.

"I need to know for sure there's nothing out there," I said. "Otherwise I can't relax. It's just a shame that I can't choose what sounds louder when I augment my hearing."

"What's it like, when it doesn't hurt?"

I thought for a moment. "It gets hard to tell what's loud and near from what's loud *or* near. Normally if I heard the footsteps of an approaching monster getting louder, I'd have an idea for how far away or big it is, but when my frame of reference changes... it messes with my understanding of size and distance and time. I can feel my vision wanting to blur so my senses aren't in as much disagreement over what I'm seeing and hearing."

She looked confused.

"Those probably aren't the right words," I said.

"It's your experience. Maybe you *are* using the right ones."

"Maybe? I can't compare my experiences to others' without using language. My ability only complicates it." It wasn't a topic I enjoyed discussing—too abstract, too potentially othering. "I hope the bike can handle whatever terrain's ahead."

"Whatever's ahead is ahead, and we can't change it," Reyna said.

I nodded. Conversation diverted.

"But let's not discuss that now. There might be things that only you've experienced or noticed. That's special, isn't it?"

I shrugged, defeated. "You could probably say the same for everyone."

Reyna tilted her head considering. "I suppose. Still, I think you might have more moments like that than other people." And she returned to her tinkering.

Did I want anything that nobody else had experienced? I wanted Andras to be healthy again, Plesmae and Earth to be safe from the Graft, to go home.

And despite the experience with my fake wings, I wanted to fly. I watched the shrouded city, wanting to borrow Dorian's memories of tumbling through its air currents.

I squeezed my fingers together, then slowly spread them, building a thin membrane between them. I held my hands over the fire and felt the faintest push upwards from the rising hot air. My fingers were only warm, but between them, it felt like I was holding the fire itself.

Of course, there were makhali who could summon and cast flame. But I'd like to think that when they held it, they didn't feel it heating the blood that circulated through them quite like I did.

"I almost forgot," Reyna said suddenly. "For when you're not on watch, of course." She handed me a pair of tinted glasses and hearing protection.

"You made another set?" I asked.

She nodded. "They were in my go bag, just in case."

"Reyna, I've never had friends who do so much to help with my sensory issues before I came to Plesmae."

"Some new things are good," she said gently.

Of course I wanted to go home. But I also wanted to keep my friends, and those two paths felt mutually exclusive.

20

———————

My turn to sleep ended when my ear was tugged. Veras was trying to remove my translation earring. I batted his hand away.

"Ella," he said, sounding in a great deal of pain. "*Please*."

I removed it. He didn't even want the thing. Veras walked a few yards away and then screamed in makhali until his face was a deep, oxygen-deprived bronze. I put my earring back on when he was done.

"It just fully hit him that he was, and will be, sleeping on the ground," Reyna whispered to me. "And that he's had his last shower for a while."

Veras was still catching his breath. "Don't smirk like that," he told Dorian. "I learned it all from tending to you soldiers. The things I've heard..."

"I could teach you more."

Veras grimly shook his head, but he gathered himself by the time we'd finished eating, hydrating, and stretching. We split up again, regrouping at the edge of the city.

Up close, the storm was so full of dust it appeared to be a solid wall. I pulled my underlayer's cowl up over the lower half of my face. We linked arms and kept Reyna's bike between us like an anchor as we passed through. I followed behind Dorian, half blind, struggling through a good twenty feet of whirlwinds that almost deafened me before they spat us out, understanding why an unintelligent creature would balk at passing through.

At first glance, we could've been in a human city in the dead of winter, thick wads of dust falling like snow and covering the streets in an undisturbed layer of off-white. The damaged skyscrapers had clearly been planned out neatly, set in a square grid and reaching straight up; looking down a street and seeing some of them out of alignment and at an angle carried the discomfort of discovering a loose or crooked tooth, somehow worse than some of them having multiple levels or massive chunks missing.

Reyna tried to rev her bike, but the wheels got stuck in the knee-height dust, so we kept together on foot. Even if we hadn't been dragging the bike and our supplies with us, running would've been impossible, any sudden shift of weight making my legs sink in too deep and causing me to trip. Veras practically vibrated with pent-up, agitated energy from being slowed down, but we had no way of communicating long-distance and so were unwilling to split up beyond line of sight.

Despite my own worry about Andras, and the discomfort of feeling like a tourist on a dead world, I felt somewhat sleepy. Last night had been a rough one, but I'd never been a stranger to difficult nights. The falling dust reminded me of December nights when snow cast a muffling blanket over everything. I found it difficult to concentrate, absentmindedly scratching at my bare arms and wishing for damp cold instead of this unbearable dryness.

Dorian, meanwhile, seemed outright angry. His hands kept rising towards his face, fingers running down the underlayer he had pulled up over his nose and mouth as if he could hardly bear to wear it. We got barely ten blocks in before he seemed to snap.

"Let's step inside for a minute," he said. "Just enough to take a breather."

"We just got here," Veras said.

"I said, only for a minute."

Dorian reached for the door of the nearest building, but Reyna stopped him.

"Nobody open anything until I check for structural flaws," Reyna said. "I can check a material's integrity with my magic. Felar's inhabitants had some strong projectile weapons, and the city's had years to fall apart." She frowned. "Not complaining, but I'm surprised more buildings haven't collapsed. I suppose their engineering was another discipline they declined to share with us."

Reyna ran her hands over the wall of that building, frowning, and moved along to the next without a word. I tried not to think about what might've happened if we'd gone barging in. We continued down the street, Reyna questing with her magic before finding a skyscraper she deemed suitable. I had my own hesitations.

"Will there be bodies inside?" I asked, stomach churning.

"Haven't you killed monsters?" Dorian said.

"*People* bodies."

"If there's anything left that isn't Graft, it should at least be dry."

"At least?"

"Would you prefer I lie to you?"

"Possibly."

Dorian scratched at his cowl. "Just get inside so I can take off this awful thing." He wrenched the door open.

He was greeted with a wall of red, wet biomass. It was like half-set gelatin in a mold, beginning to squirm and ooze through the opening. I slammed the door shut. It didn't want to stay closed. I braced my back against it.

"Rocks," I gasped. "Barricade it."

Dorian and Reyna dragged rubble over to brace against the door. I could've sworn I felt a heartbeat pulsing against my spine, something else's body heat warming my back, and broke off contact as soon as we'd jammed the door in place. We retreated down the street, not sure what a minimum safe distance would be, but nothing came after us.

I started to say, "how much of the building do you guys think is—"

"Don't," Veras said. "For the love of all that's good, Ella, just don't. I thought we'd prevented something like this from happening!"

Dorian grimaced. "Whatever was left over must've taken shelter from the wind. Don't know what it's been living off of, but…"

"For the sake of our mental hygiene," Veras said, "we are going to make a note of this to mention to the Citadel on our return, and then try to move on. It doesn't seem to be hostile. Maybe it's just… storage. All other function lost for the sake of survival. That would be alright, wouldn't it? Especially since, I mean, I would *hope* this is the only building like this."

He looked between the three of us as if seeking support. I nodded. I hoped that too.

But as we kept walking, I dared to look in the windows of the buildings we passed, finding them dark and full behind the scratched glass. I felt an intense disgust at the thought of that much flesh gathered together, disgust that manifested as a tightness in my throat and guts, and a horrible itchy, crawling feeling over my uncovered arms. I scratched at the back of one hand, trying not to bring my claws out. I wondered if my whole body would change if I sneezed too hard.

"Ella, that looks a bit alarming," Reyna said.

I looked down. A gauzy square several inches across hung from the back of my hand. Had to be a layer of skin. I tugged at it, and more tore off my hand like a flimsy glove.

"Is this a normal human body function?" Veras asked, tone making it clear he already knew the answer.

"When I've shed like this before, it's because my skin got contaminated," I said. If I concentrated, I could feel the outermost layer of my exposed skin swelling as it sloughed off. I pulled my attention away, revolted by the other details I'd noticed, the breakneck rush of blood and fleshy thickness of my hands if I zoomed that far in.

"You *were* sick last night," Veras accused Dorian.

Dorian tried to protest, but stopping to cough mid-denial didn't help his case.

"We should get inside so we're not being exposed any longer, then

I can examine us. Ella, I know you…" Veras trailed off, looking ashamed.

"You can say it," I said. "It could just be a sensory reaction. It wouldn't be the first time."

Reyna drew our attention to a squat building that was solid concrete, a metal gate blocking the way down.

"Tunnel system beneath the city," she said. "Not sure how far it goes. Before the war, visitors were expected to stay aboveground. Hopefully there won't be as much dust down there, and we can get closer to our destination before needing to come up again."

She started to fiddle with a rusted box full of wires on the wall, but Dorian gathered red energy around his sword and chopped at the gate's hinges, breaking them off. He threw the metal sheet to the side, getting us access to a wide set of dust-covered stairs leading down into darkness.

"Can I go first?" I said.

They all stared at me. I didn't exactly *want* to go first, but I knew my senses were the best in this environment.

"Sure," Dorian said, probably thinking the same strategy I was.

"Are you kidding?" Veras said.

Dorian put an arm around my shoulders. "You can be tied for first, deal?"

I nodded. Veras looked frustrated, but he and Reyna fell into line behind us as we began our descent. Reyna touched the electric lamps we passed, accidentally burning out a few before she figured out how to coax them to life. I scoured the path ahead, trying to be ready for anything—and with an entire alien universe to contend with, that was an especially tall order.

With augmented eyes, I noticed a small shift in the dust ahead of us, even though the rest of the ground and the air was still. This planet had already surprised us. I didn't want to waste time and slow us down pointing out every little odd thing, but noticing things others might not was what I brought to the team.

"Could just be some ventilation system," I told Dorian, pointing it out. "But it kind of reminds me, we have aquatic animals on Earth that come to the surface to breathe and—"

He was already moving, silently gliding down the stairs. He passed over it and then flipped around, sword cleaving down in an arc. The pale dust was stained brown as something writhed, the sword buried in its shoulder, flinging dust everywhere. Dorian wrestled with it before wrenching his sword free and sinking it home somewhere closer to the vitals, killing it.

I saw more dust further down the stairs shifting and approached it with light steps, picking out the shape of the buried monster. Standing behind it, I clasped my fists together, adding bone and muscle. When the graftling emerged I swung my hands down like a makeshift hammer, hitting the back of its neck. The shock of impact vibrated up my arms, carried by the extra bone. The graftling didn't get up. One less threat between us and saving Andras.

"That wasn't too bad," Dorian said, his breathing ragged. His blade was briefly engulfed in scarlet flame, burning away the thick blood coating it. "I've never seen a monster bury itself before. What can you tell us about it?"

Veras's voice shook as he spoke, perhaps fighting off nausea. "I haven't done morgue work before, so I'd appreciate some patience." He steadied himself. "Ella, would you mind moving it around for me so I can get a better look at its features?"

I did as asked, only touching it with my claws, dragging it out of the dust and turning it over. It smelled like I imagined mummies would. Still and observable, it looked like an alligator, leather-baked with a long mouth. Its tiny dull eyes were lifeless.

"There are some already obvious adaptations," Veras said. "The nostrils and eyes are small and on top of the head so it can see and breathe while it remains hidden. Its skin is loose and the stomach appears shrunken, but its muscles aren't atrophied. It doesn't look like anyone's been this way in a long time. Who knows how long it was waiting? It might've dragged itself down here at the end of the last war. It's unusual to see graftlings not actively involved in searching for prey or organic material."

"We should keep an eye out for any potential food sources," Dorian said. "I'd rather not believe it's been hiding here in some kind of hibernation for that long. Our solution was to starve them out, and I'd hate to think even that can't be counted on anymore. Blacksmith, I hope you're writing all that down."

Reyna was, and making quick sketches, all while she took in deep, calming breaths.

"These," Dorian said, gesturing to the graftling remains, "are proof that we'll run into trouble often, and that it may take unexpected forms. Everyone had better be prepared."

Veras nodded as he sanitized my hands, brow furrowed in concentration. I winced, but it didn't feel as bad as expected.

"If you hold extra still," he told me, "I can make sure you feel it as little as possible."

I cooperated, and he did too. Veras didn't argue against my being in front anymore, which was good because I had to navigate us around several more slumbering monsters as we descended, the dust gradually petering out at the base of the stairs, where we found a finally clean room that reminded me of ticket queues at train stations.

Dorian ripped his mask off as soon as we were away from the dust, his strained breathing audible. He scratched at the underside of his wings, shedding fine particles.

Veras pressed his hands against his chest, eyes narrowed in concentration.

"It doesn't seem to be contaminating anything," he said after a full, stressful minute. "Dried-out matter usually doesn't unless rehydrated, but even once it comes into contact with mucus membranes, it's not doing that. It reminds me more of an allergic reaction. It'll make us sick in a more traditional sense with exposure, but it won't... turn us into anything. How sick, I don't know yet. Dorian, can I examine you?"

"I don't need—" Dorian's protests were cut off by a coughing fit. "There's nothing wrong with me." He went still when Veras touched his forehead, one of the few uncovered parts of his body.

"You've got inflammation in your throat and lungs," Veras said. "Have you experienced chronic breathing problems in the past?"

"No."

"Well, you're experiencing problems now." When Veras was using his magic on someone—someone he could actually help—his eyes seemed to unfocus, looking loosely at whatever body part he was focused on. They went to Dorian's wings, and a strange expression took over his face. I couldn't tell if it was concern or pity or surprise, but any one of those scared me in this context. "Dorian, you—"

"I'm *fine*." Dorian pushed him away.

Veras stepped back a little too far and a little too quickly to match his doctorly tone. He checked on Reyna, whose uncovered arms had light patches where the falling dust had touched her.

"It's working on skin contact," he said. "I've never seen anything like it before. If something like this appears on Plesmae, it... this whole city is a trap. The quicker we leave, the better."

"What's making it?" Reyna asked.

We all looked to Dorian, who shrugged. Reyna wrote in her journal, hands shaking.

"We'll need to cover up more when we return to the surface," Veras said. "I hope there's another exit further in."

"It reminds me of a transit center back home," I said. "I'm sure there is."

He didn't look too convinced. That expression changed when we went further down the tunnel and stepped into a giant underground atrium. Beneath the surface, away from the bleaching sunlight and eroding storm, everything was white marble and chrome, an entire metropolis contained under a ceiling set high enough for a makhal to comfortably fly beneath. It was all still and dead, the perfectly preserved corpse of a city. Glass tubes hung from the ceiling and were posted high up on walls, curling and knotting like cursive, full of color-changing liquid like lava lamps. The vast underground cavern sprawled out ahead of us, shopfronts and stalls and big metal boxes attached to rails, more unknown urban landscape stretching beyond the closer wonders.

And, as if all that hadn't been enough, the occasional stairwell led further down still.

"Maybe we try a little harder next time to be less judgmental about what we don't understand?" I said.

"Why would they hide all this from us?" Veras said, stunned.

"It sounds like your species' relationship wasn't great? They might not have trusted you."

He merely nodded, still dumbfounded. Reyna was fondling an abstract sculpture of wire and stone; I figured she was probably taking things in step by step, and left her to it. Dorian had located a map, the big labeled kind you might find in a mall.

"I can't read this, but it seems obvious enough," he said, jabbing his finger at a drawing of a dome labeled with cuneiform-esque writing. "We shouldn't need to worry about going aboveground again."

"Nope. And you know what's even better?"

He raised an eyebrow.

"We may not even need to walk or fly the whole way there."

Reyna was still touching the statue, but her eyes were elsewhere, so I disentangled her from it, putting a hand on Veras's shoulder to lead him along as well.

"Who wants to ride alien public transit?" I asked, guiding them towards one of the railways. "Assuming you can get it working, Reyna? It looks pretty intact."

"I've never even been allowed to board one before," she said. "I would be honored to try."

I slid the door open. The inside was familiar enough, the seats admittedly wider and deeper than I was used to, but there was an obvious control panel. One removed metal sheet and some lucky guesses later, Reyna had hot-wired it, a few lights on the control panel coming to life. I pulled the big lever.

The tram began to glide along its rails, startling everyone but me. By my standards this was a boring ride, just slow movement in one direction, but it seemed to amaze them.

"Based on the map, we should be able to take this most of the way to the rift," I said.

"It's so nice to be moving together without effort," Reyna said. "All our carts need to be pulled, pushed, or have levers turned to make the wheels go. Even my bike needs to be recharged with my magic. Would've made schlepping all our equipment and supplies during the last war so much easier, though I suppose that would've required rails to be set up."

"You can have big moving vehicles that don't need rails," I said.

I could almost hear the *click* of Reyna placing that in a mental filing cabinet for later. We crowded to the windows that lined each side of the tram, watching our surroundings. I wished it had been under better circumstances, but I was enjoying this, showing my friends applications of technology they'd never seen before—when I wasn't being thrust into the role of chaperone, anyway. Despite all the tools she had lashed to her belts, Reyna could move almost silently when she wanted to. But *zap* was a rather unique noise, and it caught my attention.

"Reyna, please don't risk breaking the tram or electrocuting your-self," I said.

"I just want to learn how it works," she said.

"I know. But I don't want to, I get that there's nobody here, nobody to mind, but we don't want to disturb anything more than we have to, right? It's not what they would've wanted."

That seemed to make her sulk, but she extricated her arms from the mess of wires beneath the control panel, joining us at the windows. The tram occasionally squeaked, likely from disuse, but it was otherwise impressively silent. I shut my eyes for a moment, lulled down memory lane to thoughts of school buses and falling asleep in the backseat of the family car as a little kid. The memories had a distance to them I found painful; you usually don't pine for driving when it's still an everyday experience.

Dorian broke me out of it by mashing my face against the seat back.

"What—"

"More graftlings."

I peered through the gap between two seats, trying to keep out of view, everyone else similarly crouched. The white stone, the still-shiny metal, even the neon lights clearly fit together. The scene the tram was passing by did not.

This must've been some kind of business hub, multiple levels of open area on either side of us. The Graft had fully moved in. The tram glided past at least a half mile where the entire floor was covered in plant-like forms growing in clusters. The entire underground had been well lit so far, and until now I hadn't considered that might be a bad thing; the pseudo-plants grew up towards the lights, fleshy leaves spread wide to drink it in. Between their raised roots were clumps of red spongy material. As we passed by, a monster—not something desiccated and crusty, but sleek and new—gobbled some of the sponge down before carrying more off like a bird seeking twigs for its nest. Many other monsters were involved in similar tasks, the bright light glinting off dark plate-covered sides and backs. Giant rectangular prisms many yards wide stretched from the bottom floor to the ceiling. I had to swallow back a wave of nausea when I realized that it wasn't that the residents of Felar had a penchant for dark red, but that the prisms were translucent and something dark red had... moved in. There must've been literal tons of raw Graft material in just this area alone.

With rather horrible timing, the tram slowed as it pulled up to a station. It was obviously a big moving object, but I wasn't sure if the dozen or so graftlings I could spot within earshot cared about big moving objects they found inedible. Since the tram still had power, there might be other machines that were automated and still running that they were used to. So far, they seemed unbothered.

The tram stopped, and its door automatically slid open with the loud, clear ring of a bell. Every monster turned its head.

21

———————

Dorian shoved us all off the tram before leaping on top with a powerful beat of his wings, stomping on its metal roof, an obvious distraction. I looked between him and Reyna and Veras, torn. The monsters were yowling now, so I felt the time to be quiet was past.

"Dorian, come on!" I yelled.

He waved me off. He had the high ground, and a confident smile to match as the first graftlings climbed up the side of the tram to meet him. The first lost its head to his blade, the others' throats pierced with quick jabs before he kicked them off.

His smile faded as a truly horrendous number of monsters approached, dozens clambering up from lower levels of the atrium, previously unseen others dropping from the ceiling and filling the air with their bat-like wings. I clambered up the tram, grabbed his ankle.

"Dorian!"

"I—"

"I'd rather have one hundred alive monsters and one alive you than one hundred dead monsters and one dead you." Thanks, brain. Very cogent.

Dorian wrapped fire around his blade and blew hard on it, struggling through a coughing fit, creating a blinding blaze of red magic as a distraction for the winged graftlings. He dropped down with me and the four of us ran, pulling Reyna's bike and our supplies with us. We went down a side street into a warren of hallways. Dorian kicked open the first door after we rounded a corner and broke line of sight, getting us into what must've been an apartment. He and I grabbed the closest piece of furniture, a heavy desk with a stone top, and barricaded the door with it. I paused, listening closely with sharpened senses, trying to tune out my friends' ragged breathing. Outside: claws scraping against tile, guttural calls. Felar's underground was built strong and solid, chambers packed together like honeycomb, sounds vibrating through shared walls and floors. I couldn't tell if the other unidentifiable noises I heard were biological or mechanical, if they were small and nearby or distant and titanic; behind me, the sound of Reyna desperately digging through her bag could've been a far-off trash compactor at work. The air was vibrating with waiting magic, heat from Veras and Dorian gathering in the undisturbed coldness of our hiding place. I pressed my ear fully against the door, needing less to sort through.

I heard monsters draw closer. I breathed with them, lungs falling into an unfamiliar pattern of gasps and growls. Three individuals, different in pitch, snapping their jaws at each other. I tracked their paths, found them checking each others' work, too dull to properly work together. All it would've taken was one of them staying behind, and eventually we would've made a noise it heard.

The thought of fresh meat must've been too exciting for them to practice patience. I didn't say anything when the graftlings rushed on, and no more took their place. I just slid down the door, and that communicated enough to my friends.

Reyna let out a panicked laugh that quickly crumpled into a sob. Veras tried to hold her but she seemed to find squeezing a bag containing her tools to her chest more comforting. She crept further into the apartment, finding a quiet corner to recover in.

"Was that... normal?" I whispered.

Dorian let out his own strained laugh. "No, Ella, that was not fucking normal."

Veras was going through his medical supplies in one of the bike's saddlebags. "Even graftlings that come from plant material are animals that need to eat. We sometimes think of them as an ecosystem, because they have a lot of body diversity and different roles, but they don't actually have lower trophic levels, organisms that can make their own food without eating anything else. They're not *supposed* to."

"If they're able to feed themselves now?" Dorian said. "For years at a time without new food? We're screwed. We'd have to wipe out every last shred of them on this planet to be sure they'll never come back."

"If the Graft here have figured it out, does that mean there are more like them on other planets?" I asked.

Veras hesitated. "It's complicated, because we don't understand how much they 'know' or can 'tell' each other. We've seen traits become more common in a specific population, and then spread to other populations when two of them meet up, but we've also seen separate colonies display similar forms at similar times without being in contact with each other. As far as we knew."

"Oh. Cool." I looked around for a comfortable-looking whatever to collapse on. Everything remotely suitable was sort of bucket-shaped, fit for a species other than my own, but I made do with something that was like a foam tub with one long wall missing. It was a bit too scary to consider what that news meant for the universe at large. The closest I could get was, "Berith's going to be just thrilled to hear that."

"Maybe we should go back," Dorian said uncertainly. "Just to tell him—"

"Either it's happening already on Plesmae and they'll find out for themselves, or it's not and it can wait," Veras said. "I'm continuing on, regardless of if anyone else is."

"Got a plan, boss?"

"We rest long enough for me to check on everyone and get some strength back," Veras said.

Nobody argued. Veras checked my hands one more time for contamination before making his rounds with Reyna and Dorian. I took out my phone, wanting to see pictures of my family again. Already this journey was so much more overwhelming than I could've imagined. I'd tried to keep most of my letters to them optimistic, but did it make sense to have a final goodbye written, just in case?

No more thinking about that. I distracted myself with poking around the apartment. I wandered up to a wall covered in decorations. Most of it was abstract lacquered paintings, but there were smaller pieces too. Framed pictures of several alien individuals, dark-shelled bipedal creatures of varying sizes. They felt... familiar.

When I'd read through that book of alien anatomy with Andras, he'd never mentioned the shelled species I'd tried to copy had come from a world so close to Plesmae.

I looked at the odd-shaped furniture, the kitchen with its rectangular faucet and kiln-shaped oven. There was even a bathroom with a toilet, which was great because I needed to vomit. The ration cubes didn't leave much behind in my stomach to spit up, but that didn't stop me.

Veras rushed over and placed a hand on my back. His magic burned, falling in that confusing space between discomfort and pain, and I instinctively shoved him away before I could find out which it was. I stared at him, feeling tears start to form. Why would he do that to me?

"I'm sorry," he said. "I have a headache, wasn't thinking." He touched my forehead, probably checking for fever. I didn't let him do that either, couldn't stand being touched at the moment. "Ella, you did your job earlier, now I need to do mine."

"Just leave her alone," Dorian said, pulling him away.

"We still don't know the full effects of—"

"When you're a soldier sent out into the field, and that field used to be people's homes, you see things like this, and it hurts. You weren't enough to stop it, and you feel even more like shit because you're tearing apart the place too, and maybe even what became of the people who once lived there."

Veras sounded surprised, apologetic. "Dorian, I..."

"I wouldn't expect you to understand. The hurt were brought to you. You never saw this part. Give her space."

Dorian wasn't wrong, but that wasn't the only reason my stomach was rebelling. Copying that species' anatomy suddenly felt obscene, just like the Graft taking them over was, and I felt renewed bitterness towards my ability. Copying just felt safer. Both in terms of my health, and... maybe it was easier, emotionally, to be halfway between two existing things than to be something new altogether.

Whatever it took to prevent more disaster, I had to do. I had to learn. Eventually I calmed my breathing, wiped my face clean, and returned to my friends.

"Reyna, are you doing okay?" I said.

She looked down at her hands. "Probably not, but this world has never wanted me on it, so I'd like to be off it now."

I touched Veras's arm. "How about you? It's okay if you're not ready to move yet."

"I'm far more used to war than you are," Veras said. "You don't have to doubt me."

"I'm just worried you could be sick."

"You don't think I'm strong enough to get through it?"

"I didn't mean it like that," I said, just then realizing how dark his mood was and that those words could also mean yes.

The look he gave me was surprisingly hostile. "Be grateful for what you have. I'm practically powerless here."

"At least your magic has never led anyone to treat you like a monster."

His face flushed bronze. "I've said sorry. What do you want me to do about that now?"

"I want you to know that on this journey, when I change into something that makes you afraid or disgusted, I'm doing it to protect you," I said.

The words were out of my mouth before I could stop them, and they made Veras look like he'd be the next one to start retching in the bathroom. There were plenty more things I could've said, that I was angry with myself or missing my parents or terrified of how tired I already was, things that would've helped him understand how I was doing. But I didn't.

"Arguing will only delay us longer," Dorian said, somewhat swaying on his feet. "Are we ready or not?"

I wasn't sure of the answer, but Veras and Reyna nodded. I could see the shakiness in Veras's hands as he packed up his sleeping bag. He was ill, and he'd have to deal with the consequences of it. He was a healer. He should know that.

I looked to Reyna for comfort, but she wouldn't meet my eyes. "You're both my friends. I can't take a side between you," she murmured to me.

"I'm not asking you to."

"But it might come across that way. I'm sorry."

Fine. Whatever. Why waste time talking when we could be moving? I returned to the bathroom, letting my noise guide me through its cabinet's contents.

"I don't know if this is deodorant or perfume, but I'm sorry either way," I said, giving Dorian a thorough spray with an aerosol can. This was not the time for the old spray-wait-walk method of scent application. This was body odor erasure time.

"That's actually more pleasant than I was expecting," I said, while Dorian gagged on my violent application of damp-cave smell. "Doesn't even smell organic. Hopefully it'll cause some confusion."

Veras and Reyna grimly presented themselves for their own spray-down. Yes, I did save myself for last so I could acclimate to it. I again listened at the door, making sure there was nothing on the other side before opening it.

We snuck along a walkway at the edge of the atrium, huddling behind waist-high walls of advertisements. More flying graftlings nested on the ceiling, where they had their own thick layer of developing biomass to tend. A cluster of them hanging upside down like a colony of bats shifted as we neared a gap in the wall.

Dorian flicked his wrist at Reyna. "Quick. Something small and heavy you won't miss."

Reyna stared at him as though he'd spoken a new language, but she searched through the saddlebags and handed him a rough metal ingot. She made a small noise of protest when he flung it, the monsters' attention drawn by the sound of shattering glass on the other side of the atrium. We rushed past.

The main atrium tapered into a big hallway up ahead, signs with pictures of a dome pointing us in the right direction, but we didn't get to leave without more trouble. One of the glass prisms shattered near the bottom, releasing its contents.

It would make sense, I reflected, to have your aboveground-inside and underground-inside be connected, so you didn't have to step out into the desert to pass between them. And it would also make sense, if you were a species of weird alien goop monsters with aspirations of universal domination, that if you needed a space to stash all your work-in-progress biomass while still giving your individual monsters room to run around, you'd take advantage of that.

The sheer amount of organic material that came pouring out of the cracked glass could've flooded a football stadium. Instead of spreading out and growing thinner as it covered more area, it stayed waist-height as it rolled towards us.

Reyna straddled and revved her bike, the engine stuttering from the dust it had ingested. Dorian threw Veras over his shoulder and booked it. I shoved the bike from behind, the engine engaging, and ran after them. The biomass moved slower than we did, but not by much; its pace was steady, untiring. It followed us along walkways and around corners, more than just a mindless landslide.

Finally we found stairs, the first steps in our ascent to the surface, shallow enough to give Reyna a bumpy but manageable ride. Unfortunately there was a gate, set below a decorative archway. Unlike the first gate we'd encountered, this one seemed built to withstand a riot. Dorian dropped Veras so he could focus on gathering his magic around his sword, but the metal was too thick to bend or break easily once it was heated. Reyna went straight for the electrical box on the wall while Veras and I stood with our backs to the gate.

The ooze hit the bottom of the stairs and began to rise up the stairs like high tide covering the coast.

"Blacksmith, if you don't have that open soon—" Dorian warned.

"I'm trying! They never let me learn!" Sparks flew between her fingers. She shocked herself, crying out in pain, kept going. The gate neglected to obey her requests; they must've been incorrectly worded.

"The lights!" Veras said.

I looked up. More of those colorful lava-lamp tubes decorated the archway.

"I had a patient, he was working on a light when it broke, he got some of the fluid on him. It's highly toxic to their species. If all of *that* is made from them, it might still be hurt by it."

Like mercury in a thermometer, I thought. All fun and games until something leaks. I could make myself strong, yes, but strong enough to rip a four-inch-thick metal pole out of the ground? Strong enough to climb up the slick walls and break the glass? That I wasn't sure of.

I became aware of a low groaning noise that I first thought was the biomass. Reyna was squeezing one of the poles. Sweat ran down her face as the metal distorted like taffy in her hands. She twisted with her whole body, the metal screeching. One side of the arch bent, reaching a point of no return where gravity demanded the other half follow suit.

The whole contraption had looked so light and delicate from below, but by the time it came crashing down on the sludge it was huge, gallons of colorful fluid spraying everywhere, for a moment painting the biomass in bright shades. Then the spots and puddles darkened. The biomass seemed incapable of vocalizing, but the fluid sizzling where it made contact was sound enough to communicate suffering. Its edges withered and receded; whether it was a complete or only localized death we were seeing, it stopped the biomass from pursuing us further and gave Reyna time to work her magic on the electrical box. Finally the gate creaked open and we rushed through, shutting it behind us. As we continued up the stairs I could hear the slithering, skin-on-skin noises of the biomass beginning to follow us again, though we were able to leave it far behind.

We'd navigated correctly, and reached the surface, finding ourselves in a great glass dome ribbed with metal struts, its giant entrance to the aboveground street thankfully sealed shut by the makhali on their departure. In painfully recent times this would've been visitors' first glimpse of Felar, and it was suitably grand. The rift swirled in the center, surrounded by empty queue lines and what might've been a security booth. I went to lean up against one of the dome's walls, forehead pressed to it so I could cool down.

The sun had disappeared while we were underground, the scratched but otherwise clear glass of the dome letting us see our dark surroundings. After what I'd seen underground, it was harder to imagine I was in a city on Earth, especially without any electric lights on. The darkness made the otherwise familiar shapes of skyscrapers into malicious looming shapes. Some of them were already irregular from damage, but I thought I saw movement and sharpened my night vision.

The tops of the skyscrapers stirred as what had appeared to be rubble unfolded to reveal water-rich petals and release showers of fresh, contaminated dust. No wonder Dorian hadn't seen any of this. He'd flown through at the wrong time. I explained this to the others.

"So at any point," Veras said, "we could get killed by something we hadn't noticed because we weren't looking at the right time or in the right way."

This seemed too negative to me. "We're better prepared now than—"

"Don't try to make it good."

I kept my mouth shut as we left this ruined world. One more rift. One step closer to saving Andras. One step further from home.

22

The land on the other side of the rift must've been controlled by Felar's residents in the past, though it appeared they'd only fed on it, leaving behind a smattering of distant towers and old roads. Nearby was a crumbling and much smaller version of the station we'd just left, and a tower whose central shaft was drilled into the ground, perhaps something akin to an oil rig. From Dorian's maps, I knew it was mostly uncolonized worlds between us and Glashower, which was now my preference after what we'd just dealt with.

We set up camp barely a mile from the rift. We'd escaped the dust, but not its effects: Dorian was taking great, wheezing breaths that didn't seem to supply him with as much air as he needed, and my three companions were struggling to walk straight, eyes and noses streaming, hands and wings shaking. Veras got out his medicines, looking for anything that might help.

"If we're following the assumption that this is like an allergic reaction, then I may only be able to manage symptoms until the irritant is gone," Veras said. "Dorian, I can't burn the remaining dust out of your lungs without harming you. And we only have so much water to clean up with."

I was already shedding the uppermost layer of my exposed skin to remove any leftover dust. The others were stuck using damp cloths. Dorian especially was struggling with brushing the dust out of the short fur on the front of his wings, so I helped him comb through it. I could feel him trembling with exhaustion through his wings.

"Maybe we could, um, do a group cathartic scream?" I suggested, feeling it might help us all leave that awful place behind.

"Why," Veras said, "would anyone want to do that?"

"You had your swearing fit *literally* today."

He glared at me. I glared back.

"I'd do it if my voice wasn't shot," Dorian said. "Later?"

Reyna was still trying not to pick sides, which seemed to mean pretending not to exist. I wanted to do the same, to become something untouchable and safe until I was ready to face the world again, but that was beyond my ability.

That power may have kept me safe on Felar, but even I felt unwell. Brittle, somehow. Like I'd shed too much and only had one microscopically thin layer of skin left. But I had the most energy out of the group. Once Veras had doled out what help he could—makhali medicines that I, the alien, could not safely take without the risk of being poisoned—I told them all to sleep while I kept watch. Dorian protested at first, but even he couldn't stay awake for more than thirty minutes. I figured I'd wait for someone to wake up on their own, or until I couldn't stay awake any more to get my own rest.

That left me with hours alone to kill. Reyna had spent much of our time that first watch quietly coexisting with me, and that had been enough. I couldn't understand why I felt so much more lonely and bored when she was still right next to me, just asleep. I fidgeted a while before getting out my phone, my thumb hovering over my reference album. How many times had I changed myself since leaving home? How many more would it take? I scrolled through my photos with a casual curiosity that quickly skewed obsessive, not daring to stop on one for more than a second in case I realized I'd created a new, permanent normal for myself. I ran my hands over my calves, rolled my wrists, squeezed my hips. The only way to be sure was to have someone else check for me, but I could imagine how that would go. Dorian would probably point out every new muscle fiber and tell me I should be proud. Reyna might get too distracted handling a functioning phone. Veras would likely suggest this wasn't healthy.

I'd always known it wasn't.

I turned the skin of my forearms into different textures, trying to recreate the feel of tree bark and moss and leaves from the Glade here. It calmed the obsessive spiral my brain had been stuck in, but substituted it for homesickness, for Earth and Plesmae. I missed Andras. I missed my parents. I missed having someone around to be strong for me, and while I didn't regret my choice, I hated that I—that this body of mine—suddenly had so much riding on my shoulders. I knew from experience that was an unstable foundation.

ALTHOUGH EVERYONE WAS SLOWLY on the mend, Dorian and Veras weren't feeling well enough to fly for the next few days. We took turns on the bike, either Reyna and Veras or Dorian and I, while the other two walked. Veras especially wasn't managing the increased time on foot well. Mornings, or whatever we called mornings as we traveled across worlds whose day-night cycles weren't synced up, were uncomfortably quiet between us, a bitterness entering the air each time Veras examined himself and Dorian and realized today would be another slow day.

In a small stroke of good fortune, we came across a clean-running river the third day, which let us not only fill up on fresh water but wash up. Dorian and Veras let Reyna and I go first, finding somewhere else to be and look. I tried to be quick. I wasn't sure why Veras hadn't pushed to clean up first, but knew that he needed it soon.

"Do you think he ever takes it off?" Reyna asked when we had finished and the men were taking their turn.

"What?"

"Dorian. His armor."

Taken aback, I could only stare.

"I'm asking as the person who made it," she clarified. "Magical items eventually need maintenance, especially with heavy use. And he sleeps in it."

"I mean, logistically speaking, he has to take it off sometimes," I said.

"I made it to be comfortable, but still," Reyna said. "The amount of wear it must've experienced—"

Dorian was suddenly striding over and, sure enough, fully dressed in his armor, which he'd also cleaned. He sat beside us and stretched his wings to bask in the sun, momentarily content, and then looked between our startled faces. "What?"

"Reyna has a question for you," I said.

"Actually, I believe Ella was the one with the question," she said.

We stared each other down.

"What's the question?" Dorian asked.

I didn't answer.

"Alright then," he said with a shrug, and went back to enjoying the sun's warmth, eyes closed.

It was odd to see him like this, awake but still, like finally getting a clear photograph of something from my Enigma back home. The thin, short hairs at the edges of his face appeared almost pink against his pale skin. The same happened where his eyebrows grew sparse at the ends. His face had a delicate bone structure, it was just hard to believe that when the expressions it held were usually so intense.

One brown eye opened and met my staring. "Remembered your question?"

"You seem to have bounced back from... the awfulness," I said.

"That's not a question."

"Guess I still can't remember it."

"Your hair's going to be a mess if you let it air dry like that," he said.

"What is it with you and hair?" I asked.

"It can get in the way when you're fighting for your life," he said. "But it's also a means of self-expression, so I don't want anybody to feel like they have to cut it. And when you're wearing all armor from the neck down, it's the main part of you that can look disheveled."

"I wasn't expecting that serious an answer."

"Why not?"

I shrugged.

"You have to take care of your body," he insisted. "If you want it, that includes hair. The trick to hair," he sounded not just serious but on edge now, "is that you can't be too gentle with it."

I laughed.

"You need a firm, guiding hand."

I had to keep holding back my laughter while he messed with my hair, strong hands finger-combing through it. Dorian left a few shorter locks loose from the braid at the edges of my face for security.

"Is that enough?" he said.

I wanted to say no so that he'd have to do it all over again. It was just the pressure on my scalp that I wanted, not Dorian specifically doing it, but asking was still too embarrassing. Reyna was right next to us but preoccupied with her bike's engine, melting into the background. "It's good. Thank you."

"No problem. Your hair is straight, like mine, so it's easy."

"I'm glad at least some part of me is easy to take care of."

"Are you really that complicated?"

"I don't want to be," I said quietly.

He tugged on my exposed earlobe. "Overdone it yet?"

"Not since I was in the hospital."

"Can't be that hard to take care of if you learn from your mistakes."

I... had no idea what was happening right now. I didn't know what flirting looked like, if this was it. I'd never done it, never had it done to me that I knew of. "Any sign of Veras yet?"

Dorian looked in the Forbidden Direction. "Nope."

"It'll probably take him a while to get as clean as he wants," I said.

I checked the unadjusted time on my phone, experiencing a sucker punch of wrongness from seeing it was almost midnight at home. After another half hour, Veras still wasn't back. Dorian went to the river and returned alone.

"Still there," he said. "Says he isn't done yet. He's decent, if you want to bug him yourself."

I'd made a promise to Andras. I found Veras kneeling on the river's shore, scrubbing his arms.

"You've been at it for a while," I said.

"I'm not done," he said, keeping his back to me.

"Is there something tangible you're trying to remove, or the thought of what could be there?" I asked.

He didn't answer.

"I don't mean it in a rude way."

Still silence. I sidled up to him. His arms from the elbow down looked like he'd taken sandpaper to them. But he kept doing it.

"You'll scratch your skin off if you keep this up."

When that didn't do anything, I looked him over. This seemed to require intervention, I just had to figure out how to do it in a way that wasn't even more harmful.

"Veras, come rest," I said in my gentlest voice, reaching for his shoulder. "I'll bring you more water from the river to wash up with later, but you need a break first."

He smacked my hand away before it got anywhere close to him.

"Now that you've touched me, do you need to clean yourself again?" I asked before I could stop myself.

Veras made an awkward escape, wet wings making takeoff hard but not stopping him from flying off in a random direction. I trekked back to our campsite and stood there, defeated, not sure how to describe what had just happened.

"We saw," Dorian said.

"How do I fix it?" I asked.

"I wouldn't worry. He's on the most important mission of his life, he'll be back. I don't mind having a bit more time to get over the last of these damn breathing problems. Better to have a rest day and go far tomorrow than strain ourselves today."

"What if something happens to him?"

"He's not stupid. He sees something bad, he'll come running straight to us for help, and then we'll deal with it. Come here?"

I sat beside him. Dorian gently squeezed my scalp, the pressure helping me relax. He knew. Not everything, but enough to get me through right now. I took the chance to sleep for a bit during the day and then took first watch by myself, sans veil.

Veras returned soon after it got dark. I faced the fire as he slumped to his sleeping bag, not sure if I should apologize for trying to touch him, or ask him what the fuck I was supposed to do when he was in a crisis. It felt like I should do at least one of those, but my throat cinched tight around the words.

"Ella?" he whispered.

"What?"

"Your... thing. Your autism. How long have you had it?"

I wasn't in a teaching mood. "People are born with autism."

"Oh. Never mind, then."

"What?" I repeated, getting irritated.

"My other question doesn't make sense anymore. Forget about it."

I shut my eyes, trying to convince myself it was cozy here and I could unwind.

"How have you dealt with your sensory issues for so long?" he asked.

"I thought I was supposed to forget about it."

"I'm scared," he admitted. I turned to face him. He appeared small in the dim light of the fire, perched on his sleeping bag with his wings tightly wrapped around him.

"Of?"

"Of having my hygiene fixation for the rest of my life."

Oh geez. It was certainly something I could relate to, but I didn't... I'd never been expected to give advice to or comfort another person about anything like my sensory issues. But I did want to, even if I wasn't quite sure how to go about it. "How long have you had it for?"

"Four and a half years."

"You've managed to live with it for this long," I said. "Not to minimize what you're dealing with, but this moment, this trip, it's not what life will always be like."

"Is that how you cope?"

"I don't like to use that word. Coping to me should be a rare occasion, not something I do every week." That was often the case, but not using that word made it easier to lie to myself.

"But is it?"

I shrugged. "It doesn't help me much when I'm suffering. And I have to assume it'll get bad again. You should probably talk to someone else about this."

"Who else is there?" Veras asked, miserable.

Of course I'd be the last resort. My face was hot and wet. I wiped my eyes dry.

"Ella, I didn't mean—it's not like I don't want to talk to you. And I know you were trying earlier. We're different, but similar in a way I haven't encountered before."

Veras dragged his sleeping bag closer and squeezed my shoulder. I did not react.

"Ella?"

"We're different," I said. "And you keep holding that against me."

He retreated, dragging his sleeping bag away. There was a tired frustration in his voice, that of an adult not in the mood to argue with a child, when he said, "You shouldn't be keeping watch on your own."

I ignored him. This was supposed to be what I was good at, being alert. I closed my eyes and rested my palms on the ground, covering them in the most sensitive skin cells and delicate, vibration-detecting hairs I could. I could feel movement on the ground but not its direction or distance, meaning it likely wouldn't be a useful ability most of the time, but it was something new and it kept me occupied. It told me when Veras stopped trying to stay awake and lay down, and when he stopped fitfully moving around. We shared no more words that night.

~

Travel day 6: Arrived on our fourth world from Plesmae yesterday. This one has some life on it, even if it's only roots and grass. Thick algae honestly might be more accurate than grass. Not sure if that's all there ever was, or all that's left. The landscape here is layered and uncooperative. On top are lopsided rolling grassy hills as far as you can see, but the ground is split between them. The cracks started out just an inch wide, but they've gotten wider as we've traveled, to the point where Reyna and I have to keep getting off the bike to get it over the gaps. At least the boys are flying again. Right now this world is frustrating me, but I almost wish I could return someday and properly explore it. Once the cracks widened, I could see that below the hills is one continuous cavern. It's like giant termites carved out a home for themselves, leaving dirt-filled roots to form a shield of earth to protect them from even larger birds. If you look down at the right angle, so your view is aligned with the sunlight, you can see it's a drop of at least forty feet. Maybe more until you hit solid ground, since the cavern has a layer of water at the bottom. When the wind blows, I can hear it passing through below us. It's eerie, but it feels like it's inviting me down there.

Extra tired today from passing the bike and supplies across the gaps. Has to be done carefully now that there's several feet of open air between the hills. Reyna threatened me with an unknown but horrible fate if I dropped her bike. She's been extra fussy about our supplies today, even more than the rest of us. We're all aware that if we lose them, we're screwed. I think she might be missing her stuff from home. I try not to worry about if she's upset with me anymore, but I did almost fail to grab the bike. My body is here, but my mind keeps wandering. I feel lost and alone even though I'm neither.

~

I WAS RELIEVED for quite a few reasons when Veras and Dorian felt well enough to fly again, the most selfish of them being that it gave Veras and I some distance. As the landscape grew wilder, Veras and Dorian split up to scout out the best path for Reyna and I on the motorbike. Dorian soon landed beside us, hitting the ground a bit harder, I thought, than he probably needed to, as if the whole armor-clad-angel-descending-from-above bit wasn't attention-grabbing enough for him. I didn't like that I could feel the impact through my soles; it was most calming to assume the ground we were on was sturdy and stable. I watched Veras circle and hover around the hill we were currently on, wishing he'd just accept he'd have to touch the dirty ground already. It wasn't his fault, I knew that, but it was still irritating me.

"You were walking on it yesterday," I called up to him, trying to keep my tone reserved and logical instead of snappy. Okay, I supposed there was a bit more exposed mud here compared to before, but—

Damn, Veras looked pale. He dropped like a rock, almost landing on Reyna and I.

"Go," he whispered, shoving us towards the next hill. "Just pick a direction and go. *Quietly.*"

Dorian drew his sword as we moved towards the edge of the hill. Reyna jumped across first, barely ready in time before Dorian shoved her bike across the gap. Veras followed her, almost slipping on a muddy patch when he jumped and when he landed. I frowned. Most of the exposed patches of earth were just random blobs, but the two he'd stepped in were fan-shaped, more of them extending out in either direction; the indents went deeper on the side I was on, as if something had clawed into the ground.

Tracks.

I motioned for Veras and Reyna to keep going. I sharpened my hearing, trying to listen past the keen of the wind as it swept through the caverns below us. I could hear a peculiar squelching sound. Holding my breath, I clung to the hill's edge and looked down into the gap.

Below me, the limited sunlight that angled through the gap struck thick sludge and a set of glossy eyes that, on meeting my gaze, dilated.

I leapt back from the edge, my body language communicating all I needed to. Dorian was battle-ready, but the red lightning wrapped around his sword was erratic and faltering. I had to make this quick. If Dorian grew tired, I couldn't trust him to flee before he was too exhausted to. I wasn't going to lose him.

My arms and legs lengthened and swelled, shoulders and under-layer stretching to accommodate rippling muscles that would let me crush and rip with my sharp, thick claws. I pulled my underlayer up over my nose and mouth, my vision darkening as an extra eyelid slid into place to protect me from splashing blood.

Graftlings came crawling up from below, thick front legs and gnarled claws reaching over the edge of the hill to leverage the rest of their fish-like bodies up. They shook themselves, blinking away sleep.

I put myself between the dozen monsters and Dorian, Reyna, and Veras. I should've been scared for my own safety, but that felt like a secondary concern. I didn't know how the monsters before me were constructed, but until I had a reason to think otherwise... I imagined a snapped neck or spine, a lacerated throat or crushed windpipe, was universally fatal.

I lunged at the nearest one, catching it by the throat and squeezing until something cracked. I kicked at another, my leg gaining extra weight mid-swing, some part of my upper body growing mass to keep me balanced. The impact of my foot against their chest should've hurt, but it was deadened by the additional soft tissue I'd grown; it left the graftling floundering in the mud, a deep indent in its side. Hard plates appeared on the back of my arms in time to stop a slicing blow. I clawed at throats and smashed bones and threw one enemy into another, aware that Dorian was at work with his sword, but he was moving around me, doing clean-up. *I* was the threat.

The skirmish couldn't have lasted all that long, but it left me feeling heavy and weak while Dorian finished off the remaining monsters. I stood panting among their corpses, unsure if the chaos was over. Dorian's sword and armor were covered with dark, sticky blood, but he appeared fine. We moved to a new hill, rejoining Reyna and Veras on cleaner ground.

"Looks like you went all in," Dorian said.

"Whatever it takes."

"I've just never seen you like this."

I shrugged, disliking how heavy my shoulders felt. There was a weight over my whole body that grew worse by the second. We'd left a horrifying tableau behind us—*I* had left it. Dorian's fighting was much cleaner than mine, and didn't create painfully bent and split bodies. I didn't realize my sense of smell was reduced until it started to return, bringing with it blood and rot and spilled guts.

Veras hovered his hands over my arms. The filth on them burnt and fell off in thick clumps. If I didn't look behind me again, if I breathed in the smell of scorched keratin from my decontaminated claws so that it drowned out the other stenches, maybe I could move on for now. Put thought of the violence I'd dealt somewhere else.

You're not good at knowing how other people are feeling, I reminded myself. Try not to think about how Veras isn't meeting your eyes right now.

"Thanks," I mumbled.

He nodded and did the same for Dorian. And then he crossed his arms and waited, glancing at my modifications.

"We'll be here a while if you're waiting for me to undo my work," I told him. "I won't have the energy to replace this until I've rested, and we need to make up for lost time."

"If you're exhausted, we need to stop."

"I didn't say I was," I said, frustrated. "I'm saying replacing this *would* exhaust me."

"So you're close to exhaustion."

"How many times do I need to say I'm fine? You don't understand how tiring doing this can be. This is," my mouth had realized it before my mind, "this is the most I've ever changed myself."

"I know. You hardly look like yourself."

I started walking. Veras had never been able to physically keep me from doing anything.

We stuck together on foot for the moment, worried about more graftlings appearing. Despite my insistence on pushing ahead, the others went past me. Maybe it was the slight hunch to my back, but I wasn't moving too quickly. I tried to speed up, but stumbled. My hands and feet were going numb, a problem I thought I'd learned how to fix. Why was it back? It would just have to sort itself out as I walked. We'd already lost so much time. I put all my concentration into crossing the gaps between hills, needing to carefully coordinate my exhausted body. We traveled far enough and the air smelled clean enough that I was confident we were past the tainted water.

The distance between my friends and I had grown, so when my legs buckled and I fell on my face, nobody noticed at first. The numbness had crept up to my knees and elbows. I gasped for words, struggling to speak and not knowing why.

"You're not taking watch tonight," I heard Veras call out. I couldn't have responded even if I tried.

Veras turned around and was running to my side in a moment, the others close behind. His warm hand settled on my back. He was saying something I couldn't understand. Everyone was talking and it was all nonsense to me, panicky meaningless sounds added to the already overwhelming noise of my own heartbeat.

"Breathe," Veras said in English.

I sucked in air, but there was nowhere in my chest for it to go. Veras tried to help me even though it had never worked before. His magic was a burning star, a punishment, against my skin. He tried to adjust my posture to clear up my airway, but the growth I'd added made that difficult.

"Tell me what you changed. Right now," Veras said.

I just pointed at myself. Wasn't it clear?

"Did you change your mouth?"

No.

"Your throat?"

No.

"What about your lungs or heart?"

Of course not.

"It's like you're suffocating. You must be using up oxygen faster than you can get it. Remove your modifications, now."

I stared at him with frightened eyes. They wouldn't go away.

Not when I felt so vulnerable or had people to protect. Not even though I could feel the extra muscle mass in my chest, stuck beneath thick, immobile layers of keratin, compressing my lungs. I couldn't trust my body to relax back into its proper shape once I passed out.

"Then augment your heart and lungs."

"It'll go wrong," I managed to say.

"It won't. You've got me looking out for you."

Turning my attention inside my abdomen was immediately disorienting. Below the skin and muscle were thick-walled bags whose functioning I did not understand, always one silent tear away from killing me. They could be crushed, ripped, twisted, distended, misplaced...

Veras took my cold hands in his own, rubbing them together. "Breathe in deep," he said. "You're not going to leave me, are you?"

Space. My insides needed space to work. I could barely make myself examine them, to find opportunities for expansion, so I'd work from the outside in. I just needed to move some muscles outwards first, maybe... adjust my ribs? No, that made me think of my chest collapsing like a demolished building. Just the muscles. The change itself was simple, but my body resisted making it. I clenched my teeth and forced it.

I screamed as my back split open, skin torn from the inside. My modifications melted away from shock. I lay stunned while Veras cursed and removed my armor and cleaned and stitched, closing up three long ragged tears running from my shoulders to my waist.

"I told you not to hide when you're in medical distress," he said, pissed. "You had to notice something going wrong!"

"Something's always going wrong," I said, voice small.

For a moment the hard set of his shoulders softened, and then he was furious again. "You'd better learn from this experience. Understand what's going on beneath your skin before it has a chance to come to the surface."

"I don't want to think so clearly about my insides."

"This isn't about your *wants*, Ella. You could destroy yourself." He tied off the last stitch. "I can't remember the last time I resorted to sewing someone up. It's an awful thing to have to do."

I sniffled.

"More breathing problems?" he demanded.

Veras realized the answer himself, and turned me over to Reyna and Dorian. They seemed unsure of if I wanted them close by or not. I reached out, and they sat next to me as I lay on the ground.

"I should've kept some clay in my bag," Reyna said. "I'm sorry."

"I don't want clay anymore."

"Maybe we'll come across something a little different?"

"I don't want anything like that," I said, and some old resentment came to the surface, drawn out by failing to defend myself from Veras. "I want my old coping mechanism back. You took it from me."

Reyna was very quiet.

"I just need people who don't understand how I work to stop telling me how to function," I said, tearing up.

She tried to offer me my journal, but I didn't want it. Reyna instead took one of my arms and kneaded it, making a few clumps of leftover added muscle melt away. Dorian removed his gloves and worked on my other arm, then my legs, while she examined my shed pieces of armor. Some of the connections between the metal plates had snapped.

"We'll need to return to the drawing board," she said softly. "I'm sorry about that too."

"It's not your fault. I didn't give you great specifications."

"Should I fix this, or would you be better off without?"

"Fix it, please." I rolled my shoulders, felt a throb of pain. "Could you fix me too while you're at it?"

"You're perfect the way you are."

"I feel like a dumb monster."

"You're not a monster," Dorian said. "I would know, I've killed plenty. And you're certainly not dumb either."

"Thanks," I mumbled.

He took the jacket from my bag and draped it over me. "Stay warm."

Reyna handed me my phone to look through and plunked down in the grass, taking out her journal. More Graft encounters, more notes. Veras stared into the distance, constantly brushing his short hair aside and smoothing down his feathers. I considered telling him right then about why his magic didn't work on me, but I didn't see what it would accomplish if I didn't have a solution.

INTERMISSION

What used to be the occasional skirmish has gotten so much worse, entire fields razed to oblivion and rendered unlivable for both our sides. My people tell me that, given time and rain, we can coax life into those torn and torched places, but the sight of such destruction still fills me with rage. I don't understand how this damage has happened. It doesn't feel like we're losing, we have more settlers every day, and while we still push on into new lands our progress has been slowed. There's much I don't understand about what's happening, and times when I want us all to retreat and try to solve this issue another way, but always there is the greater purpose surrounding and guiding us, and so we push on. I try to go out to see my troops—

For a moment all of existence is pure white and silent, and then the world returns and it *hurts*. The air burns my skin, boils in my lungs. I feel stunned, shocked, like I've fallen and hit the ground too hard, except I have not moved. I can barely drag myself away. I trip over one of my companions, their body burnt to a crisp. Everything is —everyone is—it's like I've been looking at the world through a dirty window, and now everything is clear and sharp and I don't like it, I don't like what I see, the bodies I'm seeing are too burnt to tell what exactly they are but they're so twisted they can only be—the way I'm moving doesn't make sense—I—

I collapse away from the flames. Gradually the pain fades and the purpose returns. It's a shame to have lost settlers, but we will make more, and even this burnt area can be renewed. We just have to keep going.

23

———————

I was in low spirits for the next few days, spending much of my time as dead weight behind Reyna on the bike, trying to ignore the tugging pain of my stitches when I moved the wrong way. I had to do better. I knew what would've happened if we'd been attacked while I was collapsed and everyone else distracted. It was at least a relief to be off this awful world, even if the other places we drove through were depressing wastelands. You'd think dead worlds were dead worlds, all the same, nothing more to be said, but I soon learned this wasn't the case.

"I don't like it," I said, surveying the newest part of our journey.

"It's been fully used up," Dorian said. "We shouldn't be here long, which is great because I doubt we'll even find water."

I scuffed the ground with my shoe. The landscape didn't seem eroded, it seemed chewed on, a million mouths having consumed every useable bit of material until they reached bare rock. Off in the distance were buildings that only stood because they were made of stone. There was no life to move, no clouds to drift, not even a whisper of wind. It was like the planet itself had been killed. In that terrible stillness, even the soft hum of Reyna's bike felt disruptive.

Maybe that was why the wolf didn't attempt to hide, but stepped out from behind an abandoned building and sat neatly in the bike's path.

Reyna skidded to a halt about ten yards away. Dorian dive-bombed to land between us and it before the wheels had even stopped spinning. Veras landed behind us, out of harm's way. Dorian, damn him, had the nerve to be excited when he should've been scared like I was.

"Wait!" Dorian said, motioning for me to stand down. He took a step closer to the wolf. "Did you follow me?"

The wolf stared back at him, tilting its head. I hadn't seen it since... right before the invasion, outside Vanguard Base.

"Guys, I think it followed me," Dorian said.

"If it did, which way do you think it went on Felar?" I asked. "Through the sickening dust, or underground past the monster hordes?"

"Ella, we have to hold onto hope. Sometimes it pays off."

The wolf tilted its head a little more, then a lot more, until its ears were parallel to the ground, too far for visual comfort. Its mouth opened and dripped thick, stinking sludge.

Dorian's expression was a mix of shocked and offended. "Oh."

It paced closer. Distance had hidden its true nature from me before. The mess of teeth in its mouth stuck out in all directions. Its legs had varying numbers of additional small joints, extra knees and ankles.

This might be my second Graft Fortress.

"Why can't anything stay good?" Dorian mumbled, and drew his sword, anger overtaking his hurt expression.

"Couldn't we just run?" Veras said. "Just another rift or two, and we'll be on Glashower—"

"From those long legs? Not forever. If it's followed us this far, I can't imagine it giving up here," Dorian said. "Better to deal with it now. You two find a spot to hide. Stay safe, keep low, and we'll meet back up with you."

Reyna drove away, Veras clinging to her. I tried to hold back my fear. The wolf's size didn't mean it couldn't be killed, just that there might be more thought and effort needed. "I'm going straight for the eyes," I told Dorian. "I hope you're okay with that. I know that's gross and savage and you used to like—"

"It's a graftling," he said, furious. "Just don't get in the way of my blade."

"You don't have to tell me."

He nudged my shoulder. "We'll kill this awful thing together, and then you can feel safer."

I hoped it would be that straightforward. It was hard to keep even that simple of a plan in mind as the wolf paced towards us, driving every one of my nerves towards fight-or-flight. Freezing wasn't an option. For a moment I was at war with my body's instinct to lock up until the massive predator went away—the wolf lunging forward, jaws ready to snap shut at head-height, forced me into action. Dorian and I dove to either side and out of its way. I came out of my roll with built-up muscles and claws.

Already split up, we flanked the wolf, Dorian's sword slashing towards its gut while I leapt at the side of its giant face and sunk in my claws before I could slide off its mucus-thick fur. It thrashed, forcing Dorian back to avoid being trampled. I wrapped my legs around its neck, my joints locking in place through the growth of hard plates, and palpitated the edges of its massive skull for vulnerable arteries.

The corner of the wolf's mouth stretched back, separating skin and muscle, forming new teeth that gnashed and tried to tear me apart. I went for its eye. The wolf tossed its head back, far further than its neck and spine should have allowed, rising into a contorted bipedal position. I was thrown to the ground, my already injured back screaming. Dorian stood between me and the wolf while I caught my breath.

"You made it worse," Dorian said.

I looked up. The wolf's nightmare jaw hung open. Two tongues coiled in its mouth, dotted with what might've been strange new sensory organs. It was a shame that we couldn't know for sure what it had developed, if it had some special way of tracking us. I just hoped it hadn't passed any new traits on to other monsters, since we'd always seen it alone so far.

"Try to stagger it," Dorian said. "I'll aim for the neck. That thing'll bite me out of the air if I try flying at it."

I ran at it from the side. Knock over something twice—sorry, now *four* times—as tall as me? Sure, why not? Dorian charged at it head-on, a fire-powered kick against the ground launching him to the side before one of the wolf's disjointed front legs could swipe into him. His sword clashed against its claws, sliding him back from the impact, but he managed to bloody its paw.

I threw myself against the wolf's back legs, forcing the left behind and past the right, locking my and its limbs in that tangled position. The wolf's back crackled as its top half twisted to land on its paws, not crashing to the ground as I'd hoped, but it was enough.

Dorian's sword pierced the wolf's throat, two and a half feet of sharp metal sliding in without breaking the other side. The wolf merely blinked for a few seconds before its tail smacked me away. Dorian was beneath it and weaponless, and I was facedown in the dirt. This was the perfect opportunity for it to—

It bolted, the hilt of Dorian's sword sticking from its neck.

"GET BACK HERE!" Dorian screamed. "Berith gave me that sword, you piece-of-shit Fortress!"

We ran after it, Dorian shouting obscenities, some of which must've been new to the universe because they went untranslated.

"It's headed for a rift!" I yelled, seeing a patch of swirling darkness ahead.

"Catch it first," Dorian snarled.

It was too swift for that. The wolf stopped before the rift.

"Let's try to draw it away," I said. "It can't be that smart."

But the wolf wasn't done surprising us. We crossed some invisible threshold and it leapt, suddenly high overhead; it landed behind us, and then it charged.

"Ah, fu—" Dorian said.

Like me, he'd probably just realized that we were between the wolf and the rift.

It didn't feel like an impact. It felt like a gap, a moment where I felt and thought nothing. When the pain came, I couldn't tell the difference between the enveloping sharpness of it and the keen of air racing past my ears; I'd've thought it hurt the region of my brain responsible for vision if I hadn't seen Dorian next to me, the both of us falling through a dark sky. I caught a glimpse of a tar-like ocean below us as I tumbled.

Dorian cried my name and reached for me, wings spread to slow himself. I hit the ocean—not water, a rubbery surface, too thick to be cushioning. Tendrils crawled up my sides, and again I was falling, the material below me splitting apart to pull me under, reforming above my head. The ocean held me from every side, hot with the heat of a thousand bodies, dragging me deeper. My claws raked through it, but it was too big to hurt. All I could do was keep my mouth and eyes shut and seal off my nose and ears. The only air was that which I'd brought with me, and as it ran low, I blacked out.

I WOKE up to the worst pain I'd ever experienced, but being able to feel at all was a blessing. I sat reclined against something smooth, yielding, and hot, the warmth doing little to ease the ache that tormented every muscle in my body. There was a terrible pounding in my skull. The air was dense and stinking, doing my lungs and throat no favors. My vision was blurred, showing me a strange mix of colors.

"Dorian?" I whispered. Had he fallen in too?

I squinted, vision gradually returning. I was... clean, in a way. The reek of contamination was nearby, but not on me; my clothes, skin, and hair were damp with some other clear substance that smelled faintly acidic. Something or someone had acted to ensure my injuries wouldn't be fatally infected while I was unconscious.

I tilted my head back as my eyes cleared, needing to be procedural about taking in my environment. Hundreds of feet above me was an endless ceiling, the sort of brown-gray achieved by mixing too many colors together, that flexed and dripped like a living thing. The ceiling was supported by spread-out pillars with an off-white color and thinner middles reminiscent of bone. They cast an unearthly glow that dimly illuminated the... cavern? I was in.

Further down, the world became varied in color and texture. I lay among what could've been soft living statues that rhythmically pulsed in place. It was like someone had taken a three-dimensional anatomy model of a giant alien and scattered its organs around. A wrinkled beige mound ten feet tall throbbed as if deep in thought. A set of bones, ends stuck in the ground, had curtains of soft tissue and stringy fibers strung between them like drying laundry. An emerald scaled limb, its three digits twitching occasionally, lay like it had just been bloodlessly lopped off a shoulder. I was propped up against the abdomen of some headless quadrupedal thing, the echoes of its internal workings barely audible. Several yards away from me lay something vaguely horse-shaped, the only creature I'd feel comfortable saying was a complete whole rather than an excised piece. But, being surrounded by such varied life, I couldn't be sure what was an entire alien, and what was a fraction of one.

All of them did have one thing in common: dark red tubes the thickness of my finger were attached to them. The tubes met at nexus points that were like glowing jellyfish caps several feet across. Cloudy liquid swirled within them. Nutrients? Some sort of life support system? I traced the path that one of the tubes—such a clean word, tubes—took as it snaked towards me, and didn't like what I found.

The tube split into three bone-colored needles at the end. Each needle was barbed and about four inches long. I knew this by touch, not sight; it was impossible to see these details, because the needles were buried in my torso.

There are other times in a normal human life, I thought in an attempt to hold back panic, that foreign objects invade the body. IVs. Surgery. Medical devices. If I could think of this mess as an organic version of that, I might be able to contain my screaming until later. The plate of armor that protected my chest had been removed and lay next to me. One needle had been stuck under my left armpit, barbs hooked into my lung; another's tip was deep in my intestines; the third entered my heart. My insides had closed up around them, keeping me from bleeding out. I dug my fingers into the ground, which was like sand littered with bits of broken seashell or bone. I had to get out of here, but with the needles present, I was scared that attempting to move might kill me.

The sound of footsteps caught my attention. *Something* approached. A cry for help died in my throat as they came around the corner of a giant dismantled ribcage.

It looked as if the Graft had built a roughly humanoid person from spare organic parts, clothing, hair, and all. A person with long hair and an ankle-length dress thicker than hair or cloth should've been, sheets of tissue instead of strands. If the face had been set in fury or animalistic hunger it wouldn't've been so bad, but on a being whose eyes were set diagonally in their face, whose lower jaw almost seemed a separate creature dangling by hinges from the upper, whose features were bare, molded bone at the high points with thinly covered muscle stretched between them, a serene expression was terrifying.

The creature knelt in front of me. The uncovered arms revealed skin that, up close, was made of hundreds of overlapping diamond shapes, each moving on its own as if the arms were covered in an unbroken layer of alien remoras. The hands, though, those looked normal. Hands were important, after all.

It tore at my underlayer, creating a big rip around my abdomen. I tried not to shake, couldn't imagine fighting back in that moment. Aside from being tall, the creature itself wasn't that big. I couldn't see any sharp teeth or claws, no powerful muscles. But it moved like a person. Shifted the folds of its "dress" as it knelt, like a person. Brushed hair from its face, like a person. I didn't know how to deal with a person who wanted to hurt me.

In its own mind, or whatever it had, it probably wasn't hurting me. Its touch was incredibly gentle as it exposed, and then unzipped, my midriff.

Now I did scream.

It didn't even hurt, but the sight of a five-inch-long vertical gap opening in my body drove me over the edge. There was no blood. I was like a medical diagram, insides cleanly visible to an outside viewer. The creature thumbed through the layers of skin, fat, and muscle like the pages of a book. Its fingers entered the gap up to their final joints, my inside-sense forcing me to experience it poking and squeezing different organs.

"Stop," I whispered.

"Stopppp," it said back, the syllable drawn out and full of strange clicking noises.

It stroked my throat, bloodlessly splitting it open, and kneaded something inside. I wanted to recoil but was terrified of having an artery torn.

"Ssstoppp," it said in a voice that sounded like a distorted version of my own.

I was too stunned to respond.

"Stop," it repeated, a much more accurate mimicry. "Stop stop STOP." The word grew in volume while still sounding like a hoarse, terrified whisper. But the creature's hands were all enthusiastic interest as they continued to explore my anatomy, closing up my throat and delving again into my open torso, fondling the curves of my digestive tract.

"Stop," I said again.

The hands plunged deeper.

"You can't take them. I need them."

Something inside me was pinched.

"That's mine!" I screamed. "It's not for you!"

I whipped my head forward, making hard contact with its chin. Its jaw cracked inwards like a broken egg. The diamonds of its skin scattered from the broken lace-like bone structure, crawling over me on too many pin-thin legs and then running off. It made no noise of pain, but it did step away. The creature glided over to the brain-looking mound and pulled off a fist-sized clump of tissue. This it put on its lower jaw, smoothing the alien flesh over its cracked face so that its chin now looked like exposed meat.

And then, in the greatest mercy I had ever experienced, its attention wandered from me. It turned instead to the horse-like creature, grabbing the alien by its tail and dragging it away.

Once it was out of sight I writhed in place, resisting the urge to cry. It had left my abdomen open. I glanced down before I could stop myself, catching a glimpse of wet red shapes before I squeezed my eyes shut.

With trembling fingers, I pressed the separate sides of my split flesh back together. It was like closing curtains, always a gap between them no matter how much they overlapped. I wasn't currently bleeding, but running around like this seemed like a good way to start. Or have... the things inside me come spilling out.

No. Couldn't let that happen. Even if I couldn't escape, I... I just wanted to be closed up again. Swallowing back nausea, I focused my attention on the open edges of my abdomen. Where there should've been a wound exposed to air was instead a covered edge, lined with a membrane of my own cells, skin where it shouldn't exist. I certainly hadn't done that, and I despised the creature for having reshaped me. I broke down the membrane and formed a new layer of muscle, padding, and skin between the two halves.

Okay. Sealed up. Didn't have to feel the dank air against my insides or see my own guts anymore. Small improvement.

I focused on my digestive tract. I could feel the barb inside me, its tips surrounded by more of that membrane the creature had forced my body to make. In a moment of courage or stupidity or both, I grabbed the tube in my lower abdomen and yanked.

I wasn't strong enough without augmented muscles to tear it out in one go, and only weakness kept my scream from echoing across this entire world. It wasn't just the pain. It was the very detailed information I was receiving as the barbs tore up my small intestine, the awareness of ragged edges rubbing against each other, the displacement of my insides as blood pooled and infiltrated the cracks between them.

"I'm sorry," I choked out. "I didn't mean to do that to you."

Was delirium making me apologize to my body as if it was

another person? I'd often thought of my body that way, because doing so gave me an outside force to blame and hate and be afraid of. But this was still the one body I had, and I'd just ripped up its—*my*—digestive tract. The wound was messy and rough and would surely be slow to die from and I knew any graftling would've been happy to inflict that on me but I never would've wanted to hurt one of them in such a way.

Why the fuck was the thought of doing such damage to another creature harder than the thought of hurting myself that way? Whether I liked it or not, the gross bits I'd just torn up *were* me. I knew that. I hated that I was built this way, that I had to experience being in such an easily breakable body that I could feel every little detail of, but it was better... it was better than being one of the vivisected things around me. It was better than being formless biomass. And if I didn't like reorganizing my own insides, than it was certainly better than letting the Graft warp them for me.

"Really, Ella," I murmured. "If you can figure out your arms and legs, surely you can do this. It's not like you can trip over a misplaced kidney. You know how complicated hands are? Just don't squeeze anything too hard."

I drew together the walls of my intestine. There was a right shape for it to be, but I didn't need to worry too much about that; the other organs around it meant there wasn't enough space for me to make any big mistakes. I closed off the open blood vessels one by one. I tried to split my skin and abdominal muscles open bloodlessly, just like the creature had, discovering in the process which directions the muscle fibers ran and how to seal up an open edge. When I pulled on the barb again, it slid out painlessly, and I closed up the small hole that was left. It wasn't healing in the way that Veras did. This felt more like a stopgap, a temporary fix that might have mistakes. But it would do.

Carefully concentrating, I forced the other barbs out of my heart and lungs in the same way. I felt also where I'd messed up in sealing the split in my abdomen. The new join was off by a centimeter, with a bump of tissue at the top left and bottom right where the extra had bunched up. I slowly opened the wound again, letting bisected muscles, veins, and nerves find each other rather than forcing them together.

I put my armor back on and got to my feet. This might not be the end. I clambered over a severed, twitching, ten-foot-long arm, squeezed between two cast-off shells that might've belonged to the universe's biggest turtles, tried not to look too hard at a myriad of other squishy things on life support as I hunted for the end of this awful garden.

The landscape past it didn't make much more sense, a patchwork of different environments. A meadow butted up against a copse of craggy trees. Reeds that sprouted from a pond of unknown fluid swayed in the still air. And, strangest of all, there seemed to be a small neighborhood existing here alongside the Graft.

I went for the latter option, thinking it might at least have more hiding spots. The structures resembled houses in the same way a young child's drawing of one does. They were made of the same material as the pillars, with rectangular indents where doors should've been, shiny dark squares for windows, even overhanging roofs. Patches next to the doors glowed weakly like bioluminescent porch lights. I struck a window with my elbow. It cracked, sludge leaking out. No sanctuary there for me.

As I crept to the edge of this area, I noticed one of the pillars spread out at its base to form a dome. The violating creature stepped out from the dome's cave-like entrance, without the horse-alien this time. I pressed behind the corner of a fake house, feeling panic begin to set in. I asked my heart and lungs to slow to a more regular pace, which didn't get rid of the stress and fear but did help keep me quiet.

Once the creature was out of sight, I approached the dome. Incomplete skeletons big enough for the likes of Pillbug littered around it, color and material suggesting they'd come from several different creatures, now knitted together by liquid muscle that dripped from a tube dangling from the ceiling. The dome's entrance dimly glowed the strange green of organic light. Inside, it was partitioned off into multiple nooks set into the walls. The first few held only tattered tissue that dangled like ripped curtains. One of the other nooks was occupied by a giant chrysalis, its surface oily and opaque. Gas vented from an opening at the top, releasing the scent of ripening grass. Something being changed rather than created from scratch, then, most likely the other victim that had been chosen instead of me.

There was one more nook, unoccupied but not empty. I caught a glint of metal, out of place in this organic hell. I slipped my arm through gaps between the tissue and managed to pull a piece of it out. I held it up to my chest, and while it was scabbed over with dried gunk and too big to fit me, it was clearly armor.

I removed what I could from the nook. There seemed to be a full set of armor here, as well as a spear. Once its gross coating was removed, the blade was still sharp and the shaft decorated with swirling patterns. I ran my thumb over the ridges, finding them charged with magic, the energy fizzling against my fingers. I didn't know how dangerous the violating creature would be if I faced it unrestrained, but unless killing it made this whole place fall apart, that would mostly be for my own benefit.

The other magically charged item in the nest resembled the piece of armor Dorian wore under everything else, around his wings and shoulders. The one that helped him fly longer and higher. Maybe, if I could form my own functional wings and tap into it, I could—

Okay wow a makhal with wings died here without getting out which meant my chances were even lower than I thought and I'd already put them at close to zero—

Okay. Okay. That line of thought wouldn't get me anywhere. I couldn't meet the same fate. That one piece of armor, the keel plate, was shaped like a double-u. My underlayer had already torn apart when I hurt my back. Now I sliced into the slick fabric again, undoing Reyna's repair work so I could press the keel plate against the bare skin of my upper back, beneath my armor. So long as there wasn't contamination, I was well past caring how dirty anything was. The center spike lay over my spine, the two outer ones curving under my shoulder blades and arms. Powerful magic ran between the spikes and crackled against my skin.

With my next breath, I let my lungs expand past their usual capacity until my chest felt stretched tight. I discovered ligaments between my ribs, vertebra, and sternum I hadn't known existed. Once they were lengthened, the rhythm of my breath helping me decide by how much, the discomfort disappeared. My heart pumped stronger, transporting more oxygen-rich blood. I cut open my underlayer from my wrists to my armpits and then halfway down to my waist, experimenting with making my skin there sticky to hold the edges in place. For what I was planning, I needed room to expand. And, aside from wanting to make the simplest possible method of escape because of my exhaustion... my gut instinct was not to attempt to be a makhal.

I flourished my arms out to the side, putting everything I had into creating bat-like wings. I shut my eyes and imagined my hands and arms growing light, letting soft matter and bone thin out and stretch. I didn't want to just hold the air in my wings, I wanted them to *be* the air. My ever-sensitive hands told me when I was done, offering insight into the movement of breezes and drafts around me.

I opened my eyes, examined my work. I could see and feel the placement of muscles and blood vessels through translucent amber skin. My wings only connected to my side for about a foot, but hopefully their length would make up for that. Their wingspan was massive, the actual bones of my arms only a third of their length. Beyond that, a flexible hollow rod formed the leading edge. My hands, having formed the wing's supports, were nowhere to be seen, which sent me into a moment of complete panic. But they were the part of me I knew best. When I needed them back, I was sure they'd return. Right now, I needed them in this shape.

On their own, my wings would never be enough to lift me. They needed the keel plate's magic. I paid attention to how it felt on my skin, like a million needles pressing in and out, and reminded myself that no matter what I went through or learned about myself, I was still me.

I imagined the needles sliding a millimeter into me, and let the magic in.

It didn't hurt. It didn't *want* to hurt me. The opposite, in fact. It wanted to support, to uplift. It slid between and around my bones and muscles, lightening shoulders that were heavy with exhaustion. My wings seemed to glimmer, the keel plate's magic weaving into the walls of every cell, giving them power I couldn't create on my own. My old habits kicked in and the charge went away for a moment, but I welcomed it back and immediately felt lighter on my feet. So long as I could maintain that, I had a chance.

A distraught scream echoed throughout the cavern; my absence may've been noticed. Time to go. I didn't trust myself to handle the rest of the armor's weight, but I picked up the spear like my arms were normal and my hands were hidden in the sleeves of a jacket. A bit of muscle adjustment and I had ahold of it. The magic inside begged me to use it. It *did* want to hurt, but not me.

It was too late to save the makhal who had lost their life down here, but maybe there was hope for one more person. I jabbed the spear at the tissue suspending the chrysalis from the ceiling and squeezed the carved symbols on its shaft, feeling its magic surge and shake my arms. Everything around the spear's tip instantly shredded, dropping the chrysalis. It burst against the ground, sides rupturing and leaking a thick stinking liquid. Through one of the tears, the horse-creature glanced between me and the direction of the scream, terrified. They motioned with one arm, soft parts dangling from the bone like they'd been boiled, at the weapon. They were trying to breathe, and they were not succeeding.

"I'm sorry," I said, and risked gently touching their face. The liquid coating them reacted with my skin, cells bloating and melting, getting too close to blood vessels and nerves far too quickly; I flinched away and shed the affected layer before any real damage could be done. Whatever that substance was, it worked far faster than regular contamination. If they were completely coated in it... if they'd *ingested* it... "I'm really sorry."

They closed their eyes and laid their head down, twisting so their neck was exposed. I wished I could've safely comforted them in some way before I brought the spear down. I turned away, not wanting to see whatever half-formed mess the rest of their body was in, and fled the dome. I spread my wings wide and jumped off the bleached and oversized shoulder blade of a giant skeleton for some extra height.

My stomach lurched as I dropped. I don't know what I was expecting to happen, if the keel plate would just let me float or some inhuman instinct would kick in, but it was neither of them. I beat my wings down late, almost hitting the ground. The next few moments were all frantic arm movements. The keel plate's magic seemed to gather the air beneath my wings, giving me something physical to push off of. My feet skimmed the ground as I went from a useless up-and-down flap to a more circular movement and started ascending. I rose a couple inches, almost skewed sideways, made it up a yard. It would be difficult. I doubted I could hover in place like a makhal could, but that was fine. I had places to be. I beat my wings harder, aiming upwards.

I nearly crashed into one of the pillars, which reached for me with spiked tendrils. My wingbeats were clumsy, diagonal, and made my injuries ache, but I let my shoulders reshape to make them easier, going with the flow. I had to trust my body to do this, just like I was trusting the magic to hold me aloft.

A maw formed in the ceiling as I neared, curving down and in to envelop me. I flipped around, letting it grab my boots and anchor me. The spear's magic carved a path for me, shredding and scorching wherever my clumsy jabs guided it. My wings were caught, but I gave them sharp edges that cut apart anything that touched them. Whatever it took to escape and see the true sky again, I'd become. I stabbed the spear upwards with all I had, withdrew it to see a star.

I shoved my wings through the inch-wide hole and forced it wider, wider, pushing with muscle as well as lengthening bones, until my torso and legs were through and then—

I was out. I flew higher. The ceiling, now once again a sea from my perspective, tried to follow me, but was too heavy to lift much higher, while I was light and could stay in the air. Clumsily, of course, but it was enough. The patch below me boiled in frustration. Spread out across and floating on the endless sea were structures not unlike the ones beneath the surface, fibrous-looking mats, low-lying domes, strange towers that bent in the wind. The Graft were building something here, and they might've sacrificed a whole world to do it. They wouldn't sacrifice me too.

I spun around, looking for the rift I first came through. Time to leave this shitty world, before my limited strength ran out and the new muck on my skin made me sick. I sharpened my eyes—there. Distortion. A bright patch in the dark sky.

I dove through the rift and promptly hit a hard barrier too close to react to, the spear flying out of my hand, my wings reverting to arms out of shock. I slid off it to the ground, where I lay stunned. My guts ached from the impact, which sucked because I cared about those now. With some of my last strength, I lifted my chin, expecting to see the wolf's open jaws coming towards me.

"Oh, hey," I said. "Fancy meeting you guys here."

24

Veras held his glowing hands over me. The last of the Graft-muck that covered my clothes burnt away. Even though I'd shed all of the contamination on my skin, he'd insisted on examining every inch of me, including checking the function of my reverted arms. He'd been at it for the past twenty minutes, shivering beneath the soldier's jacket that hung from his thin frame, and calling me names the whole time. I'm sorry to report they weren't fond ones.

"—a ridiculous creature. Knew I'd regret ever allowing you to leave my sight—"

I focused on the left side of his chin, which was flushed from irritation. He'd grabbed me on first sight, ignoring the mess and requiring him to burn the contamination from our contact off his face.

Dorian was pacing unsteadily, having just been shaken out of the sedation Veras had put him under by Reyna. He looked everywhere but at me, keeping watch despite the wolf being long gone. One of his arms was bandaged from the elbow down. He'd refused to answer my questions about it. A small knife was belted at his waist, courtesy of Reyna. She was examining the spear and keel plate, frowning and quietly talking to herself about the gear.

"I don't understand half of what you're saying, but it sounds cool," I told her.

"Keep your mouth closed," Veras said. "I don't want you ingesting any of this."

"You already cleaned my face," I said. "And it's too late to prevent me from breathing it in. If it was going to kill me, we'd know by now."

"We can't be sure."

Taking his hand, I touched it to my shoulder, wincing. "Give it a try."

"If it won't help, I don't want to put you through that. I hate that my magic's let you down, but I have to accept it."

"It's not your fault."

"It's my profession, of course it's—"

"It's mine," I said. "I don't get to control most of my sensory environment, and it's extra hard for me here because I don't have the tools I had at home, and I didn't realize at first that I was keeping you out intentionally because it was completely automatic like covering your eyes in response to a bright light but then I was at the hospital and—"

"Ella, breathe."

I gasped in a few breaths. "—they tried healing magic on me while I slept and it worked for a second until I woke up and stopped them, and I couldn't stand to let them do any more on me even though it might've helped me recover faster but anyway I found out it's my fault."

"Oh." It took him a little while to process that, face twitching into different expressions as he considered. "...why didn't you tell me earlier?"

"Because it's one of the only things I have reliable control over, and I wasn't sure if I could give that up. It didn't seem fair to get your hopes up for nothing. My options on that awful world were to let magic in or die, so I managed that, but even now... I don't know if I can do it again."

"You shouldn't say it's your fault. Especially not when it sounds like a trauma reaction."

"I don't know if I would go that far," I said, even though his words felt horribly right.

"Either way, you don't have to blame yourself for reacting like that. And it's enough to say, 'I need things to be this way,' and leave it at that. I'll try not to push back if you do, okay? But I would like to... are you willing to let me try?"

"I do trust you," I said. "In case it doesn't work. Veras, even if there are times when I don't want to be around or seen or touched by you, I still trust you."

Veras hesitantly touched one of my injuries. His magic sat at the barrier of my skin, burning; I really did trust him not to hurt me, but with that sensory feedback, instinct still told me I would blister if he kept going. I imagined my magic—not my body, my *magic*, something that even now I hardly thought of myself as having—softening, still there but allowing entry.

As I let Veras's magic sink below my skin, the heat lessened until it was more like the warmth of sunlight, pleasant and helpful. It lasted half a second before he stopped, being ever so careful with me. He tried again, tracing out veins and the surface of muscles, slowly spreading deeper, lightly touching—hardly any sensation, gentle inquisitive whispers of feeling—bones and organs.

"I'm not seeing any contamination," he said, and then he really got to work, the warmth increasing until it felt like I was standing in front of an open oven, but it was worth it because I could feel the rips in my back closing up.

"Finally," Veras murmured. "I can finally help you."

"You've been helping me," I said.

"Not like this."

"That doesn't mean the rest didn't matter."

"I... you're not allowed to apologize for the next minute," he said. "Doctor's orders." Once my cuts were sealed up, I could feel his magic questing around my shoulder, the first of my injuries he'd ever treated. "I've constantly felt powerless around you. From the day we met, and I wasn't strong enough even to get you somewhere safe by myself. Then I was afraid of you. We started working past that just in time for me to watch you grow stronger, without me. You saved my life. And now, I've been planning this trip for so long, and I know I can't fight, but when I became sick and could hardly help anyone else, I... between you, Andras, and being stretched so thin at the hospital, it's felt like my magic has either failed to do what I want it to or outright hurt others. I started to feel like a liability, and it wasn't a good place for me to be in."

"I don't mean to make you feel weak," I said.

"I know. Obviously I'd rather you'd never gotten hurt, but I hope you don't think me selfish for saying I'm grateful I can finally do this for you."

He stopped speaking so he could concentrate, putting his everything into making me better. I had so many bruises from previous hard landings, so many smaller aches and pains from our traveling. Feeling all that just melt away was surreal.

"If I weren't tired, I'd have so many spoons right now," I mumbled.

"You and your damn spoons," Veras said. "I don't know if I can trust you with more." His magic washed over me one more time before he released me.

"That... was quicker than expected." I smiled weakly. "Guess I could have saved us both a lot of time if I figured this out earlier."

"You really are the most frustrating patient I could have possibly asked for."

"Would you have it any other way?"

Veras's face had been pale from worry. Now it flushed bronze with anger. "Of course I would! You're fortunate that I count you as a friend, or I would've... I don't know what I would have done, but you would've regretted it!"

"Don't yell at her," Dorian snapped, wings flared and trembling. "She's done nothing wrong."

"*She almost died.*"

"And what would you recommend she have done differently to prevent that?"

Veras gritted his teeth, hands and wings shaking, but he didn't seem to have a good direct comeback to that. Instead, he said to me, "Berith never should've let you leave Plesmae."

"Don't you bring his name into this," Dorian said.

"He should've foreseen this happening! To her, and to you. He's an idiot for—"

"Shut up." Dorian's injury didn't keep him from balling his hands into fists. "Of course you couldn't comprehend all the factors he weighs when making decisions, you don't know him like I do. Berith is one of the greatest heroes our species has ever known."

"Dorian, Veras is just upset," I said.

"I don't care," Dorian snapped. "Berith gave me a chance to keep fighting when some shitty, ignorant healers wanted to permanently retire me from the battlefield. He gave my life meaning again. Don't insult him."

"He basically exiled you," Veras said, incredulous.

"I offered to stay on!"

"Stop," Reyna said desperately, and they both did.

Veras gathered himself and refocused on me. "I need you to be careful. I can't put into words how much it would torture Andras and I if anything happened to you." He checked one more time for contamination before pulling me close. Reyna had returned to her muttering, which I think meant I'd really scared her. I knew I'd almost died, but seeing it affect the people around me made it truly sink in.

Veras rubbed my back while I threw up. His skin was hot as a heating pad as he drew out the pain and eased the cramping in my stomach.

"I can finally see just how similarly we're built," he said. "But you still have to tell me what you need. I can't read minds."

"Especially not mine?" I said.

He sighed. "Especially not yours."

I rolled my shoulders, able to feel the individual movements of muscle fibers if I focused. Veras had been right, back by the river. There were some worries we had in common. "Do you ever think about what we're made of and... get scared? Your magic must let you look inside your body like I can mine."

"I don't do so unless it's necessary," he said. "I used to when I started med school. Every student does in the beginning. Then you notice your blood pressure's slightly out of range or your throat's inflamed or something else gets you stressed, and you rush to get examined by a professor who tells you you're being an idiot. After a couple repeats of that cycle, I stopped checking myself most of the time."

"They shouldn't've called you an idiot for that."

"Probably not, but it was true. They'd gone through the same cycle when they were younger, so they knew what they were talking about." His warm hand drifted to the back of my aching neck, easing the tension there. "I wish you'd had someone like you to learn from, though having teachers isn't always completely positive. If I'd never gone to med school, I doubt I would've developed my hygiene fixation. It's hard to escape that cycle of anxiety when everyone keeps praising how thorough and detail-oriented you're being."

"I want to know why I didn't have anyone to learn from," I said. "Why I have magic when other humans don't."

His fingers glided down my arms, stopping at my wrists. "May I touch your hands?"

I nodded. He cupped mine in his, and I automatically tensed up.

"Let me in," he reminded me, and I did my best. Even when I did so, having his magic explore my hands was still almost unbearable.

"Makhali have a specialized organ that sits between the heart and where our wings attach," Veras said. "It's where magic is produced, and why we're able to fly at all. They're structurally different than ours, but you essentially have small, underdeveloped versions of that here," he touched just below the knuckles at the base of my fingers, "crowded between the bones of each hand. Regular exposure to magic at an early age can, rarely, cause formations like that in normally non-magical species. If you lived near that rift you told me about your whole life, it's a possibility."

I stared down at my hands. So it wasn't that I wasn't human. If anything, it was the opposite. I couldn't have come from anywhere other than the home I knew best, the one that had belonged to me and my parents.

The wave of relief that followed that news felt foreign. The wariness that accompanied it was far more familiar. "Nothing else feels... off to you?" I asked.

"Do you have anything changed right now?"

"No."

He squeezed my shoulders. "You've built up some muscle since coming to Plesmae. But don't treat being stronger as a reason to take risks and scare me so much, alright?"

I nodded.

"Good. Reyna, can you take first watch?"

Reyna nodded, not looking up from the spear.

"I'm sleeping," Veras announced, "*you're* sleeping," he pointed at me, "and YOU'RE sleeping," he finished, pointing at Dorian. "I know I won't be awake long enough to make sure you two actually rest. *Please* make good choices on your own."

He only made it a few minutes after that before he was passed out on his sleeping bag, not even bothering to crawl inside it. Once Veras was asleep, Dorian came up to me, stepping around the sleeping medic as if he were an armed mine.

"What happened after I went under?" I asked him.

"I reached in, but you were already too far down and it tried to suck me in too, and I had no idea what was beneath the surface and if it was something you could... you get the idea. I spent a while looking for you, but the contamination I got on my arm was eating through my underlayer. I eventually needed to land, make sure the Fortress hadn't gone after the other two, and then that bastard knocked me out once I'd told them what happened."

"It's hard for me to imagine you flying over that mess, looking for me," I said with my stupid tongue, and then had to clarify, "not as in hard to believe, but emotionally difficult. I hate that I scared you all so much."

"Stay close to me until we're back on Plesmae," Dorian said.

I nodded. I didn't want to be separated either.

Once he too was asleep, it was just Reyna and I up. I knew I should be resting but couldn't bring myself to relax that much. I opened my eyes when I heard the scuffling of shoes over dirt. Reyna's fingers ran over my hair like it was made of spun gold.

"Whoever died there?" she said. "We might be able to identify them once we're back, based on the spear. It's powerful and quite old."

I nodded. Reyna kept stroking my hair, the repetitive movement calming us both.

"When we return," she said, "if I'm quiet, or not around very often, I need you to know that doesn't mean we're not friends anymore."

"I know."

Reyna fell still and silent as a statue, watching the landscape. The last thing I saw before finally falling asleep was the spear, which she had reverentially laid on a spare blanket. Its presence felt like a call to arms, a charge to protect others from its owner's fate. I hoped I was up to the task.

25

———————

etween Veras's care and Dorian's pep talks and Reyna's fussing, I did my best to leave the stress of my near-fatal solo detour behind me. Alongside their many supportive words, they also lovingly forbid me from attempting to fly again unless it was absolutely necessary, probably scared I'd break my neck. We were only several days from Glashower and rushed to our destination as soon as I could reliably sit on Reyna's motorbike without falling off. As much as we wanted to hurry, stepping through a new rift always had to be carefully done: their blurred view of what lay on the other side gave away little information. I couldn't smell anything rotten through this one, and cautiously stuck my head through, Dorian ready and right behind me.

My first glimpse of Glashower was startlingly textured and rich, almost too much for my eyes to handle at once. Everywhere I looked were silvery undersides of leaves and dark clumps of moss shaped like lurking alligators and spun-sugar lichen hanging from branches, all greens and grays and russets layered on top of each other. The easiest way for me to describe it was to say all the plant life seemed woven together, trees and larger pieces of vegetation serving as foundations for smaller plants to grow on. It was hard to tell where one species ended and another began; the same could be said of Graft biomass, but this was, to the best of my knowledge, a community, not an amalgamation. And as far as I could see, it was safe. I tugged on Dorian's arm, signaling to him to follow me. We stepped through the rift onto Glashower—

And landed in neck-deep water.

In my defense, it was covered in a thick green lawn of plant matter that I'd assumed was solid ground. I thrashed, immediately thinking of the last awful thing I'd fallen into, mouth and nose quickly sealing up. But Glashower's air had already entered my lungs, and its scent was deeply comforting: sap, pine, and rich dirt, all filtered by the curving, spiraling, swooning, leaning trees that grew out of the water. I grabbed Dorian's arm and waded over to a nearby mini island before anyone could fall out of the rift on us. Even that little strip of land was covered in plants. The air itself seemed full of life, not just because it was so scented and rather humid, but from the way sunlight filtered through the branches and reflected off the water. The closest environment on Earth I could compare it to was a cypress swamp, but even that didn't match the sheer density of flora around us.

Dorian didn't seem to appreciate the view, but he might've been too busy spitting out algal water.

Veras and Reyna stumbled into the water before we could warn them, her motorbike making a huge splash that had me grateful our bags were water-resistant, but given that they'd been here before and we hadn't, that was honestly on them.

"You never told me it would be so wet," I said once they'd joined us on the somewhat-dry land. Damp feathers looked uncomfortable. Dorian especially looked scraggly with the rougher white feathers on the back of his wings slicked down.

"It wasn't before," Reyna said. "There was land at this rift when we arrived and left. The solid ground went for miles from here to the base we set up." She tried to pull her bike out of the water, struggling with vines that had gotten wrapped around its wheels.

"It was that way because the hamadryads wanted it to be," Veras said. "With them gone, I suppose the plants did what they wanted. Hamadryads liked having other species visit their world, but from what Andras told me, the plants were always indifferent. I wouldn't blame them for not wanting outsiders here now."

"I'll scout ahead," Dorian said. "Wait here, and don't touch anything."

He leapt into the air, his wingbeats disturbing the canopy's lacy network of vines and twigs. Dorian made it about twenty feet upwards before a thick branch smacked into him. He was thrown to the ground, landing on one of the few patches of hard, bare dirt.

The trees interlocked their branches, blocking us in. Reyna's bike was pulled from her hands and sucked underwater. The placid environment armed itself, gaps in the canopy closing off, thorny vines I hadn't previously noticed flexing, razor-edged leaves angling back and forth.

Dorian sat up, knife in his hands, a miniature inferno blazing around its blade. He faltered when a branch wrapped around Veras's waist, pinning him to a tree trunk—really, it deserved to be called *the* tree trunk. The larger flora in the Glade was meant to be the size it was; the trees looked like regular sized ones scaled up. This tree, though smaller than those, was still the largest living thing around. It had the cracking bark and knotty boughs needed to convey its great age. It was behind where we'd stepped through to Glashower, trunk bent forward as if it hoped to grow to completely envelop the rift someday. It held Veras fast.

"Everyone needs to calm down," Veras said, voice trembling.

"Plant matter's even easier to burn than animal," Dorian said. "On my mark—"

"No!"

More branches were wrapping around Veras, weaving together for strength. Leaves brushed over him, touching his arms, his wings, his forehead. Veras looked freaked out, but I knew how he reacted to being cornered by something threatening, and this wasn't it.

"It's not hurting him," I said. "It's trying to protect him from us."

Veras patted the branches. "Please put me down. I'm not him. I'm sorry he couldn't come too."

The tree's grip tightened, only beginning to loosen when Veras spoke to it in the same language he'd previously used with Andras.

"Try to show them you're not going to hurt me," he said.

For a moment I wasn't sure if he was talking to us, or to the plants, but there were still plenty of thorns waving around so I figured he meant us. I rubbed my palms together, adding friction so they were like Andras's skin texture, and touched an exposed root. Some of the plant life around me relaxed. I took Reyna's hand and put it next to mine, then looked up at Dorian. Looking displeased, he quenched the fire around his knife, the blade warped to the point of uselessness by the heat, and put it away.

Glashower's flora relaxed, and Veras was released from his wooden restraints.

"I thought there weren't any hamadryads left on this world," Dorian said accusingly. "So why were we ambushed?"

"I told you, the plants don't want outsiders here anymore," Veras said.

"The plants themselves?" I asked.

"They're much more active and intelligent here than you're used to," Reyna said.

"Why is this my first time hearing about this?" I asked.

"Because we never saw them be violent before," Veras said. "Or that fast. I'm used to them slowly moving towards light or water, or interacting with other trees. I've heard that over a period of years, whole forests could even migrate."

"That's creepy."

Veras ignored me. "It's not surprising they have a higher level of activity now. See how overgrown everything is, the lack of animals? I doubt this place has seen a hamadryad's touch since we left. They used to protect each other, but now it's just the flora left, and they don't have the same senses as we do."

"So the trees just didn't like Dorian's vibe?" I asked.

Dorian huffed. "You couldn't have developed a crush on a species from a less aggressive world?"

Veras ignored him too. "They could remember our battles here. Our combat magic and containment measures aren't kind to the environment, and here, the environment can hold a grudge. For example," he gestured to me.

The strap holding my spear to my back was under tension. When I twisted around, I saw it had green wrapped around it.

I unbuckled the spear from my back, slowly setting it in the water and letting the roots take it away, mentally promising it I'd return, but Andras came first. The deadly parts of the swamp retracted, and a way through the foliage opened up for us.

"I'm sorry, but I think you need to give up on your bike for now," I told Reyna. "And you need to keep it under control," I told Dorian.

"If we get strangled by roots in our sleep, I'm blaming you," Dorian said to Veras. "Plant guy is your boyfriend, so you lead. I'll let you know if you're about to walk into a 'dryad trap or monster ambush."

"He's not—" Veras stopped and sighed. He thought for a minute. "We could start near where we first met. I don't think he traveled too far from his home to our old base."

"Sounds like a plan."

Veras glared at him until he handed over a map. "We're here, right? We need to be around *here*."

Dorian waited.

"Why do you think I know which direction to go? Is there a landmark nearby we could use?"

"I don't know, I was going to find out but I was SWATTED out of the SKY by a TREE."

The ground shifted below him as the roots holding the island together squirmed. Dorian made what I had to assume was a rude gesture. Either the trees couldn't see, or they felt he wasn't worth a response.

"I don't want to be here either, okay?" Veras said. "I just want to find Andras's taproot and return to him as quickly as possible."

"I could try to climb up and get the lay of the land," I offered. "They might put up with that."

But Veras wasn't looking at me. I followed his eye and saw that in the distance, clusters of speckled three-pointed leaves growing from a vine waved as if they were calling for attention.

"Don't follow the trees, Veras," Dorian said. "They're not your friends."

"They're Andras's friends. He loves most plants, but that species is one of his favorites." He carefully flew to them, using his wings but keeping close to the water, awkwardly curling himself around a branch to examine the leaves. "You're not from around here, are you? You used to blanket whole groves near the base." He glided to another tree.

"He's like a child following a trail of candy," Dorian said.

"Then we'll just have to make sure nothing grabs him," Reyna said.

Dorian grimaced and followed Veras, though he was more careful about where he clung to the trees. Both makhali were slowed down by a lack of continuous open space beneath the canopy, but they at least had a path available to them.

"So," Reyna said.

"So," I agreed.

"At least we don't have to worry about flying into anything?"

I nodded. There weren't that many islands like the one we were currently standing on. "How strong of a swimmer are you?"

"I can keep myself from drowning."

"That's a start. Look away for a minute?"

Reyna turned around. I wanted to have my arms and legs free in case I needed to defend us. I had an idea of how to do that, and maybe it was a stupid one, but even if it didn't work... so long as I took care of my body as I used my ability, what did I have to lose?

Even then, I felt shy as I mentally reached for the back of my pelvis, borrowing the thinnest slivers of bone to serve as the foundation for a new appendage. I had more time now than I had when forming my wings, time enough to feel like I was reintroducing myself to my own body. I wasn't sure if it was ready to do this yet, but I asked, and it answered.

New bone honeycombed out from the slivers I'd taken, my under-layer splitting to accommodate the new growth. Fibrous muscle, fed by the arteries that traveled past my pelvis, spooled out from my lower back and formed a rope-like tail with thin, clear fins. I didn't like that it was the same color as my skin, which reminded me of a rat's tail; covering it in the same membrane as the fins made it appear opalescent, which I much preferred. Moving it felt strange, but I could get used to it.

"Okay," I said. "Let's give this a try."

"Did you find some sort of technique book when you were separated from us?" Reyna asked.

"No, I just realized there are enough things in the universe to be afraid of without adding my body to the list."

We went into the water. Reyna wrapped her arms around my shoulders from behind.

"Would a monster offer me a lift?" she said, and I could hear the smile in her voice.

"Only a very polite one," I said.

My tail swished back and forth beneath the surface without much thought from me. Having Reyna leaning on my back brought my face close to the water. Some entered my mouth, and I instinctively sealed it at the back. My lungs expanded without a second thought. If Reyna hadn't been depending on me I would've dived underwater and tested out how long I could go without surfacing.

A sense of awe filled me. If I really applied myself, what else could I do? Where could I explore that a normal human couldn't? Over the years I'd had so many dreams where my body changed to move in new ways, see things that used to be hidden. I'd never tried to recreate them in my waking hours, not just to avoid discovery, but because back then, actually trying to do something positive with my ability and failing would've cut me far too deeply. But now? I hadn't felt this kind of excitement in so long, I—

I needed to be able to tell Andras about what I'd seen on

Glashower, so I focused on the present. Hopefully it would bring him some relief to know that Glashower was waiting for its people to return. We passed many of what I didn't realize at first were buildings, soft-edged prisms grown from the entwined branches and roots of neighboring trees, windows open gaps in the wood framed with thick layers of lichen. Many of them were starting to fall apart, but it seemed like the trees were preserving them with shelter and structural support. During a short break, Dorian attempted to enter one, but the door held itself shut. He grumbled and moved on, catching my eye and nodding towards Veras. I nodded back.

Although Veras had done a fine job of increasing his stamina over our journey, flying in such cramped quarters must've been taxing. He landed on a flat area among the branches of a massive tree to take a breather, visibly swaying on his feet. The tree was covered in garlands of speckled vines, one of which coiled around his arm. Dorian landed too, and I climbed up to join them, Reyna *eep*ing and holding on tight as my tail wilted away.

"We should take a break," I said. "Maybe settle down for the night."

"I can keep going," Veras said. "We're close."

"Not *that* close," Dorian said.

"You said I should lead, so that's what I'm doing."

"Veras," Reyna said with stern kindness in her voice, "if we ran into enemies right now, you'd be too tired to flee. Would you have us return to Plesmae without you?"

He hesitated. Before he could respond, Dorian stretched out his wings, the movement stiff and awkward. He smirked at me when Veras wasn't looking.

"If you've been in pain from the collision all this time —" Veras said, his voice rising.

"It's just starting to feel bad now," Dorian said.

Reyna plunked down next to me and got out dinner. Dorian's smirk went away when Veras examined his injured arm. Beneath the bandages his skin was bruised, scalded, and calloused, a condition that barely improved with the addition of healing magic.

"It's just surface damage left," Veras said. "I'm sorry I don't have more energy to spend on it right now."

Dorian shrugged, quickly pulling his mended underlayer back down his arm and replacing his armor.

Veras turned to me.

"I'm just tired." And a little nauseous from learning how badly Dorian had hurt himself for me.

Veras insisted on looking me over anyway. He wasn't awake for much longer after that. He curled up on a mossy patch of the tree. The rest of us agreed to let him sleep through the night.

"Wonder what it feels like to have a whole planet fawning over you," Dorian said. "Lucky bastard."

"Be a bit nicer and you might find out," Reyna said.

"It's making my life difficult. Look, you can hardly see the stars through the canopy. How is anyone supposed to navigate like this?"

"Would you know what stars to follow if you could see them?" I asked.

"I could learn. If I came back and had some spare time."

"Dorian the tourist," Reyna said. "Imagine that."

"One gets tired of living on a lifeless rock, okay?"

"I get it, I understand the need for variety." Reyna found a spot where the bark had been scraped away and started peeling off the rest, revealing smooth inner wood. "This is nice material. It would be a nice break from working with—"

The branch she was leaning against bent at a ninety degree angle, dropping her into the dark water below. Her shriek and the resulting splash woke up Veras, who cried out Andras's name. Dorian calmed him down while I fetched Reyna. Her hands trembled as she squeezed water out of her hair.

"I'm sorry," Reyna said. "I'd never cut down an intelligent plant. Now, if I came across one that was already dead and dried out—"

"Quit while you're ahead," I said.

She curled up in the middle of the platform and pressed her face into a balled-up jacket as if worried she'd incriminate herself in her sleep.

Once we were the only two awake, I regarded my red-headed companion. He seemed painfully alert, his boots braced against the branches. I gently touched his bandaged arm.

"What, this?" he said. "It's nothing. I've had worse."

"It looks awful."

"It feels fine enough. It's easier for healers to close up wounds than it is for them to fix burns or scar tissue. Something about growing what's there versus having to remove stuff."

"I hate that you're hurt because of me."

"And you've risked your life for mine. That's what team members do. Don't worry about it." He frowned. "You've seemed off. How are you doing? You told us what was below the ocean, but not how you're feeling about... everything."

"It's so much worse out here than I thought it would be growing up," I said. "It hurts that entire worlds have been ruined. Like, what the fuck are we supposed to do about *that* world?"

"You tell your leaders about it and hope they know things you don't, I suppose," Dorian said. "I've never come across an enemy that I couldn't conceivably kill, until now. I don't like the feeling."

"It's a bad one," I said softly.

"What were you expecting the universe to be like?" Dorian asked.

"I don't know. All the other planets in our solar system are lifeless. We get excited when we find ice or little lines that could just maybe be signs of microscopic life on them. People's imagining what other worlds full of alien life would be like is a huge part of our entertainment, but it's always been just that, imagination. So many bad things have happened since I left home that I've never taken the time to appreciate what a miracle your existence is."

"Mine?" Dorian said, amused.

I rolled my eyes. "Your species."

"But I would hope you're happy to have me specifically around as well."

"Of course. You're easily one of my favorite six people in the universe."

"Six?"

"Obviously my family takes the top spots."

"You're in one of my top spots too."

"That's good. Might've gotten awkward otherwise," I said. It was good that it was dark. Telling people I cared about them was fine, if a little nerve-inducing; hearing someone else say it back made my face go red. "Like, 'oh God, I'm about to spend weeks more traveling with someone who likes me more than I like her,' that would be uncomfortable."

"'God'?"

"Just... don't worry about it." I didn't want to explain human religion to him, especially since I didn't believe in any of it.

He settled back against his branch. "I suppose I can try. Got enough to worry about already."

"Should probably quiet down so we don't wake anyone."

But I wouldn't have minded knowing where I ranked for him.

VERAS HAD to shake off a blanket of moss and vines to get up in the morning, but we were otherwise untouched by our environment. This did not make Dorian any less on edge, and when our separate travel by air and water ended with us finding the edge of the swamp, he walked at the front of our group with his wings cocked up and out like a protective mother hen hoping something would pick a fight with him. The land sloped upwards, but Veras was finding more and more of the vines we were following. He was so single-minded that I had to slow him down when I heard distinctly animal noises ahead. There was a different smell in the air that thickened as I crept closer in the lead, richer than anything plant-related, not necessarily a *good* smell, but—

"Oh shit, it's a zoo," I said.

"What's a 'zoo'?" Dorian hissed behind me.

"Nothing that requires having a knife out."

He reluctantly put it away and joined me. A few vines waved, warning us from coming any closer. Some yards away were... wicker enclosures, I supposed, acres of natural land divided up by closely woven branches, separating out different types of animals. I caught a glimpse of small flying creatures before the branches of their enclosure twisted, overlapping their leaves to block our view of them, or theirs of us. Little creatures squeaked at me before diving into their burrows, abandoning the berries they'd been pulling off a conveniently placed bush. From further away, source unseen, echoed a yowl that could've belonged to a jaguar. More good news for Andras. His world was looking after itself.

We wandered in the same direction, finding a similarly home-grown botanical garden. This we were actually allowed near, though with hesitation, maybe because the plants thought (or knew) they were smarter than the animals, and knew how to deal with us.

"Some of these plants look like they're from a different environment," Reyna said, examining a miniature garden of fleshy lobed plants that resembled succulents. They and their lighter-colored soil were cradled by tree roots and directly in a ray of sunlight. Several yards away, sheltered from the light by the bent branches of a tree, were mushroom-looking things thriving in the relative darkness and moisture offered by its roots. Another tree, nearly naked of leaves, seemed to have sacrificed itself in order to support several species of choking tendrils.

That was fascinating, but I'd noticed something else interesting and wandered off to look at it.

"Hey, guys," I said.

"This one doesn't look as much like a jackass as the others," Dorian said.

"Guys."

"Please let go, I'm coming, I promise," Veras whispered to some touch-starved vines that didn't want to release him.

"GUYS."

The ground plummeted a few feet ahead of me, straight down a rock-lined cliff at least a hundred feet deep. The cliff stretched to both sides, curving around and making it impossible to determine its true length. I hadn't felt like we were high up as we'd travelled, but now I could see that we stood on a city-sized raised section of land. There were more far off in the distance, like islands on the other side of a sea.

Not an actual sea, but an environment where we belonged just as little. Below us was a contaminated swamp, the water closer to sludge.

"So this isn't on the map," Dorian said.

"All of this used to be one altitude," Veras said. "I don't know how, but the healthy life sequestered itself."

"Life, uh, finds a way," I mumbled.

"What?"

"Nothing."

Veras was squinting down at the swamp.

"There are more of Andras's vines below, aren't there?" he asked me.

I nodded. The plants were melty, but I saw the same distinctly shaped leaves.

That didn't mean those plants were dead. Awful new life was developing, a sordid mix of flora and fauna, soft jointed limbs growing from hardwood trees, paper-thin leaves and petals swelling into flesh. The tree roots were gnarled, squelchy dirt caught up in them, but they created a decent enough path that Reyna and I could avoid swimming.

"This planet blows," Dorian said. He rolled his shoulders. "Guess it's time for some more scouting."

"If you go down mid-flight, you're dead," I said. "We won't be able to reach you in time. And if the trees up here are grabby, the ones down there could be worse."

Dorian scowled, but he relented.

"I think we at least know what direction to go," Veras said, scanning the swamp.

Off in the distance, something flickered among the trees like a failing light bulb.

"Think that's the base?" I asked.

"I don't know what else it could be. Glashower isn't a great place to find stone and metal. There wasn't as many opportunities or reasons for hamadryad technology to advance. Why develop magical lighting when you can coax a bioluminescent plant into glowing for you?"

"Because inventing things is *good*," Reyna grumbled. She was deliberately facing away from the ledge, so I could barely hear her.

"My point being," Veras said, "that if we see something not part of nature or the Graft, it's likely from our time here. Everything else is...
" He rubbed his face.

"You don't have to say it," I said.

"Let's just find a way to get down there and—"

Veras jolted away from the edge when the ground shook. The rocks that lined the cliff wall parted near where we stood, pulled aside by roots to allow one of their own to emerge into the open air. It seemed to double in size every few seconds, making me question if we really were the only people around, or if my understanding of sentience was too limited. And it just. Kept. *Growing.* A single, continuous brown root, several feet wide and unevenly flat, stretched from just below us on the cliff to the level of the swamp below.

Dorian started to speak. "This planet—"

"Why do you keep insulting it when you know it can do things like this?" Reyna asked, mystified.

"Glashower looks after its own," Veras said. "Andras told me that once, but I suppose I didn't understand at the time. We have our way down."

"Do you think they'd react again if we flew back up?" I asked. "Because it would be safer for them if they assumed we were contaminated."

"I can't make any promises, but I think they recognize Andras's magic. And if they know to let us down, then I'm hoping once we have his taproot, they'll let us back up."

Dorian shrugged. "Not like we were going to give up at this point either way. We'll just have to deal with it."

I took a nervous first step onto the root, finding it to be perfectly solid and still. I slowly crab-walked down it, everyone else's wings spread wide for balance, Reyna a step behind me with a hand on my shoulder. Once we'd all gotten down, the root retracted, leaving us to face whatever came next by ourselves. Like Felar and the consumed world I'd been on, the Graft's plan for Glashower seemed to be building up biomass and experimentation. Animal shapes sprouted from trees like works-in-progress hung up while the paint dried. Nothing attacked us, but it was like walking past a hyper-realistic paintings whose eyes seemed to follow you, everything slowly leaning towards us as we passed and making it tempting to run despite the treacherously swampy ground. But as clearly infected as they were, the plant life didn't seem hostile. They weren't healthy, but they didn't seem to be entirely grafted either. Glashower, I believed, was fighting as hard as it could to survive. I was sure Andras was too.

26

We experienced two miracles in short succession. The first was that we reached the makhali's base just before dark. By that point I felt we'd all proven we had some courage, but fucking around and potentially finding out in that mutated forest at night might've gone beyond bravery and into stupidity.

The second was that the base was still standing and, it seemed, protected. The veil flickered every few seconds like a struggling heartbeat, but it had done its job in the makhali's absence; there was a riot of color around the base, healthy flowering plants blooming beneath its safety. Reyna opened a gap in the veil, and I stepped onto firmer ground with relief. Veras disinfected our shoes so we wouldn't immediately compromise the base. The sprawling building must've been grown by hamadryads, looking like the stump of a tree big enough to rival those in the Glade. The outer walls were over a yard thick, a honeycomb of bark layers so compressed it felt more like stone under my hand. The walls curved where they met floor and ceiling, hallways softly bending around corners. Makhali crystalline lights, dimmed with age, still sputtered to life when touched, looking garish compared to their surroundings. More than a few eleven-legged Glashower equivalents of spiders went skittering into cracks and crevices at our approach. I nudged aside a couple crates that had been left in the middle of the hallway. There were quite a few objects left inside, as well as scattered around on the floor, nothing I'd categorize as trash but clearly things that hadn't been worth the trouble to bring back to Plesmae.

"What a mess we left," Reyna said. "I'm going to check near the forges for supplies."

"I'll check the infirmaries," Veras said.

"I'll make sure we're actually safe here," Dorian said. "A threat other than the Graft could have gotten inside."

We split up. I followed Veras, who seemed miserable.

"I don't need your help," he told me. "I'm not expecting to find anything. I helped pack it up, after all."

"I'm just here for emotional support."

"You should offer it to someone else."

"Andras asked me to watch out for you."

I didn't get any argument, so I followed him to the infirmary. He prodded at the magical lighting, sighing when only a few turned on. He busied himself with looking through boxes and drawers while I sat on one of the beds.

"So, what are you going to do when we're back on Plesmae?" I asked.

"Take care of Andras and everyone else who's been hurt by the Graft."

"After that?"

"Figure out housing, I suppose. I don't want us to be Berith's permanent guests."

"What else?"

"Ella, I'm tired."

"If Andras makes you feel a certain way, you should tell him," I said. "I can't believe you've gone this long just being friends."

That earned me a glare. "I didn't want Andras to think his medical care was dependent on him dating me. So I told myself that after a while, assuming I still felt the same, I would try to move things forward. But I never decided what 'a while' meant. I do love him, but sometimes it feels like when we touch, it's just... transactional. One of us fixing up the other and then immediately pulling away. So it's hard to tell if he actually wants *that* with me."

"Oh, I doubt that's you," I said. "That's probably him thinking he's dirty."

"Dirty?"

"Because of his contamination, he's scared to touch most people."

Veras still looked at me blankly.

"He told me? Before we left? Did he never tell you?"

Veras froze, his wings going stiff. "Do you think that's my fault?"

"No, he just seemed to be afraid of getting anyone else sick."

"He *knows* he's not infective. I've told him a million times."

"Facts don't always win over our feelings," I said. "We've both experienced that. He seemed to worry it would make him, um, harder to love?"

"Now that's just ridiculous," Veras seethed. "He's caring, and stable and resilient in a way I've never managed to be, and curious about new things even though new things keep hurting him, and he has this infuriating ability to just look at a person and they can't help but smile..." He stopped himself, face flushed a deep bronze.

"Shame I didn't record that for when we return," I said.

"Record?"

"One of my alien secrets. You'd better tell him all that."

"Forget about my future," Veras said. "What about yours?"

I shrugged.

"I worry sometimes about what you'll do after this," he said.

"I..."

I was saved from responding by Reyna and Dorian coming in.

"Where'd you get that?" I asked, gesturing to a new sheath strapped to Dorian's side.

"A placeholder," Reyna answered for him. "There wasn't much left."

"It's not even a sword," Dorian grumbled.

"Do you know how to use it?" Reyna asked.

"Of course I can wield an axe," Dorian said. Going by his tone, I guessed they'd already had this conversation. "I just don't know if it can stand up to my magic for long."

"It's not for forever."

"Can't you make me a new one? There were plenty of scraps you could melt down—"

"No," Reyna said, her tone final. "Not here. Not in the time we have."

He scowled, but gave up.

We got ready for an early night. The barracks' mattresses were full of dust, but they were more comfortable than anywhere else we'd slept recently, and the veil meant we didn't need to sleep in shifts. It was hard to fall asleep with so much anticipation in the air, but I thought about the push and pull of water against my body, and managed it.

～

I woke in the middle of the night. A low-frequency hum came from outside, making the bedposts quiver.

"Something's attacking the veil," Reyna blurted out.

The humming rose in pitch and volume.

Dorian and I ran outside, followed at a distance by Reyna and Veras.

Something was bashing against the veil, making it flex inward and strobe before snapping back into place. Reyna charged some lights outside the base.

The wolf winced in the brightness, almost matching my own expression from the eye-watering lights. Dorian's sword was nowhere to be seen. "The hell are you doing here?" he yelled.

It lifted a paw, rested it on the veil, and pushed down. The veil crackled beneath the pressure. The wolf's shoulder swelled in the dark, its paw encroaching further and further as it cannibalized muscle from elsewhere on its body.

"Dorian," I warned, squinting, the veil's strobing too much for me to look at head-on without feeling like my brain would explode. "Dorian, we need to do something—"

"Stay back and let me through. A blade didn't help me last time," he said, and buried the head of his axe in the ground. Red magic boiled around his arms. He took a step closer to the veil. Reyna hesitantly approached it as well, though further away. "This is for almost killing one of my soldiers."

He signaled to Reyna, who momentarily dropped the veil.

Dorian punched the wolf, the collected magic at his fist burning the side of its face as he grabbed onto it. It snarled and shook its head, yanking him through the veil when he refused to let go. He grabbed the axe, burying it in the wolf's shoulder, his magic scorching away the growing flesh that tried to seize his new weapon.

I swore, Reyna letting me through the veil to help, but there was only so much I could do without being in the way of Dorian's wild swings and the wolf's slashes and swipes. Reyna shouted, and the veil crackled with too much energy, all my senses burning. Dorian shoved the wolf into it, sending energy coursing through its system.

The beast howled and flung itself to the side, momentarily downed, its burnt and mutated features softening into a look of pained surprise. It writhed, back arching as it disgorged a brown mass that burrowed into the ground.

The trees near us shuddered as they underwent terrible transformations, becoming less plant and more animal. Dorian was struck from behind by a whip-like branch. When he turned, distracted, the wolf leapt to its feet and knocked him over, standing on his back with its front paws.

Anger overtook me. I grew out a long spike of bone from the back of each hand and protective plates around my arms. The wolf lunged towards me, jaws open. I stabbed up through the roof of its mouth. It tried to bite my arms off, but Dorian struggled to his feet and forced its mouth to stay open. The wolf's muscles started to ripple and change, but I wasn't done.

I grew out the tips of the spikes, making them hollow and strung with nerves, coming up with a new structure on the fly. The spikes branched, some of them hitting skull, others following the path of least resistance as they probed for soft brain matter...

Something wrapped around my ankle and yanked, pulling me over. I snapped the spikes off from my arms so I wasn't locked to the wolf. Dorian was kicked away. Despite the damage we'd done, the wolf still had the strength to flee into the night.

Dorian looked like he was about to scream. He'd suffered scratches around his shoulders and neck, and he had to be bruised all over. I felt fine for the moment. But again, there was a tug at my ankle. I looked down. A thick tentacle crept up my leg. I shrieked. Dorian fumbled for his axe while I kicked at it—

Veras bolted out from behind the veil, holding his hand over the thing and used his magic. It squirmed and let go. He hunched over it protectively. "It's a contaminated taproot, don't hurt it."

"Better hurry up," Reyna said. "I don't think it's happy." She pulled Dorian out of the way of a swinging, claw-tipped branch.

A final flash of light came from Veras's hand, and the taproot fell still. So did the sick forest. The four of us stood at the center of a circle made of pointing branches and groping limbs, the trunks around us containing split sections of bark that let them bare their teeth, a potential horde reduced to statues for now. The wolf failed to reappear.

"Are taproots normally that big?" I asked after taking a breather. Its roots had already sunk deep in the ground, but its main body was backpack-sized, maybe bigger.

"No, they're usually fist-sized," Veras said.

"How do you tell whose it is?"

"Not sure. Let's get it inside." He crouched down to lift it up, waved away our offers of help, and wrapped his arms around it. The taproot disintegrated into mud in his hands.

"Huh," he said. The tips of his wings started to twitch, the movement traveling further and further up his wings. He didn't blink or breathe.

"Where did Andras live?" Reyna asked.

"It was so far gone. Just contamination left. I, I killed him this time," Veras whimpered.

She grabbed his shoulders and shook him. "Where did he live?"

"Reyna," Dorian said with unusual gentleness. "Give him some time."

She practically shoved Veras into Dorian. "Heal him."

Veras took care of the worst of Dorian's cuts, cleaning them and stopping the bleeding. His hands shook.

"Where's Andras from?" Reyna repeated.

Veras gestured to the remains of the taproot.

"Until we know if it's his, we'll assume it's not. That means we need to go look, right now, in case the Fortress wants another."

Veras seemed on the edge of a complete breakdown, but I startled him out of it by punching the nearest infected tree, my arm hugely swollen with muscle and plating. The trunk shattered and split, revealing a solid core beneath its oozing exterior. It wasn't right. I didn't want to be in a universe without Andras in it.

Reyna wrapped her arms around me, my own hands instinctively grabbing her shoulders to reject being touched. I paused. Changed like this, I could break her, and I had contamination on me. Considering this forced me to regain control, though my hold on it was flimsy. Veras gently separated us and cleaned any infectious material from our clothing and skin.

"I'll find him," Veras said, taking in slow, deep breaths. "No matter what."

"You know the way, don't you?" Dorian asked.

Veras didn't seem sure, and I resisted the urge to pull him back when he got close to some of the contaminated trees to look for Andras's vines, branches slowly reaching for his uncovered face and wings. "This used to be one of his, I think."

He continued in that way, leading us through the dark swamp that could've held horrors we'd never seen before, lit only by the small magic lights the makhali were able to create. How he told one type of plant apart from the others, I didn't know. I certainly couldn't.

The leaves were dull in color and had grown soft, losing their pointed outlines. But Veras didn't falter in his path.

"Is this...?" I asked when he stopped.

"They're called sanctuaries," Veras said.

He'd led us to an open spot ringed by half-drowned trees. I wanted the life here to be healthier than the rest of our surroundings, but it wasn't.

Reyna examined the ground. "How deep are taproots usually buried?"

Veras didn't answer. He looked past the edge of the clearing. A vaguely humanoid graftling, nine feet tall even when hunched over, staggered between the trees. Its face was a mess of dangling lichen and algae, its hands fingerless masses of plant matter. It almost appeared to be gardening, lifting drooping vines from the muddy ground and attempting to tie them to a trellis; this was futile as both the vines and the woven branches of the trellis had all the solidity of soggy papier-mâché. After several tries it gave up and moved on to a tree, picking off the sickly leaves one by one, optimistically leaving up the leaves that were only wilted but not yet dripping purulent sap. As it worked its way through the branches it turned and saw us, putting Dorian and I on our guard.

And nothing happened. We were just stared at, the creature taking slow, hesitant steps away.

"Anything else about hamadryads I should know?" Dorian asked. "Do they keep plant monsters around their sanctuaries?"

Reyna shook her head. "We're on this trip partly to investigate new forms of Graft. It could be—"

"It's part of him," Veras said. "Otherwise we'd be fighting right now."

"Still looks like it might want to," Dorian said, axe in hand. "If anything, it's probably just reacting to his magic on you, like the rest of this damn place."

Veras pressed his palm to his forehead and winced. When he moved his hand, he had a circle of scalded tissue on his face, and I could no longer sense any trace of Andras.

"Veras," Reyna warned.

He lunged past all of us before we could stop him.

"It's me," he told the monster. "Hold still. It's okay. It's me. We're so close, Andras."

It seemed on the brink of fleeing, covering its face and backing away, cornered between Veras and a tree. I desperately searched the monster for any visual resemblance to Andras, and found nothing. But the way it quietly moved through its environment, pondering and gently caring, that was all him.

Dorian's grip tightened on his weapon.

"Give him a chance, Dorian," I said.

"I can't let you get hurt."

"I'm not going home without him. Stand down."

He gritted his teeth, but stayed back as I joined Veras.

"Don't touch him, or you might get contaminated," I said, fearing losing the both of them. "We'll do this together. You keep him under control, and I'll feel for Andras's magic."

Veras held out his arms. "Come here, Andras."

It drew itself in, trying to be small and turn away.

"I know it's you. Andras, I'm here for you."

"You don't have to hide," I said. "I know you don't want to be seen like this, but it's okay."

"There are parts of you I don't know as well, that might scare me at first, but I'll still care for you no matter what," Veras said. "Let us take care of you?"

One of the monster's hands moved from its face as it looked between us. I approached from the side. Now that I was closer, I could see that the monster didn't have skin. It was an animate collection of vines, strange silvery leaves reflecting our lights where eyes should be.

"A taproot's like a second heart," Veras said. "It might be in the same spot?"

I covered my arm with a sleeve of easily shed, loose skin and slipped my hand a few inches into the plant creature's side, forcing it between the woven tendrils, trying to avoid the wooden bones that lent the creature structure. It was like a maze inside, barbed with thorns and constantly shifting. The monster moaned, bark grating against bark.

"Hold still for Ella," Veras said.

Vines squeezed around my arm, cutting off circulation. "Keep him calm."

"I love you, Andras. Just a little longer."

The pressure relaxed, and I reached deeper into its chest. A whisper of Andras's magic came through one of my fingers. I shifted my hand in that direction, following it, in up to the shoulder, my face pressed against its side, one cheek covered in a thick callus I could safely dissolve afterwards. My hand closed around something warm that pulsed against my fingers. I pulled it out.

The monster fell apart into a slimy pile of plant matter, leaving me holding a rich brown oval wrapped in thin green tendrils. Veras carefully took it from me, feeding it healing magic one careful drop at a time. The tendrils stirred, turning tiny leaves to face the magical lights Reyna and Dorian carried.

Veras clutched it to his chest and started to cry. I patted his back with my clean arm, again unable to speak. Veras gave me what must've been the strongest hug of his entire life. There was so much wrong with the universe but this, at least, we could make right.

"I'm going to be the worst healer ever," Veras sniffled. "We're not supposed to date our patients."

"If he's better, he'll have graduated from being your patient, right?"

"Ella, do you think he heard me back on Plesmae?"

"Maybe?"

"It doesn't matter. I still need to say it again," Veras said. "No more taking chances."

"Once you've done that, can I… see him?" I asked.

Veras stared at me in horror, and I reflexively checked for how my body had changed, how I might be disturbing him. "Ella, if you don't go to see him, he'll hunt you down to the ends of the universe to make sure you're okay. I know you have to go home, but that doesn't mean you don't have a place with us too."

"Just checking," I said. If I focused, I could track the shape and workings of my tear ducts. They were going into overdrive. I knew I could stop them if I wanted.

No hiding unless it's necessary. Not my ability. Not how my mind worked. Not how I felt.

"Can we get out of here?" Reyna asked, interrupting.

Veras and I both jumped. He wiped his eyes, dried my face with his sleeve. "Yes. Let's."

We raced back through the woods, and I liked to think that Andras's taproot kept us safe.

27

Back at the base, I sat next to Veras while he examined Andras's taproot again, one gold-shot white wing draped over my shoulders.

"We can have a future," Veras was saying. "I mean, life might still be awful when we get home, and of course the house is gone, but this is..." He glanced at me, some of his joy fading.

"This will be better than it was," I said. "That's worth celebrating."

Veras nodded. "It feels good to have something to look forward to again."

"I thought of some things I'll do once this is over."

He raised an eyebrow.

"When I'm back home," I said, emphasizing the first word, "I want a pet. Plesmae doesn't have good pet material, which makes Earth way better."

"If you say so."

"And I'm going to get a job where I can leave for a week or more at a time decently often. So I can visit you."

His wing pulled me in closer.

"And..." Other things came to mind. Things like finding love, something I'd never let myself consider because of how much I had to hide. Exploring the world I was born on, appreciating it in ways no other human could. Grandiose things I felt embarrassed about sharing. "I'm going to indulge in hot chocolate, and fleece pajamas, and other warm things. And I'll be so strong nobody will be able to stop me."

"Why would they stop you?" Veras asked.

"I don't know. Some people don't like others having fun."

"If they do try, remember you've earned it."

Dorian stretched as he got ready to sleep. He swiveled his wings around. They seemed to get stuck partway through the motion.

"Are you really alright?" I asked him. "You took quite a beating earlier."

"I'm fine," Dorian said.

"Hold still," Reyna told Dorian. She ran her hand along the piece of armor that protected his back. "It's bent."

"Bent?" he said. "Hey!"

With a couple of deft movements, Reyna had removed the backplate to show him. "See? It's been hammered inwards. The structure is compromised and its magic weakened. I need to repair it."

"How long will that take?" he asked, running his hands over the dent.

"Few hours."

Dorian hugged it close. "Surely a master of your level could do it faster."

"Your armor is one of the best sets I've ever made, and the magic that makes it so is complicated. It's delicate work."

"Fine." He handed it over.

"Aren't you both going to sleep?" Veras asked. He'd removed and begun stitching one sleeve of his borrowed soldier's jacket into a pouch for Andras's taproot.

"I won't be able to relax enough until I do something with my hands," Reyna said.

"I'll wait until it's done," Dorian said.

"You need rest for your injuries to finish healing," Veras said.

"Repair it in the morning, then." He tried to put it back on.

"For the love of—that dent will dig into a major nerve center all night. Give it to Reyna."

Dorian shook his head.

Veras grabbed the piece of armor and tried to take it from Dorian, which seemed to push him over the edge. If I hadn't grabbed his arm in time, he might've broken Veras's nose. I could see the change in his eyes when he realized he'd almost gone too far. Reyna held out her hand. I took the piece of armor from him and gave it to her.

Dorian looked betrayed. He held his wings together like a shield over his back. "I hate you all," he said in a petulant voice, and then collapsed onto one of the beds.

"If you sleep on your wings folded up, you'd better not complain to me in the morning about soreness," Veras said, sounding like he needed to feel in charge, to get the last word, even as he shook with nerves.

Reyna sighed. "He's a soldier, he's used to discomfort." Lines of light appeared where she touched the armor, dozens of them to an inch, silver threads woven together to form a hexagonal grid. Where the armor had been deformed, there was a jagged split in the lines. Using a metal tool tipped with a minuscule hook, she began removing the torn threads of magic around the break. "You've worn down the bindings from use. You should've brought this to me for touch-ups years ago."

"How Dorian doesn't have joint problems is a mystery I have yet to solve," Veras said. He raised his voice. "*Somebody* is going to suffer some *serious consequences* to his health if he keeps this up."

"I think he gets the idea, guys," I said.

"You should sleep too, Ella. Who knows what shape he'll be in tomorrow."

I went over to Dorian, who crossed his arms tighter.

"We won't have real beds for a while, you should enjoy it," I said.

When he didn't respond, I poked him. He looked away.

"Do you feel unsafe?" I asked.

"Why ask if you can't do anything about it?" he muttered.

"Why can't I? You know you can trust me to watch your back. Please, get some rest."

He rolled onto his side, freeing his trapped wings. I sat on the edge of his bed and closed my eyes, exhausted. A light weight settled over my lap, the dark red fur on the underside of Dorian's wings brushing my hands. I felt him flinch when something sounded off in the distance.

"Just the wind," I said.

Dorian still didn't relax. Today had been a rollercoaster of emotions. I didn't feel like beating around the bush.

"Is this enough for you to feel safe?" I asked.

"No," he said.

I scooted a few inches closer, asked the same question, a few inches more, wound up touching his back.

"If you want something, you have to tell me," I said. "Dorian, it's okay that you couldn't kill it."

He squeezed his injured arm and mumbled just loud enough for me to hear. His request surprised me. There wasn't anything wrong with it, it just seemed like something I'd be the one to cave and ask him for first, not the other way around. I curled up against his back, my head pillowed on one of his wings, my arm around his waist. Dorian immediately relaxed. He should have just asked from the start. The quiet conversation happening a few paces from us stopped. Whatever. It felt good to have something warm to curl up around, even if that something was mostly covered in hard armor.

I woke up some time later. Veras was passed out, curled around Andras's taproot. Dorian slept like a log. His repaired piece of armor rested on one of the beds, but Reyna was nowhere in sight. I carefully slipped away and put it back on him. He didn't wake up.

"Reyna?" I quietly called out as I padded down the hallway. "Where are you?"

I heard noise elsewhere in the base. I raced towards it, fearing the worst.

I found her in a room that smelled of ash and copper. Blackened metal maws—old forges?—covered one of the walls, the fire long dead in their throats. She sat on one of the benches, digging through a few boxes full of sharp pointy things. I waited until her hands were free before speaking up.

"Everything okay?"

Reyna jumped, clutching for a battered short sword. "What—oh. It's you. It's just you." She said it more to herself than to me. "Is it time to go?"

"The boys are still sleeping. How long's it been?"

"About five hours, I think," Reyna said.

"Have you slept for any of that?"

She shook her head. "I'll go to bed soon. I'm looking for a few things, including a better weapon for Dorian."

"I imagine Dorian can handle himself so long as his weapon doesn't break in his hands."

"It feels like some of the things I've made have been letting me down recently," Reyna admitted. She brushed old ashes from her pants and looked at the cold forges. "Guess there's not much I can do about that right now, though."

"He's put a lot of strain on your creations."

"Your armor that *I* made hurt you."

"It was uncomfortable for a little bit, that's all. Besides, those are just a few things you've made out of what, hundreds? Thousands?"

She kicked the box. "Don't remind me how long I've been doing this. That's a sure-fire way to make me feel tired."

"You *are* tired. Come get some sleep."

"Stay?"

I sat beside her.

"This is where it happened," Reyna said. "I was working alone one night, since I preferred the quiet, when some monsters forced their way through a weak spot in the veil and entered the base, and there was nobody around to warn or protect me. Too focused on what my hands were doing to notice anything wrong until I was pinned beneath a graftling. So it's good to have a companion with me. I've spent too much of my life alone. Try not to be me like me, okay? Being lonely is hard enough, but sometimes you get to thinking you're alone because you deserve it, and there's nobody around to tell you otherwise."

"I'm here because I care about you," I said, leaning against her. "And Veras and Berith care about you too, even if you don't see them often."

"I know," she said softly. "It's strange to think that I met them both here. This is the worst place I've ever been, but I also wouldn't have either of them otherwise. You already know Veras took care of me after I was injured, and Berith... he briefly visited Glashower several times during the war, including stopping by to see patients. He was my one visitor when I was recovering in the infirmary. He was emotionally available for me, and I did my best to become someone he could lean on the other times he visited, and in the immediate aftermath of the war. But I felt like I needed to get out of the capital, and of course he was still busy, and..." She sighed. "I've never had many friends at a time. I really tried with those other artisans. But first I was probably the 'weird one' of the group, and then I... there it is."

Her hand dove between sharp edges to retrieve—

"You made a gun?" I said.

"Explain," she said.

I tried to be brief. The object she'd made was shaped like a short rifle, its barrel larger than a regular bullet would fit. Reyna held it like it might explode.

"I like knowing somebody else beat me to it," she said. "Part of the design came to me in a dream. I didn't even stop to write it down, just jumped into creating it. The other artisans hated it. Its projectiles are dangerous to make, and they seemed to feel it was... too easy to use? Magic takes a lot of intention, as do melee weapons and bows, but this one is just," she mimed pulling the trigger, "and something is dead. I made something I thought would help with the war, and some of the other artisans threatened to leave me behind on Glashower because they thought it would be bad for our society if I brought it home. I gave in to their wishes and left it here to rust, and I haven't been able to recreate it since. The parts just won't come together right. So I've come back for it, and I'm taking it with me."

Reyna clipped the gun to her belt and turned to me, breathless.

"I'm hardly going to stop you," I said. "Do you feel safer now that you have it?"

"I'm not sure. It's not the safest object to hold, and I should probably take it apart to remind myself how I made it, but... I think it does. I like the idea of being able to stop a monster from getting too close to me, of dealing with it before I can panic. Do you think I'm bad for having made it?"

"Just don't shoot people? I don't see what's that complicated about it. Those same artisans wouldn't be upset with Dorian for being born with his magic, right?"

"No, they wouldn't. I guess I'm just afraid that they've finally forgotten about it, but if I bring it back with me..."

"Reyna. You made your bike, which, if other makhali who can no longer fly have one? Makes the world more accessible to them. You've developed a more flexible underlayer and armor. You've made good things, and the one 'bad' thing you made didn't have any malice involved in it. Even if that does happen, it's their loss, not yours. I've really enjoyed having a badass motorcycle aunt or older sister or whatever you want to be to me."

Reyna managed to smile. "Let's go with much older sister. I always wanted a kid sibling I could dress up. Someone younger to be proud of me. I want to be worthy of that."

"You already—"

"I'm sorry if my seeing you that way made me push you," she blurted out. "Push you to be things I couldn't. I didn't want you to contain yourself the way I've had to, but our experiences aren't the same, and I shouldn't have projected my problems onto you like that. You seemed uncomfortable saying no, but I tried to convince myself that meant yes, which wasn't right."

"I wasn't good at saying no because it felt like I've been using you," I said. "Like you've had to buy my company by making things for me."

"I never felt that way," Reyna said. "Are we settled?"

I nodded.

She patted the gun again, and it seemed to bring her comfort. "That's one life goal taken care of. Now I just have to kidnap Berith."

I fiddled with my translation earring, fingers searching for damage.

"I mean it," Reyna said. "He can't bring himself to stop working despite how much it wears him down, and he's not the sort to let others rescue him, so I'll have to use some kind of deception. But once I've taken him away on my motorbike, he'll finally be away from all the people constantly asking the world of him, and I'll convince him to retire."

"I... good luck with that," I said.

She nudged me. "That's me taken care of. Now why do *you* look so down?"

I scuffed my shoes on the ash-strewn floor. "Can you ever tell who a monster... used to be?"

"Most graftlings are rebuilt from the ground up, so usually no. There might be a brief window of time for a person lost to the infection where they mostly look like themselves but... aren't anymore. But delicate, 'useless' structures like unique facial features are lost quickly as the soft tissues change. It's an accidental blessing."

"So if I saw my parents, I wouldn't know."

Reyna wrapped her arms around me. "You need to have hope. From what I've heard, your world has technologies we don't that could help them against the Graft, or at least help them warn and evacuate people better than we could. Let's try to focus on that, okay?"

I nodded, face tucked against her shoulder.

"Let's get to bed," Reyna said.

The rest of the night passed without incident. The first thing Dorian did in the morning was stretch his arm around to make sure that his back was covered. From the bunk above him, I watched Veras adjust the strap of his bag for Andras's taproot a few dozen times. Reyna took a bit longer to wake up, yawning, but her gun didn't get more than a raised eyebrow from our other companions, which must've brought her some relief.

Dorian had only slept off some of his fidgetiness, and kept shooting side-eyed glances at me. He loosely swung his axe, still distressed by its shape and weight. "Let's get a move on," he said. "The sooner we're home the sooner I can have a proper blade again."

"Pretty sure I made that axe too, asshole," Reyna said. "Is its craftsmanship not up to your standards?"

"It's just not the same. Some items are more important to our self-images than others."

Reyna raised an eyebrow.

"But thanks. For fixing my armor, and, uh, everything else." He chewed his words before slowly turning to Veras. "The jacket didn't look half bad on you, before you cut it up, anyway."

Veras, sporting his military jacket that was now missing one sleeve, only rolled his eyes.

"There it is," Reyna said. "Now, come along, children. We have a long trip home."

We raced back through the contaminated swamp, on full alert for the wolf but only coming across the same sluggish plants we'd previously encountered. When we reached the cliff, I began to build up my shoulder muscles in preparation to climb up it with Reyna holding onto me. I needn't have bothered. Again a massive root grew from the cliff and spiraled down to us, stopping just a few inches from Veras's chest where the taproot hung. He sterilized our clothes as we each climbed onto it. Once Veras was on it began to retract, lifting us back up to safety.

Reyna's bike and my spear were waiting for us at the top. The trees had parted, leaving a wide corridor of open airspace for flying through; their roots clutched compacted dirt to form a path for driving. Now that we had what we needed, what Glashower wanted us to have, it was helping in whatever way it could.

"Is this Andras?" I asked.

Veras touched the pouch hanging from his neck. "Without his taproot buried, he can't affect plant life from this far away. It's not *from* him, but it's probably *for* him."

Glashower taking care of its own; it certainly made sense. But when we took a quick breather by the rift that would start us on our trip back to Plesmae, a vine brushed the back of my neck and looped over my shoulders in a gentle, almost friendly way.

"Do you think they like me?" I said to Dorian, who was batting away a couple vines himself.

"You shouldn't be surprised by the idea of others liking you," he said. "Clearly, they do."

"I wasn't sure, since they're grabbing you too."

"What, and I'm less likable than you?"

"You do have a habit of trying to fight everything you meet."

"That's just the sort of universe we live in. Speaking of, everyone ready?"

Reyna revved her bike.

Dorian drew his axe, prepared in case something nasty awaited us on the other side of the rift.

"I'm right behind you," I said.

"I know."

We stepped through, safe for the moment, open land around us—nothing that could've made the grinding noise we heard right after. I put a hesitant hand up to the rift we'd just gone through, finding the way blocked by heavy stone. It was time to ward the paths between worlds. Not for forever, I hoped.

Life can get better.

And we set off towards Plesmae.

28

Travel day 13: *Mission accomplished and on our way back. No sign of the Fortress that previously attacked us, though with its long legs I expect it might catch up. We know better what to expect than we did before, high hopes for our return being faster than it took us to get here.*

Travel day 18: *V checks on A's taproot every time we stop, making sure it's healthy. Keeps worrying he's doing something wrong with it and has been beating himself up for not grabbing some Glashower dirt or a plant or anything else on our way out. Finally got him to stop by pointing out the plants might not have appreciated an attempted kidnapping of one of their own.*

Reyna and I have been talking a lot about Earth technology. I was worried it would make her feel less special if she heard about an idea someone else had before her, but it seems to make her happy instead. Talking about what we have at home is a lot easier now that I'm heading your way again.

Dorian's been training me to use a magical spear I found. There's some-

thing much cleaner about using that weapon instead of my body, but it's not my preference. It's like trying to do something else has shown me that I'm actually good with my ability now? The spear is good for keeping a monster at bay, but using my own hands lets me touch and stress-test and weigh whatever I'm interacting with, decide if it's a material worth copying. I don't think I was ever good at anything before I left home. I wasn't even good at being myself, or being your daughter. Maybe I'm still not, because part of me wants our lives to return to exactly how they were before all this so I can keep my secrets. All I can promise is that I'll try.

And I need you to be good parents and tell me how to deal with certain emotions. I don't even know how I feel when I look at Dorian anymore. I want him next to me all the time but I don't know what that means.

~

*T*RAVEL DAY **21**: *Back on the planet of the Ella Over-Exertion Incident. Fuck this world. Probably too agitated because I didn't sleep much last night. I guess I feel guilty. There must be lots of people like me out there who want to return home one day, and here we are, trying to block off rifts behind us. We're building barricades where we can, using whatever rocks or ruins or loose earth we can find. Hoping that, even if a monster comes along who could break them down, they're less interested in doing so because they can't smell another world past it. Still putting up magical barriers too. Even if they don't last, it'll be useful to know where monsters with the ability to break through them are. I'm worried that, down the line, someone will forget these are only meant to be temporary fixes, not permanent solutions.*

~

ON DAY **25** of our journey we reached Felar, standing once again in that glass-capped atrium. Whether or not we wanted to go back the way we'd came didn't matter, because when I quietly snuck ahead I found the way blocked by an organic landslide. Going outside through the dust wasn't a great option. In search of another path,

Reyna tapped the brick wall halfway up the stairs with a metal tool. She shot me an expectant look.

"You should really ask in advance before doing that," I said. "In case I'm not prepared."

She raised an eyebrow.

"Right in the middle. There was an echo."

"I knew you'd be listening." Reyna scanned our environment. "Alright, everyone behind that fallen pillar there. All limbs held close, please," she said with the tone of a kindergarten teacher. We did as asked. "Dorian, can I brace against you? Veras, move a few feet to your left. It's more structurally sound there." Coming from her, those were some of the most terrifying words I'd ever heard.

Veras was too gangly to scrunch in well, but he did his best. "Can we take a moment to talk about—"

Too late. Reyna stuck her head and arms past the pillar just enough to aim her proto-gun, her back against Dorian's. I couldn't see exactly what happened without putting my face in the danger zone, but I saw her pull the trigger, Dorian lurching forward in surprise at the kickback, Reyna throwing herself to the side moments before—

"This is why they didn't want to teach you their technology," I said. Not right when it happened. A minute or two afterwards, too late for me to sound cool, but I was too spooked to speak until the flying brickwork had resolved itself and Reyna's proto-gun, no, her miniature *cannon* had stopped smoking. It radiated an alarming aura I could best compare to a cloud of wildfire smoke, the smell and fullness of the air making me scared of another spark starting a blaze, another projectile being launched without warning.

"I want one," Dorian said, but his wings were quivering, and not with excitement.

"I can't with you people," Veras said. "I need a break from you all once we're back on Plesmae."

"We know you don't mean that," Dorian said.

"No, he does," I said. "But it's not anything personal."

"Thanks for understanding," Veras grumbled.

"Besides, he'll need to spend time with—"

Veras marched through the hole Reyna's cannon had punched through the stone wall. On the other side was some sort of service tunnel. Through trial and error we followed the dark, empty hallways out of the city, passing through the space between the open atriums below and the surface above. We escaped the underground, covered up as much as we could, and raced through the dusty streets and storm; once free of the city, nobody wanted to spend another night on Felar despite our exhaustion.

I soon wished I'd asked Reyna and Veras about what it had been like to be back on a changed Glashower, how to cope with those feelings, because they hit me the moment we were back on Plesmae.

The veil that protected Pellior's Landing looked like a bored giant had taken a pair of scissors to it, the walls pockmarked as if ill. Everything between us and there was in its own chaotic state of disarray. There were fires and craters and floods. Flying graftlings spotted the sky like vultures, while hundreds if not thousands of terrestrial monsters were spread across the few miles of landscape between us and safety. The Glade seemed frozen in time, a good deal of it still standing, but the rest like a garden of half-formed statues, sky-scraping trees bent and broken to form limbs. Several walking giants had been felled, forming twenty-foot-tall walls that were breaking down into hills of sludge. A few weeks was long enough for a million different things to happen.

"Hey, boys. You two should go," I said. "We'll make our own way, right, Reyna?"

"Yes. Get to Andras and report to Berith. Keep each other safe."

Dorian hesitated. "We could try to fly with you, Reyna. And Ella could maybe, you know."

"We'd all be vulnerable that way."

"Get going," I said. "Dorian, I'll take out a few graftlings for you."

"Just don't kill that Fortress without me."

They lifted off, flying with special urgency. They'd be fine, I was sure. They had to be. I stared across the ruined landscape.

"How are we going to do this?" Reyna asked.

"Preferably without panic, if possible?"

"Full throttle, then."

"Maybe not—"

She gunned the bike anyway, taking us around burning grasslands and liquid bodies. The air was foul with ashes and that singularly putrid smell of contaminated matter. A group of snuffling, low-to-the-ground graftlings looked up from their harvesting of the fallen. My spear cut through them. Thanks to Dorian's help it had grown more familiar in my hands, its magic begging to be used after who knew how long in hibernation, which was excellent because I'd need it. Dozens of monsters swarmed around the entry gates to the capital. When we drew near I launched myself off the back of the bike, hitting the outer circle of graftlings from behind while Reyna pulled to the side. I stabbed and slashed with the spear, slammed monsters to the ground with the help of additional muscles in my arms and shoulders, checked nobody was going to accidentally zap or burn or freeze me with honed senses.

A particularly large enemy that leaked gallons of liquid contamination from its mouth barreled towards me. Its back was protected by armor. I braced myself, preparing to stab it in its uncovered stomach once we collided—

A body sheathed in translucent magic slammed into it, driving it out of the way. He moved so fast that I didn't fully process it was Berith until the creature lay dead, neck cut open by his sword. I supposed that the Commander of an entire species would need to be good in combat, but I hadn't been expecting that level of speed or strength. He straightened, the protective magic around him having kept his armor clean of contamination. His eyes, the only part of his face visible beneath the underlayer that covered his nose and mouth, were freezing cold.

Then Reyna almost ran him over, braking hard and falling off her bike into his arms, and he was once again the person I knew.

"Reyna! Thank the universe, you've made it back safe."

"Where's the break." It left her mouth as a statement. "The break. Where. Where is it."

Berith took the opportunity to hug her before she could run off in search of something to fix. His tired eyes caught sight of me. He swayed on his feet and had to lean on Reyna.

"Are you okay?" I asked. "Should you be out here?"

"I am fine," he said. "I've kept my old body in shape. Ella..." He seemed to have lost the ability to speak.

"This is what I need to do to protect myself," I said, gesturing to my changed body.

"It's not that."

I was painfully aware of the passing of time. "Is everything under control out here? I'm going to lose my mind if I don't see Andras soon."

Berith nodded, still looking dazed, still holding Reyna tight. I knew she'd be safe with him, so I made a beeline for the hospital, weaving through ranks of armed defenders prepared to get called out past the gates, triage medics, and worryingly small stacks of supplies. A doctor had to corner me in the hospital lobby, demanding I let them remove the filth that covered my arms and legs. I was being an idiot. What if I made Andras ill again? I tried to slow myself down as I was led through the corridors. A weight settled around my ankles and crept up my body. By the time I was outside his room, it had all but paralyzed me.

Go in, I told myself. You have to know, don't you? Just knock on the damn door. You can hear voices, that one's clearly Veras, it's the right room, so just—

Veras opened the door before I could do anything, almost running into me. "Are you hurt?"

I shook my head. He ushered me inside.

Andras sat up in bed, braced against a wall of pillows. His eyes looked like they had before he'd become so desperately sick, the iris and whites separate again, and he no longer had that awful sun-starved pallor. He held out his arms.

There's a time and a place for weak, crappy hugs, and this wasn't it. I was as careful as I could be while still getting close. No smell of contamination here, just a trace of green and growing things. I let go before I lost the ability to.

"Why didn't you let us know you were outside?" he asked gently.

"I thought it was better to know no matter what I found, and then I got here and I wasn't so sure anymore," I said.

Andras brushed a strand of hair out of my face. "Now you know. I'm doing just fine, thanks to all of you." He had something wrapped around his throat. At first I thought it was some kind of IV drip, but it had the same texture as his skin. He saw me staring and pulled the collar of his shirt down. His taproot was stuck to his chest, the roots melting into him. "It won't be visible for much longer. I have to say, it feels good to be in one piece after all these years," he said.

"I'm sorry you've lost your last connection to your home," Veras said.

"A hamadryad can have more than one home. Someday I and the rest of my kind will reclaim Glashower, but that won't change the fact that I belong here on Plesmae, too." Andras turned to me. "Hopefully I can become as strong as you. Oh, come here again. I'm not *that* delicate. All these extra pillows and blankets are just because Veras insisted."

"You're still recovering."

"I've been improving for over a week. Just getting my taproot away from the Graft helped." Andras wasn't letting go of me yet. It was strange how good it felt where my hands and face brushed against his uncovered arms. I wouldn't have expected to like the rough texture, but now it meant something good.

"I have so much to tell you about Glashower," I said.

"Later," Andras said. "You're exhausted. Let other people take care of you now."

That was another understanding of mine that had changed. I used to think really maturing meant never needing someone else to take care of you, but I could see now that wasn't the case. I could be capable and still need someone to make sure it was a soft bed I passed out on instead of the floor.

INTERMISSION

I tried to make a home. I have tried so many times to make a home. The work always fails. I make a house but not a home, and so I leave it for others to enjoy and try again somewhere else. It is only a house and not a home unless he is there.

The foundation went well, but this new house refuses to be done more than any other I've seen. They tell me of a new foundation, one I think might suit him better.

All I want is to find home again.

29

I was woken by knocking and lurched to answer the door, needing a moment to get my bearings in my makeshift room down the hall from Andras's. It was Dorian. I'd been given some spare plain clothes to wear, but Dorian still wore his armor, albeit cleaned up from our trip. A new sword, not quite the same shape as his old one, hung at his waist. He offered me a plate of actual food, all things I could comfortably eat. He seemed fidgety, which meant life had probably slowed down for the moment.

"What time is it?" I asked.

"Early afternoon," Dorian said. "Almost a full day since we returned. Your hair's a mess."

I ate while he undid the remains of his previous work and combed out all the knots. He was unusually quiet.

"If the fighting works out here," I said nervously, fearful that speaking the words would make them untrue, "I think I might be ready to go home."

The comb went away, leaving me feeling momentarily abandoned, and then his hands were gathering up my hair and dividing it into equal sections. "That's good. I still want to take you home, though with all that's happening on Plesmae and beyond, I don't know if I'd be able to stick around and help you."

"I'll take whatever assistance you can give me. If I don't see my parents soon, the stress might kill me. But I, um." I didn't look up. "I hate the idea of saying goodbye to you, Reyna, Andras, and Veras."

"I can't help with the others. But the two of us wouldn't separate immediately, not until we found your parents. And even then, splitting up doesn't stop people from being teammates," Dorian said. "We'll always have that."

Didn't it though, if we weren't literally on a team anymore? Maybe this was a clumsy translation, and he meant something *bigger* than that. "We'll be fighting the same enemy."

"Exactly." He knotted something around the end of my braid. "Good?"

I pulled the braid forward to see what it was. Two ribbons, white and red. Same as his wings. I knew I should ask what that meant but was scared to. "Good."

"You're rested?"

"I'm tempted to sleep for a week, but relatively, yes."

"There's something I could use a teammate's help with," Dorian said. "The Citadel wants to hear firsthand about our trip."

"Alright. When's the meeting?"

"Soon."

"Soon?"

"Ten minutes."

"Dorian."

"I didn't want to pull you away from your friend, and then you needed sleep, and then I had to get us both ready."

"We'd better get a move on."

That had been my intention, but when we went to leave Veras was passing by on some other business, and the look on his face made me stop. I waved Dorian on, promising I'd catch up.

"So," Veras said. "You and Dorian."

"Don't get excited," I said.

"It would make sense," he continued. "Two warriors, traveling and fighting and killing together."

"I don't have to take this from the guy who spent three years unable to admit he had a crush."

Veras's face flushed. "He's my boyfriend now, so clearly I know what I'm doing. Maybe you and soldier boy can be an example. First human-alien romance."

I rolled my eyes. "Congratulations to the both of you, but you're making me late. Dorian asked for backup in a meeting." I dashed past him.

"Enjoy your date!" Veras yelled after me.

"You've been in a relationship for like an hour, you're not an expert!" I shouted back.

My favorite winged secretary was at his post in the Citadel lobby, a sheathed sword lying on his desk. He seemed surprised to see me alive.

"Saela, my dude. How have you been?" I said.

"Largest meeting room, third floor. Just go."

"Thank you." I made finger guns in his general direction, extended and strengthened my arms, and clambered up a pillar, finding it quicker than messing with all those stairs. Saela gasped. I was feeling pretty good about myself as I reset my body and checked my clothes for dust. So good, I forgot to knock before entering the meeting room. On having every eye in the room turn to me, I froze, needing to remind myself that I was wanted and needed here.

"Here she is. Ella can describe how she almost drowned in liquid Graft," Dorian said. He had a strained expression on his face. There were a lot of faces around that table, all older makhali who looked about one bit of bad news away from snapping, and the only one I recognized was Berith. I crab-walked around the crowded table to an empty chair. Dorian sat between Berith and I.

"You're alright?" Berith quietly asked me.

"Yep. What were you all talking about?"

Dorian jumped out of his chair to better point to his maps and the pages of Reyna's journal, which were spread out all over the table, listing the rifts we'd attempted to close off and describing the stages and kinds of contamination we'd encountered. He gradually relaxed, leaning on the table like he was telling stories at a bar. A few people looked queasy, and downright anxious at his descriptions of all that lay beneath Felar's surface. Berith seemed to have trouble focusing on the discussion, gaze shifting between the materials on the table, others' expressions, and me. I wanted to ask him about the spear I'd found later, as Berith was a self-proclaimed old man. I kept quiet until Dorian started talking about the different variations of graftlings we'd fought, and turned to me for help. "Give me a hand here. I'm having trouble finding the right words."

So I did. It was easier than I'd expected, and at first I wasn't sure why. But as I spoke about everything from specialized forms to entire Graft ecosystems, I figured it out. It was all a giant puzzle, breaking down my experiences to decipher what each monster's role was, opposite but equal to how I might decide what I wanted my body to do and build from the ground up to reach it. My words were strange but effective enough. And when I couldn't find the right words either, I demonstrated, growing armor and claws and membranes.

People were... concerned, but had the decency to hide their disgust.

Or maybe they weren't disgusted.

Or maybe I didn't care if they were.

Not caring was *great*, especially since I had so much else to worry about. Talking about the world where I'd gotten separated from Dorian only made the room more grim.

"It's as if they're actively, intelligently learning," Berith said. "We've always thought of the Graft as a disease that's incompatible with sentience, as contamination destroys preexisting brain matter, but that might be an outdated view. Whether they're preserving complex brain structures or creating new ones, we must stop them. I only wish that, to destroy such an enemy, we had easier and kinder options than razing that overtaken world down to its bones."

"How big was the total mass?" A female makhal asked.

"From below, it was like there was a second sky above me," I said. "If there was an end to it, it was beyond what I could see."

"We've never come across a single biomass that large," a man said. "Though if they've really grown capable of creating a self-sustaining ecosystem, it's certainly possible. They must've stripped other worlds entirely bare."

"You mentioned there were structures?" Berith said.

I described the garden and its gardener, the pseudo-city, and the half-formed creature in its chrysalis. "I found some makhali-made items there, a spear and armor, and killed that developing monster."

Berith was surprisingly quiet, his hands clasped together over his mouth. He looked at me with alarm in his eyes, and I wondered if we should've privately shared this information with him first. But I'll admit the rest of the Citadel's reactions filled me with relief.

"We can't leave that large of a continuous mass of Graft to its own devices," the woman from earlier said.

"The speed at which new forms have evolved is certainly quicker than we expected," the man said. "Our numbers are limited, especially considering our most recent casualties, but staying isolated without actively keeping our adjacent worlds safe isn't—"

He was interrupted by a massive ripping sound, like a million sheets being torn in half. The room shook. Someone pulled back the curtains. A gash the length of a football field ran through the veil, the edges peeling back from the wind.

"This meeting is adjourned," Berith said. "Everyone, prepare for battle."

The other Council members scrambled, likely running to a safe position. Berith placed a hand on my shoulder.

"You've seen so much," he said. "I know this trip was for your friend. If you need more time to recover, or you feel you are done fighting for now, you can take shelter. But if you want to fight, we're well past the point where I have any right to hold you back."

"It's not like I've stopped caring about people since returning," I said.

Berith looked between Dorian and I. "Ella, get your armor.

Assemble at the main gates. There are matters we must discuss, but there's no time now."

Dorian and Berith flew while I raced through the chaotic streets, intending to swing by the hospital to grab my gear. Half the veil sagged like a punctured balloon, the torn edges jagged and disintegrating. A handful of flying graftlings hurtled through the opening. One dove towards me. I tensed, ready to dodge and then strike it. I needn't have bothered. Something green spiked out and caught it in the side.

"Hello," Andras called out.

I swore and ran over to him. Andras caught me in a hug. He was already weighed down by a bag with my armor and spear over his shoulder, so I almost knocked him over.

"Sorry!"

"Guess I've still got some recovery time ahead of me." He squeezed and relaxed his fingers, and the trees around us took on new life, swelling in size and developing thick club-like branches. "Feels great to be able to do this without pain, though."

Veras came running after us. "Andras! You shouldn't be out of bed yet." He stopped when he saw the collapsed graftling and moving trees.

Andras ran his hand over Veras's hair, smoothing down a few fraught strands. "Hey. You don't have to worry anymore. It'll be alright."

Veras's face flushed. "I—okay. Okay. But you're not going out there, are you?"

Andras flung out his arm, and another flier was smashed out of the air by branches. "There isn't much healthy plant life outside the walls. This is where I can be of use." Snaking vines shored up crumbling spots on the wall, realigning cracked protective sigils and shrinking the rip in the veil.

Veras was so relieved, he looked close to fainting. "If either of you get hurt... just be careful. I need to get back to the infirmary." He ran off.

I speed-dressed in my armor, sticking the separate pieces of my underlayer to my skin. Andras grabbed the collar of my shirt before I could go. He gave me one more hug. "Thanks for keeping him safe. Sorry I can't help you out there."

"We've all got what we do best," I said. I put on my favorite modifications: long claws, hard yet flexible plates that covered where Reyna's armor would impede my movement, some extra length to my arms and legs. "And I've learned a lot about myself on our journey."

"You look savage," Andras said approvingly. "Take care of yourself."

"I will. Stay safe."

He waved, and I ran to the gate, where a bunch of makhali were gathering. More graftlings had arrived, dotting the grasslands like lesions. I spotted Berith atop the wall, translucent wings draped over his shoulders like a blanket, folded arms pressed in against his stomach. He straightened as I approached. Dorian landed next to us, his replacement sword already covered in dark blood.

"I take it that Fortress is Pillbug?" Berith said.

Every muscle in my body went stiff. I looked past the veil. Pillbug squatted in the ruined fields like an armored boulder. "Yeah. That's the bastard."

Dorian squeezed my shoulder. "Do you need to be the one to strike the killing blow?"

"Dorian, there's a war on. It's endangering everyone," I said.

"You saw it first."

"Yes, and now I want to never see it again. Help?"

"A small, coordinated group would be best, I believe," Berith said. "And three's a fortuitous number."

"It's the same on my world," I said.

Berith glanced at his troops. "We're as ready as we can be."

I took one more glance from afar at Pillbug and, giving in to temptation, raised a middle finger at it.

Its antenna waggled back.

It might've had nothing to do with me, but the gesture still infuriated me. It also drew my attention to something. Pillbug's antenna were uneven, one bent in half, the other shorter than I remembered.

Now that I looked closer with my augmented vision, I saw its sides were pocked with small holes, some of the plates warped as if they'd partially melted. I'd seen Glashower fighting back against the Graft, and here was proof Earth was too.

There was a waist-high fence running around the edge of the wall. I climbed on top of it, hoping the extra height would make me more visible to my enemy.

"FUCK. YOU," I screamed at Pillbug. "THE ONLY REASON YOU'RE HERE IS BECAUSE MY PLANET KICKED YOUR ASS YOU LITTLE BUG BITCH. I HOPE YOU'RE SENTIENT ENOUGH TO FEEL AFRAID YOU ABSOLUTE DUMPSTER FIRE OF A BASTARD."

My words did not echo over the battlefield. Everyone on the wall probably heard them though. I stepped down from the fence and looked to Berith, feeling self-conscious but also glad to have gotten that out.

"What's a dumpster?" Dorian whispered to me.

Berith cleared his throat, then raised his sword. "Split their ranks," he called out to the waiting makhali. "I want a clear path to the Fortress."

Pillbug raised its front legs and screeched, the sound shaking the sky. The individual monsters near the capital raised their own horrid voices before charging the gate, different forms crawling over and trampling each other in a horde so tightly packed that they might as well have been one massive beast with thousands of limbs and millions of teeth and claws. They were incapable of understanding the power of the destructive magic being flung at them, but with their numbers that might not matter. Following Berith and Dorian's lead, I launched myself from atop the gate, gliding over the horde and dodging swarms of flying graftlings. I temporarily dimmed my senses to avoid being overwhelmed by the waves of uneven limbs, the snapping maws, the stench of rot—and then the flashes of thrown magic, the shriek and impact of arrows, the sharp scent of blood. I felt weightless, unmoored, safe from a universe whose majority wanted to hurt me.

And then I hit the ground on the other side of the flood, body undergoing a wing-consuming, center-of-gravity-shifting spasm to keep me from falling as I landed in a sprint. To my left, one of my six favorite people in the universe hit the ground running and made finger guns at me. The two of us kept pace a little behind Berith as he closed the rest of the hundred feet between us and the waiting Fortress.

Facing Pillbug again, I forgave myself for feeling fear, now and in the past. As its cold presence wormed into my head, I forgave myself for not being strong enough to keep it out. And when its mental attacks started, I forgave myself for feeling pain.

I resisted the urge to cover my ears. It wouldn't help. Icicles pierced my mind, leaving frigid holes that allowed alien words and pictures in. The hallucinations felt clearer this time, more than just flashes of color and light. I dimmed my vision, my surroundings getting darker but the hallucinations keeping their unnatural vibrancy, helping me focus on what was actually happening. A voice, male and worn thin, whispered between my ears, the syllables indecipherable but the general shape of them familiar—

"I see what you mean now," Berith said. It took me a few moments to recognize that he was furious, an expression I'd never seen him wear before. "This, this cruel dredging up of painful memories, it *is* a new ability for the Graft. Hopefully killing this Fortress will cut that lineage short."

"Is that what it's doing for you two?" I said. "That's not what I'm getting."

Dorian shook his head.

"We'll have time to decipher it later," Berith said.

Berith formed his magical armor over the metal he already wore, making it appear like his whole body was covered in the same cellophane-looking substance that made up his wings. He struck at Pillbug's side, swinging his sword in an overhand cleaving motion. Pillbug skittered back, shockingly fast for a creature that must've weighed several tons, Berith's sword barely leaving a scratch on its shell. Pillbug reared up, antenna and the shortest legs just behind its face waving at Berith. He sidled around and closer to it, attempting to draw its attention from Dorian and I.

Instead it barreled towards the two of us, some of its legs swiveling around to spear forward. I rolled to the side to avoid ending up beneath it. Dorian skipped back and lashed out with a magic-wrapped sword, cracking an insect leg. Pillbug skidded to a halt. It held its broken limb above the ground, dangling like a broken puppet. Dorian stared in dismay at his replacement sword, already bent. Berith offered him his own.

"I couldn't after losing the last," Dorian said, the want clear in his eyes.

"Maybe you just borrow this one," Berith said. "We'll get you another blade that can better keep up with you later."

Dorian delicately took it, weighing it in his hands. His magic blazed around it, forming a crackling inferno, the blade a white-hot core at its center that held its shape without deforming. "Shall we find out what the melting temperature of Fortresses are?"

Berith cracked his knuckles, the magical armor around his hands and arms thickening with each *pop*. "Perhaps Reyna would appreciate a sample of its shell."

"I want a piece too," I said, craving constant, physical proof that Pillbug couldn't haunt me anymore.

"If I soften its shell with heat, think you can grab it without hurting yourself?" Dorian asked me.

I was already developing the skin of my hands into thick, leathery padding. "Down to try."

Berith lunged forwards, but Pillbug was strangely reluctant to engage with him. He grabbed one of its larger forelegs as it tried to skirt around him, digging his heels into the ground to slow it, disadvantaged by his species's lighter density. Dorian slashed his borrowed sword downwards, letting loose a wave of magic that seared Pillbug's head. There was no visual change in its glass-bulb eyes, but it lurched as if momentarily blinded. The plates that covered Pillbug's back shifted and raised, releasing a dark gas that hung around the Fortress and stole the oxygen from Dorian's fire, extinguishing the last lingering trace of it. I couldn't back away quickly enough to avoid breathing some of the smog in. It clung to my throat and lungs, worsened the pressure in my head. Pillbug hunkered down in its smog, its glassy eyes seeing all and giving away nothing.

I put some distance between myself and Berith and Dorian, not wanting to risk hurting either of them. I unbuckled the spear from my armor and activated its magic, its power vibrating in the bones of my hand.

Pillbug let out a grinding roar and charged me, breaking away from Berith and out of its haze. I leapt right before we made contact, landing on the broad curve of its immobile face. Its shell was obsidian-smooth, but I covered one hand in textured ridges to keep me from slipping off. I struck one of its half-sphere eyes, shattering it like glass, the pieces dropping into the dark hole left behind.

"You already know what this is for," I told it. I stabbed the spear deep into its empty eye, meeting zero resistance.

Pillbug's body froze. Its legs shriveled and drew in. I heard a low hissing noise, a noise of release.

High-pressure smog spewed and spat from everywhere; from its eye socket, from beneath its body, from invisible cracks in its shell. Pillbug's remaining eye shattered under the force. It convulsed, sending me tumbling. Pillbug ran from us towards the half-ruined Glade, smashing aside fallen trees and flattening lesser monsters.

I chased after, Dorian and Berith a step behind me. Pillbug went through the rift to 9F. We must have tired it out, because we caught up while it was stuck in a valley, escape cut off on two sides. The base of my spear stuck out of one eye.

"We're going to kill you now," Dorian told Pillbug, who had turned around to face us. "Any last words?"

Again with the mental blows. Dorian snarled, I gritted my teeth, Berith shuddered. Sweat ran down his forehead. He hunched forward, hands open, as if in need of something to lean on.

"Take out its legs, and then I'll leverage its shell open," Berith said.

It was only natural that I use my own weapons for this. After all, it was thanks to Pillbug that I'd developed them this much. Smoke still drifted from its empty eyes. "It's over," I told the Fortress. "I'm going to end it right here, so you'll never set foot on Earth again. Or your, um, stupid bug-leg things."

"Didn't have to add that last part," Dorian said.

"You never trained me to give revenge speeches."

"No, just actually useful things." His hand traced along my shoulder, and then it began.

I went left, he went right, Pillbug flung itself around in a frenzy. It still emitted smog, but that couldn't stop Dorian's heated blade from making contact with its legs, warping them. I snapped the smaller limbs I could find on my side, getting bruised and scratched in the process, but its screeches emboldened me. Dorian and I switched sides, and I focused on its bigger legs, wrapping my arms and legs around them, squeezing and twisting with abnormal strength and flexibility to snap its already weakened and bent limbs. When Pillbug could no longer hold its body up and its underside struck the ground, a strange noise like a heavy bell ringing echoed over 9F's empty plains.

Berith approached Pillbug. "Sorry you have to see this, children." He grabbed its head and left shoulder and began to apply force. The seam that ran all around Pillbug's nonexistent neck creaked and began to separate on all sides, like its head was corked into its body.

"Holy shit." Dorian had surely never been as excited for anything in his life so much as seeing his hero rip off an enemy's head.

Pillbug writhed, new soft gray nubs forming from the snapped-off ends of its legs as it tried to fight back. The shell cracked in Berith's hands, more gas streamed from its body, and the strength of the mental assault increased. Berith gritted his teeth and kept pulling Pillbug apart.

With a sound like a log snapping in half, Pillbug broke, its diver's-helmet weighty head falling to the ground and rolling several paces away. The smog surrounding it thinned and dissipated. Thick liquid pooled out from the base of its legs. Dorian kicked its shell, another metal echo ringing out.

"Want to do that cathartic scream still?" he asked me.

I nodded, catching my breath and preparing.

"Sir? Would you like to join us?" he asked Berith.

Berith was staring inside Pillbug's shell. "Get back," he said. "Get ba—"

Something pale reached from inside the shell. Berith and Dorian stepped away. I circled around the empty shell to see what was going on.

The dark shape became a pale, spindly arm, became a torso, became a drooping head with ragged hair that covered its face. It crawled out of Pillbug's remains, dragging the spear behind it.

Dorian raised his sword. And then my brain was filled with radio static that threatened to break my skull open. Pillbug's armor hadn't just protected it. It had kept us from experiencing the full force of its mental attack. Words and images squashed and cut into the soft tissue that made up who I was. It was too much. I understood none of it. Some of it might have been names and faces. Some of it was definitely Berith screaming.

INTERMISSION

I don't understand. I've looked everywhere for you, and now that I've found you, you don't even want me around? Is there something I've forgotten? Something I don't know? Have you become someone else? How long has it been? There is a wrongness and I don't, Berith, I don't know what to *do*—

30

The pale body lurched out of Pillbug's shell, held back for a moment by marionette-like strings until they snapped. It blinked in the sunlight before unfurling a blighted pair of wings and flying away.

"Where is he going?" Berith asked, frantic. He was on his knees, looking distraught. "PELLIOR!"

"It's headed towards Earth," I said. "We have to follow it."

But Berith didn't get up. He'd been closest to Pillbug's shell when it cracked open. Maybe he'd gotten hit by some sort of shockwave? I couldn't let Pillbug escape, but we couldn't leave Berith here on his own.

"Ella, you go," Dorian said. "Be careful, and don't engage it. I'll come after you as soon as help shows up."

An iron grip clamped around my leg. "Wait," Berith wheezed. "Wait."

Dorian and I pulled him to his feet. He kept a hand on our shoulders, keeping himself steady and preventing us from running off without him. We found some shade beneath one of the many stone pillars that decorated this part of 9F and eased him down, his grip bringing the both of us to the ground too. We lay on the gravel tangled in an exhausted heap, shackled together by Berith's arms.

"Berith?" Dorian said. I'd never heard him less sure. "I thought Pellior died, since the capital's named after him."

"I wanted him to come back," Berith said.

"Who's Pellior?" I asked.

Berith just shook his head and touched the keel plate on my back, and that was all we could get out of him before the makhali's forces caught up to us.

Bliss was one of the first to arrive, cutting through the air as she flew with a startling efficiency. She had an empty quiver on her back, but both ends of her bow were capped with bloodstained sharp metal ends.

"You look terrible," she said. "Anyone dying?"

For the moment, no. Berith finally released his hold on us, needing both hands free to pull himself onto his feet using the closest pillar. Dorian and I moved away from him before he could catch hold of us again.

"Can't believe you came this far out," Bliss said. "Come on. Let's get you safe and seen to."

"No," Berith said. "I have to find him. I have to catch up to him before something else hurts him. I—"

"You couldn't catch up to a puddle in this state, old man. You need to recover first. Capital's a fucking mess, but it's safe for now. We've got cleanup in progress. Your girlfriend's sketched up some ideas for traps to lay for when the next wave of monsters hit, but we'll need leadership present for when that happens."

"I'm not going back without him!" Berith shouted. Between his height and his wingspan, he was capable of taking up so much space, of looming; he just normally didn't. "I have dedicated every day of my adult life to the guidance and preservation of our species. Just this once, *I need you to manage without me.*"

And then he collapsed. Dorian barely caught him in time, gently lowering him the last few inches to the shaded ground.

"Can I hand something off to you one more time?" Dorian asked. "I promise it'll be the last."

Bliss sighed and knelt beside Berith. She ordered the other makhali who'd arrived to sweep the area and confirm it was safe. "Charging off again?"

"I don't understand everything that's happening right now," Dorian said. "But I know Berith is safe with you, and I know Ella needs to go home. So I'm acting on the information I'm sure of."

"Shame you're so ignorant," she said, but didn't argue. "We'll get a camp set up here. Unfortunately, not everyone is capable of knowing when to tune their leaders out."

Dorian offered me his hand and spread his wings wide. I formed my wings. He held the sturdy bone that formed their leading edge and we ran together, Dorian helping to drag me into the sky, carefully releasing me once we were aloft so his wings wouldn't tangle with mine. An intensity of rage I'd never experienced before ignited when I saw the organic mess near the rift to Earth. If the Graft's goal was to repopulate 9F, they had a fair start on creating a sickly marsh—with resources stolen from *my* world. Dorian shouted a warning when I dove toward the rift at breakneck speed, but I'd waited long enough. How could I slow down now?

I shot through the rift without stopping, needing to pull up suddenly and swing my legs forward to skid to a halt and avoid crashing. I threw my wings wide, mutant bat-like limbs fully on show for anyone who might've been around.

I couldn't care less.

Dorian joined me a few seconds later, cursing as he landed in the tainted mud. Pillbug was nowhere to be seen, but it didn't matter. I should've anticipated this. But as much as I might've developed in other ways, I still hadn't outgrown that terrible disconnect between what I knew and what I understood.

"Wait," Dorian said. "You shouldn't—"

I was already wandering, needing to rip my shoes out of the mud with each step. I had trouble recalling the exact landscape that should've been on this side of the hill, but knew there should've been trees, roads, a town or two in the distance. Instead there was only sludge. How far had I run that awful night when I'd first left home? Couldn't've been more than a few miles. Compared to the distance I'd crossed, the worlds I'd seen, a few miles was *nothing*. For me, or the Graft.

It was like I'd stepped back in time to before any human lived here.

It was like a heat ray had blasted over the landscape, melting all the plant life like candle wax.

It was like nature had taken an eldritch turn, all sinkhole bogs and trees growing animal limbs and a river that was actually a miles-long slug.

It was all of these things at once, and it was terrible.

The river bent upwards in the middle, drawing itself up into a thick shape twenty feet tall. Eyes opened all over its slimy surface. It stared at us from every conceivable angle, a long, toothed slit opening up at one end—

I lost track of time after that. One moment I was staring at the living river, muscles unresponsive; the next, Dorian was carrying me across 9F's wasteland; and then we were in a tent back at the makhali's temporary camp. I lay on a sleeping bag, my head propped up on Dorian's lap. He was staring into the distance, hands mechanically turning my hair into dozens of little braids.

I turned my head. On my left, Berith lay on his front a few feet away, several blankets spread under his sleeping bag to keep his wings off the ground. His face was turned to the side, eyes shut, face stuck in an expression far too calm. It reminded me that healers could make their patients sleep; it scared me that there were things happening in the universe that would put even someone like Berith in such a state. His limp wings looked like crinkled cellophane, dropped garbage.

To my right, through the tent's open flap, was 9F's drained earth. Off in the distance was a blue-green stretch of organic growth, and makhali burning it, turning what life was here into ash.

"Will that be all?" I asked.

Dorian startled. "What?"

"Earth. Will that be all that's left?"

"We don't know how far it's spread. I'll help you find them."

"How will I know for sure it's them?" I said.

"They were away when it happened, right? Surely they're out there, and still in one piece."

"Part of it."

"Ella, they're out there."

He jerked away when my entire body spasmed, muscle and bone rapidly reshaping in a violent fit as I lost control of my emotions. My vision strobed from near-darkness to overexposed blinding white. My skin crawled with calluses that migrated up and down my limbs. My insides squirmed. Dorian cursed and shoved a folded blanket under my head, probably so I wouldn't bash my skull open against the ground.

A medic came running, drawn by the awful wail I only realized came from me after it was over. Dorian hovered protectively over me while I continued to flail involuntarily.

"Step away from her, for your own sake," the medic said. "She must be contaminated."

"She's had a bad day," Dorian said. "Let her be. I'll take care of her."

"Soldier, you need to—"

A scalded hand grabbed the medic's shoulder, spinning her around and nearly shoving her out of the tent.

"*My* patient," Veras snapped.

"But she's—"

"MINE."

The medic scurried away. Veras knelt by my side.

"Talk to me," he said. "Tell me what happened."

I screamed instead. There was nothing cathartic about it.

I heard the crunch of wheels on gravel outside, and then Reyna and Andras came in too. She knelt between Berith and I while Andras plunked down next to Veras.

"Is B okay?" she asked, looking over her shoulder at him.

"He's had a shock," Dorian said. "So has Ella."

"Do you want me to stop you doing this?" Veras asked. "Or do you need to get it out?"

I pressed my palms over my face, claws digging into my scalp. Veras tried to heal the small cuts I gave myself, but I couldn't stand the stimulation of his magic; he pulled away as I resisted him.

"Give her here," Andras said. He pulled me into his arms. "Ella, breathe. Breathe deep."

He went from smelling like a hospital room to smelling like the plants I'd had in my room at his house. His scent shifted again, to the syrupy sweetness of his carnivorous plants. The floor of the Glade. And then a smell that was more mundane to me, not quite perfect but close enough to the forest near my home—

I shoved my face against his neck, convulsions slowing as I focused on that scent.

Veras approached me again, his magic finding an opening this time. He took care of my cuts and bruises, going slow and careful. I could tell when his magic reached my churning insides, felt it flicker and falter in surprise.

"Does it hurt?" he asked.

I shook my head. I *wanted* it to hurt so the outside world wouldn't in comparison.

"It's okay," Andras said. "We can take things back from the Graft, you've done it yourself. It's okay."

"Not... not all of that."

"You have our help. We're here for you, no matter what comes next."

"I want my parents," I said. "I want... I want my family to all be together."

"You're not quite free of us yet, I'm afraid. But we'll get there."

"I want us to all be together." If only the contamination hadn't spread, everything could've been perfect. I could've had my parents. Could've figured out a way to keep up with my friends. Would've worked towards a point where I didn't have to hide my ability anymore. But instead it was all—

"We'll get there," Andras said. "We'll get there."

I shut my eyes and drew in another deep breath to center myself, mind tracing the shapes of bones from my feet, up my legs and spine, to my head, down my shoulders and arms. I was still agitated, in flux, but maybe just wasn't such a bad thing. Yes, my body was unstable.

That just meant it could grow into what I needed.

ACKNOWLEDGMENTS

I'm fortunate to have been raised by people who fostered my creative interests my whole life. I grew up surrounded by paintings and sculptures made by my grandfathers, and, as the years went on, a *lot* of craft supplies. Whenever I finished sewing or crocheting or cross-stitching something, I knew it would be well received by family and friends, and that stayed true as my interests shifted to writing, even if I did have some anxiety around sharing my work at first. So I have to start by thanking my wonderful friends Lisa, Macy, and Alex, my sister Simone, my father Phil, and especially my mother Karen. She's been such an amazing cheerleader as I've made the transition from writer to author, and has even helped me with line editing. All that time and effort isn't even mentioning the fact that she, you know, made and raised me, which I imagine took some doing.

I'd also like to thank my former coworkers within the diagnostic labs at Seattle Children's Hospital. As I neared the end of my contract there, I dared myself to talk about my writing more, and to say yes any time someone asked if they could read it. The goal was to get myself used to the idea of others reading my work (a rather necessary element of being an author) and you were all so supportive.

When it came time to finally put this book out into the world, I was incredibly grateful to find these awesome people who were willing to give a debut indie author a chance:

Myburgh, Claire Rodriguez (yewscion), Page Alexander, Ryan B, Marie-Theres Fuchs, Johnny N, Macy Finger, William C. Tracy, Aimee Cozza, Alex Walchli, Beatrice Matarazzo, Trip Space-Parasite, Adam Nemo, Zack Fissel, Victoria P, JullesT, Per M. Jensen, Ven of the

Void, Lisa, David Harris, Gabrielle, Mason M, Joshua McGinnis, Stephanie Walchli, Jack Oskay, Tina Churchill, Kailey, kestreloo3, Chris Hawkins, Bethan Fildes, Adgee Harville, Robin Lynn, and Israel Jones.

And, last but not least, I need to thank the autistic and neurodivergent communities. I had the initial idea that eventually mutated into *Graft* right when I graduated high school, and Ella was always floating around somewhere in the back of my head as I attended college, lost a close family member, and began my professional life. We both went through a lot of development during that time. *Graft* wouldn't be the book it is today—and I wouldn't be the *person* I am today—if it weren't for other members of my community being honest and open about their struggles and successes. A big element of autism is "masking," or (whether intentionally or not) acting in ways meant to hide neurodivergent-coded behaviors in order to better fit in with neurotypical people. Although exhausting, masking can be thought of us almost like a defense mechanism, an attempt to avoid trouble by keeping one's true, non-conforming self hidden. I owe a huge thank-you to all the members of our community who share the realities of their lives, positive and negative. Nothing has been better for helping me learn more about and take better care of myself than your stories. Who knows if I ever would've cobbled together the spoons to get this book into your hands otherwise?

Yours,

Madeleine

ABOUT THE AUTHOR

Madeleine Marie-Rose is a proudly queer and neurodivergent author native to the Pacific Northwest. She started Monsters and Maidens Publishing with the goals of sharing the many stories that plague her brain with the world and learning to live as her most authentic self. You can find her at https://www.monstersandmaidenspublishing. com/, on Bluesky, or under a weighted blanket with a mug of hot chocolate.

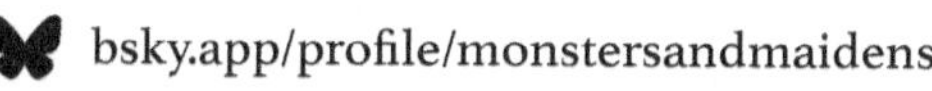 bsky.app/profile/monstersandmaidens.bsky.social